Divide by Zero

By

Sheila Deeth

An Ink-Filled Stories Publication

First released by Stonegarden.net
First paperback edition 2012
First ebook edition 2012

Republished 2012 by Beckoning Books
an imprint of Second Wind Publishing/Indigo Sea Press

.

First IFS print edition 2018
First IFS ebook edition 2018

Front cover design by Peter Joseph Swanson

Dedication

With thanks to my editor Shirley Ann Howard; pre-readers Anna O'Donovan, Jean Harkin and Sheila Harris; Peter Joseph Swanson for the beautiful cover image; my cheerleaders at Coffee Break, Writers' Mill and Gather.com; and to Stonegarden.net for giving me my first taste of being published. Thanks also to the teams at Second Wind Publishing, Indigo Sea Press, and Ink-Filled Stories for welcoming me into their families of authors. I'd like to thank my own family too, and especially my mum for her constant prayers and encouragement.

OTHER TITLES BY SHEILA DEETH
IN THE MATHEMAFICTION SERIES

- **Divide by Zero**—*a community divided by tragedy*
- **Infinite Sum**—*a woman close to breaking point*
- **Subtraction**—*the man who wasn't there to help*

ABOUT THE AUTHOR

Sheila Deeth is an English American, Catholic Protestant, mathematician writer, with a math degree from Cambridge University England and a life-long love of words. Her works include the Mathemafiction series of contemporary novels, science fiction and fantasy novellas, picture books, animal stories, and the Five-Minute Bible-Story Series. Connect with her online at www.sheiladeeth.com

DIVIDE BY ZERO

Readers say:

"What an amazing, unforgettable story… that   will leave you with challenges, perhaps regrets, perhaps renewal… This inspiring novel turned out to be almost epic in impact…" *~Glenda Bixler*

"Ms. Deeth… brings us insights into the thoughts of all kinds of people and does it extremely well. I highly recommend 'Divide By Zero.'" *~E.G Lewis*

"Like a human patchwork quilt… Of   all   the characters, my favorite was the white cat, Garnet. Mystical and fundamental to the plot(s), she was quite endearing… moments of pure poetry… "
~Aaron Paul Lazar

It takes a lot of stories to make a neighborhood. New neighbors add their tales, families multiply, and death subtracts. But dividing by zero might blow it all apart unless a little child can lead them.

Meet Troy, the garage mechanic's son, Lydia, the rich man's daughter, Amethyst with her remarkable cat, and the curiously accented Andrea. Old Abigail knows more than anyone else but doesn't speak. Meanwhile in Paradise Park, a middle-aged man keeps watch over autistic Amelia, who keeps getting lost. Pastor Bill mends people; Peter mends cars. And someone or something's going to break.

Divide by Zero

<u>Cast of characters</u>, in order of appearance

- Peter Markham, garage owner
- Mary, his wife
- Troy, their son
- Pattie, Mary's colleague
- Dan, Pattie's husband
- Abigail, Mary's mother
- Charlie, realtor in Paradise
- Todd, Troy's best friend
- Lydia Steepleton, Troy's girlfriend
- Frank, Mary's new neighbor
- Jessie, Frank's wife
- Steve Walker, new resident on Paradise Road
- Amethyst Greenwood, lives two doors away from him
- Garnet, Amethyst's white cat
- Joe Grainger, policeman, lives across the street
- Karen Grainger, his wife, a schoolteacher
- Carla, waitress at Benson's
- Sapphire Greenwood, reporter, Amethyst's sister
- Dyson Lee, her partner and friend to Charlie, the realtor
- Mason, their dog

- Andrea Blake, art gallery proprietor
- Sylvia Steepleton, Lydia's younger sister
- Jason Steepleton III, her father
- Savannah, her mother
- Jason Junior, her older brother
- Janet, Lydia's roommate in the dorms
- David, workmate of Troy and boyfriend of Carla
- Amelia Callaghan, small beautiful child
- Jeffrey Irons, construction magnate
- Shamrock, Jeffrey's red setter
- Pastor Bill at the Church of Paradise
- Simon, older boy on school bus
- Sharon, Sylvia's friend and Simon's younger sister
- Jeremy (Germ), Troy and Lydia's firstborn son
- Alison Greenwood, Amethyst and Steve's firstborn
- Nate Greenwood, Sapphire and Dyson's firstborn, friend of Alison and Jeremy
- Evie Callaghan, Amelia's mother
- Jason (JC, Jacey, Jay) Markham, Troy and Lydia's second born son
- Jeannie Collins, Troy and Lydia's neighbor
- Tracey Greenwood, Nate's little sister, JC's friend
- Marcie Kopp
- Robert Kopp, her son, friend of Alison and Jeremy
- Darryl Kopp, her husband
- Joshua, Troy and Lydia's third and youngest child.
- Jen Williams, schoolteacher
- Dr. Mary Phillips, PhD, psychologist
- And finally, Jeremy's old math professor, who knows about dividing by zero

Part 1

The Father

Summer

Storm Clouds, Hot Meal, Clear Day, Don't Leave

Peter gazed down at the golden pond of his drink. *I'm not my father* he told himself though his reflection wasn't sure. *I'm faithful, good and true. I'm not like him. I don't hurt people.*

He glanced up at the woman dancing on the stage. She was young and beautiful, unblemished and free. He watched her swirl, swinging her red skirt high above her knees. Mary had danced this way in their youth. She'd hung on his arm, long curls of hair brushing his face, filling his nose with the perfume of roses and sun. Her eyes shone like blades of new grass in a painting. Her lips brushed his, soft as petals falling in rain. But this wasn't Mary, and Peter wasn't his father. He wondered if his parents had ever known any dance but hurting and tears.

"You could try your chances with her, old man," said the friend at Peter's elbow. "See how she's looking at you?"

Peter shook his head.

"I mean, seriously, she's got all the moves. And look at those..." The friend fisted hands in front of his chest, but Peter shook his head again, making his ears ring. The conversation clattered too loud and jarring. He shouldn't have come here, shouldn't have let them persuade him. He should have stayed working, or gone home alone.

The friend of a friend from a table close by rocked a lazy hand. "Old Pete, you know, I rather think he likes..." Long fingers dangled in the air as words trailed away.

Not that Peter minded, but why should not wearing a ring and not dating mean people assumed he dated men? *Crazy world we live in.* He sighed, lifting the glass back to his lips. *Drink up. Get out of here. I shouldn't have come.*

The dance ended. The woman placed her mike back on the stand. She stared over the crowd then glided toward their table as if she'd seen Peter watching. Broad hips swayed under the bright red dress. Thick hair tumbled on bare shoulders. Her teeth were white, eyes green, but she wasn't Mary, wasn't who he wanted to see.

"I'm off." Peter coughed, slapped down his glass and added, "Got work to do tomorrow."

He wasn't used to this, the company, the drink, going out instead of going home. He had rules to keep him safe and lived by them. Now Peter staggered as he climbed to his feet, steadied himself, leaned over the table, then felt sick. Sour smells of drink, sour memories flooded in. He'd given up women long ago; perhaps it was time to give up alcohol too. It had been a mistake letting his friends drag him here, risking temptation in public. *Lead us not...* Remembered prayer? He shouldn't let friends lead him away from his silent home, or drink lead to despair; no ring, no girls, no nothing the safest way.

He remembered the smell of his father's breath and the ringing sound of his voice. He remembered the sodden thump like wood on wet earth and his mother's whimpering cries like a kitten in distress. He remembered many things and thrust them away with straightened arms. Then he struggled to find the door.

"Don't leave." Was someone calling him back? His mother, but she wasn't here. Dreams and reality mixed and melded in his mind then tumbled free. Cold air should wake him.

Peter tugged the door awkwardly and stopped, trapped somehow in a gap between yesterday and tomorrow, between outside and in. Warm air wafted behind—"Shut that door, man!" Cooler breezes blew ahead. He remembered hiding outside in the cold, under the picnic table in un-mowed grass. A rotten plank, fallen free long ago, lay splintered and soft. He thudded it hard as he could against the ground. "Take that.

Take that." It didn't drown the sound. Later his mother let the cat out; Peter crept through the line of yellow light spilling from the back door. He hugged her battered knees as he passed, smelling sweat and blood. Then he stepped around the hulking, snoring shape of his dad and climbed upstairs to bed.

In the cold air Peter remembered Mary and thanked the Lord he'd left before he could hurt her. No ring, no women; he'd seen his temper, watched those storm clouds over his head, and taken a hike. She was probably married to someone else now, had long forgotten him. She never answered his letters, never acknowledged cards or gifts he sent her for the lad. She'd stand in the kitchen cooking hot dinners for a stranger's family tonight. Peter imagined the swirl of her dress—wide, fifties style, like the picture on flour packs—her face bright and free. She'd enjoy clear days of sunshine, sweetness and light. She deserved it, for sure.

And the boy, little Troy? He must be better off with another dad too.

Peter slammed his fist into the wall outside the bar, making his knuckles bleed. Not the first time; they were thick and rimmed with scars. A couple shuffled by, heading in for a drink. "Let's get inside," muttered the man. "Let's get away from him." But it was only a wall Peter hurt. Forever, for always, for mercy, Peter wasn't his dad.

Storm Clouds

Storm clouds gathered outside; *a suitable end to the day* Mary thought. At work, Pattie had pestered her with talk of the old people's home. She'd moved her father over the weekend. Now she wanted to sort out Mary's life. "It's the perfect place," Pattie said. "Gorgeous views on the drive down. You'd love it." But Mary had too many memories of old folks ranged against walls like balls of yarn, TVs with silent pictures in the corner and radios squawking overhead. She'd promised her mother, many years ago, she'd never put her in a home, and

Mary wasn't the sort to break a promise.

"Clear day promises," her mother used to say. "Don't you go breaking them when storm clouds gather." So yes, Mary thought. It was singularly appropriate for clouds to be gathering tonight.

She stood cooking dinner in the kitchen, the small room cozy with the smell of meat in the oven and potatoes on the stove, windows steamed, fan whirring pointlessly. Three plates lay stacked on the table behind her with a tray waiting to hold her mother's meal.

"Mary!" barked a sharp ragged voice.

Mary sighed. "Coming, Mother." She left the oven mitts in a heap by the pan.

Warm bed, clean clothes, hot meals, and a servant ready to wait on every whim was all Mary's mother wanted. Five more minutes to brown the pie and dinner would be ready, but Mother had picked up her bell and was ringing, singing raggedly in time with the chimes, "Mary!"

Oh, how Mary hated that bell; its tinkle, delicate as a small child's toy; its authority louder than church bells on Easter morning. "Yes Mother, I'm coming." The bell still rang.

Mary crossed the hallway with steady, angry tread to keep from hurrying. A key rattled and scratched in the lock as she passed. The front door swung wide and her newly grown-up son stood facing her in the worn out sneakers, holey sweatshirt and hip-sliding jeans of a newly qualified garage mechanic. "Troy! Perfect timing for dinner. Just let me go to Grandma."

Troy made a grab for her arm. "We got to talk Mom."

"Later."

"No. Now." He tugged harder, fingers like iron bruising her. Mary found herself steered back into the kitchen, still listening while the child's bell, church bell rang from the other room.

"Troy, your grandma…"

"Mom." Something stern and urgent rippled in Troy's voice, reminding Mary of his father, making her turn to face him. "Mom, I'm sorry, but I really can't cope." She watched his wide mouth form the words and forced her brain into motherly, helpful mode.

"Can't cope with what Troy?" *What does he want? What does he need me to do that I'm not already doing? And what does Mother need?* Words circled silently.

Troy waved his hands like blackbirds baked in Mary's pie. "Can't cope with all this." His arms enfolded kitchen, plates on the table, windows and the sound of the bell all into one as his gaze swept the room. "With Grandma. With you, always run off your feet. No time to talk, no time for anything. I might as well not be here."

Mary withered under the weight of too many complaints, so much simpler just to answer the bell. But Troy leaned back against the kitchen door, trapping her in the room.

"I don't know what you mean. You *are* here, Troy. I feed you. I keep house for you. I'm your mom. I just don't know what you want."

"I don't want you to *keep house.*'"

Such a simple reply, it simply didn't make sense. *Who else is going to do it?* Whatever had upset Troy, Mary didn't understand. She'd missed some vital clue, some essential jigsaw piece. If a mother's meant to sort things out, she'd lost some part of herself.

Troy was talking again, hands waving, explaining, complaining, words tumbling from his mouth in endless streams. They vanished in the ringing, ever-ringing of the bell. "I have to go to her," Mary said. So Troy stood aside with a gentle smile—a smile so very like Peter's—blank and sad.

So like Peter's smile, Mary thought, clinging to memories of earlier days in her marriage. She walked around her mother's room, calming her ragged breathing, relaxing her shaking hands with familiar tasks. She plumped cushions, changed channels on TV, opened pill boxes, adjusted the shades. Her eyes saw her mother slumped in the worn-out chair. Her ears heard demands. But her mind whirled through years and disappointments to the day Peter left. "Don't go," she'd called. "Peter, don't leave."

Suddenly, hopelessly, Mary realized what Troy's smile meant. Ice dropped on her shoulders with remembered pain. "No," she cried.

"Mary," her mother ordered as Mary turned from her. "Mary!"

But Mary said, "Not now," and hurried out the room, leaving her mother tinkling the hated bell.

She ran to the front door, pulled it open, rushed down the path, and stood helpless at the gate. "Troy, please. Troy, please don't leave," but it was too late. Red tail-lights disappeared into the first sheets of rain, storm clouds dropping their load. While her mother continued incessantly ringing the bell.

Hot Meal

Earlier that evening, his work at the garage all done, Troy handed in his resignation with the same hand that picked up his pay. Storm clouds had gathered but the rain had yet to start— black skies, dry asphalt and electric air. He walked to his car, switched on the radio, and drove home.

Troy brought the vehicle to a halt outside the gate and stared at the path in front of him. So many years invested here; if he tried he was sure his arms and legs would remember stretching up against the front door, tip-toes aching, one arm reaching for the knob while the other rapped on wood. "Daddy, let me in!" His father would pull the door wide open, catching him with strong hands wrapped around his waist and lifting him high. Troy would fly, then lie with his back to the ceiling, looking down on the hallway. Mom's eyes shone brightly as she gazed up at him; her laugh happy and light, the smell of a hot meal cooking in the kitchen, the sight of the table laid out below as his father carried him. He remembered childhood's king-of-the-world perspective; three plates, three knives, three forks; three of everything, always.

Troy remembered clear days playing on grass by the path while Dad ran the mower. Warm air smelled of gasoline and daisies. Mom brought lemonade to the door, her print frock waving in the breeze. She'd sit on the step while they talked about engines and birds and the kids down the street.

Then came the day when Troy's father walked alone away from the house; not a backward glance, spine ramrod straight under the shabby brown jacket, hair hidden under a hat, battered suitcase in his hand. Mom ran after him, barefoot, screaming, "Peter, don't leave!" Neighbors opened their doors to watch. Troy gazed unseen from his tiny bedroom window while the world turned upside down. "So like your father," people used to say. But his father was gone.

His mother's face never smiled at Troy again, not even when he grew tall enough to look down on her graying head; no hands could lift him in the air.

Troy remembered walking up the path, solemn featured, solemn natured, his tiny palm held tight in his mother's hand. He felt so proud to carry his mother's shopping bags, just like a daddy would. He remembered measuring his height by whether he could reach the keyhole in the door. Mom gave him his own key eventually, so he could do his paper route without waking her in the morning. He felt grown up, felt visible.

Meanwhile his mother shrank and faded, a ghost taking her place. She came alive for his grandmother's visits of course, fussing over cooking and furniture, proving she could cope on her own. She came alive if a workman knocked at the door; came alive for the mailman; in church. But Troy walked the path alone in long trousers, shiny shoes pinching his feet, tight collar around his neck, and lived with a ghost.

At school concerts Troy only cared for one face in the audience. He watched his mother's outline in the dark, watched as she disappeared till all that remained was a rubber stamp in the passport of his life. At high school graduation they were told to wave to parents and supporters who'd brought them this far. Troy didn't move, faced forward, didn't even blink. He knew his mother wouldn't notice; she wouldn't move either.

Still seated at the wheel of the stationary car, Troy sighed. It was time, he guessed. *Get it over with.* Storm clouds lent leaden weight to the scene ahead, everything two-dimensional, grass painted sharply on broken paving stones. He climbed out, legs grown leaden too, almost tripping as he bent to the gate. Walking up the path—*don't step on the cracks*—he heard his grandmother's bell. She lived with them now, relics of her home filling their old living room. Troy's toys were banished upstairs when he was still a boy. Now like a thief in his own home, he sneaked around unseen, spending as little time there as possible.

The bell rang. Though he couldn't hear her voice, Troy knew his grandmother was calling his mother's name. Mom would rush to answer of course, her purpose in life.

When Dad left, Grandma became their metronome; a regular visitor, someone to be obeyed, someone to impress. She taught Troy to tie his tie straight, fasten buttons in the right holes, keep shoelaces from trailing. She told him to do his homework, though homework smelled of Dad and he hated it. She even phoned his mother each day to check on him. Grandma demanded perfection, while Troy's mother wilted like the flowers she planted in vases to show she cared.

When Troy was thirteen, Grandma was rushed to hospital. For days he studied school books by her bed, smelling the mixture of sickness and disinfectant and stale mashed potatoes, blinking under over-bright overhead lights. Then came the taxi, Mom helping Grandma maneuver an alien walking-frame up the path, Troy carrying her cases. A neighbor drove the rented van with furniture, then carried and squeezed chairs and tables through the cramped front door. Gray dust from the living room's new wall mixed with the clean scent of wood in the darkness of the hall—Grandma's new room. The whole house changed in the space of a few short days. As Troy lifted his hand with the key, he still saw the marks where Grandma's wardrobe had gouged the wood and scratched his arm.

The bell still rang, the hated bell, as Troy slammed the key into the lock, opened the door and walked straight into his mother.

"We need to talk," he told her at once, though he'd planned perhaps to eat and discuss it slowly over dinner. He could smell a hot meal cooking.

When she pulled away, disappearing again, Troy grabbed his mother's arm. It felt so thin, so brittle; he was afraid she might break if she wasn't already broken.

They moved to the kitchen, bell still ringing, dinner still cooking, Grandma still waiting, impatiently. They balanced themselves between the smells of a hot meal and the disinfectants of Grandma's room. Meat pie, Troy thought; he wondered when his mother had stopped making those pastry leaves to decorate the top. Leaning back against the kitchen door, blocking her escape, he told her everything. Words poured out; why he had to leave; why he couldn't cope; how he loved her; how he hated to see her this way; how he knew he just had to get away. And he saw in her eyes, she wasn't there.

Was this why his father left? Did Mom used to disappear, even back then? Troy didn't remember.

When his mother said she had to go, had to answer Grandma's bell, Troy stood aside. He even smiled for a moment recalling the view from overhead: three plates on the table, three of everything, and his mother's laughing face looking up at him.

She crossed the hallway to Grandma's room, having never really left her. She'd never really been in the kitchen with Troy, never heard a word he said. Slowly Troy placed his front door key next to the plates—only two needed now—walked to the door, and went out.

Storm clouds lent a scent of ozone, raindrops in the air like mist dissolving and beginning to fall. Troy wasn't crying, not really, but he tasted salt in his throat. Dinner. That was it. He smelled his last hot meal, and it was too late.

Don't Leave

You're a stupid old woman Abigail. Say it, said the voice in her head. *You're a stupid old woman.*

The other voice, the scratching, wretched voice, the wordless drone, tasted thoughts and tried to form them into words. "You're a… you're a… storm cloud on a clear day."

You're a stupid old woman.

If the television was on it would silence the sounds in Abigail's head; real voices, real words, real meanings; if the TV was on. And if she could get up from her chair she'd switch the TV on. She'd walk across the room, turn the knob, flick through channels till she found something worth watching; then go back to fit herself among her cushions. That's what she'd do. It was pointless but no more so than sitting, lolling in her chair, with spittle beginning to pool in the collar of her blouse.

You're a stupid old woman.

"Storm cloud."

But now, because she couldn't move, and because the TV wasn't on, and because the voice in her head refused to be stilled, Abigail shouted the one word she still knew how to say reliably. "Mary. Mary!"

It was a sweet name, for a sweet, sweet child; fair-haired dancing girl who smiled like summer. The way Abigail's voice curdled it, the name sounded like swearing. *Cursed Mary, bedeviled Mary, martyred, mutilated Mary.* "Mary!" She spat. How she hated that scratching, ratcheting voice. How she despised it.

Abigail's daughter didn't answer of course; the room remained silent. So Abigail moved the hand that still obeyed, the one that could shift just far enough for finger and thumb to grasp the handle of the bell. She began to ring; hand rocking, side to side, peaceful in a memory of motion. Abigail rang and called for Mary. The sound of the bell soothed over her ratcheting voice, so she rang it again. Again, again; drown out the words in her head.

One day, Mary wouldn't answer. One day she'd leave, just open the door and walk away. Abigail would be alone.

"Mary," she called in fear, ringing her bell. *Mary, don't leave.* But that was just the voice in her head. The one in her mouth repeated her daughter's name harshly, bitterly, over again.

There was nothing wrong with Abigail's hearing though, and something changed; something in the quality of the air maybe, or a draft under her door. It felt like someone else entered the house besides Abigail and Mary. Her grandson Troy, Abigail thought. Perhaps he'd come home for dinner. Perhaps she'd catch cold from the draft if he didn't close the door. *Close that door,* said the voice in her head. "Winter storm," grated the sound from her lips, too quiet to hear. She rang her bell again.

Doors left open in a house that might as well be heaven or hell, or prison cell. Abigail rings her bell, ignored. Only the voice in her head replies, as always. *You're a stupid old woman, Abigail.*

Don't leave, Mary.

When Mary came in at last, savory smells from a hot meal followed her, clinging to clothes, wafting from her hair. Abigail felt her blouse grow damp under her chin; drool puddling there at the thought of food to come. *Disgusting.* She grunted restless noises to tell Mary what she wanted. Mary said, "Yes Mother," as if she understood. Sweet Mary whispered like roses around the room, switched on the TV, changed channels, while Abigail's chin still dribbled untended and ignored. Abigail wanted her cushions moved. Mary moved the shades, adjusting the light. "Mary," said Abigail, but words wouldn't come. Till finally Mary came to the chair, wiping a handkerchief on her mother's wet chin.

Abigail would have thanked her if the ratcheting voice would obey.

Suddenly, over the sound of television, over Mary's *Yes*

Mothers and Abigail's rasping breaths, an empty silence froze, the absence of a noise that hadn't been noticed. A draft blew through the door again, change in the air, electricity from a storm firing bolts at the sky.

Mary jumped and hurried out the room, Abigail calling and ringing for her return. *Don't leave, Mary. Don't leave me on my own.* The voice betrayed her, rasping only, "Storm cloud. Storms. Clear day." Sweet Mary might never come back, and Abigail would die alone, one last hot meal in the kitchen left uneaten, the television channel forever unchanged.

She heard her daughter's anguished cries. She wished she could go comfort her, but this aged body had betrayed her long ago. She wished she could speak, but had no words. Mary wasn't leaving Abigail, but Troy left Mary instead. Troy walked out, taking away the last of her daughter's hope. If only she could get up from her chair, if only she could walk, then Abigail would go to her daughter, wrap arms around her, and whisper in her ear, comforting words. She would have stroked her hair, her sweet pretty Mary, left all alone. Instead she sat and rang her bell, unnoticed.

"Storm clouds. Clear day."

You're a stupid old woman, Abigail.

Clear Day

"I got a letter today. Ten years, and she writes me. I knew her handwriting and I tell you, lad, my hand shook like palsy when I picked it up. I held it to my nose, I did"—Peter waved his hand by his face—"just longing for the smell of her, but it only smelled of paper. And I cried. Would you believe it, son? I cried. Just a little, just enough to wet my eyes. I was crying for her."

The younger man stood in the doorway, hesitant.

"Ten years, and every card I sent, every letter, every check, not a single word, as if she barely wanted to believe I was alive." Peter shook his head. "I left her. Yeah, I know I'm at fault. I left her. But oh, how I loved her; how I missed her, these long, ten long years.

"If I could have smelt her on the letter, I'd've cried like a baby. I know I would. I loved her so much, can't you tell? I can see her now, like the day we met, hair like a cloud around her head. I remember her voice, like lavender on daisies, her hands like butterfly wings. Oh I loved your mom.

"And that doesn't mean I didn't love you too, my Troy, old son. You were the apple of both our eyes. You were everything to us. But you can see how it was can't you? Well"—He thumped the table with battle-scarred hands—"Well, why should you?"

Peter shook his head then, trying to dash the memories from his eyes. He paced around the plastic-topped table, watched by his grown-up son. He gathered his thoughts into explanations while his son's eyes gazed unchanged.

"Never told you about my parents, your grandparents, did I? No, I wouldn't. But me, I remember the way they used to bicker and shout all day when I was a kid. They hated each other—can you believe that?—all my years when they were still there; nothing but one of them telling me the other was no good; either one, nothing right, nothing ever good enough. So I could never be good enough either, could I? Could never relax. It was my fault; that's what I thought. Can you imagine how that is?"

Troy hadn't reacted, hadn't relaxed either, hardly seemed to care. Still, Peter wouldn't tell him anything more; Troy didn't need that hurt, that fear, didn't need to wonder whose evil genes he might have inherited. Troy was all right.

"I couldn't do it to you, Troy. When I saw it in her eyes, when I knew we were going the same way, I had to leave. I couldn't do it. Not to you, Troy, not to my own son. I loved you too much."

"Couldn't do what?" Troy asked.

"Couldn't do what they did to me. Don't you see? I loved you both. I couldn't bear to lose you, but I couldn't destroy you either. You've got to understand."

Peter walked back to the table where he'd left the letter. "Yes, I wrote," he said to Troy's quizzical eyes. "I wrote every week at the start, then every Christmas and birthdays and Easter and holidays. You didn't get the letters did you? I sent money. I couldn't send presents. I didn't know what you'd like. You didn't know?"

Troy shook his head.

"She should have told you. But I hurt her, Troy. It's not your mother's fault. You mustn't ever think that. Maybe she thought she was protecting you from me. Don't hate her Troy. Don't hate your mother. Please."

His son, still standing in the doorway, still leaning on the frame, closed his eyes.

"Anyway," Peter continued, shrugging off the moment. "I got a letter. Did I say? She says her mother, your grandmother made her write. She lives with you, right?"

Troy nodded sullenly.

"Mary says her mother kept looking at a picture on the shelf, one of us building sandcastles on the beach. D'you remember it? 1965? Sixty-something anyway. She says her mother kept looking at it, till Mary brought it over to her. Then she moved her hand—she only moves one hand now; that's what your mom says—she touched your face and mine in the picture, just you and me. After a bit your mom says she figured it out, like your grandmother was telling her to write me.

"I don't know." Peter sighed. "Women figure stuff out I suppose. It's just what she says, what she wrote." He felt like the world was running down with his words, time like sand disappearing through the spout.

"She says she doesn't know where you are, Troy. Doesn't she read? I told her you were here."

Troy turned as if he were bored of the conversation and Peter grabbed his arm.

"We have to go to her, son. We have to go to *them*."

Troy shook his head, tried to shake his father's grip.

"I don't know what she wants, not really, I don't. But I know we have to go. You can't just leave your mother like this." When Troy looked back in disbelief, he added, "Yes, I left. I know. But you're her son. We have to go."

This time it was Peter handing in his notice, though he was the boss handing control to his second in command. Father and son packed cases, closed up the neat little house with its neat little rooms and neat little yard with dead little flowers. They loaded Peter's truck with luggage in the back and a tarpaulin tied down with knots and rope. Then they drove cross-country.

"How did you find me anyway," Peter asked as the radio died, yet again, in the middle of nowhere, in plains of empty silence.

"The phone," said Troy. "I kept trying directory inquiries till I found your name."

"That easy is it?"

"No. It wasn't easy, Dad."

"Well, thanks, I suppose."

Troy's car stayed behind in his father's garage, with boxes and tools, broken cups and furniture, and newspaper clippings. It had barely made the trip out. Troy seemed happy enough with his father in control of things now. He sat while miles wore away at the silence between them till conversation filled it with long-lost dreams.

They reached their old town, their old road, where neighbors stayed silent and invisible, hidden away in their homes. Peter stopped the truck in front of the gate. They walked down the path and heard the bell.

"Grandma's bell," said Troy, striding behind. "She rings it for Mom. All the time."

Peter almost smiled as the sun came out, bright shafts of light over grass and flower beds—clear day after all, where storm clouds had dogged the weary length of their journey.

The door opened at his first gentle tap. Savory smells drifted past, Mary's cooking, a hot meal for someone, not for him. Then she stood there, fraying, graying, and beautiful. She smelled of roses still.

"Mary." There was nothing more to say. Peter leaned his unshaven face into his wife's embrace. Her arms wrapped around him, voice smothered in comfort against his chest, tears running damply and sticking to the hairs behind his shirt. Over her head, as he turned her around, Peter saw his son watching. He still heard the bell.

"I'll go to her," said Troy. "Just don't leave while I'm gone." But his parents were going nowhere, locked in an unlikely embrace that seemed warmer than dinner and longer than all the years.

Fall

Agreeable, Nodding Head, Peter Piper, Fallen Leaves

Lead us not into temptation Peter thought, looking down at his wife's sleeping form, curled tightly under the covers on the edge of the bed. She'd welcomed him back with open arms and a smile like the hottest day of summer. They'd talked all through dinner, gravy for two spread over plates for four; food ran out before the words. She'd stared at him as if she couldn't believe he was really there. Smiles pulled the wrinkles away from her mouth, stretching her cheeks, tearing back years. She touched him with fingers under the table, slid her knees to rest against his, tapped his shoulder every time she stood to answer her mother's bell. Troy had colored red with embarrassment and asked to be excused. Then evening fell, and Mary trailed fingers like silk on Peter's palm as they headed upstairs. And there, right there and then, it all fell apart.

"You've got to sleep somewhere I suppose," she said.

"I'll take the sofa."

"What sofa? We gave away the sofa when Mother moved in."

"Spare room?"

"Troy's room and it's full of his stuff."

A sudden gulf widened between them—expectation, revelation. "I'm back," Peter said softly, hoping to rekindle desire, but Mary pointed sullenly to the side of the bed by the wall.

"You sleep there, but keep your hands to yourself. Okay?"

He nodded, but couldn't sleep.

She seemed unable to bear the thought of sharing space with him. Yet she was still his wife; she'd never bothered to divorce him in all those years; and he'd never thought to wonder about that, how she couldn't have remarried if she'd never asked for divorce.

He drank her scent with long deep breaths as he leaned on his elbow over her, nodding head absorbing her sleeping beauty. The whole room smelled of Mary; *did it smell this way before?* The whole upstairs belonged to her while downstairs was sour with scents of sickness and age and Abigail, a change less agreeable, less welcoming. No matter; Peter opened his mouth drinking flowers and shampoo, tasting behind it that salt-sweet tingle of woman in the air. He wanted her, but shouldn't.

Turned on his back: *Don't touch. You haven't the right.* Marriage gives you the right.

Turned on his side: *Oh Mary. My beautiful bride.*

I'm not my father.

Peter's mother died when he was scarce out of childhood, still small enough to hide under tables and pretend he wasn't there, still young enough not to admit what he heard and saw, and scared enough not to fight. His mother never saw his wedding. She never knew Mary though he thought she might have liked her; might have noticed the bump perhaps as well. Would she have warned Mary off?—'*Don't make my mistakes*'—but marriage wasn't a mistake. They could still make it work.

Mary smelled of roses even back then. Her wedding dress perfectly disguised her pregnancy. Her arms were pink as rose-petals, bare to the sun, prettily padded with weight of the growing child. Her eyes gazed deeply into his when he lifted the veil to kiss her. Most of all Peter remembered the bliss of nights spent legally together, no fears of anyone pulling them apart, accusing them of sin. The child, their child, would be born in a perfect family, would bless and be blessed. Peter's father would never know and could rot in hell. His mother would watch from heaven and rejoice.

Peter turned onto his back again with a sigh. The bed creaked but Mary didn't move. Was she really so deeply asleep or just ignoring him? She'd always turned toward him back then. His body stirred and Peter reminded himself, stern warning, *mustn't touch. You're on trial here.*

They saved up for a house after their marriage, living in Abigail's upstairs room till the baby was almost two—upstairs from Mary's mother, just like now. Peter had scrimped and saved—they'd scrimped and saved together—until, at last, they had a place of their own, a row-house, neat and tidy, with grass and flowers outside. He carried Mary up the path in his arms, the babe held tight in hers. They must have looked like some crazy children's toy or a balancing act. He held the key between his lips while Mary pulled it out—sharp metal taste—reaching to fit it neatly in the door. Then they tumbled inside.

Peter stretched an arm over his wife, remembering. He pulled her close till her curved back rested against him, knobby bones making ridges down his chest. He clasped her small clenched fists in one hand, moving the other one lower, stroking her nightdress, feeling her respond. His body began to move against her back, comfort and warmth, remembered joy, but suddenly she shuddered awake and rolled away. "Don't you dare touch me!"

"But Mary…"

"Don't you dare!"

Peter turned to the wall. His body ached for release that clasping fingers couldn't give. So long, so nobly, so rigidly he'd kept himself controlled.

"I never betrayed you Mary," he whispered to empty space. "Not really," but she was asleep again. He heard her breath, slow and steady, didn't dare turn—he yearned for her so. He talked in muttered undertones, to wide-flowered wallpaper grown ancient and gray, to memories of lying more comfortably in the same place in younger days. At least Mary had her friends at work to talk to. Troy had what he wanted— Mom and Dad both under one roof. Dear old Abigail had her bell. They had comfort perhaps. But Peter had left his life behind yet again, left friends, acquaintances, like fallen leaves. He was getting too old for starting over, too old to learn new ways, too tempted to ignore. *Marriage gives me the right. Leaving takes it away. Pay the Piper, Peter.*

Something thunked downstairs. Abigail needing help? Or Troy? Mary still didn't move. Somewhere between waking and sleeping, between past and future, memories and fear, and the troubles of everyday life, the pictures in Peter's dreams began to turn gray.

When the alarm clock rang he pretended not to hear it.

Agreeable

Mary's friend Pattie waited for things to improve but they didn't, poor Mary getting quieter each day after Peter's return. By the water cooler she kept her eyes cast down, hands tense around the waxed paper cup, fingers fumbling with the tap, wrists trembling.

"You okay Mary?"

"Yip." She made a strangled sound, one Pattie knew well. It meant Mary wasn't all right at all, despite her nodding head.

"Things okay with that husband of yours?"

"Yip," even more strangled.

"And young Troy's all right?" Yip. "And your mother?"

That covered all the bases; everyone and no one was all right while Mary, agreeable, sweet, quiet Mary, had nothing more to say.

Pattie watched her friend walk away, thin body hunched beneath a head of graying hair, plastic cup cradled like a child, and business papers tumbling like fallen leaves from her arm. If Pattie stayed near the coffee machine, she'd catch Mary on her break for a longer talk.

They'd worked together in the same office for years, as close to friends as workmates can be, sharing gossip and lunch and occasional afternoon drives as years went by. Mary knew Pattie's Dan had put on too much weight; Pattie's father was too forgetful and they'd put him in a home; Pattie's son and his wife hadn't the faintest idea how to discipline their kids. Pattie in turn knew Mary's Peter had left ten years ago; her mother was a pain; her son a rebel; and suddenly Peter was back.

With little faith in fairy tales and much in misery, Pattie also knew Mary and Peter's new relationship was heading for the rocks. And she knew, beyond the faintest doubt, Mary's mother belonged in a rest home, just like Pattie's dad.

Halfway through the morning Mary appeared hesitantly at the coffee room door. "Sit down," said Pattie, immediately dropping her slow pretense at filing. "Sit down; I'll get you a cup." She broke out the cookies too, her secret stash from their hiding-place under the counter.

They sat on opposite sides of a coffee-room table, cold metal chairs, warm drinks. Pattie stared at her friend's bowed head and twisting hands, seeking an opening. "Tell me," she said in the end. "Tell your Pattie now. Tell me all about it."

Mary sipped from the cup.

"Tell me, Mary. If you don't, I'll only guess and you know what a gossip I am."

Still Mary didn't speak.

Then Pattie held out a cookie. "Cookie for them—tastes better than a penny."

At last Mary raised her eyes from the plastic table-top. Her lips even twitched. It was a start.

Mary told Pattie slowly, over solemn choices of cookie—white chocolate or dark, chips or chunks—how everything at home was falling apart. "It's like you said, Pattie, there's no going back. You can't turn back the clock." Her husband, home after ten long years, seemed to want a wife and relationship long dead and buried. "Oh, I hugged him all right when I saw him," Mary said. "When he turned up on the doorstep. I hugged like there'd been no yesterday. But then you step back, and he's gray, and you're gray, and there's all those years gone by. I felt sick." Meanwhile her son was happy and sad and mostly, probably confused, as if he imagined his dad had a magic wand and hadn't waved it yet.

Mary's mother—well, her mother was her mother. "Sits in her chair and rings her bell. Rings it morning, noon and night and I so hate that bell."

"And?"

"And Peter," Mary said, seemingly ready at last to complete her complaints. "Him. He sits in his chair and says, 'Hey love, d'you want to make another coffee?' as if I'm his slave. Thinks he's the Pied Piper or something, just has to play a tune and I'll do as I'm told. And Troy comes in; 'Hi Mom, Hi Dad, Hi Gran.' All's right with the world, and runs upstairs. Laundry on the floor. Stuff all over the place. Empty cups. Dirty plates."

Mary's voice grew higher, water pouring over the rigid dam of her silence. She seemed ready to cry and sucked back on her breath. "I thought it would help," she said, more quietly. "I really thought it would help having him around again. Now I feel like a nobody in my own home."

Pattie, friend, more than workmate, more than a gossip, placed an arm around Mary's shoulders. She had such thin shoulders, shaking shoulders, shuddering with struggling breaths. Pattie stood behind her with nothing to say, offering silent comfort—Pattie, the one who always talked too much— she knew she did. Then she picked up the coffee cups and plates and said at least Mary wouldn't have to wash up at work. "So, what you doing Saturday?"

"Me? Nothing. Everything."

"You're coming out with me."

Mary looked up, confused.

"You're coming out with me," said Pattie, "and there's no getting out of it. I'm taking you for a drive."

"A drive? Where to? You're nuts."

Pattie agreed, since she hadn't even thought yet where they'd go. She said she'd pick Mary up at ten. Then she left, watching her friend's nodding head slowly droop over the table.

Nodding Head

Abigail meant it to help, but she failed. She sat, stuck in the chair in her room, remembering how she'd hoped it would all turn out. If hopes were dreams and dreams came true, Abigail would be walking around the room cleaning up instead of molding like leftover bread dough.

She'd tried so hard to get her daughter back with her husband. She'd been so sure, and so right about where young Troy had gone. Then she'd been sure and wrong about how to make things right.

Of course, everyone thought Abigail was just the poor old, ancient old mother; drippy old dear with no idea what's going on; poor idiot shut in her room ringing her bell; annoying old thing. *There's nothing wrong with my mind*, Abigail thought, *and nothing wrong with my eyes. I see it all*. Not blind, not poor, just old, Abigail saw perfectly well what was happening to her daughter, darling child, ghost child, lost child, turning to stone. She wished she could help.

In the mornings Abigail heard the sounds of dawn, early traffic rumbling outside while Mary let her *lie in*. Her bed lay under the living room window where glass rattled with every passing car. She longed to sit up and peek, and wondered why people imagine the old just need sleep. But *lie in* means lie still, stay out of the way, out of sight, out of mind. So she'd listen to the morning sounds, and recognize the steps in the morning routine.

Mary's alarm rang first, beeping in the bedroom overhead, sharply stilled with the bang of Mary's hand. The bed would creak as her daughter climbed out, footsteps stumbling on the stairs, the sound of water gurgling in the kitchen, clattering cups, fridge door open and shut, faint scent on morning air of stale bedding, worn-out slippers and coffee.

Mary's feet would patter on the stairs again with her breathing too loud, a knock on Troy's door, "Hey, wake up

Kiddo," footsteps stomping to the bathroom, running water. Mary's shower was as fast as Abigail's coughing for breath, then back downstairs to pans and plates, cooking breakfast for a hardworking son before he left for the garage.

Troy's footsteps were slower, heavier, more deliberate. The hissing of sprays punctuated Troy's shower, like rustling wind in the falling leaves of autumn. His feet tapped unsteadily on the stairs, front door open, paper snatched from the step, chairs scraped back from kitchen table as mother and son sat to eat. Abigail would listen, closed in her room, while Troy and Mary ate breakfast together, agreeably sharing the paper and rustling the news. The scent of coffee mingled with toast and bacon—*ah the sweet taste of salt*. Over it all that harsh background scent drifted from whatever miraculous product Troy used under his arms.

Mary would bring Abigail's coffee in bed. "Morning, Mother." Then she'd run out again to pack lunches, make Troy's bed, sort the washing. She'd help Abigail with those thick ugly stockings that glued themselves to her feet—elastic for phlebitis; Abigail remembered how Troy, when he was little, thought fleas were biting her.

When Troy was little. When times were happier. Abigail felt like the baby now, with Troy the man.

She'd never meant this to happen. When she came to stay she'd hoped to make life easier for Mary. "You can't travel all this way to help me morning and night." Abigail's proud head had nodded for emphasis. "You should let me live with you. I'll not take much space." But here she was, in the best room of the house, Troy's records and games banished up into his bedroom, the dining room squashed with easy chairs all jumbled around the table. They thought she didn't know.

Nothing wrong with my imagination, Abigail thought. Except, if only she'd imagined this right, it wouldn't have ended this way.

Troy left for the garage, Mary for the office. The creaking house grew quiet while Abigail watched TV, wishing she could change channel, pouring coffee with shaking hand from the flask on the table, eating cookies from the plate. By evening her hands wouldn't be able to move, except to clutch the bell. Mornings were brief freedom, with no one around to notice.

Eventually the bed upstairs complained again. Eventually running water splashed. The heater roared urgently. Abigail checked her watch, hands and wrists still mobile. How could Peter take so long to get clean?

Peter whistled—Peter Piper she called him—as he showered. He sang as he dressed. Then Abigail looked up to his hurried, "Hello there, Mother" when he poked his head through her door. He ignored the empty mug and plate on her table—not his job of course.

The microwave, strange modern machine, whirred and clanked and pinged. Knife and fork scraped on plate. Coffee reheated. Frozen food cooked fast. Peter's footsteps would stumble into the cluttered dining room, newspaper rustling in food-laden hand, and he'd sit—chair creaks and groans—to watch the portable TV on his own—*wouldn't want to watch with me.*

At lunchtime Abigail heard the key in the lock as stale air fled. Mary was home, doubtless overloaded with shopping, ready to refill cupboards, make lunch for three when it should have been two, or one. Abigail's hands were stiffening up again now, though she grasped and clawed the air to keep them moving.

If Abigail had imagined this right, Peter would still be away in another world, in another life. She'd be in a retirement home, Troy in an apartment, and Mary in a pretty little place of her own. Sweet Mary, pretty Mary, beloved daughter Mary. There'd be laugh lines around her eyes and a twinkle in her smile, and she'd visit every weekend where her mother would pretend to laugh with her and all would be well.

I'm just a foolish old woman, Abigail thought, *can't even make a single word make sense. Even my imagination's giving up.*

She clawed her solid fist again though the fingers barely came together. Then Mary came to pick up the cup and plate and switch off the TV so she could *rest*. Abigail tried to thank her.

"Nodding head." Her ratchety, half-silent voice spat rubbish from her mouth. Mary looked on with weary eyes and sighed.

Peter Piper

"Pattie's taking me out." Mary pulled her coat down from its hook behind the kitchen door.

"I can take you out."

"We're going for a drive."

"I can…" Peter paused, half-out of his chair. "Going where for a drive?"

"I don't know. Why would I have to tell you?"

He slammed the newspaper down on the table, scattering knives from the plates. "Shut up!" And Mary jumped back. She'd given him breakfast, cooked it, laid it out for him—he should be thanking her. Then his voice suddenly calmed. "I can take you out for a drive if that's what you want."

It wasn't what she wanted. Mary retreated toward the door. *Be nice. Be agreeable.* "I know, Peter," she answered in her sweetest, motherly, eternally patient voice. "I know. But Pattie asked me. Pattie's my friend."

"I'm your husband."

"Ex." She hadn't meant to say it aloud. She knew it would set him off. Truth was, she hadn't divorced him and she wasn't quite sure what that meant.

Peter leapt to his feet, tipping paper like wind-blown leaves from table to floor. As Mary stumbled past he grasped at her. "Peter, Peter, Peter's ex! Piper picked a peck." His fingers tweaked her weekend skirt and her leg—they'd leave a bruise. "Picked a peck of pickled peppers didn't he? Didn't I?" He chased her around the tiny kitchen table, kicking chairs out the way.

"Peter, stop it!"

"Pickled Pattie."

"Peter, stop!"

"Peter's pecker."

"Stop it, Peter!"

"Pick a pecker."

"Peter. Not now."

When Mary halted, Peter ran into her. She pushed him away and saw him stumble. Then he lifted his eyes to hers, all innocent and agreeable, like her son's when he was small, like her son's when he wanted something, like her son's when they were arguing and he wondered if the world would fall apart again. *Poor Troy*, Mary thought. Didn't he know the world would never stop falling apart?

Still, she couldn't bear to hurt him, neither Peter nor Troy. Breathing heavily from the rush, hair damp from morning and breakfast, she stared at Peter and knew she was meant to love him. His head swayed and she wanted to make him nod. But Peter had been gone so long, too long. Now only a shadow remained, dark prophecy of her son. She saw who Troy would become someday perhaps, loved Peter for Troy with a mother's love, but had no feelings of a woman for a man toward him now. He wasn't her man anymore, just a picture and memory, lost hope.

"Maybe later, Peter." Peace offering.

Peter thunked down on the chair, face shiny with sweat. "You know, I'm getting sick of waiting, Mary." His fists kneaded the paper.

"I know, Peter. I know." She twisted the solid gold band she'd never stopped wearing. "I know. It's just hard."

"Yeah, well, it's harder for me." Peter smiled, looking down at himself, making his own jokes under the table where she could sense his desire. Mary didn't care. It would be less *hard* if he'd go out and get a job. But Peter said he needed to get a life first. Mary had none to spare.

When the doorbell rang, she shouted goodbye to her mother, left son asleep and husband buried in breakfast and the paper, while she walked toward the sun.

Fallen Leaves

They were silent in the car, Pattie driving, Mary clutching handbag and keys, as if she couldn't remember the way to put one back into the other. Pattie sighed. There'd be a right time to talk, just not now. So she drove, steadily, not so long, while it felt like miles.

"How far are we going?" Mary asked. A voice at last!

"Not far."

"Where to?"

"To Paradise."

Then Mary laughed.

"Oh Mary," said Pattie, her eyes still fixed on the road. "Oh Mary, it's been so long since I heard you laugh."

"Paradise?" Mary asked, laughter gone as suddenly as it had appeared. "Where on earth would you find that?"

Though the cynicism crept back into her friend's voice, Pattie knew they were okay. It was almost time to talk.

The next town was only ten minutes away at most. Traffic lights announced it. A new subdivision of houses lay just past the remains of a farmer's gate. Pattie drove through tree-lined streets that widened for elegant shops. Road signs pointed to changing lanes. Mary's hands clenched tensely on her bag, but at least she'd put the keys away. Pattie smiled.

"You don't like towns Mary, do you?'

"No."

"That's okay. We'll be out in the countryside soon."

Leaving the towers and glass-fronted shops, Pattie drove through fields and into the edge of a forest. For a while the road paralleled a country park with gray town buildings shimmering on the other side. Hills rolled lazily down to a duck pond resting in the dale. Fallen leaves lined the edge of the road with thick piles of brown. Sunshine dripped through red and gold, dappling the tarmac. "This is nice," said Mary.

Pattie told her it was called Paradise Park. "This is where we're going?" No.

A brook burbled gently, reflecting colors of fall. Then the view narrowed as forest thickened blackly around them. A sharp bend, roughly-surfaced bridge, and yellow lines led to another traffic light. Across the intersection, construction machinery hummed and buzzed furiously, flashing bright lights.

"New development?" Mary asked warily.

Pattie said they were building new college dorms. "Church dorms, or Christian dorms or something, for the University in town." They drove slowly past a tiny church. A label proclaimed it *Church of Paradise,* and a sign shaped like a thermometer advertised the state of the building fund. "I think there was a village called Paradise once," Pattie volunteered. "I guess the town must've grown and swallowed it up."

"Nice little church though," said Mary, smiling weakly.

"Yes."

They turned across traffic at the next junction, entering an area with a large stone sign proclaiming *Paradise Gardens.*

"Where on earth are we now?" Mary asked.

"Still driving," said Pattie. "I think I might move here."

Mary laughed, sounding more relaxed with every mile. The houses were big, new-looking, clean-painted with neat bright yards and green lawns. "These are way too big for you," said Mary, but Pattie said she was looking at the town houses down the other end.

A green was dotted with small soccer players. They fluttered like fallen leaves forming patterns of shirts and shorts. An elementary school, Paradise Elementary, dominated a parking lot full of soccer moms waiting with minivans. And a row of neat town houses hid behind drying hydrangeas and the dull pointed leaves of azaleas.

"Very nice," said Mary, head nodding, as Pattie parked the car. They sat together imagining colors of spring, watched by the squirrel sitting atop the For Sale sign.

"Come and look." Pattie opened her door.

"Why? I'm not moving anywhere," Mary complained.

Pattie answered sharply that maybe she should. "Peter pipes a tune and you follow, Mary. Well, maybe it's time you piped up for yourself once in a while." Then she smiled. "I just want you with me while I look, that's all."

Mary seemed to relax, so Pattie continued to talk as they walked to the door. "You should think about it though. Like I said, there's no going back. Even if Troy gets a place of his own. Even if your mom—well, whatever, the house would never be the same. You got to move on. Keep moving on. It'll keep you young."

"We can't afford to move."

Pattie grabbed her friend's arm. "Mary, how d'you know what you can afford?" she asked. "Your Peter had a fine house out there where he was living. That's what Troy told you, right?" Mary nodded. "And a business?" She nodded again. "Right, well, he sells that house. He'll get money for it. Sell the business. You buy yourselves a nice little townhouse here, and we'll be neighbors."

"Why would I want to live in a townhouse with Peter?" Mary asked, then added, "And Mother and Troy aren't about to leave home either."

"Buy condos," said Pattie, laughing. "A little separation would do you all good. Two condos. Maybe three or four." Crazy idea, but at least it birthed a smile.

Condominiums dominated the left side of the road, town houses on the right. Pattie watched Mary's eyes widen with dawning of impossible imaginings. Then she heard the complaint she'd known she was bound to hear.

"But where would Mother live?"

"I'll show you," Pattie answered. "Later." Luckily Mary didn't ask what she meant, and the realtor Pattie had arranged to meet strolled around the side of the building, hand outstretched, ending the conversation. He said his name was Charlie. Black-haired, almond-eyed, he seemed young enough to be Pattie's son. He almost tripped over a fluffy white cat scurrying past.

"Just ten minutes from work, for me and Dan, and *so* handy for Dad," said Pattie as they shook hands afterward. Charlie said there were several other places in the same price range. He could show them another time, perhaps if Pattie were to bring her husband with her. Pattie agreed.

"And you, Ma'am?" Charlie looked at Mary. Her face flushed suddenly warm and she stumbled back.

When Charlie left, Pattie dragged Mary across the street to the condos. "You could live downstairs," she said. "Put Peter upstairs."

"Oh yeah. Most agreeable. And I'd be his maid climbing the stairs every day to make his bed."

"Well, at least you'd have separate beds." At least Pattie and Mary could still share a smile, so the friendship stayed strong. *Scary when your friend's strung out so tight.*

Back in the car, Pattie told Mary they were finally near their destination. "Not the town house then?" *No, not the town house.* Wrought iron gates, green painted, had a sign welcoming them to *Paradise House*. Pattie parked the car in the asphalt semi-circle by the wide front door. It was an old people's home.

"No way," said Mary, clutching her purse to her chest. "No way! I won't put my mother in a home."

Pattie insisted she at least come and look, at least take a brochure back with her and show it to her mother. "And at least come in with me and say Hi to my dad." So they walked around together, two middle-aged women in a home filled with the old. Assistants and care-givers greeted and smiled, brochures were proffered, cups of tea and lemon cookies, while sunshine filled the airy blue room where Pattie's father rested, his white head nodding, a white cat lying like slippers across his feet.

Pattie tried, too hard inevitably, to tell Mary how good the place was, and how her dad was happy. Mary just nodded politely and agreed to take a brochure.

"I'll show her when I get home," said Mary, but Pattie knew she wouldn't. She took an extra one to give Troy if she saw him.

Winter

Moving on, Saying Goodbye, Let's go, Fresh Start

I'm bound for moving on. Peter sang the songs in his head, remembered the occasional bar in LA, occasional acquaintances trying to be friends. He'd thought he'd done all his moving on back then, leaving the Midwestern plains and lakeshores and towns. He'd said goodbye to wife and child long years before he could hurt them. He'd committed himself to his chosen fresh start, all work and no play, just existence, being safe. If he let himself go, went out when he had to for friendship's sake perhaps and drank too much, it was just once in a while. At least he never took anyone home with him and never hurt anyone. He wasn't his father. A quick and dirty grope while a dancer squirmed on his lap hardly counted as betrayal, just adult fantasy.

I'm bound for moving on, he thought, for moving on again. Mary wouldn't live with him now, but maybe Troy would work at his garage and they'd still be together. Peter would keep himself pure just like before and wait for her. He'd close and lock the door on temptation and be a good father, belatedly, to his son.

I'm bound for moving on. But he had moved on, older now than his father had ever been. He looked in the mirror, shaved carefully around his new beard. *I'm really not my dad.* He smiled, feeling something enormously freeing in the thought. He wanted to comb his hair differently and breathe different air. If he was older and hadn't turned out like his dad, perhaps he really could be safe.

I'm a good man. I'm a good husband, Peter thought to

himself, swallowing the mint of toothpaste, feeling fresh and well-prepared. Though, of course, his wife didn't appreciate him.

Peter straightened his tie, adjusted his collar, measured the shape of his smile. *Put your life up for sale and move on.*

Moving on

None of it would be this way if Abigail could help it, if she could tell them what she wanted, if she could make them listen to her thoughts and see what she meant.

It wasn't as if she was completely helpless. When Troy left home Abigail had known, deep inside herself, where he'd be. She'd stared, aiming with nose, eyes, head, ugly clawed fist with its useless, pointless fingers, at the picture on the shelf. She kept looking, kept pointing, kept struggling to speak, till Mary brought it over and sat with her. Poor Mary had nothing else to do except work and sit with her mother. Then Abigail pointed to Peter's face, struggling so hard to make her fingers move the way she intended. She pointed and fought her recalcitrant lips, trying to sound his name. Mary guessed, like a small child playing I-Spy. "Do you want this? Do you want that?" Till eventually she asked "Do you want me to write to him?" Then Abigail nodded, nodded till her head threatened to fall.

Yes, write him. Call him, she wanted to say. "Peter Pattie," was what came out. "Peter Piper. Move on."

So now old Abigail turned her nose to the brochure Troy left on her table.

"Don't worry," Mary said. "Can't think where that came from." She made to clear the glossy paper away but Abigail's fingers managed to hold it down. "Don't worry Mother. Don't fuss. I'll never put you in a home."

Abigail gazed into Mary's face. The pursed lips gave her daughter away. Poor Mary, doing her duty while trying to make it sound like what she wanted. Poor Abigail trying to live with and be grateful for whatever she was given. This wasn't home, or life. Abigail sighed, desperate for more, more for Mary and more for herself.

It didn't work of course. She tried to make Mary look at the brochure but it wasn't like the family picture, not something Mary even wanted to see. All Abigail could do was clutch it in her fist when her daughter tried to tidy it away.

"I wish you'd let go," Mary said impatiently. "I wish you'd stop worrying, Mother." She had no idea.

Eventually Abigail decided to try with Troy. She heard his key in the door, footsteps in the hall, and she rang her bell.

"I'll go, Mom," said Troy, agreeable, the only peaceable member of the family these days.

"Oh don't worry," said Mary, predictably. Still Abigail kept ringing after Mary came, ringing, ringing till her daughter went out in dismay letting Troy take her place.

"Hi Grandma."

Abigail put down the bell. Troy walked toward her and she tried to smile, willing her hands to pick up and hold the brochure, but they fell to her lap.

"Hi Grandma. What were you looking at? This brochure?" Troy leaned over, pouring sour garage-breath in her face, and picked up the leaflet.

Abigail struggled again to smile, building determination behind her eyes, tensing her reluctant, disobedient body like a wire. "Do you like it?" Troy asked, unfolding images, page by page, by her face. "Are you trying to tell me something?" Abigail nodded. That, at least, was something she still could do.

"D'you wish you could live there?" She nodded again.

"D'you want me to tell Mom?" More nodding head.

"You're sure?"

Mary walked into the room, a shadow crossing the threshold behind Troy. Abigail met her with her eyes and nodded as fast as she could, a nodding-head toy keeping time on top of her neck. She tried so hard to shape her face into a smile, tried to say yes and didn't even know what words came jumbling out. That jagged voice betrayed her at every turn.

Then Mary knelt beside her, holding pictures and words as they fell from Troy's hand. Mary gazed into Abigail's eyes— Mary, beautiful Mary. Slowly, struggling to force out one word, Abigail said, "Yes."

"You really mean it, Mother?"

"Yes."

"You're sure?"

Abigail nodded and Mary sighed.

Was this a smile awakening Mary's face? Perhaps a spring in her step? Could Abigail set things right for her daughter after all, make green grass grow?

Troy turned to wink at his grandmother from the door. She would have winked back if she could, but even if she couldn't move, couldn't speak, couldn't close a tear-gummed eye, she could still get her own way.

It was time to say goodbye, time to move on, time for a fresh start.

Saying Goodbye

It didn't take so long to arrange everything once the decision was made. Peter drove across the country to close his business and house. They sold straight away, impossibly fast. Mary wondered if he'd planned it all along, had the papers drawn up waiting for the day. Meanwhile Troy drove her along those same roads Pattie had taken. She signed forms for her mother at Paradise House, Troy checking the details, boy grown to man. Then they picked out a ground floor condo only streets away, backing onto grassland, Mary's new home. Troy spotted a *for sale* sign at the garage when they stopped for gas. "Dad should make a bid," he said. "We'll all be together." It made perfect sense.

Could it really be so easy?

Father and son drove down together next weekend. Peter liked the garage or the location—Mary never asked which.

They put down deposits on the business, two separate town houses doors from each other, and on Mary's condo, signed away their lives. "Signed away our firstborn too." Peter laughed, clapping Troy on the shoulder. They must have planned it all while Mary cooked dinner for her mother and herself. The money, all that impossible money, came from Peter's business, booming when no family borrowed his time.

Mary's mother seemed happy. Her lips still twisted, but almost smiled. Her clawed hand clutched Mary's after the meal, but her fingers seemed almost gentle as they groped. White clouds of hair around Abigail's head became a halo instead of an evil nest. The moving began.

Peter left first, to an empty house furnished bit by bit from both their homes. Troy drove Abigail and Mary to Paradise House, while Peter followed in a rented van. Mary's mother's room seemed to move with her, only the view from the window changing, grass and trees instead of cars. Afterward Troy furnished his own little house with leftovers and details, while Mary packed boxes in rapidly expanding emptiness.

Now she walked through the rooms one last time. Floors, still carpeted, muffled her footsteps, but walls echoed every sound. Dust and spider-webs floated in the air, their taste coating her tongue. Sunbeams drew patterns like motion detector beams to scare intruders, as if the house already knew she'd moved on.

From the doorway of the main bedroom, her refuge for so long, Mary studied lines in the carpet where her double bed had stood, deep-seated dents from the feet of her big old dresser, scuffed footprints of chair, chest and stool. All this furniture was in Peter's house now. It made sense, she knew. His house had more and bigger rooms than her condo. But memories molded in the furniture were hers, not her husband's. Peter had left this house and all it held long years ago. It seemed strange bequeathing part of it to him.

She drew breath, pursed her lips and crossed her arms over her chest. *Time for a clean break, fresh start.* Boldly marching across the floor, cutting light beams that made no alarm, she stood where the dresser once sat, brushed cobwebs from the missing mirror and imagined her image there. She'd never again run her fingers through whorls and crevasses of smooth carved oak. The glowing timber would never again remind her of holes in her life. *Yes*, Mary thought at last. *It's good.* Good to dump her wooden memories and start living again.

In Troy's room Mary leaned against the narrow window, looking down over the path and small neat yard. Troy had played there as a tiny boy, running to his father, flying in the air to be caught by proud strong hands. They'd been a family then. Later, Troy played alone, with only an overworked mother to throw back the ball, grass growing too tall and Mary too weary to cut it. He'd lain in the sun, scraggly teenager with transistor radio playing on his chest. Then he'd sulked when she made him help with pulling weeds.

Lately Troy lived his life in this room. The marks of his absence were paint peeled from walls, threadbare patches where he'd lain on the carpet with his records, stray breadcrumbs and stains of strawberry jelly and blackcurrant drinks, stronger drinks as well. Mary smelled stale alcohol. She knew where Troy's ancient TV had stood, and the bed, and the pile of dirty laundry. He'd moved everything to his townhouse, down the street from his father's, to rooms Mary hadn't even seen. Troy had grown into a man, a homeowner now. *He'll have to do his own washing.*

Mary smiled sadly, trying to imagine how Troy's little house must look. He'd taken his furniture in the rented van, bought table and chairs for his dining-room from the classifieds while Mary leaned over his shoulder with her nose rubbing his hair. He'd taken a bookshelf from his grandma's room, one of Grandma's sagging armchairs, and a bedside cabinet she'd used to hold cookies and coffee. That was it, in a two bedroom house. That, plus his father's brass curtain rods. Still, he did have a house. Just turning twenty, how many young men his age could say that? He had a home of his own and his mother felt proud.

Just for a moment, Mary waited at the top of the stairs.

Suddenly weak, suddenly homeless and scared, she couldn't take the next step. She'd lived here so long, she thought, since the day they signed the papers, since Troy was two. She'd lived here through short-lived years of happiness, and stayed through long hard years of separation. She'd lived again through the shorter, even harder months back together. Now she had to choose between homeless and free. Freedom felt like a loose step on a stair where she might fall.

"You ready yet, Mom?" Troy waited down below.

"Just coming, Troy. Just saying goodbye."

Troy laughed because he had fewer memories, or fewer he cared to keep.

Downstairs, Mary insisted on viewing each room alone, one last time. She said goodbye to the kitchen where they'd eaten through all those years, three eating together till Peter left, two till her mother came, and two again when her mother got too ill to leave the living room. The space looked bigger without table and chairs. Big enough to chase in. *Big enough to dance.*

Mary remembered the burbles of earlier joy. She saw Peter lift his son over his head, heard the giggles of a little boy's voice. She heard as well the echo of brittle laughter through recent months, Peter chasing, demanding what Mary couldn't give, Peter scornful, Peter cruelly insistent. No, she told herself. Listen instead to the quieter sounds of moments shared with her mother, Abigail ready to move to a home, seemingly content after all.

Mary said goodbye then to Abigail's room, seeing the ghosts of its previous incarnation behind the dust and dents of her mother's furniture. There—where her mother had kept the TV—Mary and Peter used to sit on the sofa, arms around each other, comfortably married. There—where her mother's bed left a layer of dust on the carpet—Troy used to play his games, wooden trains pushed noisily around grooved wooden tracks, plastic bricks built into concrete jungles, cardboard boxes filled with counters and cards and dice, cartoons on TV.

There, behind the coffee ring, was the stain from Troy's

blackcurrant juice. Peter had laughed. "Boys will be boys," while Mary wept for their first major spillage in her perfect home—perfect marriage waiting for the dream to go sour.

The dining room—Mary had to look there too. She had to remember its former glory before all the furniture piled on top of itself when her mother came to stay. She remembered candlelit dinners enjoyed while Troy slept, late night meals with Peter, dinners with friends, bridge nights even, when they were young.

Mary remembered, sorted the memories, dusted them, and put them away. With no furniture to hide them in, she simply folded thoughts between her hands, tucking them into pockets beneath her clothes. Time to move on.

"Let's go," said Troy. They went.

Let's go

Troy and Peter hired the van from a company in the next town. They got a good rate because Peter had bought the local garage in the subdivision. Peter offered a deal on services in exchange. *So many deals.* Even Troy's house purchase came through faster because of his father's business. Troy's new job would be working at his father's garage, though it was hard leaving where he'd trained all these years. They gave him a party his last day at work. Troy drank too much, and his best friend Todd brought him back sprawled on the seat of his car. Troy's last night in his childhood home was spent on the floor instead of bed. There was something ironically appropriate about it, Troy thought now, as he waited for his mother. "You ready yet, Mom?"

She wandered around rooms saying goodbye while Todd and Troy loaded the van with boxes and last bits of furniture, his mother's mattress—the bed had already gone to his father's house—kitchen table and chairs, the cross piece from the cupboards in Troy's bedroom. Boxes were stacked and tumbled, squeezed against each other to keep them from moving, numbered to protect against getting lost. Most of them would be delivered to Mary's condo.

Grandma moved the week before, her furniture gone too, making the new room a miniature of the old, same pictures on shelf and wall, same cups and plates on the same embroidered cloth. She was content, Troy thought.

Troy's father left a month ago, moving to his new house as soon as he took over running the garage. He seemed happier too, finally resigned to knowing his marriage wouldn't work. He'd offered to drive today but Troy said no. The condo was Mom's fresh start—she wouldn't want him there.

"What about you?" Todd asked of Troy as they finished loading the van. "How do you feel?"

"Lonely," said Troy. "Hungover. How d'you think?" He thanked his friend for his help, agreed to meet for a drink sometime soon. "Call me." Then he waved goodbye.

Troy's mother drifted downstairs, meandering like a ghost through the remaining rooms, eyes lost in the past.

"Come on, Mom. Let's go."

Finally she let Troy take her arm and help her into the van. "It's so high." She giggled like a child. Troy felt cold, wondering if, like Grandma, she'd turn into a helpless dependent one day.

Ghosts of past and future met on the path: Troy's father in the old brown coat, mother barefoot and running, Troy reaching for the lock. If he listened closely enough he might hear Grandma's bell, quietly demanding, or warning, trying to deliver a message words couldn't spell. The ghosts passed through him now and moved on, taking nothing away with them. Another van approached down the road, new owners ready to fill the house with new dreams. Troy turned the key to start the engine, glad his mother could turn the next page of her life.

Fresh Start

Paradise House, it said on the red brick wall by the wrought iron gates. "That's where your grandma is," Mary told Troy, and he nodded. "Have you been to see her yet?" He nodded again. "And your dad? Has your dad been to see her?"

"I don't know."

Troy drove the van down the next side road, stopping at the curb by the condos.

"Here we go." Mary felt old as Troy helped her down from the van and walked her to the entrance. "I'll bring in the boxes and the table," he said, "then I'll go unload the rest on Dad and me." She hardly listened.

The condo was already fully furnished. Part of her knew it was Peter's furniture—small modern stuff from his *other* home. He'd said it would be more practical. His house was bigger so he needed the big old furniture. Mary had been too tired to disagree at the time, but now, as she looked around the neat tiny room, she knew for once in his life her husband had been right. The neat little table and chairs fitted perfectly into their alcove. The two-seater sofa filled the length of the back wall. The bookshelf would hold her library and videos while the tiny TV, bought second hand, would work fine by the window with the curtains closed, on its stand bought by Troy through the paper.

Mary had thought it might hurt to know some of these were Peter's things. But everything was second-hand. She spared the past no thought. Transitory items, they were hers for the present, devoid of memories. It was good.

The bedroom opened from the narrow hall, neat single bed, white dresser, white drawers, clean and bright. If there were stains from Peter's coffee cups, she'd soon cover them. They wouldn't be her stains, not part of her life. Peter wouldn't touch her now.

The furniture and rooms smelled musty. They didn't smell of Peter. It was good.

As Troy brought in boxes, Mary put the kettle on. She spared a moment to feel lonely, wishing Pattie and Dan had moved as well, but perhaps this was better, a completely fresh start, her unencumbered unknown. She wondered what her neighbors would be like, and felt her shoulders straightening to the challenge. Peter? He'd be a friend, she knew. She doubted they'd fall in love again, but at least this way they wouldn't fall out any further.

The kettle whistled its tune and she brewed the tea.

Spring

*Measuring Time, Keys to the Heart, Cradle Snatcher,
Wildwood Flowers*

He slept in the big double bed, measuring time as the hours ticked away and, each second, remembering her. He woke alone in the big double bed, damp with memory and pain, knowing though he was rejected she still held and turned, oh so tortuously twisted the keys to his heart. He buried his face in the weft of the mattress and smelled her memory there, roses and violets and wildwood flowers, freedom and sunshine and pain. Closing his eyes to drive back the sanding of time he remembered the cradle, sweet baby's breath, how it snatched with its promise from night.

Then he thought how she wasn't so far from him now. He could easily drive to her house. He could watch through the window and follow her shadow's sweet image where curtains revealed it. He could break down the door and pin her to the wall... *But he wasn't his father.*

Measuring Time

The clock was a wedding present from Peter's grandparents, meant to measure the hours of a marriage they always knew wouldn't last. They were right of course. They were always right. They'd given his parents a clock on their wedding night too. His father smashed it eventually.

In early days of wedded bliss, Peter and Mary would laugh and dance to the beat of the clock, radio songs competing with its all-pervasive disapproval.

"We're in love." Tsk.

"We'll last forever." Tsk tsk.

"We're going to have a baby." Tsk, tsk, tsk.

They'd sit in front of their borrowed TV in Abigail's upstairs room, wrapped in the warmth of each other's arms, and still the clock would tick. Mary would struggle from her seat to turn up the sound. Peter would make a fist as if to destroy the measurer of hours. Fist for the clock—no anger for Mary back then.

When they moved to their own home, the clock still measured his presence and his absence, timed meals when he was late, kept count of every detail and every offense.

"Where've you been?" Tsk tsk. "Out with your fancy girl?"

But Peter had done nothing wrong. He knew, because he wasn't his father. He had no fancy girls, loved Mary too much to hurt her that way. The clock didn't know it.

The clock, fake gold filigreed around its face in a pattern of wildwood flowers, breathed deep with the years. It measured the beat of Peter's growing desperation. Its steady sound ticked undeterred as the household fell apart. The clock snatched Troy's sweet cries from the cradle, poured out its scorn as the child learned to walk, as he went to school. Then Peter left, the timepiece ticking its triumph over seconds and minutes, weeks and months, ten long years weighed and measured till his return. The wildwood flowers stayed bright behind the glass, dusted daily by Mary's patient cloth.

Tsk tsk… Tsk, tsk, tsk…

The wooden case looked just like his parents' own clock before his dad broke it, even the gold scrolled petals behind the glass, even the scratches on the glow of dark polished oak. Their clock too must have counted hours and days of what shouldn't have been, before it lost time.

Black eyes, sprained wrists, broken arms and sobbing cries, all to the steady tick of his parents' clock—they happened far too often even for a child to believe. But it could always have been true, she might've fallen downstairs, though Peter never saw it. He saw closed doors, heard muffled cries, and hid in corners, under tables, or out in the yard, wondering if he would inherit his father's cruelty or his mother's clumsiness.

"Your dad likes things right, doesn't cope well with mistakes." *Accountant, numbers, order.*

"Your mom's just careless, son."

As a small child, Peter pulled wings off flies and legs off ladybugs. He screwed up his face and concentrated on the actions of fingers and nails, measuring dexterity to prove he wasn't his mother. Then he felt sorry for what he'd done, pitied the helpless creatures he destroyed. So, after all, his heart wasn't hard. His hands might yet be all thumbs. Peter was just a lost little boy, flightless and scared.

When Peter's mother asked his father about *your nice fancy women,* Peter believed she meant the secretary at work in her fancy tight clothes. She was called Lacey and smelled of flowers. She handed out candy from a jar and had red fingernails. Lacey wore big red glasses to hide her eyes under the strip lights in the office, but Peter learned to see truth underneath.

One day, Peter's father came home late and drunk, wearing lipstick on his collar. It couldn't have been the first time, just the first time his son noticed it, first time he remembered. Young Peter was good with colors. He could recognize the age of a bruise just by looking at its shade. So it wasn't hard for him to notice the pink of the lipstick wasn't right, neither for his mother nor for Lacey. That was the day he guessed there were other fancy women in his father's life, not just colleagues at work. He wondered if they all wore dark glasses, if their arms and legs hurt in the morning, if long sleeves or slacks and jeans hid bruises beneath.

I'm not my father, Peter told himself as a nine-year-old sitting alone in his bedroom, drinking in pictures from forbidden magazines. The images excited him, women unblemished, unclothed flesh as smooth and pure as fruit on a supermarket stall. The magazines came from a pile under his parents' bed, on his fathers' side.

I'm not my father, Peter told himself again, nearly a teenager now, clenching his fists in anger as he stood by his mother's coffin. "I'm not my father," when the police knocked at the door.

I'm not my father, Peter told himself, a boy who lived with his grandparents, watching other boys date the prettiest girls, afraid to ask them out in case he might hurt them. Mary asked him to dance, not a boy at all by then, and she smiled prettily, taught him to trust himself.

Gentle Mary, delicate, fragile little Mary, green-eyed beauty like an angel with a halo of fluffy fair hair. They dated and all Peter wanted was to share his life with her, so they chose to be married. She completed him and he thought she could keep him safe. For a short while he'd forgotten husbands are meant to protect their wives.

Peter wasn't his father, but the clock could just as well have been his father's clock. Though Peter never attempted to hit his wife, nor touched another woman, he saw the signs of his marriage crumbling away.

"Where've you been?" Tsk tsk.

"Out with your fancy girl?" Tsk tsk... tsk, tsk, tsk.

"You didn't know," Peter told his son, when the ten years were done, just before he came back home. "You couldn't have known how it was. I had to leave."

Afterward the clock continued to tick on the mantle. Mary wound its mechanism and dusted its smooth clear glass through lengthening days. It ticked disbelief while Peter tried his hardest, while what he'd broken proved beyond his skill to mend. It ticked, steady and sad, when Peter moved out to his own lonely home and Mary to her shiny new condo. Peter took the clock, his turn to wind it now. It carried the memory and reminder of what might have been. His grandparents won.

The clock ruled the mantle of Peter's new home, watching over his living room. He used a remote, new-fangled toy, to turn up the sound on TV, sitting alone with no wife or child to warm the empty chairs. But the clock ticked on. He aimed a fist but, instead of smashing his accuser, carried the clock out carefully and left it in the car. Just a few weeks listening to its litany of memories proved just a few weeks too many.

Next day Peter stood the wooden clock on the counter at the garage. The sounds of engines and machines drowned its voice. Books and ledgers overruled its authority. A working business always has need of a good timepiece.

The clock was never dusted there, the glass of its face never washed. Still Peter took care not to let the springs run down, keeping the key in the drawer.

Tsk, tsk. "Where've you been?"

Tsk, tsk. "I've been working, old friend." *I'm not my father.*

Keys to the Heart

Keys to his house, keys to the garage, keys to the cars, to the desk, to the safe, keys to his son's house, his ex-wife's condo, the home where his mother-in-law lived, so many keys, so many pieces of his life. Peter kept his keys on one wide ring in the pocket of his jeans, its weight familiar as flesh against his leg so he felt unclothed without it. If he left the ring on a shelf he felt un-tethered, as though he might look in a mirror and find he'd disappeared, snatched away on a cloud.

Just as Mary disappeared, he thought. Just as his son was disappearing now, new interests, new girls in his life. *Just as dreams disappeared.*

Peter kept the other ring, the gold one, on his finger, its smoothness growing familiar and soothing again. Though he'd taken it off through their time of separation, he wore it religiously now. Though he knew Mary would never have him back, he had to keep the ring. He wore it because it identified this new self, father-of-Troy, ex-spouse-of-Mary, because taking it off would turn him into someone he didn't know, and because it made him look safe.

People came to the garage for help, teenage girls, women afraid their transport would let them down, stranded motorists. The ring told them their mechanic wasn't a threat but a solid family man with a wife waiting at home. So they could talk to him.

"Mr. Markham?"

"Yes."

The woman shuffled nervously against his counter, her gaze wandering from cash machine to clock. Peter wondered if she guessed why it measured time there with its gold filigree flowers and broken promises.

"Look," she continued. "I know you've stayed really late to fix my car."

"No problem. It's my job."

"No, I mean it's really kind of you. And I guess…" She moved her gaze to his hand. "You know, if your wife wouldn't mind, I'd really like to buy you a drink or something."

Peter smiled, the unfamiliar beard still scratching his chin. The woman was pretty, a stranger in town, sweet ship passing in the night. Still, it wouldn't do to set a precedent. "Very kind," he muttered politely while the keys in his pocket jangled, tangling him, and the clock ticked on. "Very kind." Then he added, almost silently, "No wife though."

"No wife?" She listened well.

"We're separated, divorced almost. We just, you know…"

The woman said she knew and Peter believed her. He wasn't sure why. Something in the way she looked at him he supposed, in the sadness of her eyes, as if she'd seen too much of life in her small number of years. He filled out the forms, accepted her money, jangled coins and gave her back her keys. Then, somehow, he ended up turning out the lights as she left. He locked the garage, held her hand, gazed deep into her eyes. *What a cliché.*

"About that drink?" she asked, hips swaying just the right way, chin at the perfect angle to highlight the hollows of her neck. "D'you know a good place?"

Peter drove through town in front of her car, waited when

she missed the turn, and led the way to a restaurant on West Point Road, with a motel out back. He checked his mirror over and again as he drove, trying to remember her face and the wildwood flowers on her skirt.

After a meal they booked a room and stayed the night. It had been a long time—a really long time—and a stranger's lap-dance in a bar was no substitute.

Next day the keys felt lighter against Peter's leg as he walked around the garage. He wondered if he should give back the ones to Mary's condo and Paradise House. He wondered if he might take off his ring too, once in a while, and hide it in his pocket. He felt younger again.

Not my father. I didn't do anything wrong. Not my father. Just a man with natural needs. He'd just spent a wonderful, beautiful night with a woman he'd never see again. Of course, the clock ticked its weary accusation from the counter, but Peter didn't need to answer. The sounds of machinery drowned its voice.

The touch of a woman was sweeter than honey and stronger and richer than beer. *Time for a new life* Peter thought. *Time to step free from the past.*

Cradle Snatchers

"So, Mom, I've met this girl."

"You've met a lot of girls in your time, Troy," Mary answered. They strolled the grounds of the old peoples' home, Mary pushing her mother's wheelchair while Troy strode a few steps behind on the narrow path.

"Yeah, but you know what I mean."

"So, tell me about her." Mary slowed her steps to listen, picking words out of the crunching and wheeling of gravel. She'd dreamed for years Troy might find someone special. Would this be the one? But as he muttered, sighed, described, and her mother's wheels kept turning, Mary found herself drifting back into the quiet of her own thoughts.

Troy lived alone in his two-bedroom house near his dad, a nice enough place, well enough kept for a bachelor. He worked at his father's garage, where he earned good enough money. He dressed in clean clothes under his overalls. He bathed. He washed his hair—a fine young man. Yet he drifted from girl to girl, never seeming to look for commitment either from them or himself. Had Mary and Peter spoiled it for him? Had their broken marriage made him an eternal wanderer, picking the wildwood flowers with a smile and a kiss and throwing them away?

Still, she listened with at least half an ear, and noticed the name of the girl, Lydia Steepleton. She heard Lydia lived in one of the larger houses, in the posh part of the neighborhood, and was still in school.

"Troy," Mary warned. "Don't go cradle-snatching, please."

"I'm not," Troy answered.

Mary stopped the wheelchair and turned to him. His long dark hair blew around his face, but she could see his eyes, clear and honest, unfettered by guilt. He looked well and confident, better than Mary had seen him look in years, so she believed him though she worried just the same.

"Take things easy," she advised. "Give it time." Troy answered he was giving it time.

"Don't rush." He wasn't rushing.

"Don't be hasty," until she ran out of different ways to say the same thing.

At the door of the home, Troy hugged his mother and grandmother before leaving. He said he hoped they'd enjoy their tea, and Mary invited him to join them. She always did. Troy refused, again as he always did, but gave a new excuse.

"I'm meeting Lydia."

"Well, have a good time."

"We will. We're going to a movie."

Mary almost asked which one, before she remembered the name would mean nothing to her. She recalled her days of courting and movies, when titles measured the passing months, and smiles of anticipation lit her face. Troy held the door then waved goodbye.

The smile still tugged the corners of her mouth as Mary pushed her mother. Scents of sickness couldn't wash it away. Strips of sunshine from windows lay like bars across the floor, but didn't threaten her mood. Watery light floated out from the quiet Blue Room where they would drink tea. Mary pushed Abigail's chair against the wall and watched her thin hair puff with the breath of each snore, white strands shaded blue from the curtains. She brewed tea with the tiny electric kettle, pouring water into a wildwood-flowered pot to steep with the leaves. Then she carried cups and pot to the small polished table on a wildwood-flowered tray.

Abigail's cup steamed, cooling quietly. Mary rested her elbows on the table, sipping contentedly at her own dark brew, tracing the outlines of the pattern on white china.

"Hello Frank." She smiled as her neighbor walked through the door, pushing his wife in her chair.

"Mary." Frank nodded.

"Nice day for a walk."

They agreed indeed the sun was shining, the elderly and sick were sleeping peacefully, and weekends were good. Tea was warm still in the pot, the grand old clock measured time on the wall, and sunlight drifted, blue-shaded from heavy drapes.

When Mary poured a drink for Frank, their fingers touched. Mary smiled and pulled away, while Frank took the easy-chair on the other side of the round coffee table. Frank's wife slept in her chair to his left. Mary's mother slept to her right, white hair and skin contrasting with dark and gray.

"So, my Troy says he's met a girl."

"Anyone I know?"

They smiled and talked, like friends, and it was peaceful to converse. Mary wished she could believe they were just another old couple drinking their afternoon tea. Though she wasn't so old herself, and their companionship might be frowned on.

"Lydia lives in one of those big houses," Mary explained. "Lydia Steepleton, Troy said."

Frank said he'd heard of her. "Dad's some kind of big businessman. Isn't she still in school?"

Mary said yes. So they talked about age gaps and relationships, each treading carefully around the fragile friendship growing between them, neighbors, one downstairs, one up, in the corner building, one visiting her mother and the other his wife.

"Do you think it's serious?" Frank asked eventually, his brown eyes concerned as if Troy were his own son.

Mary thought back to Troy's open face, the way his eyes looked straight into hers, no longer searching the ground for answers. She'd almost forgotten, he had blue eyes, just like her mother's. "Yes, it's serious," she replied.

Then Frank stared at Mary's hands holding the delicate cup, wiry fingers curled tight around the warmth of fine white china. He stared at her knees held primly together, and the pattern on her blue print skirt. He gazed at her face, open and smiling, mysterious green eyes, with once-fair hair lightly curled and tucked behind her ears. He called himself a cradle-snatcher and worse as he looked at her, and he wasn't concerned.

Wildwood Flowers

The quiet evening danced slowly to the sound of Frank's fiddle, playing a mournful melody he called *Wildwood Flowers*. Mary sat in her chair, invisible below his balcony, quietly enjoying the sound. She watched shadows descend till the flowers, wild and tame, disappeared into gray. She watched the shades of night draw in, street lights and car lights flashing like firebugs in the sky. A white cat vanished as it hunted in shadows of grass. Mary smiled contentedly.

She and Frank had met as strangers at the home where Mary visited her mother. She saw him as a fine looking man, long silvered hair, wrinkles of wisdom, dark skin and a smile like sunshine. His wife was the gray-skinned silent one, the one Mary's mother would have called *gone* if she still used words to describe anyone. Frank would sit looking at his wife's empty face in the sunlit room, long legs angled under the sagging blue chair, arm stretched over her chest, fingers shadowed dark against gray hair. Gone she might be, but something shone in her gaze when Frank held her, and vanished when he left, some knowledge perhaps of being loved. Mary envied her that.

Sometimes Mary looked in her mother's clear eyes and thought Abigail envied Frank and Jessie's love too. Then she'd think of all the missed conversations, times she could have asked about her parents' relationship, asked about love. She'd look at her mother's gentle face, cursing the wasted years. Abigail would never talk now, not beyond maybe saying her name and adding some totally meaningless phrase as if it were pregnant with importance. Yet her mother wasn't *gone*. She stayed ever-present, very watching, very knowing. So yes, Mary did get something from visiting her.

She got Abigail's sweet smile when she looked at Frank. She got a pat on the hand when she mentioned his name, and her mother's approval.

A few months ago Mary and Frank started timing their trips to coincide, walking their charges in spring's cold sunshine and meeting in the Blue Room afterward. Mary would make a double pot of tea, saving some for Frank. A few weeks ago they skipped the tea and met at the coffee shop instead, ignoring the stares of summer crowds. A few days ago Mary was formally introduced to Frank's tiger-striped cat. Yesterday, they held hands and kissed. She loved his dark skin's contrast with her light.

"Would you like a nightcap, Frank?" Mary stepped out onto the lawn to look from her condo up to his.

The song slowed and stopped. "Yes, Mary," said Frank. "Yes, that would be nice. I'll bring my fiddle, maybe play you a tune."

"A happy one?" Mary asked.

The gentle voice called back, "Can't it be happy and sad?"

The wildwood flowers were happy and sad, their faces turned up to the sun in the day and down to the shadows at night. When Frank played again, his sherry glass empty at his side, Mary heard laughter rippling behind the pain. The music sang of how their lives would be measured, Frank wed to a wife who'd gone away by accident, Mary to a husband gone by choice. United they were, in love and sorrow, like wildwood flowers growing where they land.

They held the keys to each other's hearts perhaps, or to each other's condos.

Two cats strode slowly across the lawn as Mary turned out the lights, Frank's hand touching her arm. One cat was small, dark, tiger-striped, the other large and white. They serenaded wildwood flowers with their own caterwaul in the quiet of night.

Part 2

The Neighbors

Bridge Players

White Cat, Bridge Night, Pack of Cards, Coffee Cup

*Y*ou get to know people when you live near your work, when you run a garage and repair your neighbors' cars to keep them on the road. You get to know who's patient and who's in a rush, who puts the pedal to the metal, who always stamps on the brakes, who drives like a pro and who's forever sliding on winter snow. You can discover a lot by servicing somebody's car.

Peter's garage stood at the north end of town, just south of the Paradise lots—Paradise Gardens, Paradise Mansions, Paradise Cove and the rest—just down a side street from the church. He serviced the pastor's little white van, rich mansion-dwellers' limos, condo-owners' tiny runabouts, teenagers' first cars with weary wheels and doors falling off, mommy-mobiles with room for soccer teams and babies in back, swish speedsters, sturdy roadsters, even the yellow school bus. He learned to match addresses to vehicle types and to people, to recognize which women might play the field, to measure his chances, though of course, he was still married, still faithful, except... *A man can dream.*

He learned which parts of town might make good places to meet someone, just in case, not as if he ever did, where he'd take her, where they'd eat, and play, and sleep. Two years now since he'd returned to his family, no harm in imagining, but he'd only slipped once. Peter was strong.

He learned which parts of town might be good for his son to set up house, after he married, after his girlfriend got pregnant maybe. Not that Troy seemed in any hurry to get hitched, the way he fixated still on that rich man's daughter. "Rich men's daughters don't marry car mechanics," Peter said over coffee at the garage, but Troy just smiled. "Well, if you're getting married, if you're needing a bigger house, I'd say Paradise Road's not a bad place to try."

"Why, Dad?" The boy's voice carried a smile as he bent to his work.

"Well, they play bridge."

"I don't play bridge. And how would you know that anyway?" Troy bobbed up with a white cloth turned almost gray.

"Seen their packs of cards," said Peter, tossing a clean rag to the floor, "and bridge books tucked in the box with the maintenance manual. Used to play with your mom."

"They sell bridge books?"

"Bidding rules and all that."

"Well, all the more reason never to play bridge."

"They have nice houses too."

Troy came up for air, face shiny with sweat and dark with the soot of engine oil. He answered that he already had a nice house. Still, he had to agree, agreeable child, his home wasn't built for a family.

"You do want a family don't you, son?"

"One day, Dad, maybe. Not yet."

"You can't always plan these things you know."

Troy laughed. "Just in case you're asking me, Dad—and did Mom put you up to this?—well, anyway, we're not."

Of course, Peter and Mary had *done it* many times before they were married. Like father like son, Peter thought. Except, he reminded himself, *except, I'm not like my father.* "Paradise Road. I've had some nice cars in from there. There's a real nice girl too, not married, named after a jewel, Armadillo, Ammadiamond, some kind of name like that. She'd be perfect for you."

"Dad, I've got a girlfriend."

"I'm only saying. She's got a cat. Big white cat to go with her jet-black hair. You always liked cats."

"I hate cats."

"She's got a figure, gorgeous Italian curves and swerves, and she's available..."

"Dad!"

Peter laughed, but felt a catch in his throat behind the smile. *If Troy didn't want her...*

White Cat

Steve Walker went from the hall to his living room, flicking the light switch and looking around at well-organized furniture, books like packs of cards all stacked together, coasters square to the edge of the coffee table, cushions evenly spaced on the large white sofa. He hadn't intended to leave the window open behind the sofa. Its draught disturbed him so he set off across the room to tug it closed. Traffic hummed quietly at this hour, distantly passing the end of Paradise Road. Summer flowers scented the breeze. Then something moved.

The something was a cat—large, white, pale as the sofa's soft bleached leather, and hairy as the sheepskin rug. It jumped as Steve approached, then walked slowly away, lifting dark-rimmed paws, delicately extracting needle-sharp claws, hopefully not leaving a mark. The proud feline head faced one way then the other, till its gaze settled with green slits for eyes looking straight into Steve's startled face.

Steve shuddered, feeling the creep of carpenter ants in his stomach. He used to laugh at his sister for running from insects but sometimes, now, he found a glint of sympathy. Little Sally, screaming, curled into a ball against the wall—he'd like to curl up too. Sally's small hands would hug her abdomen while she buried her chin in her chest, just because a bee was trapped in her room. "Throw a book at it," Steve suggested but she didn't dare. So instead he marched, big brother to the rescue, placed a cup over the exhausted insect, slid some card underneath and released it through the window.

Steve smiled slightly, leaning on the wall and resting in

memory's distraction. The tale of the bee had played out handsomely. Sally's bedroom was upstairs in their childhood home. The stunned creature plummeted earthward, closely watched by both children, till a huge black bird, probably a crow, swooped and ate it. Sally cried.

But cats always land on their feet, Steve remembered, coming back to the present. It would take a very big cup, even a very big bucket, to cover this creature. He wished, oh how he wished, he hadn't opened the window, but he needed the breeze. He just hadn't needed or wanted a large white cat.

Steve wasn't really afraid of cats, but something about their purring set his teeth on edge, electricity in their fur made his skin crawl, their knowing eyes made him feel like all his secrets were tumbling free. But he wasn't scared. His heart beat in his ears, and palms grew sweaty because of the heat, not fear, not like a little sister. He stood alone in his own proud home, apart from the cat who, uninvited or not, seemed determined to stay.

The cat had a red jewel set into the middle of its collar, just under its chin. Steve watched the gemstone wink at him as the intruder tilted its head and began to purr. He gritted his teeth. Throwing a book was a tempting idea, except it would surely damage good reading material. He backed away.

A red jewel, Steve thought, rubbing his chin with his hand, *ruby or garnet maybe*—he liked knowing the names of things. The purring grew louder and Steve shivered, teeth chattering in spite of summer warmth. He did *not* like cats. But he lost the battle of wills and went into the hall, leaving sofa and room to the enemy.

Rubies and garnets circled his mind, and his neighbor was called Amethyst. The connection felt like the ghost of an idea, imagination as likely as memory, but he fastened on it as possible salvation. Steve and Amethyst had met earlier in the street, simultaneously refusing invitations to play bridge with a neighbor. They were the two newest people on the block, an obvious *couple* though they were total strangers to each other. Amethyst had smiled into Steve's face as she said no. "Maybe another time," she added, before calling her cat and heading up the path. *Her big white cat.*

Steve grabbed the key from its hook by the door and rushed out. "Amethyst," he shouted toward the open windows of his neighbor's house. "Amethyst, are you home?" He'd feel very silly if she wasn't. In fact, he already felt silly, thrown out of house and home by an invading ball of fluff.

At his second call, Steve saw a raven-haired figure waving from the kitchen window. Amethyst disappeared and came to the door. "Have you lost your cat?" Steve asked, leaning forward over the gate. Amethyst frowned. She looked first toward Steve, then back over her shoulder, as if the feline might suddenly appear. Meanwhile Steve described his guest, pantomiming with his hands. "White, fluffy, huge. Little diamonds and a big red jewel in its collar?"

"Garnet!" Amethyst jumped like a small child with delight. It was rather endearing really. "Why, have you found her?"

"She's making herself at home in my living room," Steve answered, "and I really don't..."

He intended to say he really didn't like cats, but Amethyst invited him to make himself at home in her house instead. They could share a cup of coffee perhaps while Garnet shared Steve's sofa. Steve found himself smiling, *a pretty good exchange.* Perhaps he'd have to conquer his fears and let the cat visit more often, though the thought made him shudder, even with Amethyst's sweet perfume soothing his senses.

Still, in time, even scared little Sally learned to tolerate insects. With a brother like Steve, she'd had to.

Bridge Night

The bridge players were Joe and Karen Grainger and they lived in the house across the street. Joe was a policeman and Karen a teacher. They seemed to have taken it upon themselves to provide a social focus for their small neighborhood.

"Your predecessor played bridge," said Karen Grainger one evening, accosting Steve as he climbed out of his car.

"My who?"

"The guy you bought your house from."

Steve wondered if Karen meant the house had some kind of bridge aura, so he'd have to learn. When Karen told him Amethyst already knew how to play, he saw the attraction. Soon he was borrowing books and packs of cards from her, just in case. He bought a strange metal and plastic machine called a bridge computer, but didn't let anyone see it. And he tried to like cats.

The next time Karen caught him carrying his groceries from the car, Steve looked around for Amethyst. "We need an extra player," Karen said this time. *Not an extra couple?* Maybe Amethyst had already agreed. The white cat watched with emerald eyes and slowly swished her tail through fall's first leaves as Steve said yes.

Steve and Amethyst arrived together, meeting on the road and shyly walking up the path. The door opened in welcome, spilling yellow light into misty gray. Karen's tiny body bobbed and twitted like a bird. "We were waiting for you." She held out a hand like a broken wing and Steve shook it nervously, afraid its feathers might fall off.

"Sorry," he said, while Amethyst approached the dresser where coffee cups and wine glasses waited. The room was filled with small square tables, strangers murmuring, walls dimly lit, which surprised Steve as he thought of trying to read numbers from the cards. A thin haze of coffee and candle-wax

drifted by the lights. The cookies were a mixture of homemade and shop bought—*should he have brought some too?*—with coffee in a jug and wine in a box.

Joe led them both with practiced cordiality, arms laden with glasses and plates, to a table where an older couple was seated. The shadowed man held out a hand in welcome, eyes and teeth bright, while the woman, pale as he was dark, smiled politely. Steve didn't catch their names. *Not a couple though*, he thought. The woman wasn't wearing a ring.

Amethyst looked so confident taking her seat opposite Steve. He saw her slightly quizzical glance around the room, and wondered how often she'd done this before. More often than never, he thought. *More often than me*. Then someone dealt the cards. Steve should have noticed who, but he'd been dreaming. He had a feeling it mattered—*person on the left of the dealer bids first* or something? He couldn't remember. Dry leaves rustled outside.

"Steve?" Amethyst reminded him.

"Oh, sorry. Is it my turn?" He looked at his cards.

Fourth highest of the longest, strongest suit. No, that's when you're playing—defending? How did it go? This is the bidding, so count up, thirteen cards. He tried to add points and remember, *fifteen to seventeen means* what?

Whatever he said, it must have worked. Suddenly it was Steve's turn again, and he made another bid. With each turn he found himself growing more nervous. This wasn't what he'd planned—he'd imagined having time to sit back and watch what other people did. All too soon he'd bid to game, so he had to play.

The older man's wrinkled hand laid down a card. Amethyst placed her cards face-up, ordered by color, by suit, by number, each edge neatly aligned. Then Steve tried to plan.

The king and the queen will win, unless one falls to the ace, and then I have to make the ten, except the jack… He struggled to work it all out. Amethyst had left her seat and he felt her move behind him, smelled her perfume and looked up.

"No problem. You should be fine," she said softly. She meant to comfort probably, but only made him more nervous. Now when he failed he'd have only himself to blame.

Their opponents glared, obviously biting back an accusation.

"I'm not helping," Amethyst defended herself. Steve silently agreed while she sat down again. He tried to smile and messed up the neatly ordered cards as he picked which one to play. Amethyst's well-groomed fingers tidied them again.

Cookies helped. And wine. At least it made him feel better. And not being first to bid made life much easier in later hands.

"I think that went pretty well," said Amethyst as they left. They'd shaken hands with their hosts, Karen's broken wing still limp and boney, Joe's grip firm and strong, and they set off down the path.

"Yes," agreed Steve as limply as Karen, while Amethyst firmly and strongly led the way.

"Want a nightcap?" she offered.

Now, that will really help.

Pack of Cards

Joe Grainger paced the living room, window to door to window, when everyone had gone. Meanwhile Karen busily tidied the debris from the bridge evening. Joe marched with his policeman's tread, steady, relaxed, and ready at a moment to go, his I'm-in-control walk, while Karen took charge of everything.

"I think that went pretty well," Joe said, the first time he changed direction. Karen agreed and continued stacking plates and napkins on the table.

"Don't you think it went well?" he asked the next time. Karen said yes, while collecting empty glasses and coffee cups, adding them to the tray.

"Young Steve's walking Amethyst home," Joe told her, striding away from the window.

Karen said, "That's nice." But of course it was simply what she'd hoped. It was she, not Joe, who'd invited fair-haired Steve and the sensual Amethyst, who'd carefully arranged things so they might make friends and perhaps become regulars. If the evening went well it should be to her credit because she'd planned it well.

Joe marched toward her as Karen slid the last deck of cards into its packet. He stared critically. "You need to check all the cards are there before we put them away."

"I counted them," said Karen but Joe took the packs from her hand anyway and sat down, dealing decks into suits. At least he'd stopped pacing. Karen carried the tray into the kitchen.

"Don't put the glasses in the dishwasher, Karen." She continued to wash carefully, as she always did, rinsing each piece individually under the faucet.

When Karen returned to the living room, clean glasses on the tray, Joe told her he was missing a three of spades. He looked oddly triumphant.

"But I counted them," Karen answered.

"But I checked them," said Joe.

Karen took the box from him and asked where he'd put the jokers.

"Over there." Joe pointed to the fireplace where Karen fanned them out to reveal the missing card. "You must have got it caught there when you put them away," said Joe. Karen agreed—much easier and kinder than arguing the point.

Back on his feet, Joe paced the room again while Karen put the glasses and tray away. She folded card tables and stacked them against the wall. Joe stopped pacing long enough to heave them to the cupboard under the stairs, then walked back to the window.

Karen began tugging the sofa into place. "I'll help," said Joe, lifting the other end with his light easy grip when she struggled and strained. When Karen put her end down, Joe promptly let go, leaving it crooked for her to set right.

"Don't you think we should we close the curtains?" Karen suggested, joining Joe at the window. He dropped a hand to her waist while they stood together. Lights shone through the mist across the short front yard of Amethyst's house.

"I think Steve's still there," said Joe. "Think they've gone upstairs…"

"And they say women gossip." Karen leaned her head on her husband's chest.

"Hey, you're supposed to be the romantic one." Joe bent to nibble her ear.

"And you're the controlling one."

"Of course," he agreed. "But it did seem like a good idea, telling them to be partners."

"Given they were the only new players."

"My idea to invite them wasn't it?"

"Of course. You're a genius, dear," said Karen, remembering it was hers. "Now close the curtains, genius. Let's go to bed."

Joe stooped and Karen stretched to match him arm to arm and hip to hip as they climbed the stairs. Karen, who wasn't the controlling one, glanced back at the kitchen cupboard where her secret cat-treats were hidden. She, not Joe, had been inviting Steve and Amethyst to play for months while they just ignored each other. *How foolish*, she'd thought, two beautiful people, evidently made for each other and living all alone. Karen told Steve how pretty Amethyst was, but he took no notice, while Amethyst determinedly ignored Karen's hints about Steve's eligibility. Till at last Karen lit on the perfect solution, tempting Amethyst's cat with a trail of treats leading to Steve's open window. Even so, it had been weeks before the cat jumped inside.

You had to admit, Karen thought, they made a very nice couple, even if Steve did keep saying he wasn't keen on cats. She steered her husband around the corner to their bedroom and pondered how fine is the line between controlling and control.

Coffee Cup

Summer turned to fall, and the rain would soon turn to snow. As the latest downpour ended, pale specks like burned-out fireflies fluttered under cones of city-center streetlamp light. A bedraggled white cat sat at the roadside, fur speckled gray and plastered to skeletal frame. Amethyst rushed, head down, feet kicking up sludge, black hair dripping around her face, purse clasped to her chest.

With squeal of brakes and shriek of tires a dark van cast a tidal wave and sloppily sloshed around the corner. Amethyst had almost stepped into the road, but the white cat, gliding along the curb, sent her sliding to a lamp post instead. The van missed her by inches.

"What the...?" Amethyst bent to touch the cat, for luck maybe, but it had gone.

Meanwhile, leaving Paradise, Steve drove too quickly past the church. He'd rushed home after work, cursing himself for leaving the box on his bed that morning. Having picked it up, he checked his pocket again—*still there.* The storm had slowed him and he was going to be late. Traffic lights slowed him more. He checked his watch.

Benson's Restaurant beckoned Amethyst with a welcoming glow from its windows. She crossed the road carefully and a waitress met her at the door.

"Hi, my name's Carla. That must have been scary." Amethyst nodded. "Those delivery guys drive way too fast. 'Specially in this weather."

Carla offered a towel, much better than cleaning up with paper in the bathroom—*such luxury.* Amethyst thanked her and asked if her boyfriend was waiting. "Steven Walker? Table for two? I think we had a reservation."

"He doesn't seem to have arrived yet. You go finish washing up and I'll get your table ready. Will you want a hot drink?"

Amethyst nodded then pushed on the door to the ladies room. She turned to ask, "Did you happen to notice the cat?" Carla didn't seem to hear.

The stream by Paradise Park swelled thick and black. Water boiled and roared upstream of the bridge, roiling in the faded light. Rocks and tree-limbs bounced and a loud crack split the night. Tarmac vanished into mud and mire.

Steve's car had turned the corner now and sped toward the bridge, wipers pushing away the drips still falling from leaves on the trees. He was late, rushing to the restaurant by his work where he'd agreed to meet Amethyst, late and hungry and tired.

He drove too fast, hunched low over the wheel, gazing through steam and gloom, till suddenly his headlights picked out the shape of an animal. Pale and furry, it raced across his path, green eyes, a fleeting flash of red. Steve swerved, braked, swore, and his car nosed helplessly into the nearest ditch. *Was that Garnet?*

"I—hate—cats!" Steve shouted, banging his hand in frustration on the steering wheel.

Meanwhile Amethyst had cleaned off her skirt and tidied her hair. She sat down at a table.

"He's probably stuck in traffic," said Carla, offering coffee.

"But he works just down the road." Amethyst hesitated. She wanted to ask if she could borrow the phone, but thought she'd sound naïve. *Do they let you make phone calls from restaurants?* And who would she call? Steve's office? They'd probably just say he was on his way.

The restaurant wasn't too busy yet. Unpredictable weather had driven some customers away, though air drifted cool and dry through the window now, its earthy smell competing with warm scents of cooking.

"You like cats?" Carla asked, picking up on Amethyst's comment from earlier.

"Yes. I have a white Chinchilla, called Garnet. Got her when I was a kid."

"Nice."

Amethyst felt like she had to explain since Carla still stood watching her. "It's just, you know, there was a cat ran in front of me, looked a bit like Garnet and made me step back. Saved my life I guess."

"Cool cat. Well, I'm sure it's okay," said Carla. The door opened and she turned to seat another customer.

Out in the forest, Joe Grainger drew his police car to a halt and looked at the vehicle nosed into the ditch. He paused to notify the dispatcher before getting out. "Got a problem?" he asked, then stepped back in surprise. "Oh it's you. Steve Walker, right?"

"Yeah me. Some stupid cat ran out in front of me." Steve

shook rainwater from his hair.

"And you do so love cats."

Steve smiled. *Had it been so obvious when they chatted over cards?*

"Well, give me a minute. I'll see if I can help," Joe offered. "Just got to check on the bridge around the corner."

Joe strode downhill to the bend in the road. He whistled when he saw the storm damage. "Looks like you may owe your life to that cat, Steve," he shouted. "Or whatever it was. Have you seen what's ahead?"

Steve strolled to join him, paling at the sight. He could have been there, he and his car. He could have been dead but for a cat-like animal. And he hated cats. Meanwhile, Amethyst, who loved them, waited at the restaurant.

"Ah, we'll have you there soon," Joe reassured him when Steve explained his rush. "Don't worry. Let's move you out of this ditch first. Go back past the church and over William's Way then through the town center. Should get you there."

Steve frowned, trying to memorize the route. The two men maneuvered his car out of the mud. Stepping back, Steve straightened his trousers, wiping off splashes with a handkerchief. "Not too bad."

"Could have been worse." said Joe. "So, know your way?"

Steve sped eagerly to William's Way. Amethyst sat in the restaurant tapping her watch. And Carla stopped at her table with the happy news. "Just got a call. No worries. The police station let me know your young man's on his way. Got caught on the wrong side of town and the bridge is out."

"No problem," said Amethyst, sipping her coffee and wondering vaguely why Steve hadn't just come straight from work. "I'm happy waiting." She put down her cup.

Outside the window the bedraggled white cat had returned, speckled black with grit, green eyes staring, and a bright red jewel on its collar. It purred, unheard, to the listening night. When Steve arrived, almost equally bedraggled, the feline guardian left.

Steve had a ring in his pocket, white stone, not red, and Amethyst said yes.

Artists

Absent Muse, Jumping to Conclusions, Art Lessons,
Felicitous Feline

*F*elicitous Feline saves lives, the headline said. Below, the Arma-diamond lady smiled—A. Greenwood, Peter read from her entry in his ledger, open on the counter by his hand. She hugged the huge white cat in her arms while a smiling young man draped himself artistically on her shoulder. "Ms. Greenwood and Mr. Walker were particularly pleased at their narrow escape on this, the night of their engagement. And for interested readers, yes indeed, Ms. Greenwood said *yes.*"

Ms. Greenwood. Ms. Greenwood, the gloriously diamonded Greenwood wore a ring. The byline said S. Greenwood too, *sister, brother perhaps, or Dad?* So much for pairing the diamond lady with Troy, *or with me*, Peter thought, but the boy was still dating his rich-kid high-school graduate anyway. Peter slammed the paper onto the counter. "No happy ever-afters you know," he said to the empty office. "No happy anythings."

He searched his ledger for the name of the woman he'd slept with—was it really almost two years ago? He was tired of skulking around, tired of hunting what couldn't be found in dark places where memories haunted him. A bright motel, out-of-town stranger, comfortable lack of commitment, that's what he needed. She'd phone him perhaps, arrange to meet in some other neutral place. But she'd disappeared. *They all disappear.*

K.J. Kingston. That was her. She'd paid in cash. No phone number. No address. No bank account.

The young man's smile, Mr. S. Walker, mocked him from the newspaper photograph. A happiness brooking no loss, a confidence declaring *I've got it made.* "Yeah well, *I've* got it made too young man," said Peter, unaccountably angry with a stranger he'd never met. Perhaps the feminine beauty of the cat-girl had him bewitched. She pressed her hip to her lover's thigh, the grip of his fingers firm in the hollow of her shoulder, where skin's so smooth and bones ache to be filled with kisses and love. Peter rolled his fingers along the counter top, imagining the warmth of flesh to welcome him, smiling at the memory of a woman who'd invited him for coffee and let him stay the night. *In a motel. In a nowhere place.*

His body clenched. Had she never meant to come back? Was that why she paid cash? Was she just looking to get laid? Was he?

Troy found me, Peter thought. *Why shouldn't I find her?* What had the boy said? He'd used the phone. Well, Peter could do that too.

"K.J. Kingston," he said after dialing directory inquiries, then added, "Ms."

"What town?"

"How should I know where she lives?"

He slammed the phone to its cradle. A woman who didn't want to be found probably didn't use her own name anyway. Peter sighed. Perhaps he was just jumping to conclusions. He should give her more time and maybe she'd come back. Or maybe she'd used him as some kind of muse to drive away her pain. Perhaps he counted as practice for her lessons in the art of seduction, a toy for her to play with and throw away, a mouse on a string.

He imagined the angel-cat's tail curling around the angel-cat woman, sliding deep into her slick warmth. He didn't even care if K.J. Kingston had used him, just wished she'd reappear and use him again. Then he shuddered and sighed.

"No happy ever-afters you know," he said to the absent Ms. Greenwood and Mr. Walker as they stared from the page, wrapped in the heavenly glow of their *felicitous feline* friend.

Absent Muse

Amethyst's sister, Sapphire Greenwood, worked as a reporter for the local paper.

"*Felicitous feline!* You make Garnet sound like an angel or something," Amethyst had complained, visiting from her smart new house in romantic suburbia. Sapphire said maybe a demon, but they don't save lives.

"They have red eyes," said Sapphire.

"Garnet's are green."

"She's got a red eye in her collar."

But that was in fall, when Amethyst got engaged, rain washed out the bridge, traffic dissolved in chaos, and all the schoolchildren had to buy fancy shoes and backpacks for another year of lessons. Sapphire's muse had taken a hike since the rush of Christmas at the newspaper. Now she sat in the cramped apartment, writing her column slowly with fingers pecking at typewriter keys. She'd been assigned to cover arrangements for the church's Easter fair, and she stared at her notes. Even with the glorious Savannah Steepleton's youngest child declaring Amethyst's feline *an Angel in Paradise,* and painting angel cats, Sapphire couldn't make herself muster much interest. *There's a limit to how long no-news can be news.*

So what if guardian angels are Catholic. She scratched a line through another woman's comments and wondered, *who cares?* So what if Paradise's pastor says angels are in and saints out. *And demons? What about them?* So what if the sweet old dear in the gabardine coat jumps to the conclusion the cat must be a devil? Sapphire sat, fingers poised over keys, with nothing to say, and closed her eyes.

"Tired?" asked Dyson from across the room, lounging in comfort far away from the paper-piled desk.

"Nope. Not really."

"Hungry?"

"Nope."

"Thirsty?"

"Nope. Just looking for my muse."

Sapphire heard Dyson's lithe footsteps on linoleum as he walked to the kitchen. She heard the sucking sound of the fridge door opening, the padding paws of their dog in search of food. Ice cubes cracked, one dropping, plopping, into the dog's water dish. More cubes clattered musically in glasses, faint hiss as a bottle was opened and the gurgle of pouring bubbles mixed with the lapping of wide dog tongue. Dyson placed a ginger ale at Sapphire's side.

"Thought I'd get you one anyway."

"Thanks," said Sapphire, as Dyson plonked himself loudly on the sofa again in front of the TV. Ancient springs creaked despairingly.

"Mind if I switch the TV on? Will it distract you?"

"I'm trying to write."

"It could be inspiration."

He kept the sound low, kindly he probably thought, while Sapphire struggled either to hear or ignore it. Music danced to the fizz of bubbles bursting on the surface of her glass. She turned around while she drank, stroking Mason's furry ruff as he snuggled beside her.

Ah, the sweet, sharp, bitter taste of ginger ale on her tongue. She should write drink ads. Then she surely wouldn't miss her reluctant muse. But could she still write stories?

Dyson flipped through channels as usual. She saw him stop at the news. An art teacher lectured on music therapy to a reporter Sapphire'd met from Channel 5. She knew the voice. They'd talked cats and demons together as they recorded the church fair meeting. She leaned forward to watch but the picture changed to a medical program now, body parts artistically strewn and a quiet analytical voice describing their fate.

Sapphire's thoughts swung to the mince thawing for dinner. The imagined smell made her gag. Running to the bathroom, she struggled not to lean over the bowl. *Please no,* she thought, then found her eyes fixed on the shelf, and on the future. Not the televised body parts making her ill after all; she'd jumped to the wrong conclusion, forgetting her own body part. The stalk from the pregnancy kit waited lonely and bright, inexorably blue.

Of course. Why not get morning sickness in the evening? It was time to tell her secret.

"Dyson," said Sapphire, stumbling back into the living room. He stared at a report of a stalker in the park and Sapphire wondered vaguely who was covering it. But other, more important thoughts claimed her attention.

"Dyson, I'm pregnant."

"Ah." Dyson sat back, eyebrows raised, eyes narrowed and drink in hand, almost toasting her. "D'you suppose that's where your absent muse has gone?"

"Huh?"

"Too busy inspiring real life instead of fiction?"

Sapphire sighed. Sometimes Dyson said the strangest things, though sometimes they almost made sense. She watched him put his glass on the floor, oh so carefully where the dog could tip it over—Dyson's concept of careful never quite the same as Sapphire's. She watched him struggle free of the sagging sofa, waited while he walked unsteadily toward her with arms outstretched.

"Sapphire, Sapphire," he whispered softly, his lilting voice so well loved. He rested his hairless chin on her hair, wrapping himself around a waist that would surely soon be growing.

"Love you, Sapphire, so much."

"Love you too, Dyson Lee."

"I'm going to like this muse."

Jumping to Conclusions

Sapphire stirred tomatoes into the mixture in the pan. Sprinkled herbs were good for her queasy stomach. Lasagna bubbled and softened. She checked. *Don't want it to turn to glue*. Then she looked at her watch.

Dyson's friend Charlie would arrive for dinner soon. Time was getting on. The Paradise Church Fair demons glared and Sapphire whispered fear at how her schedules grew out of hand. She tossed meat and red-eyed tomatoes into the casserole, layered with pasta, layered like her life.

"Don't worry," said Dyson. "Charlie's always late. Probably showing a house and *almost* making a sale. You know how he is."

She remembered Charlie finding their apartment for them, donating his ancient sofa and chairs to the cause. He seemed an okay guy, one of Dyson's friends from high school. All he ever needed was dinner once in a while, and his favorite was lasagna.

"Wonder how he's doing?" Dyson mused.

"Why?"

"Well, I think he's listing some new house out where your Amethyst bought. Paradise Road or something?"

Sapphire sighed. Maybe one day, when she got her big break, with kids in tow and a life full of hope, maybe then they'd buy near the park and Charlie would help them.

Meanwhile Charlie sat waiting in his car, dinner a far distant prospect as he sighed and gathered his papers. He should have known not to expect too much from this visit. Any phone conversation starting with "I'm not sure I really want to sell" is bad news for a realtor, but this second house was only two doors away from the first one, so he'd agreed to call.

The first client was a youngish man—Mr. Walker he said. He'd greeted Charlie effusively at the door, almost an hour earlier, "So glad you could come," and proceeded to offer to show him all around. Of course, Charlie wanted a chance to back up his credentials and detail the package he'd offer, but Mr. Walker insisted.

At least the house appeared clean, cluttered but clean. Mr. Walker clearly had a Mrs. Walker or housekeeper. Sure enough, just moments after Charlie's arrival, a startlingly beautiful raven-haired young woman marched in the front door.

"Don't worry about me," she said breezily.

Charlie wouldn't have worried, but she proceeded to follow them from room to room, adding her own critiques to each of Charlie's comments, disagreeing with everything he said.

"You'd want to move some of the furniture out, to make the rooms look larger," said Charlie.

"But not the bookshelves," said the erstwhile Mrs. Walker.

"Well you might move *some* bookshelves. Buyers like to see walls."

"Books add character."

Charlie sighed and thought of Dyson and Sapphire's downtown condo, with floor to ceiling books. Maybe Mrs. Walker was a writer like Sapphire. "It's up to you of course, Mrs. Walker," he said politely, through gritted teeth. "Though in my experience, buyers like to imagine their own character."

"No, not Walker," she interrupted. "I'm…"

Charlie didn't hear her name. A rather large, rather fluffy white cat leapt through the window, landing in not-Mrs. Walker's arms and muffling her mouth with its tail. Charlie wanted to ask her to repeat herself, but she murmured sweet nothings to the feline, so he got by with weak smiles aimed in her direction instead.

Upstairs, Charlie suggested fewer chairs in the bedroom, fewer beds in the spare room, and fewer bookshelves on the landing. The dreaded cat-lover knew better of course, so Charlie had to sweetly pretend to agree. Chairs let the buyers sit down, *yes indeed*, and especially if they've got kids. Extra beds show a room has plenty of space. *Space for kids,* thought Charlie, *though they don't seem to have any.* Mr. Walker gazed adoringly at lady and cat, always taking her side.

Charlie had seen it all before, controlling wives who keep their own names and boss their husbands around, cat or child kept close at hand and never criticized. Still, something almost made him disagree with himself. Somehow, despite everything she said, the woman didn't seem so controlling. If he didn't know better, Charlie would say the cat controlled her.

Green eyes gazed up at him now, sharp eyes like the sharp dark claws he knew were hiding under fur. Slowly Charlie struggled against the urge to get away. He wasn't wanted here.

At last they'd viewed the whole of the house, even the kitchen, stunningly immaculate, tidy and spacious. The cat stood to attention in the center of the spotless countertop. Charlie tried to ignore it.

"This is the room I'd show first," said Charlie. "I'd probably have some cookies baking, to give it that welcome-home feeling, maybe a fresh-washed towel or two." He tried to smile at the cat, which smiled hungrily back. Meanwhile not-Mrs. Walker frowned, so he added they could always put store-bought cookies on a tray in the oven and set it really low to get the same effect.

Charlie spread papers on the kitchen table. He showed pictures of similar properties—told them the average price per square foot, explained how redecorating, and yes, even moving bookshelves, would increase the price they might get, described how the photographer would shift things around, suggested, warily, the cat might need to be out when buyers came. They listened, nodding to everything, but neither of them asked him to leave his brochure. As conversation and time ran out, as the next appointment drew close, the cat paced, waving its tail. Charlie offered Mr. Walker a business card, said goodbye, and left.

So here he waited in his car in the snow sorting papers. His next appointment began in ten minutes. Trying to look busy for those last would-be clients who stared through their kitchen window, he held his notes in front of his face as though reading.

Five minutes later Charlie walked two doors up the street, toward the intersection. A red station wagon hadn't been there when he entered the Walkers', so someone must be home. He followed the gravel path between wild roses and tame floppy weeds. Then Ms. Greenwood, his next customer, opened the door before he could knock.

"Hello again," she said smiling. A rather large, rather fluffy white cat leapt into her arms. "Amethyst Greenwood," she introduced herself. "This is Garnet, and you know Steve of course."

"Steve Walker."

Charlie shook hands, smiled warily, and wondered if his day was looking up. "Will you be selling one of the houses?"

"Oh yes, I think so," said Amethyst and Steve in unison. The cat began to purr.

Art Lessons

"No way!" said Sapphire, when Charlie told them the story over dinner. "My sister can't move out. She only just moved in."

Charlie had only just realized his erstwhile client was his friend's wife's sister. Black-haired both, but they didn't look alike. Meanwhile the scent of lasagna in its incongruously circular casserole, made his mouth water. He gazed pleadingly, as Sapphire started to serve. "Just wait till I see her!"

"No way!" said Sapphire to Amethyst when she visited the next day.

"Yes way," said Amethyst, petting the dog, and feeling as if they'd turned into schoolchildren again.

"You're going to sell your new house and move in with him?"

"Or him with me."

"But you've only just got it sorted."

"Only just got engaged." Well, there was always the ring, and one of them would have to move. "And besides..." Her voice trailed away, keeping secrets.

Sapphire made coffee while Amethyst piled newspapers off the sofa onto the floor. Then Sapphire announced her own news with pregnant delight.

"No way!" said Amethyst.

"Yes way!" Schoolchildren again.

"Me too!"

Sapphire shrieked in surprise, while Amethyst mused that their babies would be schoolchildren together and start the next generation.

Meanwhile Steve had gone to the art store to buy a little gift for their new home, still not quite sure which of the houses they'd choose. The store had opened recently, in the block where the old *House of Cards* used to stand, down the hill from Benson's restaurant. The proprietress was a girl Steve had known back in high school.

"Hi Andy, remember me," Steve announced breezily. The shop was empty except for Andrea reading a book behind the counter.

"It's pronounced 'On-DRAY-uh.'"

Steve stopped, taken aback, and checked she was indeed the girl he'd once known. "Yeah, right Andy. So what I want is to get a nice little picture for our new living room."

"We don't do *nice little pictures,*" Andrea replied in a breathy voice, not quite sneering or smiling. She still hadn't got the accent of refined superiority quite right. "We do works of art," (she pronounced it ay-AH-art). All the same, she led her customer to a wall where smaller paintings hung. *A sale's a sale*, thought Steve, guessing she really couldn't take offense, not even at an old colleague who wanted to annoy her by using her unsophisticated high school name.

A set of four pictures, one for each season, hid in a corner of the display. Steve found his eyes drawn to them, or maybe to the price tag, but they did look nice.

"Ah yes." Andrea used a slow, high-quality, perfect-pitch sales voice now. "YAY-es. Bill's collection. He's getting quite a following these days. Bill Brightman that is—I'm sure you've heard of him."

Steve said no, but found himself searching memories. Brightman? Wasn't there a Jack Brightman in high school? A relative perhaps? And didn't Jack date Andy at some time?

"Well what a shame. Bill's really up and coming," Andrea continued. "You should look into him. His use of color is quite unique. They say, if you'd just examine the detailing in his brush strokes here…" She leaned forward. Steve didn't.

"Actually, I was looking at the pictures, not the brush strokes."

He saw a flash of anger in Andrea's eyes but it quickly stilled. A true saleswoman. He guessed she'd be as patient as a doctor when she chose, especially if it looked like he might spend real money. So Steve gazed at spring, summer, autumn, and winter, and Andrea gazed at Steve while the silence lengthened.

"Sooo, do you like them?"

"Yeah probably," said Steve. "I'm just not sure we have room for all four though. I'll call my fiancée—see if we can meet up and look together. That sound okay?"

"Certainly," said Andrea, though it sounded rather more like "SAIR-ten-LAY." She didn't seem too worried anyone else would buy the pictures while he waited. Not really great works of undisputed talent, but Steve was looking to put things on the wall, not take art lessons.

Steve slipped out of the art gallery, waving as he left and trying not to laugh. Andrea had been just one of the crowd at high school, not particularly good at anything, and definitely not an artist, nor an upper class twit. But she'd always had a good head for money.

He walked to the end of the street to the public phone, treading carefully on new-fallen snow. Amethyst was visiting her sister in the old apartments by the creek. She agreed to meet for lunch at the Old Town Café. "Don't you want to see the pictures before we eat?" Steve asked, but Amethyst said no. She knew she'd like them if Steve said he did, knew they'd fit, and knew all she really wanted was an excuse to spend time with him.

"D'you want to bring Sapphire?"

"No, she's still working on that Paradise Church Fair thing. All that fuss over Garnet and the Steepleton girl's angels. I'll see you soon."

Steve browsed the book store while he waited, then rushed

out as Amethyst approached. Arm in arm, they strolled to the café, ordered, ate and relaxed, even kissed once in a while. They paid their bill, tipped the waiter, and collected their coats and scarves against the cold winter air. As the waiter bowed and smiled his thanks, Steve and Amethyst drew deep breaths, tried not to giggle, and headed across the road to the art gallery.

"She's a bit overpowering, the shop lady," said Steve. "Seriously."

"And what d'you think I am?" Amethyst smiled back at him. "Trust me. I'm an artiste."

The glass door opened wide at Steve's touch, cool-scented gallery air blowing out to meet them. *Paint, paper and money—that's what it smells of*, Steve thought. Then Andrea came striding forward, smelling of expensive perfume, black-gloved hand outstretched in greeting.

"Hi, Andy," said Steve.

"Well, hell-ooo again. I'm On-DRAY-uh."

Amethyst held out her own gloveless hand, lordly and limp. "And I'm accompanying this gentleman."

Steve looked around in surprise. Amethyst's voice had taken on an accent all its own, rounded out with apples and plums.

"Amethyst Greenwood Walker," she continued, shaking the air in front of Andrea's fingers. "I'm sure you'll have heard of me, one of the Trinity Boscombe Greenwoods." She twirled around, slowly, so elegantly. Ah, Steve could watch her forever, especially if she called herself Walker. She looked as if she were examining all the gallery's glorious contents, and lighting, and walls. "I'm here to look at my old friend Billy Brightman's paintings. I do hope you're giving them all the exposure they deserve."

Invisible exposure, Steve thought, and On-dray-uh seemed to shrink into her high-heeled shoes. Amethyst continued her monologue, Steve only hoping she didn't bump into anything as she pirouetted.

"Such an intriguing collection," Amethyst pronounced, like the expert she wasn't. *When did she last take art lessons?* "And dear Billy"—imaginary Billy, possibly—"he really is quite the up-and-coming young star. A wonderful career ahead of him, I shouldn't be surprised. And you," she turned to the hapless Andrea, "you'll be playing your part in it, I'm sure, Andy— wasn't that your name?"

Steve tried not to laugh as Amethyst ran out of breath. Andrea fluttered her hands nervously, face reddened in embarrassment, still trying to squeeze in the words she so clearly couldn't think of.

They bought the pictures, very reasonably priced after all. Andrea, still looking very confused and very subdued, packed them neatly in layers of tissue. Then Steve and Amethyst said their goodbyes and giggled all the way back to Steve's car.

"The name's On-DRAY-uh," laughed Steve.

"Not at all. The name's Amethyst."

"I'll drive you back to Sapphire's if you like."

Felicitous Feline

In the end the cat would make the decisions of course, always the cat. Though their neighbors, Joe and Karen, were convinced their lessons in conniving bridge nights had brought the young couple together, Steve and Amethyst always knew the cat was in charge.

Garnet, Steve learned as their relationship grew, was a pure-bred Chinchilla with delusions of royalty. She hunted mice and birds and power with equally delighted aplomb. But no one would ever find out if she'd hunted Steve for himself, for Karen Grainger's treats or for his house. Garnet was a cat of strong opinions and great inscrutability.

The realtor, Charlie, noticed her technique first. When he showed Steve's house to potential buyers, Garnet would pad behind through every room, menacing them with green-eyed gaze, making Charlie feel like he'd brought guests to dinner and they were the main course. When he led them two doors up the street to Amethyst's, the curious feline was nowhere to be seen.

"Everyone jumps to the conclusion she's yours," he told Steve when they met to discuss progress.

"No way," said Steve with a shudder. "I don't even like cats." Garnet eyed him suspiciously till he tossed a fish-shaped treat from a box on his shelf.

"Looks like you're stuck with that one." Charlie checked another failure to sell from his growing list.

Meanwhile Amethyst's and Sapphire's bumps grew gradually in tandem as spring turned to summer. Who would have known? Dyson and Steve debated if it had something to do with sisterhood—"not really our faults at all"—while the girls debated names.

Charlie nearly sold Steve's house to a couple who came back with three small children. Unlike Steve or Charlie, these children loved cats. They chased the bundle of furious fur in strange and wild abandon from room to room till suddenly the smallest child was trapped in a corner and began to scream. The sale was lost.

A brooding man came to an open house one weekend—he didn't leave his name but Charlie recognized him from the garage near Paradise Church. The cat hated him and spat in fury as soon as he appeared.

"Terribly sorry," said Charlie.

"No problem. I'm just testing the waters for my son. He's getting married soon."

Eventually the man's son and his girlfriend would show a serious interest in Amethyst's home. Garnet, all sweetness and light bright delight, would purr over them, nuzzling the young woman's ankles and sitting demurely beside the young man as he examined seals on windows and wood on windowsills. When they settled at the kitchen table to sign, Garnet leapt into the woman's lap like a child.

But now the lovers leaned back luxuriously on the sofa in Steve's white living room, Garnet kneading Amethyst clawlessly. They watched TV, drank wine, discussed how blackcurrant juice would stain when the baby arrived, and agreed that if at all possible, this would be the house where they'd live all their lives. So Garnet won. She even decided which curtains would move with Amethyst, by ripping apart the ones she didn't like.

"I'm sorry," said Charlie to the next potential buyer. "I know we said Ms. Greenwood would leave the curtains, but the cat… Well, I really am sorry."

"That's okay," said the woman with voice as sharp and cutting as the felicitous feline's claws. "I didn't like them anyway and I'm not so sure about the house." Which was just as well, since Troy and Lydia were still discussing wedding plans and hadn't seen it yet.

Part 3

The Wedding

The Graduate

Sad Surrender, Spicy Peppermint, Graduation,
Day of Decision

A wedding? Were they really getting married, Troy and his sweet little schoolgirl all grown up? It seemed only yesterday she still lived at home, followed Daddy's curfew, kept Troy on a silver leash. Then she moved out to that church-built dorm. Poor little sister getting all the flack of course, that Sylvia child. Where had the time gone?

And Peter? He ran the pages back through memory—road to a wedding, a future, family. He bet the bride was pregnant.

Nearly two years ago, he'd taken Troy to a bar for his twenty-first. It's the sort of thing fathers do with their sons. *Show the lad a good time. Help him to grow up. Daddy's home, little son.*

And Mommy's gone, suddenly taking up with her fancy man Frank.

Peter's father never took him anywhere—not fishing as a kid, not to playgrounds nor movies, not even to other kids' parties. Peter's father was never there except when Peter wished he wasn't. Then his mom would disappear, lying late in bed or going to stay with a friend. Dad would get Peter up in a morning, tell how his mother was clumsy and lazy and needed a head-doctor more than anything else. "Get out of that bed or you'll end up as lazy as her." At the weekend Peter would walk to the park and sit all alone on the swings. When it rained he got wet.

But I'm not my father Peter said to himself. If he'd missed out on the fishing and playgrounds and movies with young

Troy well, never mind. He'd take his son to a bar like a good dad now and all's forgiven. Besides, the boy was puppy-dog weak, all dewy-eyed over his stupid teenager. *Time to introduce him to riper fruits, give the boy some choice.*

"I'm not sleeping with her," Troy told him over and again till Peter almost believed it. "Not sleeping with her. I wouldn't." But was Mary sleeping with Frank? Seemed like she might be.

Smells of sweat and beer and perfume settled in his nose. The performer flounced with waves of lacy fabric like a tail, spice in her eyes, peppermint promise in the way her mouth devoured some wodge of gum before tasting the mike. She raised a voice thick with haze and smoke. Notes graduated into the thumping beat of a man's temptation, offering more than she could give, filling the smog with desire.

"Now that one, over by the bar." Peter tried to steady his voice, directing Troy's gaze to a group of women laughing loudly together.

"What about her, Dad?"

"She's giving you the eye lad. See? She's looking at you."

"Maybe she's looking at you." The boy turned his gaze back down to his drink.

What's he made of? Pretending his body's made of steel. "Just look at her, son."

"Dad, I'm not interested. I'm listening to the song."

Peter squirmed on the hard wooden seat. He was listening too, but not to any music ears could hear—more to the promise underneath. "Troy, you know…"

"I *don't* know, Dad. I don't know what you want, and I don't know why you've brought me here. I could be out with Lydia, having fun."

"But you wouldn't be would you? Always letting her set the rules. *Lydia's* studying tonight. *Lydia's* Dad won't let her out. *Lydia's* got to go to church." At least he managed not to say aloud, *She won't even let you have fun and sleep with her.*

"Dad, I love her."

"How long will you wait?"

"As long as it takes."

Peter turned his gaze away from his son and searched the room. Other women, available women, real women who wouldn't say no to a good-looking guy with money in his jeans—they stared at him. They licked red tongues between sweetly parting lips. They tipped their heads back, long white necks, smooth skin, milk-scented and pure. They blinked smoky eyes, tossed waves of hair like curtains behind their heads. For a moment Peter thought he saw Mary, but no, *she's out with Frank*. Perhaps the magical woman from the motel danced past, but why would she reappear? He thought he saw an amalgam of both and thought she smiled at him. Sweet surrender that, let himself go, touch an occasional drink, an occasional bride, his arms around an occasional woman's body and flesh warmed inside.

I'm older than my father ever was. Older and wiser, Peter thought; older and safely separated, he'd never done any harm. He'd kept Mary secure. He was old enough now, perhaps at last, to let himself go.

As for the boy? He was young enough, Peter supposed, to keep dreaming, waiting for that girl who dreamed about children's toys and lived with her parents. They'd both grow up. He just wished young Troy would hurry up about it instead of staying frozen in a place where he loved a child not even graduated yet. *What's a father to do?*

Sad Surrender

A wedding? Was his daughter really getting married? Jason Steepleton waited, resting a hand on the smooth-grained wood of the banister, but his mind swung back to last summer, Lydia's graduation, endless arguments about her future and she so certain, so rightly certain it seemed, she was going to marry Troy. He'd stood here then, trying to block the hallway as she swung downstairs from her room. "Sweetheart." She'd swayed to the side, attempting to pass. "Are you sure you're all finished studying?"

"Yes Daddy."

"You've got finals coming up." Jason remembered maneuvering himself to block her path, his trim flesh scarcely wide enough but the hallway thankfully narrow.

"Yes Daddy. I know."

"And you need the grades."

"Yes Daddy."

But he saw it in Lydia's eyes—she thought her father a fool. *How does she expect to get on in the world*, Jason wondered. She hadn't even bothered to apply to university on time, in spite of all his urgings, seemed to think community college would be plenty good enough. When her father talked to her, she didn't even pretend to understand.

"I'm serious. You're eighteen now," said Jason.

"I know, Daddy. And I've studied. Honest I have." He watched her squeeze against the wallpaper to pass. "And I've done my homework. And I've earned my keep. And I'm going out."

"Lydia, please." Jason held out a hand, but she was gone.

The front door slammed. Jason heard his wife cooking in the kitchen. *Can't she hear? Why doesn't she intervene?* But Savannah left all the difficult conversations to him. She seemed as lackadaisical as her children about planning the future—he'd expected more of her. Still, people change. She'd probably expected more of him.

Jason leaned his head through the kitchen doorway. "So, Lydia's not staying to dinner?" he asked pointedly. Savannah, chopping vegetables, replied that Troy had called on the phone earlier. They were going out for the afternoon.

"She sees far too much of that young man," Jason replied. "You should have said no." Then he stormed to his office.

Troy Markham was nothing more than car mechanic—a good one, Jason had to agree, who'd done a good job fixing Savannah's car after her little accident with the wall in the yard. But Troy was a car mechanic just the same, not at all the type of person Lydia might be expected to date. Lydia said he'd graduated high school with no problem, got a scholarship in math no less. She said Troy was bright and intelligent, but as Jason tried to impress upon her, there were far more important things to be intelligent about than cars. She said he earned good money. Jason, as a father, had different and better informed opinions.

All Savannah said was, "Troy's nice in his way."

"Don't push her," she'd tell Jason, in earnest evening conversations when the girls were upstairs. "You'll push her away." Or other trite phrases. "You've got to let her make her own mistakes." And, "She'll come around in time."

Time was running out, Jason thought—passing too fast, with summer and graduation day almost here. A job at the old people's home and a place at community college to study art was not what he'd planned for his daughter. His son did well enough in his little job downtown. He lived in a condo not too far away. Little Sylvia was far too young to worry about. But Jason wanted the best for Lydia, his favorite child. No one seemed to understand.

He read his financial magazine in silence, considered investments he'd decided on earlier, and fumed. Meanwhile his wife cooked dinner. The smells of meat and vegetables soothed his mood and stirred his stomach. Eventually, Jason wandered back to the kitchen.

"Not ready yet," said Savannah smiling.

"Glass of sherry?"

"Mm. Nice."

Jason poured and they sat at the kitchen table, a shared moment, toasting each other. He gazed adoringly at Savannah's food-warmed face, so like Lydia's, so serene.

"I just want her to have a good life, like ours."

"I know, dear," said Savannah.

"I just want her to do well."

"And she will, dear. I'm sure."

He sipped his sherry again, deep dark flavors of spice and smoke, even a hint of peppermint. Almost perfect. "You're sure she'll get over him in time."

"Yes dear, I'm sure."

Was that a flicker of doubt Jason saw? Did Savannah's hand shake just a little now as she put down her glass? Jason wondered what secret she might be keeping from him. When she offered no trite phrases he found he missed them.

"Too many women in this house," he said morosely, putting down his glass in sad surrender. Savannah promised dinner would be ready in a moment.

Spicy Peppermint

A wedding? Was he really getting married? Troy remembered the day he decided to buy a ring. They drove to the beach on his day off from the garage, Lydia taking time out from her studies. Damp air blew in Troy's face while whispering waves soothed his ears. His arm rested lightly on Lydia's shoulders as if it was meant to be there. Hers balanced on his hips while they walked. The top of her head, fair-haired and smooth, bounced gently against his chest. He remembered the breath of her voice tickling hairs beneath his open shirt as he bent his face to her fragrance, fruit-flavored shampoo.

Seagulls shrieked and Troy looked up, missing some words. "Just wondered if you fancied ice cream," Lydia repeated. Troy couldn't resist kissing her up-turned lips, hearing that voice in his head declare *This is love, the real thing.* It felt good. It felt warm, despite the evening chill.

The sun began to sink, tourists drifting back from the shore, coolness descending damply on the air. The young couple turned down an alley already cold with shade. Troy slipped his jacket over Lydia's shoulders. Ahead the lights of an ice cream parlor shone into the gloom. *Thirty-three flavors* it said on the sign. "Let's try there."

Lydia shivered.

Inside the store, air conditioning cooled the already chilled air. Troy held the jacket open so Lydia could slip her arms into the sleeves while he searched for prices. Chrome surfaces gleamed and strip lights reflected like bars of a futuristic prison. Glass-fronted displays cut the air with sharp-shadowed shapes. A sign buzzed overhead, neon streaks of green and red.

Lydia whispered her choice, "Cherry chocolate," and Troy wanted coffee. When he found the menu he only had cash for one dish.

"Let's try something different, something we can share."

Summer Daze maybe—blue raspberry and white chocolate swirled like clouds in a cool vanilla sky. But Lydia's eye had been caught by the brighter shades of Spicy Peppermint, vivid green and red like the buzzing lights.

"Looks like Christmas to me," Troy laughed, but Lydia claimed it for their own, Troy's green work overalls and her red dress.

"Which red dress?"

"The one I wore the day we met."

This is love Troy thought, that they could laugh and neither of them worry that he didn't remember.

"I was with my mom. You and your dad fixed her car."

They sat in a corner of the store, sharing sweet coldness on plastic spoons, pressing frozen lips into kisses as the impulse moved them. Strangers wandered in and out, scented with Italian food from the pizza place next door. When they'd eaten, Troy leaned over the table, resting his forehead on Lydia's, breathing her perfume and spicy peppermint tang, and looking down her perfect nose to hands lying flat on the table. He slid his forehead lower till his eyes peered down her shirt. Lydia pushed him away. It tickled and he smiled.

He would buy her a ring, Troy thought suddenly. He'd slide it onto a finger of her beautifully manicured hand. He was sure—well, almost sure. *How much do rings cost?* Buy it before she graduates.

Lydia's new wristwatch beeped the hour. It must be time to leave. "Did Daddy tell you I'll turn into a pumpkin if I'm late?"

"I thought the princess's carriage did that."

"Well if it does, you could carry the pumpkin in the back of your truck."

They walked out. Tires, tools, oil cans and other singularly unromantic items strewed the bed of Troy's truck. Lydia's cardigan lay across the seat—clean seats because Troy had wiped them. She handed the jacket back to him and electricity ran through their fingers as they touched.

It would be easy to park on the road, rest warm and comfortable, twine their arms together, body's desire, clothing slipping away. Windows would steam and the car would gently rock. But Troy turned the key and Lydia studied the ring she'd been given at church. It would be so easy, yet they both knew she wanted more.

As the truck trundled into the subdivision, Lydia asked Troy to stop. She wanted to use her check book to get some cash at the supermarket.

"You need cash?" He'd imagined she had more than enough.

"I always need cash."

"What'll you buy?"

Lydia laughed and grabbed Troy's hand, dragging him behind her.

Neon lights flashed over the parking lot. Bright fluorescence spilled from the store. Troy and Lydia walked cold empty aisles, arm in arm, bodies perfectly matched, held together by warmth.

Lydia stopped by the ice cream display. "Look," she said. "Spicy Peppermint. They've got our flavor."

Back in the truck, Lydia tucked the paper bag into the well in front of her. "It's breathing cold on my feet," she complained. Troy laughed blowing warmth at her face. Her house was only a few streets away, past the Paradise Mansions sign with its old-world lamp and fancy scrollwork. Troy stopped, made her wait while he opened the door to help her down, then escorted her, gallant suitor in a pick-up truck, along the clean-swept sidewalk toward her gate. He bent to kiss then pulled back, seeing the little frown on her face and knowing her father might be watching. It was 10:04.

Warm light streamed from the front door, a glowing river on paving stones.

"Where've you been?" Mr. Steepleton's voice boomed fit to wake the neighborhood.

"Out."

"You're late."

"Hardly."

"I was worried."

"I'll bet."

He must have noticed the paper bag tucked under Lydia's arm. "What've you got there?"

"Ice cream, Daddy," said Lydia, stopping with her hands still on the gate, Troy's arms wrapped around her waist.

"Really. Why?"

"I wanted some."

"A whole container?"

"Yes Daddy. A whole container of deliciously spicy peppermint." Troy held her more tightly, offering support.

"Can't think what you want that for."

"I'll take it to Troy's if you'd rather."

Her father sighed. "Just bring it in."

Troy released her to her father's waiting arms, his fingers trailing behind her, grasping only air. Lydia walked as if on ice and looked back, small face fading into warm-lit wallpaper. Troy mouthed, "Spicy Peppermint," and waited till the door closed before returning to his truck

This is love, he thought. *This is love. And I can give her more than this.*

Graduation

Was she really about to get married? A year ago and it seemed scarcely more than a day, she and Troy had planned how they'd meet at her graduation. Now they kissed at the end of the path. "See you tomorrow." "Sleep tight." "Sweet dreams."

Troy drove his truck to his father's house, his own place already sold. Meanwhile Lydia walked back to her father's arms.

On Graduation Day Lydia finally committed to making her own decisions—she just wasn't certain what she'd decide—love, life and the future all clamoring for space. She stood on stage, capped and gowned, folder in hand, with the rest of her class all around. They'd *walked.* They'd sung the school anthem. They were ready and waiting to toss their caps in the air, though Lydia knew she'd mess up and fail to catch hers as it fell—*would she toss her veil tomorrow or just the bouquet?* She'd barely looked anywhere during the graduation ceremony except at Troy, hardly thinking of her parents. Her father's new camera recorded the whole event of course. Her face gazed overly large on telephoto, ready to be shown to guests for years to come. Daddy would call her ungrateful, absorbed, or absent-minded, depending on his mood, depending on what she chose to make his mood. And he rarely liked her choice.

But on Graduation Day Lydia felt proud. She understood herself at last. It wasn't procrastination holding her back from college applications. It wasn't laziness keeping her from interviews. It wasn't hopelessness, as her father said, but rather hope—her hope, not his.

Hats flew. Lydia grabbed, grappled, retrieved. The orchestra played and students filed from the stage.

Somehow Lydia found herself in the foyer, mist in her eyes and silence in her ears. Around her, students screamed with joy, cameras flashed, names were shouted over crowds. Lydia stood in an emptiness all her own.

Troy found her first. She felt his breath on the back of her neck, turned around, and leaned into arms that wrapped her close. Even with the bulky folder between them, Lydia fit perfectly. This was where she belonged; she knew it at last. Her hands rested in the small of Troy's strong back. Her cap was tucked under his chin where it wouldn't slip or fall. She breathed the sweet pine scents of his chest as she relaxed.

When Troy's muscles stiffened, Lydia knew her parents

were here.

"Lydia dear," said her mother's milky smooth voice. "We were looking for you."

"Turn around for the camera," said her father's deep growl.

Lydia's body, obedience ingrained, shifted away from Troy. His arms still held her loosely around the waist. Her back still felt his warmth and rocked to his breath. She still smiled.

Other parents took their pictures, lights flashing in unshielded rhythm, but Lydia's father stood out from the crowd and stood still.

"I think Daddy wants a picture of you on your own," her mother advised, but Lydia didn't move. Savannah's smile froze and slipped. "Afterward we'll go out to dinner."

"We were thinking ice cream," said Lydia blankly.

"Spicy Peppermint," Troy whispered, tickling her ear so she smiled again, feeling alive.

"Your father has a table reserved. At Benson's."

"Can Troy come?"

They didn't answer. When the silence lengthened beyond the realm of politeness, Lydia felt Troy's arms slide backward from her waist. *Don't go*, she wanted to say, but said nothing instead.

"Maybe it's a family affair," he whispered.

Ever-gracious—it wasn't graciousness she wanted to hear.

"I want him there," Lydia demanded.

No answer.

"Please."

Lydia's mother held her purse like a shield, blue-gray, matching her blue-gray shoes, unblemished leather, cup of celebration Kool-Aid incongruous beside it. Her father held his sword, his camera.

"Let's take that picture now, Lydia. Come along."

Troy's hands still touched her back, so light, so gentle. His fingers trailed along her palms, feathered the tips of her nails, one finger, none. Sadly surrendering, Lydia stepped out alone. When the flash freed her eyes from its mangled red, she looked back, but Troy was gone.

Day of Decision

She never wanted Troy to leave her, ever again. At least that part of her decision was made. But what about college, qualifications, earning power and jobs?

"Lydia, will you please just consider it?" said her father.

"Lydia, I'll wait for you," said Troy.

"Lydia, it's your future we're talking about." That was her mother of course.

Then, "You choose," whispered her brother, Jason Junior.

"Stay here," said Sylvia with quiet pathos.

Lydia didn't even know what she wanted to do. She liked to paint, loved to write, but most of all, longed for Troy. She'd stay with him she knew, come what may, married and forever. The only important question for her was when.

Lydia sat on the edge of her bed, twisting the ring on her finger—not an engagement ring, not yet, just the silver promise band from church. It committed her to waiting. *How long?*

Downstairs, Lydia's father collected papers and lists, ordered brochures according to college rankings, and spread the results across the dining room table. Lydia walked in and saw him, then tried to walk out again. He made her stop and look with sad surrender and solemn care. "But Daddy, the dates are all passed."

"Nothing's final. Shouldn't stop you from applying."

They ate dinner in the kitchen, not just that night but every night for a week, Lydia's mother permanently harassed because she couldn't clean. Sylvia complained there was nowhere to put things down. Meanwhile Jason Junior stopped calling around after work. Without his whispered *You choose,* what chance did Lydia have?

She sat in the kitchen with her mother, dinner on the stove, time passing, papers and plans all wearing her down.

"So what should I do?" Lydia asked, twisting the ring distractedly again.

Her mother surprised her by not throwing back a solution. Instead she stood up and stepped away from the table, resting her hands on surprisingly slender hips. It was a somewhat unaccustomed stance, too young or too decisive. Savannah looked uncomfortable, almost artificial or comical.

"Mom?"

"Do you love him?" Savannah's voice squeaked.

"Love Troy? Yes of course I do!"

"Then you shouldn't go away."

Lydia stared at this new side of mother in surprise. *A decisive answer? An answer supporting me?* "Mom?" she asked in tones of disbelief.

"You should stay in town," Savannah repeated. "Go to the U. Live in the dorms. There are some nice ones by the church. That's what you should do."

Lydia wrapped her arms around her mother, danced amongst pans and plates, and hugged her tight. "You mean not live here? Will Daddy agree?"

"I think he'll have to." Savannah smiled—just a tiny smile, a tiny determined smile.

Lydia's mother looked truly beautiful and spicy then, powerful like the scent of peppermint. Suddenly Lydia felt proud of all the times she'd been told she looked like her. "Mom, I love you!" she exclaimed.

"You love me today," said Savannah, and both of them laughed.

The Student

Freedom's Price, Dark Walk, Long Wait, Love Promises

Peter followed Troy's truck sometimes. Little boy with his high school graduate, newly engaged. Peter knew what they were doing—of course he knew! He watched them halt by the side of the road that clipped the edge of the forest. Then he drove his car around the corner where he couldn't be seen, hidden under trees. He heard doors slam, voices too low to comprehend the words. Two figures ambled hand in hand through shadowed undergrowth, dark walk to the stream. They stood, entwined as one; *two-headed beast* thought Peter, surely drawing life from itself while the world disappears. He imagined his son's hands slipped beneath folds of garments, soft skin pressed to skin, sweet warmth, and the taste of a woman's lips, legs opened wide around a strong man's back. He imagined he heard the sharp-drawn breath, the panting of desire, and he waited, touching himself, deeply longing as he gazed through the trees.

Love promises: "I've sworn I won't," said Troy, like father like son, like Peter had sworn he'd touch no one else after his wife. "I've sworn I won't..." But he'd touched the woman in lamp-lit dark motel and she melted in his hands. She tasted his flesh, nipping his chest. He tasted hers. He'd touched... he'd seen... he'd known... in the woods, in the dark. He wanted more.

He'd tasted flesh, young flesh—it was sweet. Now Troy tasted his college girl, licking spicy peppermint from her face—from eyes, from neck, from breasts, from underneath...

Peter spat angrily. *Troy tastes everything while Dad gets nothing at all.*

"I've sworn I won't," but who believes love's promises? Somewhere in the trees they'd get naked, Peter knew, where no one could see. A father could tell.

Freedom's Price

"You realize, when I live in the dorm, the parents'll have no one to fuss over but you?" Lydia closed the last drawer in the dresser. Sylvia nodded miserably from the bedroom door as Lydia continued, "Don't worry, Sis. It won't be too bad."

"That's what you say," said Sylvia. "But you're moving out."

Bags and boxes stood in the center of the floor. Childhood books stood guard over empty spaces on the shelves. The rest of Lydia's reading materials, pictures and ornaments poked out from beer and wine boxes brought by Jason to help her pack.

"Everyone'll think I'm an alcoholic."

"So, hide them under your bed when you're done. Or throw them out."

Sunlight shone through curtains pulled back too tight. The room looked bare. A white closet door made a black hole in the cream walls. Inside, weightless hangers presided over shelves emptied of clothes. Two old sweatshirts lay on the floor, next to a pair of fluffy slippers.

"Can I have those?"

"Be my guest."

The final moments ticked away.

The bed sagged and groaned under the weight of sisters, bags and boxes. The girls giggled. "Wonder if we'll make it collapse."

"What would Daddy say?"

Then Lydia stretched lazily, while Sylvia asked the question she'd been waiting for all day. "Why d'you have to leave?"

Tears prickled in her little sister's voice—they clogged Lydia's throat as well, but she couldn't let them out. Instead she gazed at the ceiling overhead, shadows that seemed like pirates or aliens as she grew up. *Why break away from family, home and security? Why not stay?* She'd registered for a full load of classes at the U, but lots of other students commuted, even some of her friends. Then Lydia thought of her father checking up on her, telling her who she could and couldn't date and how late she was allowed to stay out, shooting his superior critical looks at Troy for every failure of accent or manners.

"I need my freedom, Sis." She pushed herself upright on the bed to hug her little sister. How thin Sylvia was, all arms and legs. *When did that happen? Is she ill?* "I'll visit. Don't worry." But already Lydia worried about a child grown suddenly old—too tall, thin, sad, and scared. She worried her sister would have no one to share all her secrets in long dark nights. When she came home there'd be nothing to say. Lydia the stranger. Sylvia grown up. Just the way things go.

Their father's footsteps stomped on the stairs and the girls jumped quickly to their feet, the moment gone. They pretended business as Daddy strode into the room. His presence, even before he spoke, commanded the empty space between home and away.

"Let's get moving." He yanked two bags into his arms and Lydia called out, "Careful, Dad." They trooped downstairs in a sullen line. The sun cast fewer shadows, gentler shades, outdoors less empty than before.

Lydia's father drove the short distance to the college dorms. Her mother unpacked her clothes and made the bed. Her sister sorted books onto shelves. Her brother came by from his apartment with a pillow.

Plugging devices into walls, untangling wires, sorting connections—too many chargers for clock, cassette player and radio, unless they positioned them just right on the strip—Jason Junior crawled under the desk while Lydia passed wires through to him. Sylvia shouted instructions. The parents sat together, unspeaking on the extra-long, extra-hard bed.

"You'll phone home every day right?"

"Sure, maybe"

"You'll do as your mother says, young lady, or you'll come straight home right now."

Lydia's new roommate, Janet, winked from across the room, her family long gone. Then Lydia and Sylvia caught each other's eyes. They collapsed in stifled giggles while Daddy frowned. Jason Junior said goodbye.

The room felt empty when everyone left. Janet lay reading, her case unopened on the floor. Lydia waved from the window as Sylvia disappeared along the path. Night turned the evening sky black. Inside the room bookshelves and closets bulged. Clocks blinked. Chargers hummed. Carpet and curtains held secrets all their own.

Lydia felt like a visitor meeting a friend. Bed springs creaked as she sat, book held listlessly, wondering what Janet was reading while pretending absorption. Both of them looked up together.

"You local then? Your mom and dad stayed late."

"We live nearby."

"Your parents worry?"

"Yeah."

"And your sister? She seems nice."

"Yeah, she's okay."

"What are you studying?"

That night, Lydia lay unsleeping on smooth clean sheets. *Your parents worry?* Truth was her parents never stopped worrying. She'd phone, answer questions, though maybe not every day. She'd go around for dinner on Sundays probably. But the echo of worry would follow her, from dorm to class to home to party to the front seat of Troy's rusty truck. Meanwhile Sylvia, sweet innocent child, would stay shut in her bedroom keeping her secrets to herself.

Lydia called every second night from the public phone in the basement. She tried not to listen to her father's litany of instructions, or her mother's despair, before they put her sister on.

"I might as well be invisible," Sylvia whimpered.

"And I might as well have stayed home for all the freedom I get."

"Don't stop calling us, will you?"

"I won't."

Dark Walk

The bell in the clock tower tolled midnight as Janet entered Paradise Park, hurrying to her dorm by the shortest route. Leaves left by the day's windstorm rustled under her feet. Behind her, students partied noisily, loud music, muffled laughter in the streets, but the park swallowed sound. Janet wondered for a moment where her roommate, Lydia, would be—back there in the crowds perhaps with her car-mechanic boyfriend, or maybe romantically watching the night stretch over town from the comfort of his truck. Or she could be asleep. Lydia never seemed to work as hard as Janet, never even needed to, an art and journalism major with talent to spare. *Talent's easier than brains.*

Janet had spent her day in the library, studying and snatching food from machines in the lobby. Lydia's exams would be essays and opinions, portfolios of sketches and ideas, but Janet's head hummed to the sound of equations and theorems, plusses and equals in rhythms of integer steps. She counted rings of the church-bell and forgot to stop, "fifteen, sixteen, seventeen..." Feet moving onward, brain too tired to think.

White lamps hummed, casting ghostly shadows from their tall metal stands. Damp earth and warm leaves scented the air. Janet strode on, around the hill, past the pond and into the night-shrouded trees. Gravel rustled underfoot while she still counted in her head. In the bushes something moved—only a cat. White and fluffy, it sprang to the path then disappeared.

Then the lights went out.

Janet froze. It felt like sleep, like dreaming. No sound. No sight. Even the music and numbers stopped while the world drew breath. Had the windstorm cut the power?

In a moment she heard the rumble of traffic again. Ambient light from headlamps drifted through trees. Student voices sang their brittle tune. Candles and flashlights flickered in windows while insects fluttered flame-like over leaves. Slowly, the shapes of lamp post and tree trunks appeared.

Janet walked on, more cautious now on the shadowed gravel path. One step. Two steps. Somewhere behind the noises didn't fit. Three awkward shuffles, tapping, gravel slapping, to her two…

"Who's there?" Janet called. No answer. So she continued, eyes wide, striding faster as the following steps gained speed. She stopped at the next lamp post, clung to its cold metal and peered back. Something moved, slid off the path before she could focus—someone hiding in shadows under trees.

Footsteps rustled behind her and Janet jumped.

"Sorry," said a deep, quiet voice. "You all right, Miss?"

"I thought someone was following me."

"Back there?"

"In the trees."

The stranger was tall, hair blond, almost white, well-muscled body dressed in long-sleeved shirt with a narrow red tie. Green eyes glinted in the gray and he had a gentle smile.

"You headed for the dorms?"

Janet said yes.

"I'll walk with you. Keep you company. If you like."

The light above buzzed suddenly, bathing them in white as power returned. At the edge of her vision, Janet saw branches move, eyes watching, something waiting to catch her alone.

"Don't worry," said her escort. "There's only one of him and two of us." He spoke loudly, making Janet feel oddly reassured.

"What's your name?" she asked, meaning really to thank him but fumbling for the words.

He paused. "Steve," he said.

"Like Steve Austin on TV?" Janet laughed nervously,

wondering why she was so helpless at conversation. "I'm Janet. Hi." They walked in silence.

At the edge of the park a dark haired woman waited by a car. "Garnet, Garnet. Where are you?"

"Did you find her?" the woman asked, as Janet stepped toward the road.

"No," said Steve.

Janet asked who and the woman answered, "My cat. She's white with a red stone in her collar."

There'd been a white cat on the path before the power went out. "Maybe…" Then a car zoomed past distracting her.

When Janet turned back to the woman, Steve had disappeared. A fluffy white cat meowed in the shadow of the trees, bright red jewel under its chin. It rubbed its fur on Janet's leg as it strode past, green eyes gazing intently back at her. Then it leapt into the other woman's arms, purring contentedly and loud.

"Oh well. Goodbye," said Janet as the woman climbed with cat into the passenger side of her car. Janet frowned distractedly. "Goodbye Steve Austin?" she whispered, then laughed at herself as she watched the car disappear.

Long Wait

Troy steered his truck into a parking space outside the dorms, wheels rumbling on gravel at the curb. For a moment he sat facing the dark, neither he nor Lydia ready to move or speak. Then he turned. "Well, Cinderella," just as Lydia began to say something else. Troy smiled. Lydia laughed and waved a hand at him. "I got you home before midnight didn't I?"

"Just." Lydia glanced at the watch on her thin wrist. Troy looked at the dash. Still four minutes to go. Pretty good timing for him, he thought. Then they sat, still and silent between the dark of park and watching lights of dorm. Eyes averted, they breathed just a little too heavily in the night. The windows were open, cool air whispering in.

Troy jumped as the streetlamps snapped off, Paradise Park absorbed by night, windows and doors suddenly dark. "The power's gone out. Must have been the wind." Shadows deepened around the truck. The path to the dorms, tree-sheltered, faded to gray.

"I could walk you to your room."

"No visitors after eleven." Lydia twisted her ring.

"But you said your roommate's out. No one would know."

"She'll be back by now."

Silence, again. Sounds of late night traffic wafted toward them—a car horn, hum and roar, brakes and muffled voices. Headlights gleamed false brilliance through the windshield, etching shadows on Lydia's face. The scents of night drifted in through the open window, cold and earthy, fumes and flowers.

Lydia began to unbuckle her belt. Troy watched the way she looked down at her hands, fingers fumbling for the catch. He studied the mound of her breast as she pulled the belt back behind her, then watched her twist the silver ring on her finger, around and back again, before she looked up at him. Lips parted, eyes half-closed, hands limp in her lap—he simply had to kiss her.

And, like all his goodnight kisses, it was fruitless, like kissing a photograph instead of a living girl.

Troy pulled back, tension filling him till he thought he might choke. He leaned away from his love's sweet smiling face but she pulled him back, hands linked behind his neck. He felt the ring, smooth and cold on the prickling hairs above his collar. Then she pressed her small, half-open lips on his, reached into him.

Didn't she know?

Lydia's breasts pressed, squeezed against Troy's chest, and his body filled explosively, even his wrists aching as he clutched at her. "Lydia," he mouthed with tongue sliding low to her neck to taste the word. "My Lydia." Then he felt her hands, thin-boned, so delicate, as she pushed him away. He didn't have to let her. He could keep her, clutch her tight to himself—he was much stronger than she. He could press his flesh back into hers, draw the tautness of her body's peaks against him, and swallow her whole. He could fill her, make her part of himself till he found release. Her face, slightly flushed, her glowing skin, the rise and fall of her breath—he could see she yearned for him too. But she pulled back.

"We have to wait." She twisted the ring, sacred silver, sign of bondage, keeping her from him.

"I know." Troy's voice sounded strangled. He knew, because she'd told him before, because she kept telling him, as if she wanted his sympathy and thought herself the only one struggling with this. "I know, Lydia." He shook with passion.

They kissed chastely now with closed lips. Outside, the power returned, street-lights humming as shadows washed away. Lydia smiled weakly. "Don't get out of the car. I'm fine now. Really I am." Then, while Troy still drank her scent and her words, she gently closed the door.

Troy breathed slowly, sinking back into the seat. He watched through the window of the truck. His body longed for her and burned beneath his belt. Then he turned away. The clock on the dash read ten past midnight—time for him to go home. His key woke the engine. The radio crackled its noise.

Across the street Lydia's roommate stood outside the park by a red station wagon. Was she watching someone leave? Was Lydia watching Troy? But no. She'd be walking up the stairs by now, chatting with friends or silent, alone with her thoughts, and probably still twisting that promise ring.

Love Promises

Lydia shouldn't have said it. She realized before the words left her mouth, but it was too late—the thought already on its way—her tongue well-prepped. If it wasn't this, she'd only have said something else, something equally wrong. It's the way things went.

"I don't live here anymore. You can't tell me what to do."

She got the lecture again of course, the scent of Sunday dinner still on the air. Daddy gave her the predictable text about finances and who pays the bills, as if she were just another utility like gas or electricity—if she didn't give good value her father might spend his money elsewhere. Lydia stayed at the table while he spoke, continued pretending to eat dinner, and twisted the ring on her finger, around and around. Then she followed her mother to the kitchen. That too was how Sunday dinners at the Steepleton home always went.

"You can't blame him," said Mom as she always did. "He's just worried about you." As he always was. Daddy just worried Lydia might be accosted in the park like Janet nearly was— such a serious concern Lydia thought scornfully, as if she spent her time in the park while driving with Troy in his truck. Daddy was worried because dear roommate Janet, who thought a white cat might be a guardian angel, also thought a ground squirrel was a rapist.

"She calls it Steve Austin. Six million dollar guardian angel cat. She's a certified loony."

"Your father's just worried."

So Lydia sat by the kitchen counter, twisting the promise ring on her finger, around and around, forward and back, till her knuckle ached. She watched her mother pile plates into the dishwasher, closing it noisily and tugging open the drawer for her oven gloves. Savannah bent for the pudding and Lydia stared, her familiar mother growing suddenly old, caregiver showing signs she might need to be cared for.

The dish steamed. Apple turnover, Lydia's favorite, its smell began to chase away her mood. "Now just help me carry the plates in to the table," said her mother. As always, Lydia followed and obeyed.

"Why did you tell Dad about Janet anyway?" Lydia whispered to her sister as she sat down.

Sylvia frowned and Lydia followed her gaze to the empty spoon next to her placemat. Sylvia's slim fingers—she was really getting thin—toyed with the wooden handle. "I didn't mean to tell him," she whispered, and Lydia sighed. "Well I didn't! Miss Parker phoned and told him she wanted my picture back for the exhibition."

"Your picture?"

"Yes. I painted one of Janet's guardian angel cat, like the cat that was in the paper—you remember." Their father snorted disapproval, evidently listening from the end of the table. Lydia smiled. "I hung it on the wall of my room because I liked it. I'd like a guardian angel." Their mother groaned.

Such a wonderful conversation, Lydia thought. Daddy snorts and we know he thinks we're talking rubbish, as if painting could ever be important like a calculus exam—*poor mathematical Sylvia.* Mommy sighs because she doesn't approve of angels, or cats, or something. So they send us to academic schools because they want us to get good jobs and be just like them. And we go to a good Christian church, and everyone wants us to conform. It's all planned out then they groan and sigh because we turn out to be ourselves and not whoever they wanted us to be.

The sisters talked quietly over dessert, a semi-private conversation their parents wisely avoided. Lydia felt briefly as if she'd never left—so many years, so many tears around this table. But all the dynamics were different now, Sylvia the one jumping at her parents' every word, Sylvia waiting with bated breath to be criticized, hoping to be ignored.

Meanwhile their parents talked loudly about the girls, but not to them, their own independent diatribe. They hoped Sylvia would settle down soon, hoped Lydia was working at her classes, and hoped she wouldn't throw away her life on a whim. On a boy, they meant—on Troy. Lydia felt like a tennis net hearing their words lobbed overhead.

Most Sundays Lydia stayed for coffee. Most Sundays they sat in the living room together while their father told the girls what he'd been saying to their mother earlier. Lydia would promise to do as she already did: be responsible, work hard and pay attention. But today she'd had enough. She told them it was getting late—might even get dark, so she really ought to go. "Wouldn't like you to have to worry about me, Daddy."

She phoned Troy from the kitchen to ask for a ride, because she did want to scare her father really, and she needed someone lean on, just for a while.

"I don't know what more he wants of me," Lydia complained to her mother as she waited for Troy. Daddy had gone to drink coffee alone in his office. Sylvia had gone to hide away in her room.

"Daddy just wants the best for you," said Savannah.

Aren't motherhood and apple pie, and the warm sweet smell of baking supposed to be best? But Daddy's best was success and good grades and awards and a well-paying job, something he could boast about to his friends, a good return on his investment.

"It's not fair," Lydia answered looking down at her hands. Then she turned to her mother and recited her list, fingers counting the points. "Daddy's got what he wanted hasn't he— I'm going to the U, getting good grades. And you've got what you want—I come home every Sunday." She twisted the ring on her finger again, pulling it almost to the end, almost letting it fall, then sliding it back. "God's got what he wants too—I'm wearing the ring. And the only person who doesn't get what he wants from me is the one I'm going to marry."

"You don't know that," said her mother gently.

"Yes, Mom. I do."

Lydia pushed the ring too far and let it fall, rolling along the table and down to the floor. What did it matter? A promise made to a God who wasn't interested in helping her—no sex before marriage, no hope, no release.

The truck's horn sounded outside. Troy didn't come to the door anymore, easier not to meet her father. Lydia wanted to go out to him without picking up the ring. But already her fingers fumbled restlessly, no silver to twist and turn and slide on them. She'd worn it so long it seemed a part of her. So she bent down, picked up the band and slid it into place, smiled weakly at her mother, and walked out the door.

In the front seat of the truck, Lydia reached over the gear shift, falling into Troy's arms before she'd even thought of wearing her seat belt. Troy didn't complain while her tears dampened his shirt. He didn't demand she tell him what was wrong. He didn't start the engine or ask where they were going. He just sat, someone who loved her just as she was, just where she was, whatever she was doing. He waited, as he always did, till she was ready to tell him, "I'm all right."

The Bride

Wedding Announcement, Wedding Day, Wedding Gift,
Wedding Remembered

It was dark in the park, deep under trees where shadows made a blanket, safe and warm. He could forget the inane conversations there—women going home to their husbands, pretending to flirt with the garage man because he wears a ring, because he's safe and hubby knows I'm here. It was dark in the park, and Peter could disappear, letting the whisper of wind in the leaves blow over him, pretending its touch on his skin was a lover's caress. *Yes, there were lovers in the park, in the dark of the park.*

Peter walked, letting the beat of his feet match the pulsing of blood in his ears. He marched till his energy was spent, then felt renewed. Unsure what he'd do without the park to escape to, he strolled this universe all his own which nobody owned, where no one knew him because no one was there. No need to smile or pretend their separation was amicable. No need to watch his son and future daughter-in-law, pantomiming joy while his body pulsed with pain at what they shared. No need to match clever answer to false innuendo and get a name as a funny man, or match wits with shiftless employees and know they call him a monster.

It was dark in the park. No one announces their wondrous wedding day there, no gifts, no plans, no memories, just dark in the park. And sometimes there were lovers lighting the dark.

Wedding Announcement

"So they're getting married this summer. I expect you knew that, didn't you? Well, as much as you know anything." Peter paced the floor of the Blue Room in Paradise House while Abigail sat trapped in her chair. He waved his arms, waved spittle, waved his anger. Meanwhile she drooled into the collar of her blouse, unable to help the way her body behaved.

"She's still in college," Peter railed. "Did you know that, or do they try to keep it secret? Don't know how they plan to support a family, but then, her daddy's rich. No good their asking me for help I'm telling you. And I'm not going to give him extra time off at the garage either. No way. If he wants to pretend to be a married man then he can behave like one. You tell him if he sees you. I'll expect him working twice as hard with a family to support.

"Yeah, and I'd like to bet she's pregnant. I see them evenings you know. I see how she stays late, lights on up in his bedroom. No way they're behaving themselves. Then they're off to church on a Sunday morning, all lovey-dovey innocent.

"Yes, I thought that would please you, Abigail. She's a churchgoer, is our lady Lydia. They're getting married with a pastor and all the trimmings. And she's got this stupid promise ring on her hand. You never made Mary wear one of those did you? *I promise to be virtuous.* Except in the bedroom when she thinks nobody's looking, that's what I say.

"Don't believe me do you? Well, what do you know? How would you know? She's no more virtuous than your sweet Mary. Did she ever tell you that? Oh I'm sure she didn't. Such a credit to the church she is, isn't she? Waltzing around with her fancy man, and his wife not even dead yet. You've seen them I'm sure, him here to see his wife while she's visiting you? I bet they think you don't know. Well you know now."

Of course, Abigail can't answer. She hasn't spoken in years, and though she hears Peter's voice she doesn't always listen. The words don't matter anyway. She feels the shape of his speaking, like electricity tingling before a storm. She might try to nod or shake her head, but she knows he won't see her. He's not really talking to her anyway, just using her as a chance to let off steam.

Abigail sits and waits for Peter to go, his words like a hail storm throwing stones while inside she's still smiling. The truth is Abigail knows so much more than Peter thinks, and more than he knows. She's seen Mary and Frank. They visit her together. She's seen the smile on Mary's face, joy shining out from her heart. It's not conventional of course. It may not be completely right in the eyes of the church, but it's good, Abigail knows.

Abigail tunes herself to people's emotions now, rather than words. Frank is a deep still pool, refreshing water to Peter's storm. Mary's a fluttering bird, almost afraid to rest. Frank's wife, who never stirs, never speaks, is a wise old goldfish swimming deep in the water, always there but hard to see. She's happy. She doesn't think Mary's a threat. There's room in Frank's pool for two.

And young Troy? He's like the clouds, sometimes clear, sometimes hazy, sometimes a gathering storm with a touch of his dad. He visits his grandmother often, as if to recapture childhood innocence. He even asked her about Lydia before he proposed. "D'you think it's okay, Grandma? Is it okay to ask?" She moved her head—can't move much but Troy sees. Troy uses his eyes. Then he showed her the ring.

Another time, storm clouds darkening him, Troy asked, "Grandma, what if I'm like Dad? What if I let her down like Dad did Mom? I don't want to hurt her." It was Abigail's fear as well. The answer would depend on Lydia, on how strong she was.

Afterward Troy and Lydia met her together. Abigail saw how beautiful she was. She watched Lydia's face light up for Troy and the way her hands found his, gently, not needy. She listened to Troy's rainwater voice tell of peppermint ice cream and lazy days at the beach. Lydia held him back, making sure he didn't betray their private lives, which meant she could control him; she'd keep him safe from becoming his father.

The next time Troy asked, while Lydia made tea, Abigail pulled her lips into a smile. She tensed the muscles of her neck to move and carefully nodded her head. Troy saw, she could tell. The clouds in his eyes blew away and he was pleased.

"They won't invite you to the wedding you know," Peter continued. "Won't be room for wheelchairs and the like. Wouldn't suit Mommy and Daddy's perfect image, not at all."

But Abigail was invited. She'd seen the invitation. She wouldn't be there because the doctor said it wasn't safe, but she was wanted, loved and invited.

"I bet Frank'll be there, but not his wife. He'll be all over your sweet Mary he will, drooling over her. So much for church and morals and all that."

Peter ranted while sunlight faded from the walls of the blue sitting room. Then he looked at his watch, turned around and walked away. No goodbyes. Abigail didn't mind. Troy and Lydia always kissed her goodbye. Mary and Frank too. But Peter wasn't there for her benefit, just for himself.

She felt glad to see him go. Now she could relax back into her chair, resting from the onslaught of his fire. Muscles that couldn't smile at will might smile in contemplation of the wedding to come.

Wedding Day

In the summer time, when the weather is fine… Carla listened to the tune in her head, unsure why she was here, standing with her party dress swirling in filtered heat under pines trees in the churchyard, canned music throbbing from speakers overhead. She'd served the bride's family at Bensons of course, but they were clients with miniature tips and Carla, long-suffering and silent, was invisible. She'd loaded groceries into brown paper bags for them at the supermarket too. Her boyfriend David worked with the groom and his father at the garage, but it didn't make them friends.

"His dad's actually closing down for the wedding," David told her in amazement when he invited her.

"What, like no sales, no service? No way!"

"Yeah. Says he doesn't want his son's side of the church to be empty. Seriously, he's trawling everyone he knows and asking them to be there."

David was far away by the door of the church now. Carla watched him, waved, but he probably didn't see. He stood importantly with the groom and best man, while Carla hid by the drinks table next to the bushes.

The bride's family was out in force. Steepletons had lived in the subdivision since the first homes were built, and they knew everyone. Savannah Steepleton walked around with glass in hand, cultured voice perfectly modulated, greeting friend and stranger alike.

"What a beautiful little girl!" she said, stooping in front of a tiny dark-haired woman and her motionless child. The child had one thumb planted in her mouth while the other hand held a stuffed rabbit. "Amelia, isn't it? And you're Mr. and Mrs. Callaghan?"

"Yes, that's right. We think she's gorgeous too, Mrs. Steepleton." The man beside the woman stood ramrod straight and uncomfortable, spitting words like nails.

"How old is she?"

"Nearly two."

"And does she talk yet?"

"No."

Carla wondered why the mother didn't say anything. Was she overwhelmed by the great Mrs. Steepleton or was there something wrong with the child? The tiny figure stood neatly, hand firmly held, not struggling or trying to wriggle away. Clear eyes gazed straight ahead under rumpled hair, never flickering right nor left, no smile, no frown—ethereal beauty resting in eternal distance.

"Pretty child." Mrs. Steepleton walked on.

Jason Steepleton III, the bride's proud father, was all

business of course, shaking hands with the movers and shakers of town, exchanging business cards. Carla watched his fingers reach into his pocket again, more monogrammed rectangles, more influence, as each new face approached. His voice boomed out. "Good to see you. So glad you could make it."

"Jeffrey Irons." A heavily-built, well-suited stranger introduced himself loudly.

"Good to see you. Good to see you."

Bride and groom stood in the doorway to the church for their pictures. A reporter from the local paper scribbled notes. Carla had to admit, they made a beautiful couple—Lydia, as expected, in a frothy white dress, fair hair coiffed and threaded with flowers and pearls. Dark-haired Troy looked amazing too in a suit. Usually Carla saw him covered in grease at the garage, or else sweat-stained in ratty jeans and tee-shirt, mowing his mother's grass outside the condos.

Troy's mother bought her meager foods from Carla at the grocery store. She stood now, stubbornly refusing to look at Troy's father. They'd been together for the photos of course, but now Mary Markham backed into shrubs on the other side of the path. A tall, silver-haired man paid her studious attention. He'd given her a glass and stood behind her as they both drank, she lifting her head to smile back into his eyes after each sip. *Not quite young love*, Carla thought, but love just the same. Which was nice. She'd always felt kind of sorry for Mary when she checked out her shopping and watched her scrape pennies from her purse.

Troy's father, Peter Markham from the garage, stood alone near the wall. His gaze dropped to the watch on his wrist at regular intervals. Carla wondered just how long he was prepared to risk keeping his garage closed.

She sighed and sipped her drink—so many half-known strangers and no one to talk to. It's what happens when you work in a store or a restaurant, or both. All the people turn into blurs of half-remembered events, meaningless names with no faces and no distinction. No one sees you. She wished David would look her way—wished he'd introduce her to someone—

wished it was time to leave. The scent of pine and flowers mixed with sweet strawberry punch made her head swim. Music throbbed. The sun beat down too bright, shadows moving till Carla lost her patch of shade. She made herself walk around the table again, wishing she could force her feet not to keep time with the music, wishing she had courage to move further away.

Something brushed against Carla's legs. Red drink splashed forward to the pale tablecloth when she jumped—no one near enough to notice. She looked down at a large white cat, almost a bride itself with ruffled fur like a veil over its head. The cat slipped between the table legs to be scooped up by Amethyst, a regular at Benson's. *Now there's a name you remember after running the credit card.* She was dating a guy called Steve Walker, if Carla remembered it rightly. Or more than dating— she looked pregnant.

An older couple stood talking under the trees and Amethyst approached them, so much more confident than Carla. She chatted easily with the tiny woman while her husband rocked slowly on his heels, gazing down at shiny shoes. Policeman's shoes? He looked different out of uniform.

"You could get some more drinks Joe," said the wife, her voice oddly loud for such a small woman. Carla watched Joe take their glasses in his hands. He approached the table and she quickly stepped out of the way.

"Friend of the groom?" she asked, seeking something neutral to say when he looked at her.

"Not really, no."

"Bride's side then?"

"No. We live across the street from where they're buying. Troy's father said we should come."

"Oh," said Carla. More people invited to fill up the son's side of the church.

"Hi Joe." Amethyst's Steve was here after all, looking really quite startlingly handsome, well-muscled under his shirt, with whitish hair, and freckles on his nose. Carla smiled but wasn't flirting, too old for her.

Joe hurried away while Steve fumbled the glass in his hand, gazing restlessly around the churchyard. Carla could smell his aftershave, and tried not to stare. He seemed to be avoiding her eyes, but then, he seemed to be avoiding everyone, even Amethyst.

"You know anyone?" she asked.

"Yes and no," Steve replied, but seemed at a loss for other words.

"Aren't you and Amethyst… Like…?"

"Yeah, we're engaged."

"Getting married in church then? Like this?"

"Next weekend." It probably explained why Steve seemed so uncomfortable. Carla told him she was here with her boyfriend who worked at the garage with the groom, more for something to say than because she thought Steve might be interested. Steve said Troy and Lydia were buying Amethyst's house. Then a stranger approached with a ready smile for one or the other of them.

"Remember me?"

"No… Jason?" Steve asked. "What brings you here?"

Jason who?

"Brother of the bride."

"Good Lord!"

"Didn't you know?"

So this was Jason Steepleton IV. He didn't look much like his father. Thin fingers fumbled with his jacket pocket, as if he were counting threads rather than searching for business cards. He balanced nervously on one foot then the other, eyes flickering restlessly as he tried to sound relaxed.

Carla's boyfriend approached with the best man in tow. "Todd, meet Carla." They shook hands. "Nearly time to get back."

Then the bride's mother advanced, limp wrist outstretched. "So good of you to come." The same phrase her husband kept using, and exactly the same intonation. Savannah shook Todd's hand first, then David's with a frown, then Steve's, and then Carla's. "Jason, I'm so glad you're meeting old friends." Jason smiled as he refilled his mother's drink.

"This is what summer's all about isn't it?" Savannah announced, waving her hand at the crowds in the wide churchyard. Drips from her drink flew outwards. Carla scrubbed them from her dress. "Weddings. Family. Friends." *Funerals*, thought Carla. "Ah yes. This is it. This is what summer's all about." Savannah twirled lightly, facing the church then road then church again. Even when she stood still, her eyes continued to spin.

Something sad blinked out of the bride's mother's face. Carla couldn't quite place it—perhaps just the sorrow any mother would feel on losing a daughter. *Would my mother care?* Or perhaps she struggled with that desperate need to enjoy something unenjoyable. Carla had seen it so often in her own mother's eyes as she grew up. "Are you all right Mrs. Steepleton?" she asked.

A younger girl wrapped her arm around Jason and smiled. "Come on, Mom. Daddy's looking for you."

"My little sister, Sylvia," said Jason over his shoulder. "She's too young for you Steve."

"Me? I'm nearly a married man."

Jason looked like he wanted to stop and ask more, but his mother pulled him on.

David tugged Carla's arm. His boss approached commandingly, a businesslike look on his face as he tapped his watch. "Yeah, I think it's time to go."

"Don't we need to say goodbye to someone?"

"Why? Nobody knows us."

Carla slipped her purse over her arm, smiled vaguely at Steve and Todd, who really didn't know her, and followed David's lead out of the churchyard, back down the busy road.

Wedding Gift

"We should go to Paradise House before we leave," said Lydia. Troy smiled. He loved her comfortable manner with people, the way she always listened, how her instincts always placed her three steps ahead, easily knowing what would make them happy.

And she was his wife, he thought suddenly, kissing her quickly while she still looked up at him. He couldn't quite believe it. She tasted the same, almost, though her skin seemed softer, her mouth a touch sweeter, her eyes glinting brightly and filled with unworldly light. Lydia was his wife.

"Well we should," she repeated, disentangling their lips, and he agreed.

"We could go on our way to the airport," he suggested. "Leave here in good time and stop for a quick visit." But Lydia said no. She wanted to go now, dressed in all her fluffy finery. She wanted to show off the dress and veil, and the flowers, and the pearls in her hair. She wanted the old folk, all of them, to see Troy in his rented tuxedo.

"It'll make their day, month, year. Seriously." Her eyes sparkled at him.

"Let's do it then."

Of course, Lydia's mother wasn't pleased. Troy explained they'd take their going-away clothes with them, drive to the rest home, visit his grandma and anyone else awake, then look for a room to change in before doing the rounds again. "We'll be back to say goodbye."

Savannah interrupted him. "I wanted to help you get dressed, Lydia."

"Mom, really. I'm a big girl now. I can dress myself."

"But this is special."

"Yes Mom. And I want it to be special for the elderly too."

Troy's mother just smiled when they told her, genuinely pleased by the gesture as they'd known she'd be. Old Frank seemed grateful too. Troy looked around to check with his father, but he'd already returned to the garage so he clearly didn't mind.

"Which car will you take?" asked Lydia's father. They wanted to borrow his because it had hooks where they could hang clothes to keep them nice. "Don't get any oil on my upholstery, young man," he ordered, as if Troy's tux might get oily just by being worn, but perhaps it was a careless attempt at a joke. Lydia squeezed her new husband's hand. Troy smiled, not planning to let anyone offend him today. Then Lydia's brother offered to drive. He promised not to watch the lovebirds kissing in the back. Troy promised to return in plenty of time before they left for the airport. And everyone promised to wait and throw confetti.

Jason Junior steered carefully and watched the road, while the happy couple was free to kiss unobserved behind tinted glass.

At the retirement home, Troy helped Lydia out of her seat, unfolding the furls of her dress, inexpert and amused. "I'm fine, I'm fine," she said, smoothing lace with white-gloved hands.

They walked through cool stark halls. The scent of Lydia's flowers battled disinfectant and boiled cabbage, and won. The soft light of her dress and veil battled the overhead fluorescents and shone, victorious. Her gentle voice humming *Here comes the bride* cancelled out the sound of radio and TV till the assistants switched them off.

The couple knocked together on doors, slipping lightly inside, smiles for the bedridden, a touch for the sick, a swish of soft material to quiet the hum of electrical machines. They walked into sitting rooms, green room, yellow room, and blue. Curtains swished open so afternoon light could enhance the bridal glow. Eyes beamed at them. Memories flowed with tears of happiness. Lydia wiped the tears of strangers, whispered sweet words Troy couldn't hear, and brought smiles to every face.

Even the old man who swore all the time stopped swearing long enough to call her pretty.

In the Blue Room they stood by Abigail's chair. Troy kissed his grandma awake, Lydia kissed her to sleep, and Jason took their photograph. The blue light should have been cold on Lydia's white, but instead it flowed warm, like deep water, glowing with promise and hope.

An assistant offered them Abigail's room to get changed in. They tripped over discarded slippers, dodged around tissues damp from nameless fluids, and laughed at the pleasure of nakedness under a glowing light bulb as they dressed each other.

"And your mother wanted to help you get dressed," Troy whispered, hand on bare skin.

"Not today." Lydia smiled.

They paraded their new finery and everyone turned to admire them. Jason took more pictures, promised copies, collected wedding garments inexpertly folded, and escorted his relatives back to the car.

Narrow back roads led to where the reception waited on grass outside church. Everyone threw scraps of colored paper, brilliant snow storm, as they climbed out of the car. More drinks. More talking. Then time to leave with Jason Junior driving again. The crowds cheered as Troy and Lydia leaned back against the warm upholstery. The airport beckoned and they waved their tickets delightedly through open car windows. But their dearest memories came from the joy in old peoples' eyes, more real even than the happiness of friends, somehow more permanent even though it belonged to people whose memories faded fast. It was the nudges, the *Did you sees?* and sparks of recognition. It was something light in the touch of caregivers' hands, the clouds of years temporarily dispersed. It was gift immeasurable, joy unmistakable, treasure given and received, sustaining hope for their new life just begun.

Wedding Remembered

"There's somebody here to see you Abigail," they'd whispered, as though they thought she didn't know—as if she wouldn't have felt the change in the air, stale dust filled with light—as if she wouldn't have heard the swish of silk and the rustle of voices. "Did you see? Do you remember?" Just because Abigail's eyes were closed didn't mean she was asleep. She could still smell the perfume, and taste the wine.

Abigail carefully opened her eyes to a vision of wonder and joy. Lydia stood in cream and white, her veil with pearls nestling neatly in folds of fair hair, tiny, white-gloved hands held out in greeting. She pirouetted on delicate sandal straps, and smiled with delight while Troy's face glowed with pride above the neat black bow of his puzzling tie.

The word was buried in Abigail's memory and she tried to speak. She'd practiced all week long. "Con," *not a con Abigail*—it's for real. "Con-gra," *not a conga*, though she's sure the young couple would dance it well.

The sputtering stopped at Abigail's lips as she found herself transported through the years. She remembered dances when her husband was alive, congas down dusty streets of a sunny little town, festive flags overhead, arms and legs in the wind while friends swung them around like paper dolls in the lanes of her mind.

"Congra-tul." *Two. You two are one. We two were one,* she remembered, feeling again her husband's hand pushing the ring on her finger, as Troy's must have done for Lydia short hours before. Did Troy have a ring? Abigail couldn't ask him, couldn't see.

"Congratul-ate." *Eight. Two. How many children?* She'd only had the one, and Mary too had only the one child, Troy.

"Congratulation," but they weren't *shunning* her. They were good, these young'uns. They'd grown up well, to share their special day and their love with the old—their wedding day.

"Wedding," Abigail shouted in triumph, and didn't know, never found out if the word she'd practiced had managed to leave her lips. "Wedding, wedding, wedding." She bounced in her chair, weary springs creaking and the wood of threadbare arms trembling under her hands. She heard church bells ring in her ears, wedding bells, wedding march, the merry wedding organ beginning to play. "Wedding, wedding."

Lydia reached out and held Abigail's hands, as if inviting her from her chair for a dance. "Yes Grandma," she said, loudly, happily. "Yes Grandma. You're part of our wedding." Jason's camera flashed.

Lydia's brother looked good too in a tux Abigail thought, though not as good as her Troy.

Troy and Lydia posed by her, one on each arm, while Jason snapped, flashed, snapped and Abigail smiled. She didn't know if it looked like a smile but it certainly felt like one, from ear to ear. She didn't even care if her collar lay straight, or if drool had pooled in its creases. Till she was tired, and then she closed her eyes.

It was only a moment, but the young'uns were gone. Sunlight faded from the room. Still, the shadows were gentler than before, filled with memories and hope. Faces and voices were light around Abigail, time's fabric grown thin.

"Abigail." A hand touched her shoulder again. No, she wasn't asleep. "Abigail, they're here for you again."

Lydia stood before her, dressed in lemon and lime, her smile lighting up the Blue Room's gray as the sun began to set. Troy wore a lime green shirt to match his new wife's dress. He looked so like his father. *But no*, Abigail thought. She could see a touch of his grandfather too. Something in the set of Troy's chin, or the depth of his blue eyes, or the brows nearly meeting—something reminded her of her wonderful husband so long dead and gone.

Abigail gazed in silence at them, filling her mind, her memory, and the depths of her day. The *oohs* and *aahs* of her neighbors were better than dinner and didn't drip on her clothes.

"Well Grandma. We'd better be going," said Troy.

Still she gazed.

"'Bye Grandma. See you later."

Abigail struggled again with the word, wet lips spluttering. She wanted to say, "Congratulations," but her ears heard only "Wedding!" *Close enough.*

Part 4

The Family

Brother of the Bride

Open Door, Missed Opportunity, Park Bench, Job Interview

Sweet little rich girl. Let's all bow down to the rich girl shall we? Prostrate ourselves before her on the ground. Here she comes to the garage in tee-shirt and jeans like she's slumming it. Sweet little, pretty little, foolish little rich girl.

I know about her brother, Peter thinks with a smile. He knows Jason's out of work, not so sweet, not so stinking rich anymore. Daddy's probably terribly disappointed. But would dear Jason ever come here for a job interview, work in a garage? Good heavens no. Wouldn't want to soil his pretty little hands.

I know about her sister, Peter thinks, closing his eyes. Little angel wandering alone in Paradise Park where nobody sees, thinks she's so innocent. Hugs trees because no one bothers at home to please her. Lies down on park benches pretending to read and keeping her eyes turned away. Poor little rich thing.

Sweet little rich girl, our lady Lydia. Troy just bows his head to her every command, holds doors open for her like he's converted to gallantry. *Come on Lydia.* When you going to confess you're *with child,* dear little girl? No way you'd've married him if you weren't. Take your brother with you when you tell your daddy though won't you, 'cause my Troy'll be working here, not carrying your train. Take your brother. Don't let him miss the opportunity. Might make a man of him.

Open Door

Jason Steepleton IV liked his job well enough until he lost it. He liked his condo well enough but without more money for the mortgage he'd lose that too. He liked his sister well enough, but she'd just got herself married. So asking Sis for cash was out of the question. Asking Dad? Instead, he asked his mother.

"Whatever happened to your job?" Savannah responded, as if he hadn't already told her, over and over again, as they stood in the kitchen by the open back door.

"They shut us down, Mom. It happens."

His mother couldn't seem to understand.

Jason continued, "So anyway, Mom, I've got to pay the mortgage next week, and I'm really going into debt, so I just wondered…"

"Yes, of course." She tossed him the answer like money to burn.

Jason, knowing his mother never made decisions without Daddy's agreement, wondered what was going on. "I'll pay you back."

"Of course."

"When I get a job." *Why didn't she ask more questions?* "But I don't know…"

"That's all right Jason," his mother said decisively. "A door will open soon."

Jason pushed the kitchen door closed behind him, propelling Savannah to a seat by the cluttered table. She was obviously too distracted to hear. Something huge must be weighing on her mind, and any other time he'd ask what, but today he needed money, nothing else. He marched around the kitchen furniture repeating, explaining, and waving his hands in the air. He tidied papers, stacked books and recipes, piled dinner plates in order with largest on bottom and smallest on top. Through it all, his mother smiled serenely. It was very annoying.

A picture on the kitchen wall caught Jason's eye. It hadn't been there last time he visited. The photo showed three children, small and innocent, a memory of youth. Jason tugged a corner straight, saw the oven reflected in the glass, with towel hanging crooked on the rail—turned to straighten that too. Then he set the extra chair beside his mother's bench, square-footed with the pattern of gray-tiled floor.

"How do you know I'll get a job?"

"Because."

"Because what?"

Instead of answering, Savannah took photos of Lydia's wedding out of her purse and began to show them. Jason pulled the chair out again, evened its feet between the tiles, and sat at her side. His fingers counted threads on the buttons of his coat while the other hand held and stacked full-color images, taking care not to bend them.

"And this one's from just before Troy's father went back to his garage," Savannah's voice droned, "and this one… and here… and Daddy took this when you were driving to Paradise House. Here's where you came back."

Jason gazed patiently, began to count threads on another of his buttons, then moved to finger the stitches on his belt.

"Oh, and this is Jeffrey Irons," said his mother with a curious little smile for the fat man in the photo.

Jason asked, because he knew he had to, "Who's Jeffrey Irons?"

"Oh, we go way back." That smile again, then Savannah laughed nervously. "He's got some openings at his business in town you know. Daddy said you'd get an interview."

"Daddy said."

"Jason, don't be cross. He's only opening a door for you. It's a great opportunity." His mother sounded so worried, so sad, Piggy-in-the-middle as always. But Jason really needed a job. He resented his father's interference, but even he wouldn't look such a gift horse in the mouth, not with the red ink flowing so dangerously free in his bank account.

"I'm not cross." He kept his voice even, quietly obedient. "It's fine Mom. But don't I need to apply or something first? And what are you not telling me about Jeffrey Irons?"

Missed Opportunities

A photo of the wedding hung on the garage wall. Like the wedding ring, another way for Peter to look safe.

"That your family then?" asked the round-bodied man as he fumbled, tugging his wallet out of his pocket.

"My son and his new wife," said the garage proprietor gruffly. His fingers were long and thin like his body, thick-knuckled, oil under the nails. Dirt clung to his pores and peppered his beard. He shuffled papers like an expert keeping the customer satisfied.

"Isn't she Lydia…?"

"Steepleton. Yes. You know them?"

Of course Jeffrey knew them. The girl in the picture looked so like her mother. *Savannah! Ah, my beautiful Savannah!* If he'd paid more attention to Savannah, he wondered, back when they were young… if he'd followed his own path instead of unthinkingly treading behind his father's? What if he'd taken better care of his health, kept his weight down, married, and had children? Memories of all the roads not taken wound like vines around Jeffrey's feet. These days he could only walk where the vines chose to lead, from car to garage to house to work to park bench high on the hill, his ample belly marching before.

He saw a young mechanic look up in the back room. The son, obviously. *Like father, like father, like son.* Jeffrey wondered if this lad unthinkingly followed his father's footsteps too.

It had all made sense back in the day. Moving away wasn't entirely unthinking. Jeffrey's father advanced to the big city office and Jeffrey got a place at university to study business. Hope and a future all planned themselves out, with money for the taking. Meanwhile his beloved Savannah talked of the future too, but her ideas and Jeffrey's proved so very different. They both wanted marriage and children one day, but Jeffrey wanted career and business first; stability, security, with money behind him to pay for everything a family needs. He chased his dream to another world leaving Savannah behind, sweet unclaimed prize, for another man to find; missed his opportunity.

There were other girls of course, plenty of girls in university and town, eager to please a rich businessman when the job went well. But Jeffrey had no one to care about, no one he missed now he'd moved back to Paradise. Perhaps he never gave himself time to know them, work commitments hiding the gaping hole in his life. Now he filled his loneliness with food, sharing hopes and dreams with an Irish setter... who was barking with her leash tied to a metal post outside.

"Sorry... My dog..."

"No problem. Just sign here and initial here... X marks the spot."

Papers covered the countertop, which towered at just at the wrong height. Jeffrey leaned his stomach against the wood, pushing his face forward, hard to breathe with neck bent low and elbows sticking out. The papers looked clean and official like those a successful business might use, so maybe the son wasn't wrong to follow his dad.

It was just bad luck, Savannah's son Jason being out of work, bad luck like marching feet getting tangled in vines. Jeffrey's job disappeared when the economy went south. He moved back here to his dad's old office—not his choice, just another inevitable tug of the vine. He moved his father, now aged beyond health and memory, into that glitzy retirement home on the hill with the overstuffed name, Paradise or something. Jeffrey got cups of tea from the intern, Savannah Steepleton's pretty daughter, newly married and still working her way through college.

Married to the garage man's son, to a car mechanic no less. Jeffrey tried to imagine Savannah marrying so far below herself. But she'd met Jason Steepleton III. The rest was history.

Like all Jeffrey's old friends, Savannah had roots and branches here, family ties he'd lost. Jeffrey had nothing but the feeling of being a stranger in a place he'd called home. Forests where he used to climb trees had been absorbed into Paradise Park. The church out in the fields sprouted classrooms from every corner, residing now on the edge of a subdivision. Fields were houses. "You can never go back," his father said when they first moved away. Now at last, Jeffrey knew what he meant.

The irony was if they'd stayed in town Jeffrey could have earned a fortune from construction in the subdivisions.

"Need your address sir, if you don't mind." The garage man pointed to a line just above the signature. Jeffrey listed his king-size suburban house that stood with grounds and vines on the southern edge of town. He lived alone except for his dog and furniture, and a maid three times a week. He drove north in his king-size, super-sized car, to his skyscraper office every day, enjoying wide-windowed views over Paradise Forest and Park while his spirits flagged.

When the super-sized car's spirits flagged, he gave Paradise Motors a try because his secretary said they might offer a discount.

Jeffrey's stomach rumbled. He had sandwiches in the car, bought earlier from the store downtown. When this was done he'd go eat in the park, find his favorite wide wooden bench and let Shamrock run free. Jeffrey's eyes would follow the drama of other people's lives while regretting his own. Mothers played with children in the wide open spaces, teenagers stole kisses under trees, young boys rode their skateboards and bikes along the paths, and ducks got on with their noisy feathery lives around the pond.

"That do?" The garage man marked the form and Jeffrey handed over his money. Shamrock barked and the vines tugged again. *Time to leave. Time for routine.*

"Have a coffee 'fore you go if you want." Garage man

turned away from the counter, heading back to his son. Coffee glugged like brown sludge in the bottom of the pot.

Tomorrow was Sunday. Jeffrey's king-size body would wake at 10am in his king-size bed, his own super-efficient king-size coffee maker grinding beans for a single lonely cup. Stumbling downstairs, he'd let Shamrock run in the king-size yard, while he bent awkwardly over his stomach to pick up the Sunday paper with its king-size ads. He'd eat a king-size brunch of leftovers, toast and marmalade, reading the paper and dreaming of might-have-beens—the chatter of family life, smells of home-cooked pancakes and bacon, orange furniture polish, the shining of silver cleaned by a wife who cared, the comfort of a daughter like Lydia Steepleton, but it could never be. So Jeffrey left, without coffee, casting a final regretful glance at the photo on the garage wall.

Shamrock panted happily when Jeffrey stooped to free her. He walked to the car, watched her leap into the passenger seat. Her wide mouth drooled and teeth smiled whitely in anticipation. Her tail shed red hairs high into the car's stale air. Then Jeffrey drove through the midday streets, told the dog how hard it is to find a good mechanic, and watched at the light for businessmen returning to work.

Tomorrow he'd watch for well-dressed, Sunday-dressed families going home from church. If he timed it right, he might see Savannah with her husband and maybe a daughter or two at her side.

If he'd married, Jeffrey wondered, would he still go to church? But Sunday was his one day off, his day for lazing around in baggy jeans and a worn out sweatshirt. No one would see him, the invisible fat man watching from his bench on the hill. Shamrock would chase after cats and ducks and children until it was late, till the light grew slant. Then Jeffrey would drive his king-size car back through empty Sunday streets. The vines would wind their trunks comfortably around the windows of his king-size house, and fence him in.

Park Bench

Fall sun poured its mixture of warm and cold over the park as Saturday ended. Leaden clouds hung behind the trees while bright colors splashed incongruously over grass and flowers. Jeffrey Irons sat on his favorite bench looking down, gauging the weather, and wondering how soon he'd have to drive home.

He had a picture in his hand sent by Savannah after the wedding. He carried it everywhere. The note on the back said simply, "I thought you might like this." Neutral. Unconcerned. Just keeping a door open to further conversation. He tried to imagine what children he might have had with Savannah had things turned out differently, and he thought of Jason, Lydia and Sylvia.

Young Jason needed a job, or so Jason Senior said at the wedding. So Jeffrey would give him an interview. For friendship's sake, for memory's sake, the boy would surely fit the bill.

Ducks flapped their wings on the steel-gray pond as a lady went by with a stroller. A dark-haired mother walked behind holding a small child's hand. Both ladies were pretty, Jeffrey thought, and both belonged. But sitting on his bench, meatloaf hands on tree trunk knees, Jeffrey felt more like a pigeon among ducks, ungainly, unable to swim against the tide. Mothers with children were the cats, vaguely threatening, parading a future he'd lost.

Jeffrey watched as a white cat stalked from the trees and followed them, stiff-legged with back arched high in the air, tail sticking up. He wondered if Shamrock might take it into her head to give chase. The little girl walking with her toys seemed lost. She'd left her mother and followed a path winding deep under shadows into darkness. The cat turned around and trailed behind.

So many paths not taken, Jeffrey thought, looking at the faint map of veins on the back of his hand. A spider web of life's possibilities, all turned to dust. Savannah's son would pass the interview. Jeffrey would phone her with the news, an excuse to hear her voice. In the evening he'd visit the rest home, remembering his father who wouldn't remember him, and accepting a cup of tea and a smile from Savannah's sweet newly-married Lydia.

Little girl, cat and dog had all disappeared. The stroller-less woman turned around as if she'd forgotten something. Then barking erupted. A streak of white followed by red exploded from the black forest shadows. Cat leapt over the edge of the pond. Dog fell in. Baby cried, splashed by the spray. And small girl, unconcerned, unresponsive, strolled from the woods behind them, rabbit and doll dangling from her hands. The mother's voice echoed, "Amelia," as she ran forward, waving arms, mouth opening and closing, a black hole in her face but the child stood still, stick figure who looked like she'd prefer invisibility.

Stomach rumbling, Jeffrey, the truly invisible fat man, called his sodden dog and went home to find more food.

Job Interview

Yesterday, when nobody cared, the weather was sunshine and warmth and clouds of pale gray. Today the planet shifted. Late summer sun turned to early winter and rain. Jason's suit jacket flapped as he ran for the cab. One hand struggled to hold his tie in place while the other clung to his folder. His pen slipped to the ground.

"Where to?" the cab driver asked as Jason slumped in the back. He gave the address, memorized from the interview letter, then opened the folder to check he'd got it right. *Everything that can go wrong should go wrong*, the adage said. But the address was correct. He'd done one thing right. Time to sit back and relax.

Straight away, of course, Jason began to worry. If he'd got the address right, he had to mess up the interview didn't he? It was all about balance, this jobless world of right turned into wrong. Lost the button off his jacket—counts as wrong. Met up with the cab—one right. Correct address—two rights. Something else needed to go wrong, but of course, he'd dropped his pen earlier.

Jason pressed the top of his pen, hoping it still worked. But now he was one, maybe two rights ahead, which didn't look good. He made a list, like solving a math problem, and wished he'd studied architecture instead.

Silent cab driver in a city of noise—right or wrong? Then the driver spoke. "Traffic's bad."

Predictable. Jason added another mark to his mental list and they passed the park.

"Traffic light's out."

Two wrongs.

They waited a full ten minutes for the light, Jason checking his watch and smiling inanely because if enough things went wrong he just might get the job. Missing the interview was one problem he couldn't afford though, so he asked, "How far is it to walk?"

The cab driver answered, maybe five minutes. "Great." Jason paid and walked the rest. Cab can't complete the journey, another wrong.

Jason's jacket flapped open again, missing its button. Rain started falling, which would make his shirt wet, maybe transparent, embarrassing, circular patterns drawn on his tie. Too many wrongs made his list too far from balance but at least kept his mind from the interview. Puddles formed on the path and splashed Jason's shoes. Would the interviewer notice? Black leather stained brown and his socks grew wet. Mud spattered his trousers.

Jason rushed through the door and waited for the elevator. A pretty but heavily pregnant lady waited beside him, looking like she'd never set foot in a puddle in her life. Jason smiled nervously as she held the door, long black hair brushing his hand. He kept his eyes to the floor and walked carefully, avoiding her bump. Soothing music. Jason's heartbeat sped up, even as the music called for quiet. They stepped off at the same floor and this time Jason held the door for the lady when they approached the same waiting room. Was she interviewing too? *Do pregnant women apply for jobs?* Too many wrongs—he needed time to stop and check his list. Life hadn't always been like this—safe, father-dictated choices used to mean security.

"Jason Steepleton?" the secretary asked. "Mr. Irons will be with you in a moment. Why don't you sit down?" Then she turned to the lady. "Steve said you should go straight in."

Jason sat on the low padded bench. The cushion sagged beneath him, holding him down like the music in the elevator, ignoring his heartbeat and keeping his body trapped. His knees stuck up at too steep an angle to steady the folder while he read.

"Jason?" A voice spoke in welcome and Jason lifted his gaze from shiny shoes and well-pressed trousers to clean blue shirt. The speaker looked vaguely familiar from somewhere. Then Jason struggled to his feet to shake hands and noticed the man's white-blonde hair. Not a stranger after all.

"Steve. I didn't know you worked here."

"You should have said you were applying." They both spoke at once.

How did this fit into Jason's lists? Good that he knew Steve, bad, they'd not been in touch, balanced maybe? The woman from the elevator turned out to be Steve's wife, Amethyst, who Jason might have met a few weeks ago at his sister's wedding. She hadn't known him either though, so he wasn't too embarrassed.

Jason glanced through the open door, seeing a large photograph on Steve's wall, Steve and Amethyst with a fluffy white cat wedged between them. The cat had a large red jewel on its collar. Amethyst had a jewel on her necklace and Steve wore a red tie. Jason remembered the necklace from the elevator, red like the floor-numbers. He'd ignored it as being neither wrong or right.

Now a larger, older man approached with hand outstretched. "I'm Jeffrey Irons." He had an oddly booming voice.

"We met at Lydia's wedding of course." Then he nodded at Steve. "You two know each other?"

"Yes," said Steve. "From school. Way back."

"Yes indeed. Well, interesting. Let's go."

Jason found himself ushered into a dark-paneled, well-appointed room with framed certificates and leather furniture. No pictures of smiling faces or collared cats here.

"Sit down, Jason. Just relax a moment and I'll tell you all about the job."

Jason didn't know how to relax. Instead his mind raced—back to the traffic light, the cab, the dash for the cab, back all the way to the moment he left his house, the phone call when he ordered the cab, the job he'd held and lost, his father's I-told-you-so, to shattered dreams and parental influence. Slowly he fixed his thoughts on Mr. Irons' conversation. Slowly his suit became less of a disguise. Slowly his socks dried out.

It was still raining when Jason left the building. His suit-jacket flapped as he ran to a waiting cab. His tie flew in the wind, catching drips, painted with circular stains. He clutched his document folder in one hand, waving the other in the air, holding tight to his pen. He'd got the job!

Just to keep things in balance, the cab left the curb before he reached it. Jason stood in the rain with wet shoes and wetter socks while a passing vehicle splashed. He smiled.

Sister of the Bride

Guardian Angel, Walk Alone, Something Borrowed,
Something Blue

Peter was nearly a grandfather now, Troy a father-to-be, and pretty-girl Lydia was wide as a car. The sunlit, spring-warmed green of Paradise Park was the child's promised world. Lydia would sit on a bench with the baby. Troy would take his sandwiches from the garage and eat at her side. And Peter would watch.

A fat man lolled on a bench on the hill, mouth open to sky as if he thought raindrops were wine. Discarded toys lay incongruously at his side. Mothers and children strolled past the pond, unconcerned. They'd run faster if it started to rain. Or they'd shelter under trees. School kids would come out later, chattering, splattering words like seeds. The in-crowd would hang out together, loud and lumpy, while those on the fringes withered and wasted away. Some would go home. Some would wander the long paths all alone. And some would stray into sleepier parts of the forest, where nobody played.

Safest of course to stick to the path, well-measured, entrance and exit well-planned. Or else walk by the pond, playground, wide grassy fields where everyone is seen, everyone understands. If you have to stray in the forest, keep your straying quiet. Shadows gather and angels guard these trees on borrowed time.

Peter liked the quiet of the forest, walking the untracked land between tree trunks, far more invisible than any fat man trying to lie still on the hill. Peter's shadow stirred the undergrowth, a part of nature, at one with the birds and the bees. Collar pulled up and cap pulled down, baggy coat fastened over his beard to hide the shape of him, he was nobody. Mary couldn't stare at him here, comparing him to her lover, every smiling glance a reminder he didn't measure up. Troy couldn't question him sharply, doe-eyes accusing, "Did you betray her dad?" Lovely Lydia couldn't offer her ever-innocent dewy sympathy. Carla from the supermarket couldn't pretend he was her favorite customer—Carla who thinks she knows everything but doesn't, who smiles like she's someone else when she dresses up to serve at Benson's—and Pastor Bill wouldn't have to ask, "Are we going to see you on Sunday?"

Blue skies hid in the shadows of gray, and clouds suited Peter's day. It was quiet in the park, for now, till the schoolchildren came. Sometimes even they could be quiet for a while.

Guardian Angel

Sylvia Steepleton, youngest child, was the academic of the family. Her brother Jason had already finished college and begun his new job—not a genius, just an all-around nice guy, and their father would never approve, no matter how he tried. Lydia studied art and journalism at the U, neither of which qualified with Daddy as real work—and she was married, even worse—and she worked at the retirement home, hopelessly beneath Daddy's dignity. Sylvia was the mathematician, straight-A student acing every test, destined to go far. Not Daddy's favorite of the three, she knew—Lydia would always be that. But Sylvia had the honor of Daddy's greatest expectations.

She was painting a picture this afternoon in art class. She'd made her father let her keep taking art. He called it a waste of time, but Sylvia didn't listen. *Mathematics is art.* Daddy said it would distract her, but Sylvia called it relaxing, her one rebellion, her one safe place where she could hide herself in the images she made.

Around the room other students were absorbed, each in their own creative bubble. A hum of voices murmured requests for scrap paper, borrowed paints, or color advice. Sometimes the teacher spoke, giving prominence to someone's catchy idea or bright new technique. Sounds washed the room like paint brushes in water, muted with background blue, giving shade but no texture.

Overhead lights kept the room bright, and windows onto the school yard let in the sun. All around, easels lazed at crazy angles, tall like walls, each person's secret hiding place with only their backs in view. Paint-splashed images decorated the wall space between the windows—hidden meanings resting in frames, hopes and fears in doctored photographs.

Sylvia's painting probably seemed like a fluffy picture-postcard till the teacher looked closer. Sylvia heard her sharp intake of breath, felt as she leaned over her shoulder, invading her space, and sensed when disapproval turned to surprise. She was glad she'd decided to paint it again, to try out a more grown-up style, more suited to Senior High. The fluffy white kitten of past attempts was blessed now with pale feathered wings.

The white cat rested in the center of the page, washed with light blue shadows, purple bruising the sky behind the fur. Sylvia added pale streaks over gray, thickening and slimming softly under her brush. Feathers had their tiny tips retouched with the smallest pen. Green eyes shone, though Sylvia wasn't quite sure how a cat's eyes should gleam. A red stone glowed like a secret third eye watching from the kitten's collar.

Sylvia leaned back, pleased with the effect, then stretched to add a spark in the cat's wary gaze, flipping her brush to streak dampness on the tiny black nose. The diamonds on the collar hadn't come out so well—they looked more like multi-colored dust. Still, she liked this picture better than last year's attempt.

"That's really quite pretty, Sylvia," said her teacher, breaking the silence and easing Sylvia's tension. "What do you call it?"

"Guardian angel cat." She hoped no one would hear. Not that she was embarrassed at the name—just didn't like disturbing the silence.

"Where did you get the idea?"

Sylvia stared at the page, unsure what to say. There were two stories after all, one in the paper, one just family. "My sister's friend says her guardian angel's a cat, so I thought I'd paint one."

Understanding or memory flickered in the teacher's eyes. "No, I remember don't I? That couple who were getting engaged? Didn't you paint something in Junior High for the competition?"

A boy spluttered nearby—no matter. Boys always snickered, whatever she said. More important were the quieter sighs of admiration from the girls. Some of them came to look. Their *oohs* and *aahs* made Sylvia feel good. Painting made her feel good. Appreciation. Recognition of talent. Being able to communicate without having to speak.

The final bell clanged. "If your pictures are dry you can take them home now," the teacher announced. Sylvia's angel was still wet. All the same, she'd feel wrong leaving it behind, like ignoring luck, or leaving beauty to the beasts. She took a blank sheet of paper to protect the paint, then laid both sheets in her folder, lifting the padded blue rectangle like a shield in front of her as she ran for the bus.

Outside, fresh air, the breeze laden with gasoline and diesel, replaced the closeted fumes of art-lab paint. Wind pushed the folder against Sylvia's body, pressing it to her chest. She struggled not to squeeze it with her fingers, not wanting to risk sticking paint to the covering sheet.

"Got your pictures, Syl?" asked one of the boys, as she scrambled to the bus.

"Yes, I'm fine."

"Going to show us?" "Show us. Show us," the students chanted, something in their insistence scaring her. She felt pressured, too many eyes staring. But she needed to know the picture was safe, not smudged or glued, so she opened the folder to reveal the cat anyway. Someone cheered. Someone jeered.

"It's beautiful," said Simon, hunky older brother of Sylvia's best friend. He smiled, the first boy really to smile at Sylvia, first boy to say he liked something she'd painted and sound like he meant it. Sylvia smiled back, but didn't push her luck. She sat in her usual place, half way down the bus, half way between people she only half knew, and a world away from the most beautiful boy in the world.

At home no one noticed Sylvia come in. They hardly ever did. She rushed upstairs to place the folder on her bed. Her previous angel cat picture ended up back in school, but she'd always fancied having a guardian of her own. This time Sylvia swore she'd keep her luck at home. An old painting she'd done of a millhouse by a stream hung on her wall. The frame seemed about the right size. Sylvia switched the pictures, wondering as she did if anyone would see the difference. Since Lydia got married all they asked was that Sylvia keep clean, obey the rules, and do her homework on time.

The cat kept watch from its picture frame now, green eyes following Sylvia around the room, swaying from side to side as they struggled to see from their window in the wall—Sylvia's picture, her secret world, her own to do with as she chose.

The cat was her guardian angel, but she'd met it too late. Even cats with wings can't turn back the clock or undo the memories that left her thin and broken and brittle as glass.

Walking Alone

"Where were you then?" Sylvia asked the picture, wishing the memories didn't keep coming back. Two years, and she'd never escaped them. "Why didn't you protect me? Why didn't you make me walk some other way?" But the cat didn't reply. "Why didn't you tell me what he wanted?"

She remembered heading home that afternoon from Junior High, all innocence and youth. She didn't follow the wide bright open causeway through the park, not even the trail under the trees, but cut across through tangled branches and weeds. You're not supposed to walk alone nor wander off the path, not when you're a brand new teenager anyway, and not when your parents and teachers and friends, sister too, all want to tell you what to do. Which is one of the reasons she'd chosen to take the shortcut, to prove their warnings untrue. The other reason was rain. She wouldn't get as wet under the shelter of trees.

She pushed the hood of her sweatshirt from her face, making her hair feel less sticky, less enclosed. Fat blobs of water splashed from leaves down the back of her neck, but thirteen-year-old Sylvia didn't mind. Drips weren't half so unrelenting as rain.

Walking slowly, wandering, she had nothing special to get back for. The homework could wait in her backpack. She'd either be ignored or get in trouble when she walked in—for being late, not phoning, missing the bus, delaying dinner. Who cared anyway?

Lydia cared, she supposed. Lydia always cared. But Lydia was contemplating college and dating Troy back then, hardly ever around.

It hadn't really gone dark, not yet. The days were getting longer with spring, and the leaden gray of rain blinked through leaves and branches, almost refreshing after winter's cold. Underfoot, damp undergrowth still crunched with bones of frozen leaves, grass and weeds. Ahead, a ray of blazing sunshine filled a clearing with echoes of heaven. Rain like a waterfall splashed to guard the entry. Sylvia stood entranced.

The sound behind her didn't disturb her—probably just animals, or acorns falling down. Then heavy hands reached over her shoulders, clasped her chest, and pulled her off balance.

Sylvia opened her mouth, just to gasp, not scream, sure some crazy kid from school was playing tricks on her. She found herself turned around by a stranger, face pressed into the oily cloth and sweaty smell of work clothes. She struggled to move and the stranger tilted her head back painfully, almost sideways, pulling on her hair. Beyond his shoulder she saw sky while he held his face to hers, his features just a shadow against the light. Thick lips slithered over hers while sandpaper skin scraped her cheeks.

Sylvia pushed and thumped with her hands, but the stranger tightened his arms and held her still. She heard breath rattling in his lungs, felt his heart beat fast, and shuddered at the cold of saliva on her skin. When she stopped fighting, the man's hold became almost gentle, one hand around her waist, the other clasping her head, molding her body as he bent her back. She kept her eyes shut, unwilling to see, while his tongue, wide and fat, pushed between her lips against her teeth. But it didn't hurt and being held was oddly comforting. Then he pushed her away and she almost pulled him back. Some part of her whimpered, wanting him stay and keep her safe.

"That was good," the stranger said, panting slightly, face still hidden in shadows and dark. "Thank you." He hurried away.

Sylvia straightened her clothes, wiped her face on a tissue from her backpack, and headed home. *Parents can kiss you,* she thought, *sisters, friends.* Why should there be anything wrong with a stranger's kiss? She smiled, trying to taste his tongue again, a tinge of rebellion thrilling her. And hey, she hadn't even said anything, so she hadn't broken the rule about not talking to strangers.

She should have told someone of course. But Mom was arguing with Lydia again, and Dad—well, she couldn't tell Dad. When Lydia and Troy kissed in the truck, Sylvia hugged her silence to herself and said she didn't care. Then, not caring, she waited till another rainy day and returned to the woods. He wouldn't be there if he wasn't meant to be. And if he was, she'd know it wasn't wrong.

She watched the figure of the man approach this time but still couldn't see his face. He wore his cap too low, his collar too high, hiding his chin. He never quite looked straight at her. He walked too fast as well, almost rushing toward her, as if to sweep her off her feet, or catch her before she could memorize how he looked.

He held her again, hugged her, warm and tight against his body. "I thought you wouldn't come," he gasped. "I'm so sorry. I thought you wouldn't come—should have trusted you."

She'd thought she wouldn't come—thought he—thought she—couldn't untangle her thoughts. But it was good to have pleased someone, to be worthy of somebody's trust.

The man's voice rustled gruffly over Sylvia's head. He wrapped his arms around her back, knuckling her spine, holding her tight. She pressed herself closer to the metal scent of his shirt, so nice to be held and wanted, and she wondered if Lydia felt this way when Troy hugged her.

The stranger mashed his mouth against Sylvia's again, just like last time, and she closed her eyes. His tongue thrust instantly between her teeth. She let it because he needed her, because he'd gone out of his way to meet her again, and because he cared—*no one else did*. She let his hands glide up and down her arms, tickling and cold. She leaned toward him as his arms wrapped around her back, fingers rumpling her shirt then kneading the skin under the waistband of her skirt.

One hand slipped under Sylvia's tight-fitting top and began to stroke, cool and smooth along the hollow of her back. Goosebumps lifted then settled down. Sylvia wriggled more comfortably, stiffening just for a moment when the stranger's other hand insinuated coldness between their bodies, pressing hard against her belly. His fingers brushed the edge of her first-bought bra, then slid over satin. She felt their pressure, muffled, odd, but there was nothing improper about his approach, she told herself—no attempt to undress her. He kissed her neck and it tickled and Sylvia giggled. Then he undid the top of her blouse, flicked his tongue against her throat, kissed deeply as if drinking her in, and stepped back. *Like a vampire*.

"Thank you," said the stranger, breathless again, before he left. He appreciated her.

The stranger's kisses were Sylvia's secret, as Troy's had

been Lydia's, the stranger's tongue her talisman against indifference. She'd always wondered what older teenagers were doing, what it felt like. Now she knew. It wasn't bliss or rapture but if he wanted it, it was okay by her. No one else kissed her at home anyway. Or hugged her. They were all too busy arguing about Lydia's college plans—and the dreaded Troy.

Okay, it wasn't the gentle kiss of a parent. But it was okay.

Sylvia missed him the days he didn't turn up, when she walked home too early or too late. Did he miss her too? It was routine, like any other. She didn't seek him out, but she waited for him.

The stranger's breath puffed in short heavy gasps. He pressed her back against a tree, held her tight, with his legs wrapped around her against the trunk. Thin-fingered hands fumbled under her blouse while lips pressed to her face. She felt him grope underneath her bra, fingers touching, circling, touching again, palms cupping, caressing her skin. She felt him slide one hand between her legs, underneath the short tight skirt. She winced at the catch of elastic as his fingers squeezed under her pants. Then he stayed so still, so very still, barely breathing, while his heart thumped hungrily.

"You're so good," he gasped, drawing back sharply. "Oh, you are really good. You're so good to me." Then he left again, his face still a secret shrouded in mystery. She realized now it was a secret she wouldn't even try to discover.

After a while, you don't think of telling anyone 'cause there's too much to tell.

One day the man pushed her down from her perch against the tree. He stretched her back over his arm then straddled her struggling body, till she lay on the ground. He pressed himself heavily on top of her, squeezing the breath from her lungs. His mouth sucked hard around her lips, around her face. She was sure he was bruising her, his thick tongue thrusting sharply inside till she struggled and almost choked. He folded a wide hand over her face then, sliding on slick saliva, covering nose and mouth and keeping her silent. His other hand dropped over her unformed breast as he leaned back from her, fumbling to undo her clothes, each button and clasp a challenge, his fingers all thumbs. Sylvia wriggled, leaves scratching where bare skin lay exposed. Head and lips pressed down on her shoulder, scraping with unshaven beard. The stranger's tongue lapped hungrily at her throat, under her arm, then slid down naked skin to suckle her stomach. He pushed her bra out of the way, wrapping his lips around the tiny buds of her, while fingers twisted, groping on hot palms, pushing her skirt till it too came undone. She felt him slide his hand on the inside of her thighs, up over lacy underwear till fingers hooked and tugged on the elastic. He pulled her pants down awkwardly around her legs as he spread her knees. Then, stretching her, he stroked and touched, creeping higher, intruding under damp folds of skin, and she heard him gasp. She saw his eyes—only his eyes— never looked for his face. Then she tried to fight him away as his body pressed and crushed her. Breath squeezed from her lungs. Space opened inside of her, fingers, more, thrusting suddenly, urgently, in the gap between her legs.

She felt herself buried in deep yielding earth and scratched him in fear. Suddenly he drew away, stood over her looking down from the blackness of his shadow, then fled. She heard his voice mutter something that might have been *sorry,* but nothing more.

Pulling her clothes together, fastening buttons, brushing off dirt, there was something damp on the inside of Sylvia's thighs, dull and sticky, she wiped at it. She wiped her mouth, wiped and wiped and wiped, and never went alone to the woods again.

If only she'd had a guardian angel cat back when she needed it.

Something Borrowed

By tenth grade Sylvia had a reputation as an artist and mathematician, and a geek. She studied too hard, took her painting too seriously, didn't have enough friends—didn't have a boyfriend, that's what they meant. But she planned to change all that. She was going to dance at the high school Christmas party. She'd relax and prove she could be just like everyone else—Sylvia the beautiful, the desirable. Of course it didn't work out.

She drove home carefully, her first time borrowing Mom's car, first time driving all on her own, and felt like a first-time beginner and failure at life. She had to stop and climb out to clear snow off the windshield. The wipers were broken. She could barely see the road markings and kept worrying she'd find she'd parked illegally. Would a policeman ticket her? Would he smell alcohol and test her breath? She hadn't drunk anything, but she wondered now, could you get drunk on fumes? Would he think the car was stolen? She didn't know where the paperwork was kept.

As she brushed snow again from blue sloping glass, Simon's face seemed to peer from the reflection but he wasn't there. He'd never be there. Hot tears mingled with snowflakes on Sylvia's cheeks—would they make the snowflakes steam? The windshield wipers of her eyes were broken too, thoughts dripping back to the surface of her mind as she swept them away.

She liked Simon, Sharon's big brother. He combed his hair, kept his nails clean, wore freshly ironed shirts. He had a tiny yellow beard and a very sweet shy smile. But his breath had smelled of drink tonight and his hands were hot and clumsy. Sylvia cried, leaning over the hood of the car.

Simon had called her something, she remembered, as she struggled away, leaving the party, terrified by his kiss. She'd felt guilty until he shouted but she couldn't hear. The silent roaring in her ears drowned everything out.

"You're a..." *something*. "That's what you are."

Then Sylvia rushed through the door marked *exit*, out of the way of sounds and smells and faces, out of heat into the cold. In the yard one girl was throwing up, another holding her head. "What you staring at girl?" Sylvia wasn't staring. "You think you're teacher's spy or something? You going to report us to the school?"

The beat of the music followed her, clattering voices, brittle bright laughter like the roar of an express train on the tracks.

"You're a good student," the English teacher said, when Sylvia discussed her college hopes. "You'll get lots of offers."

"You'll have a great career in math or science," said the math teacher.

"You're very talented."

Sylvia's mother said she was her good little girl, then that she was growing up fine, then that she wasn't too old for a spanking yet, and should do as she was told. "Take that look off your face."

Sylvia's brother Jason called her a heart-breaker. Her sister Lydia called her a doll. And whenever Sylvia was angry or sad they all said, "That's not like you," as if they knew her.

"You're beautiful," Simon said earlier, before he called her something else. She didn't feel beautiful. She gagged when his breath mingled with hers, eyes going slack, his tongue pressing slimily against her mouth. She wasn't who he thought she was.

Sylvia stopped the car outside the house, the ground too slippery for her to risk parking on the drive. Snow fell in endless flakes of white, and lights shone from windows downstairs. She checked her face in the mirror, eyes red from crying, makeup smudged. Knowing she couldn't get into the house unobserved, not this late at night, she wondered which persona to wear—helpless child struggling with broken windshield wipers, grown up daughter home from the dance, famous scientist, mathematician, pretty girl, ugly duckling, maybe she should think of something else.

"You're a..." Not that. Whatever it was. *Nobody knows*

what happened in the woods.

Sylvia had borrowed the car from her mother, borrowed the blouse from Lydia, borrowed Simon from her best friend. "I'm just something borrowed," Sylvia thought, someone who fills her emptiness with other peoples' lives.

Something borrowed. Something blue. She took a deep cold breath and marched inside.

"How was the party, dear?"

"Boring."

"Not like our Sylvia to sound so down in the dumps."

Sylvia might not have got in unobserved, but nobody had seen her.

Something Blue

"Why did you do that?" Sharon asked. Sylvia just shrugged as they walked the tree-lined path in silence. "You always do it, don't you?"

"Not always," Sylvia mumbled.

"Oh come on!" Sharon stopped short. "Come on. Tell me one time you didn't."

"Didn't what?"

They walked on. Dried leaves from long-gone fall crunched underfoot. The air smelled heavy and sickly sweet, pine needles dripping on the outer branches of trees. Light shone brighter as they came to the end of the path. Running water, shouts of children playing and adults calling names drifted nearby. Sunlight slanted through bark dust floating on air.

"Let's stop here," said Sharon when they came to a bench, so they sat. Sylvia gazed down at her hands, firmly, primly clasped over her knees, skirt pulled down, legs together. Beside her, Sharon threw herself into a sprawl, arms and legs akimbo on wooden slats. Then she stood again, stepping forward and back.

"No," Sharon said as Sylvia started to move. "No. You stay there. Let's talk." She faced her friend. "You listen, Sylvia.

You just sit there and listen to me for a change." She turned back to the tree-hidden sky, gathering thoughts from the air. "Okay. So we're at the party and it's snowing outside." Arms thrown out dramatically. "Everyone's happy. Right? Great music. Great food. Nothing bad going on. Nothing our mothers wouldn't approve of, right?"

Sylvia nodded and groaned.

"And then my brother, my dear sweet Simon that you've been going all gooey-eyed over forever, my brother that's only there 'cause I told him I wanted him to meet you—'cause you told me *you* wanted to meet him… Yeah?"

Sylvia nodded again.

"My brother asks you to dance, and you stand there like a brick. Then he tells you you're pretty—I know, I was listening—he tells you you're pretty and you run away like he's threatened to murder you or something."

Sylvia's head angled down. Tears splashed on the backs of hands tightly clasped in her lap.

"Why?" Sharon asked, reaching to comfort her friend. "Why, Sylvia?"

But Sylvia didn't answer. Her sobs were quiet, though they drowned out the birds and the water, children and parents too. The rest of the park belonged to a different world as Sylvia wept in her secret circle of shame.

"Why, Sylvia?"

A mother walked by, holding a small girl by the hand. "Amelia, this way." The child hummed tunelessly, trailing a red-dressed doll and stuffed rabbit behind her.

"Why?"

A bunch of schoolchildren, youngsters with bright happy shouts and flashing feet, burst from sunlight into the trees. They raced past the bench with parents following. Sounds of tears and laughter stayed behind, waiting for seasons and time.

"Will you tell me sometime, Sylvia?"

"Maybe. But I don't think we should stay in the woods on our own. We should warn those kids."

Mother of the Bride

Party Dress, Sunday Dinner, Church Fair, Money Matters

"Warn the children," it said on TV. "Paradise Predator." Perhaps he should walk the park and keep watch because, after all, the predator couldn't be him. *Not my father*: He never hurt anyone. The almost-women in their tight tops, short skirts, swerves and curves smelling of burgeoning womanhood—they threw their words and charms abroad with vaunted innocence. Drawn like moths to the flame—no, that was wasn't it—the girls were the flame and they were drawing him—did the *Predator* draw them? Hair spun and waved in wild abandon, long soft limbs, small buds of beautiful promise. Meanwhile Peter hid in the shadows and kept away because he wasn't his father. He kept watch, kept safe. He hadn't hurt her—he'd been strong—but still she haunted him. Every time he saw her, every child he saw like her, every young woman.

He wondered sometimes if she'd give him away, but felt safe as she grew older and years went by. *One little girl's wild imagination versus the word of an honorable citizen, upright gentleman with quietly wayward wife, vital member of the community.* Perhaps Peter should start going to church, then he could add pillar of the faith to his vital statistics. Sunday dinner with the pastor maybe, a helping hand with the church fair, the odd bit of monetary aid in the way of free service for the youth group's van… That kind of thing. The child would never tell.

He saw her sometimes but she never walked alone—she who'd waited for him, encouraged him with parted lips, alluring smiles, and a willing way with buttons on her party dress. She didn't look for him now though, didn't make any sign. She was never alone in the forest anymore.

And Peter was. Peter was horribly, terribly, wearily, endlessly alone. But he wasn't his father.

Party Dress

By her last year in high school, Sylvia had grown beautiful. Savannah was in awe of her daughter's smooth perfect skin, the soft washed flow of her hair, intricate fingers, delicate nose… Taller than Lydia, thinner than Jason Junior, quieter and more serious than both, *how had she grown?* Now little Syl was Aunt Sylvia to Troy and Lydia's Jeremy, who'd been born unannounced in the local hospital while Savannah, still at home, awaited the call.

"I wanted to hold your hand, to be there for you."

"Yes Mom. But we wanted it to just be family."

"I am family." *How long would it be till Sylvia deserted her too?*

Young Simon called to date her most weekends, taking her to suitable movies and youth group dances at church. Today the invitation to Senior Prom lay in Savannah's hand, tucked in its neat blue envelope. She might open it—after all, her name was Ms. S. Steepleton too—but Sylvia would probably complain. So Savannah took the envelope back to the table by the door. When her daughter slung in, laden with backpack, Savannah held the invitation out.

"We could go shopping for a dress together," she offered eagerly.

Sylvia slid a finger under the envelope's seal. "No Mom. I'm going with Sharon."

Pity. Still, Savannah would cope. She didn't believe she was the sort of mother who tended to smother her kids. "Should I drive the two of you then?"

"No," said Sylvia. They'd probably just ask Simon.

Just Simon? Savannah smiled.

The doorbell rang on Saturday morning and Sylvia rushed outside with purse and measurements and plans. Sharon greeted her with laughter, then Savannah smiled again. "Buy something nice, girls," she called after them, thinking *just Simon* and checking which child got to sit in the front seat beside him—Sylvia of course.

Back in the kitchen, Savannah hummed though she knew it drove Jason up the wall. She pondered how an empty nest might feel, then hummed some more.

Simon dropped the girls in town and told them to hurry. "Can't stop here," he said. "No parking. I'll meet you at five. Be ready. Okay?" Then Sylvia took charge.

She led the way, like a proud big sister, to Mason's—"The very best for clothes; you really must try them." The ancient façade still dominated High Street with white carved stone and windows tall as the sky. Marble columns marked the entrance just beyond the clear blue glass of Benson's restaurant— "Don't you think their super-burgers are to die for? Even Daddy likes them." Sharon's family, of course, never ventured beyond Old Town Café. "This way. Come on."

Sharon froze in the super-modern bright atrium revealed beyond the door. But Sylvia strode confidently, fully in her element, smiling at moving stairs and pointing to signs. "This way. Third floor."

Fabrics floated like visions of angels in heaven. Cream oceans, silky smooth and glowing with expense—delicate imprints of flowers draped on the smooth pale skin of lifeless models. "Not my color," said Sylvia, but the dress on the mannequin was everything Sharon might have dreamed. Unfortunately, the price tag was more like a nightmare.

They wandered slowly from rail to rail, from posed individuals to groups of three in silent conversation. Sylvia delighted in great new styles while Sharon searched for numbers and dollar signs. "It's no good," Sharon said for the fifteenth time. "There's no way." They came from different worlds.

Sylvia tried on yet another gown. She twirled in front of the gilt-edged, floor-length mirror. "You could borrow something of Lydia's," she volunteered. "She's about your size."

Sure, but Sylvia's sister was also five years older, happily married, and many months pregnant now with her *second* child.

"I meant something she wore to a high school dance," Sylvia laughed.

Sharon straightened her expression and forced a smile. Her stubborn streak still wanted a dress of her own for the senior prom. Something borrowed just didn't seem right.

Sylvia shrugged back into her own clothes again. Another reject. "Are you sure your brother won't mind being my date?" She sounded suddenly more like her schoolgirl self instead of sophisticated shopper.

"Quite sure. Let's keep looking."

By the end of the day, Sharon and Sylvia stumbled on aching feet. Bright parcels hung from their arms. Sylvia had bought a dress at last, green as her eyes, smart, proper and demure as a maiden in church, but definitely classy. Sharon had bought material and a pattern from the fabric shop.

"What's your mom going to say?" Sylvia laughed as they waited for Simon and the car. "D'you really think she'll make the dress for you?"

"Well, she'll either say yes or she'll teach me how to use a sewing machine. Or both I expect."

Savannah sighed when Sylvia related the conversation over dinner. Jason frowned the *unsuitable husband* frown that met all mention of Simon. "Not everyone's like us in money matters. You should keep that in mind," he advised. Sylvia wondered how on earth anyone could *make* a dress for a prom while Savannah imagined how Sharon's sweet mother would delight in designing something for her grown-up child. Knowing her, the dress would be the best one of all. Sharon would dance and be queen of the ball.

Sunday Dinner

Sylvia's eyes were a little red after dancing the night away. She seemed a little unsure on her feet in those unsuitable shoes, a little quiet—really just her usual self. In church she sat sulkily after the Prom, Savannah keeping guard between daughter and father while grandson Jeremy peeked around his parents across the aisle. The pastor had hijacked the end of the service to tell how the church steeple needed renovation. If bricks or tiles fell on anyone, the church wouldn't be insured. Not unless they hired a contractor, and they needed money for that.

Familiar news, Savannah thought, as they shook hands after the service. *Another reason to make a grab for cash.* She wondered how long it would be before the phone started ringing with friends full of ideas—summer fair, autumn fair, Christmas fair, church fair, whatever…

"All they ever preach about is money," said son-in-law, Troy.

"They only ask when they need it," countered Savannah, patiently.

"Yeah well. They always seem to need it."

Lydia tugged Troy's arm, as she often did when the young family met with her parents, clearly trying to keep the peace. She smiled apologetically and Savannah smiled back. She didn't mind Troy's complaining so much, but Jason would relish any excuse for an argument, and it was Sunday, Lydia was pregnant, and they had Sunday dinner all planned.

Luckily Jason was busy following his grandson who was climbing the walls, arms stretched out like a tiny monkey, tough little fingers grappling between the stones. Jeremy reminded Savannah of Lydia, into everything just as his mother had been. At least Jason seemed more tolerant of children's behavior these days, now his own were grown up.

The families walked toward their cars. Jason, Savannah and Sylvia climbed into Jason's dark blue beamer. Troy, Lydia and

Jeremy would follow along in the beat up little Ford, a replacement for Troy's truck. Of course, Savannah wanted to ride with Lydia and talk of pregnancies and children. She wanted to strap her little grandson in and listen to meaningless babbling all the way home. But it couldn't be. Instead she listened to her husband's learned criticism of the sermon, accepting his teaching, pondering the lonely quiet of Sylvia's silence, and that was life. No point trying to change it.

Meanwhile Troy was still talking about money when they got to the house.

"What with one arguing finance and the other arguing theology," Savannah complained in the kitchen. "What else can we complain about? It's Sunday for heaven's sake." Lydia and Sylvia just laughed, which made Jeremy giggle. The happy gurgle at least made Savannah feel less mad.

Then the phone rang.

The chair of the church-women's committee wanted Savannah's help raising funds for the steeple—*now there's a surprise*. "A summer fair perhaps?" Meanwhile Lydia had turned down the heat on the potatoes, just *after* they boiled over.

Then the phone rang.

Would Savannah and Sylvia maybe run a stall at the fair— just little gifts, little crafts, nothing complicated. "You're always so good at that sort of thing." Meanwhile the gravy Savannah was so good at making grew lumpy as glue because Sylvia hadn't stirred it enough. Savannah had to struggle to whisk it smooth.

Then the phone rang.

Could Sylvia make some guardian angel cat pictures to sell at the fair.

"Cool. But I thought I'd make brooches this time," said Sylvia when her mother, tight-lipped and disapproving, passed on the message.

"Why?"

"Because I've been doing some metalwork this year."

"Well, *I* thought..." Savannah didn't have time for what

she thought because the phone rang again—the committee chair who had more time for her own thoughts than anyone else's.

"For heaven's sake, Savannah, don't let that daughter of yours get in there with guardian angel cats again. It's ridiculous"—her voice so loud it carried across the room.

"It's not ridiculous; it makes money," said Sylvia from her spot by the stove. Lydia wanted to know what was or wasn't ridiculous. Troy said he always knew money was all that counted.

"You keep out of this," said Lydia.

"It's ridiculous because it's a Christian church," said Savannah, hanging up the phone. "I can't think why the pastor allows it really, but who am I to argue? There's no way guardian angel *cats* are Christian whatever you think." She stressed the word *cat*, repressing a shudder of horror. Not her favorite animal.

"What's not Christian about them?" asked Sylvia, as if they hadn't had this argument every year since the newspaper first mentioned the mythical cat.

Troy chipped in, "What's Christian about begging for money?" Lydia chased him out the kitchen, where he complained now he'd have to talk to his father-in-law. This earned him a rather obvious, rather long and loving kiss, leaving Sylvia and Savannah to argue alone.

"Angels *are* Christian," Sylvia persisted, draining water from potatoes and tumbling them into a bowl.

"Guardian angels aren't."

"Why not?"

"They're Catholic."

"What's wrong with Catholic?"

"Nothing. They just aren't."

"There's nothing wrong with guardian angels," cried Lydia, returning to the fray. She drained the peas and let them rattle and roll in another bowl. "Nothing wrong with cats either."

"They're pagan, maybe," said their mother uncertainly, cutting meat with a very sharp knife. The two girls stepped theatrically each out of reach, carrying their bowls with them.

"Catholics aren't pagan, Savannah," Jason called lugubriously from the hallway. *How on earth had he heard?* "I thought you knew..." *Oh no—not another blessed theology lesson...*

"Not Catholics. Guardian angel cats. Aren't they Egyptian or something?"

"No angels in Egypt."

Jeremy shrieked and bounded on the stairs. Jason, thankfully, turned to rescue him. But the girls still had answers for everything, just like their Dad. And the church still needed money. It was all so confusing and never seemed to get simpler.

Savannah wouldn't win the argument though. She never did. Sylvia would make and sell her cats, the steeple would be saved, and the theology of feather and fur would continue to be debated in stores, in leaders' meetings, in vestibules and halls. Whichever side was arguing, Savannah always lost.

The phone rang again and Sapphire Greenwood from the paper asked for an interview. "About the church fair next month." *Well, that was quick.* And dinner was ready.

Church Fair

The weather stayed fine for the fair, clouds threatening, but no thunder showers to dampen summer flowers. Cars rushed past on the road outside church. Horns shrieked, tires squealed, and the parking lot on the edge of Paradise Park filled rapidly. Traffic lights played their chirruping notes as people crossed the road. The air was full of the chattering of neighbors and friends. "Did you see?" "Have you heard?" "Did you know?" Music accompanied words, piped to speakers overhead, bright sounds mingling and meandering like curtains on the breeze.

The cake stall tempted with sugar and spice by the lavender patch. A lucky-dip barrel of fall-scented hay dominated a stall full of toys. Bookshelf rejects piled high on the book stall, the moldiest offerings tumbling on one end where a moody teenager listened to music through headphones under his hood. A roaring trade in miscellaneous knick-knackery drew crowds to a stand labeled *gifts.* Teenage girls shared perfume profusely while elderly women walked by holding their noses. Little children rode push-along toys at fifty cents a time while bigger children, from the church youth group, chased after them, or after their money.

"Come on Jeremy Germ. It's time to get off."

"Don't want to."

"Ah, but you must." The logic of superior height was followed by stubborn wails, excited shrieks, and tears from a tiny tot who tripped and fell.

Pastor Bill walked around with his smile pasted on, greeting everyone as potential friends and flock. Meanwhile the high school group wheeled old people from the rest home around the flower bed because they hadn't worked out how to get wheelchairs through the crowds.

"Did you want to go to the gift stall?" Pastor Bill asked an old lady struggling from her chair. The wheels slid forward and the teenager jerked to a halt. Bill leapt to rescue her charge.

"Yes, yes," said the lady as Bill caught his breath and fastened her straps more securely.

"Let me help." Pastor Bill straightened his collar and adjusted his smile. "I'll lead the way." Then a line of chairs began to snake through the crowds, with the pastor calling "Make way, make way," as he forged ahead.

Lydia grabbed Jeremy's hand when he threatened to fall under passing wheels. A small girl scrambled onto an old lady's lap and was welcomed heartily. The newspaper photographer took pictures while Sapphire Greenwood pointed out what was needed. Her little son Nate stuffed gravel in her purse. When Sapphire said no, he shoveled it into his mouth instead.

"For heaven's sake, Nate!" Sapphire scooped up the boy, trying to balance her notes on his corduroy leg while still writing her report.

"What you doin' Mommy?"

"I'm trying to work."

"Why Mommy?" *Why indeed?*

The lady from the art gallery, Andrea Blake, strode toward the big white table covered with gifts. Sapphire made to follow, smelling news, while Nate pulled her hair. "Put me down, Mommy." By the time she'd picked up her purse; tipped out the gravel; and reinstated pencils, notepads and money; Andrea Blake was already saying farewell to the Steepleton's sulky youngest daughter behind the stall.

"What was that?" Sapphire asked.

"Oh, Ms. Blake asked me to sell my guardian angel cat brooches at her store," said the teen. She almost smiled. Her mother, Savannah, on the far side of the table, gave a look reminiscent of the one Sapphire had thrown at her small boy.

"Success story then. Can we get your picture please?" Sapphire asked.

"Yeah sure," said Sylvia, but photographer and child had both wandered off.

Wheelchairs were taking over the fair—the pastor's refrain, "Make way, make way"—the sound of wheels on gravel—the disconnected shrieks and sighs of very old and very young. The afternoon sun drifted lower behind a cloud, but the chatter and laughter continued while music played, repeated itself, and traffic hummed on the road. Church bells tolled the hour, then were silent in a steeple standing in urgent need of salvation.

Money Matters

They used the office behind the children's room to count the takings. Pastor Bill supervised, a gently-used frown replacing the overly zealous smile he'd worn during the fair. Someone switched on the lights "so we can see what we're doing." Someone else switched them off "to save money." Most people looked like they really didn't care either way while their oldest member twittered from desk to table, blinking owlishly.

Savannah Steepleton sat in a corner, counting notes and checking columns of figures. She and the all-important chairperson were avoiding each other's eyes again.

"Your Sylvia's brooches were so good," gushed their oldest member. Savannah smiled weakly. "I mean really, really good. They sold like hot cakes. And that Andrea Blake. How about that? Her asking your Sylvia to sell at the art gallery, well how about that?"

Savannah's smile grew tight, the skin of her cheeks seeming too thinly stretched. Pastor Bill could see she and Sylvia had endured another argument. Not that he was sure he'd call them arguments as such. Savannah would say one thing. Sylvia would say another. Then, as if they'd used up their allotted time, they'd go their separate ways. Perhaps Savannah's older children had drained her dry, or Sylvia had run out of life when brother and sister grew up. Except, as Pastor Bill remembered it, Sylvia changed from excitable schoolgirl into mouse quite a while before Lydia's marriage. *Typical teen.*

He steered the old lady to the table to pick up more envelopes, then patted Savannah gently on her shoulder. "We appreciate all your help," he whispered, hoping she'd realize he included her Sylvia in *you.*

"Don't *you* think the brooches are good?" The white-haired woman grabbed Pastor Bill's arm and he wondered why she could only hold onto long-term thoughts at the wrong times. By now she was too close to the ever-officious chairwoman and too far from Savannah Steepleton.

"Will you please just shut up about Sylvia's cats," said their illustrious chair. "You know what I think."

"Oh, I'm sorry. I forgot."

Of course, their chairperson had to launch into a long explanation then, just in case people really had forgotten—all about why it was *inappropriate* for a Christian church to subscribe to such pagan mythology.

"Well, they're just good luck charms really aren't they," said someone else peaceably, which made everything worse.

Still they'd met their goal. The steeple would be saved. Pastor Bill looked at the beloved ladies of his flock and prayed they would be too.

The next week, far across town, brooch-maker Sylvia Steepleton made her way with a bag of samples to Blake's art gallery. "The name's On-DRAY-uh," said Andrea Blake, displaying a limp hand in greeting as the teen entered.

"Yeah right," said Sylvia, wondering if she was meant to shake the hand or kiss it.

"Did you bring your stuff?"

It's not stuff! Sylvia laid out brooches, pins, tiny framed pictures, and ceramic ornaments no larger than a thimble. They covered the white-clothed counter by the cash register. Then she looked up. "So? What do you think?"

"They're okay," said Andrea. She'd seemed a lot more interested during the bustle of the fair. *They're saleable* Sylvia guessed she meant. "They're smart, original, local," *and they don't take up space.*

Sylvia found herself reading behind the syllables, watching the older girl's eyes for words she didn't say. The gallery's voicelessness echoed around her, pictures listening warily, piped music soothing a customer's fears, encouraging laid-back ennui and overspending. She could see her art would fit well, right by the register, tiny gifts tempting buyers who thought they were just looking, a trinket to remind them and bring them back, because surely they meant to buy more than that, a simple memento perhaps. Her cats, whatever her mother's friends said, would be just the thing—local, quirky, even spiritual.

"So, how many can you make, and how often, and how much d'you want for them?" Ms. Blake was all business.

"I have to pay for materials."

"Of course."

They haggled and computed and eventually agreed to sell at fifty percent more than at the church fair.

"We could give some of the profits back to the church," Sylvia suggested.

"Why?"

"So the buyers'll think they're doing good. So you'll get their goodwill too."

Andrea smiled, clearly liking the thought.

Didn't think I knew much about business did you? Maybe one day Sylvia would ask if she might be employed in the store, perhaps over Christmas when she came back from college or next summer.

"You'll bring more when we run low."

"While I can. I'm going to college soon."

"Here, to the U?"

"No way." She'd picked her college as much for its distance from home as for its courses. "I'm going as far away as I can."

"But you'll be back for summers?"

"Yeah, I guess." She'd definitely ask about vacation jobs soon.

The doorbell chimed while they tied hand-lettered price tags to the ornaments.

"Hello there. Welcome. The name's On-DRAY-uh." Andrea walked to the strangers with hand outstretched while Sylvia continued labeling her wares, each string neatly tied by nimble fingers, each tag positioned just so on the clean white cloth. She left quietly, just as the customers asked Andrea about the cats on the counter.

"So, is there a story behind these?"

"Well…" Andrea began, concocting a fairy tale of dogs and mice, steeples and pigeons, and the magical flight of a kitten that fell from the belfry.

Part 5

The Children

First-Born Son

Ten Days, Baby Names, Toddler Group, Different

Mothers sit down to watch their toddlers play. Children chase. A middle-aged man, verging on old, eats sandwiches on a bench at the top of the hill. Schoolchildren snack, filling their lunchbreak with laughter, calling each other names and running merrily in the sun. Teenagers stray while Peter, taking a break from the garage, strolls happily down the path toward the woods. This place holds no fears and no threats for him now, nor for the *Predator* who seems to have disappeared from the news. Loose women offer no temptation, though he'll smile wryly at the scantiness of their clothes. Peter is safe, sure and secure, for he'll never be his father. He's different and proud of it. He has grown to be a grandfather, he's finally found true love, and all is well.

The woman enters the trees by a different path. He sees the splash of color from her coat and knows, though surely she's too far away to be seen, it must be her. They'll meet at the bench hidden under shadowing leaves—whoever gets there first will sit and wait till the other appears. Then they'll go without acknowledging each other, each separately, each clearly and privately alone, off the path into the undergrowth. No one will ever dream they're together.

He's built a hut for her down near the stream where nobody goes. Metal roof, wooden walls—it's rough-carved, buried under scrub, and almost invisible to passers-by; *nobody passes by*. They're always careful to approach on different paths, wearing away no trail through the weeds, leaving no record, no tracks for anyone to follow.

She's first to the bench of course, eager for his touch. Ten days apart is too long for her he supposes, but Peter keeps things safe and regular, well-planned. He listens to her rustling footsteps through the undergrowth, making his own way more quietly. Then he watches her stoop to the low wooden door, the shape of her body straining deliciously at the seat of her pants. His breath comes faster, catches in his throat. He swoops across the clearing to take her in his arms, her back to his chest. They stagger, two bodies entwined as one, through the rough-carved hole serving as entrance to their home. Then he pulls the leather-hung doorway closed behind.

Inside it's dark, shadowed and cold. The air smells of earth, wet wood and mold but they don't care. They fumble with buttons and clasps, fingers stumbling in a race to undo each other's clothes. They laugh, arms wrapped around each other, skin to skin, chest to chest, face to face. He lays her down on the sleeping pad then joins her, pulling a ragged quilt to warm their nakedness. He kisses her, drinks long at the well of her neck. His body swells with the taste of her, salt of longing, sweetness of sincerity. His strength releases into her now, feeling her strong enough to hold, wide enough to contain. No innocent, no wary stripling child this woman of his, but tight and firm. He fills her willing body, pumps his seed with glorious wild abandon. They roll together, hold eternity, and wait while their world falls still. The hut, the sleeping pad, the air around is all that matters here. This and the wonderful fact that they belong.

Mary might still have her fancy man, and Frank might not be so bad—a bit thin, too strict, too tall. Troy can have his pretty young wife who pops out babies one after another, scarce days to breathe or name them in between. The boy can dine with his fine neighbors, Steve and Amethyst and their precious babified cat. He can pretend he's not different if he wants, pretend he really belongs in their grown-up world. But Peter belongs here in a world of his own, safe world, safe secret passion, and everything's good.

Leaves rustle with the wind. Water bubbles as a bird

sweeps down, snatching insects in its path. Far away the traffic roars—not here. The garage waits and the clock on the garage counter measures time.

Ten Days

"I feel huge," said Lydia, stretching her arms around her stomach.

"You are huge," Amethyst confirmed.

"Right. You're no help."

The toddlers, Amethyst's Alison and Lydia's Jeremy, played happily in Amethyst's kitchen, play-dough covering the table and falling to the floor. It smelled so good the thought of it made Lydia want to throw up. She wished this baby would just be done with it.

"D'you remember how big you were with Jeremy?"

"Oh, don't remind me."

"Or how big I was?"

Lydia laughed. She remembered Amethyst insisting on driving Steve to the airport when she looked almost ready to pop. She scarcely fit behind the steering wheel. Lydia joined her as the new neighbor, her pregnancy still unconfirmed, offering moral support. She worried she'd end up having to drive her new friend to the hospital before the end of day. "But it all worked out okay."

"Yeah, and d'you remember that other trip the next spring…"

"After Alison was born…"

"Before Jeremy. And your brother went with him…"

"Oh boy! Jase had just started work…"

"And we'd just got the van." Amethyst's mommy-mobile was big enough for car seat and stroller, diapers and diaper-bag, food, and baby too. "You were huge by then, but you always looked so cool and calm and collected and squeaky-clean."

"Who? Me?" Lydia raised her eyebrows in disbelief.

Amethyst told how hard it had been back then, the agony of shrugging her brain into gear when they set off from the airport leaving Jason and Steve behind. "You know how you let off the brake with one hand and you're signaling, moving out into traffic and somebody's bound to hit you or the baby will cry and you'll get distracted and you'll hit them instead. All that plus no Steve." She'd been so scared with Steven missing ten whole days of their baby's life, though Lydia remembered Alison as a perfect child, sleeping peacefully.

"You sat there all cucumber-cool while I drove," said Amethyst.

"Me? Cucumber-cool?"

"And you asked me was the baby always this good."

"So what did you say?"

"I'm not sure, but we almost got side-swiped by a bus."

Lydia shuddered. She hated driving in traffic now, with Jeremy distracting her, with the stranger soon to be born. She certainly wouldn't dare drive the mommy-mobile. Her bump wobbled and she pressed her hands against it, glad Amethyst was going to help her shop this afternoon. Somehow everything's bigger and faster and louder when you're pregnant; buses too wild, cars like darting hornets waiting to sting, people unpredictably stepping out with hands held high to halt you. If you breathe too hard or turn the wheel too sharply, the baby inside makes you feel like you're going to be sick.

Amethyst continued talking about Steve and Jason's trip. "Don't you get scared when Troy goes away?" she asked. "Like there's a hole opened up in your head and you think you're going to fall in?"

"Troy doesn't go away."

"Well, what about your dad? Did he ever leave your mom on her own?"

"Mom would've hired help." Lydia watched as Amethyst rolled her eyes. *Okay, so Jason and me were Steepletons and a big name in town. It doesn't mean we had everything go our own way.* She tugged herself back to the conversation, Steve's trip, Jason… "How long was Steve gone that time?"

"Ten days again. Always the same."

"Not too long."

Amethyst laughed.

"Well, what could happen in ten days?"

"For starters, I thought you might have the baby. Then we'd've both been laid up."

"Not me. I wasn't due for ages."

"And you always do everything on time, I know." Amethyst sipped her drink then began listing problems on her fingers. "Alison could've grown a tooth. The store could've run out of milk."

"You don't really worry about that sort of thing do you?"

"Oh, you'll see. Just wait till your Troy has to go on a trip."

"Never happen." *Garage mechanics don't go on trips.*

"You wait. It might."

Lydia insisted Amethyst tell what really happened while Steve was away. Surely nothing so dramatic.

"Well… Garnet disappeared. Alison got an ear infection. The freezer broke down and the ice cream melted and dripped all over the floor."

"Oh, yuk."

"And it was orange! I remember it well." They laughed together. "Then the repair man's car leaked oil on the driveway—we'd only just had it done. Then Garnet came back and threw up on the carpet. And Alison wriggled all over it…"

"Over what?"

"Over the cat vomit! And I lost the car keys and the house keys—they were on the same ring—and I banged my head on the cupboard while I looked for them—I was sure I'd nearly knocked myself out. Then Alison decided I was a horse and climbed on my back, and threw up on my shirt."

"Wow!"

"I'm telling you, baby vomit doesn't look a bit like cat vomit. Not a lot of people know that."

"Was that all?" Lydia asked.

"Well, the furnace broke down, the toilet leaked, the light socket went on the blink and smelled like fish…"

"You should've called Troy to help."

"Ah but, you see, you always seemed so perfect and perfectly calm. You were dressed up all the time and your hair all fastened back and your make-up and all…"

"Who? Me?"

"I didn't want to look like a failure to you."

"You idiot! You looked like everything I wanted to be."

Ten days later Amethyst had rushed out of the house, hair straggly from housework and sweat. Her tee-shirt, un-ironed, looked moderately clean, pulled on at the very last minute, with only a tiny stain from Alison's orange antibiotics. Her jeans were ratty because she'd spent all her time washing baby clothes. And her socks didn't match.

"I never noticed. Seriously."

Amethyst piled Alison into the baby seat, holding her down with an elbow while she struggled against the straps. Arms and legs kicked violently and a screaming voice alerted the neighborhood. Alison's little face was a mucus mess, her once-clean dress now badly stained, and her diaper needed changing. "Happy days! Oh yeah!"

Lydia smiled.

Amethyst declared she'd almost been screaming herself. "And there were you, cool as spring, dressed in your mint-green maternity suit with lemon silk blouse and your jewelry just so and your make-up and your hair, and oh…" Amethyst waved her hands in the air, "just so."

"Was I really so bad?" Lydia remembered the maternity suit, bought at great expense by her mother. She hated it.

"And you asked me, 'Is the baby always like this?'"

"And you said?"

"I said I didn't know."

Baby Names

Was I really so bad, Lydia wondered later, the shopping piled away in the cupboard, the toddler safely taking his nap, and Troy still at work. She tried to look back, remembering when Jeremy's bump was still part of her, unnamed stranger waiting to take his first-child place in the world. Was she really so bad? And was he really just a nameless little boy still dreaming of being born?

Lydia remembered singing strings of words to him. Would he have heard? Would the music have blended with soothing sounds of her heartbeat? Would she have filled his growing heart with joy? She remembered how easily joy faded as panic took its place. She'd silently pace the room, then break into sobs while her nameless infant waited, wriggled and turned in his tightly cramped space, preparing for birth.

Mint green maternity suit and lemon blouse? Yes, Lydia remembered them, gloriously fitted, bought by her mother, smoothed and shaped over her blooming bump, resplendent in colors of spring. Mother's baby. Not hers. And Mother full of how sister Sylvia might have a boyfriend called Simon at last and be growing up. Meanwhile Lydia, growing quieter and fatter each day, had stood behind a stall every Tuesday morning at church, selling knick-knacks and pretending her legs didn't ache. She took happy little jaunts in her neighbor's brand new van, pretending she wasn't terrified of meeting the child to come.

"Is the baby always like this?" Oh yes. She remembered asking Amethyst that and feeling so scared.

She took up painting again, part of an artist's group meeting every Saturday morning in the church hall. Young Sylvia still painted her guardian angel cats, much to their mother's dismay, though she'd promised to study math at college so Daddy was okay. Lydia painted still-life images in the rain. When the sun shone she added spring-shaded scenes of village churches and duck ponds to her repertoire. But every stroke of paint became a black mistake as the child's birth drew near, like the cracking of her voice.

She was writing again too, but all she wrote were dirges to sadness and loss.

Nine long months Lydia's stomach ached and moved without her volition. Meanwhile her body stopped moving, drained of energy even while the world filled with life. It felt like fall in spring to Lydia, winter in summer as the baby's birth approached. The child had no name.

Back home from church, from painting, from helping Amethyst, she waited for Troy. When he came in, tired and oil-stained, weary with cars, she'd ask him, as many times now as the birds sang in spring, "What shall we call it?" Troy said she was the creative one. He trusted her, left the job to her and thought it kindness. Till she cried and they decided to make lists and charts together.

Is Paul better than Peter? "Pall of death," said Lydia, sarcastically.

Is Margaret better than Mary? "Oh Sweet Maggie May." Maybe not.

They'd ended up with squared sheets of paper, one for a boy, one for a girl, each name compared with the others, plusses and minuses adding up to numbers in columns and rows. The unnamed child was a shopping list.

Not Jason, because it was Lydia's father's name. Not Peter—Troy's dad. Not Troy, too confusing for sure.

One day she felt the bump fall lower and heavier, promising light. She phoned the garage in a panic. "It's now, Troy. We're going to have a baby." Three days early, she didn't mind. She didn't phone her mom.

The unnamed babe seemed kind of pleased to be released from his cocoon, and they called him Jeremy… but now this new little stranger was growing there instead. Time to make those lists and charts again, to wish she could write or paint but motherhood leaves no opportunity. Better keep the little one amused and wonder what she'd do when there were two.

Toddler Group

"There's a group meets at church," Lydia told Amethyst as they sat in the kitchen. She'd picked up a flyer on her way out from last Sunday's service. "Moms and Toddlers: Need a break in your busy day? Invite a friend." She needed a break as bump and toddler grew large, but inviting a friend sounded a bit *evangelical.* Lydia wasn't sure the label fit, not really her scene. Though she didn't fancy going alone to a strange new group either.

"It's not like… I'm not trying to convert you or anything," she apologized.

"So?" Amethyst asked. "What is it?"

"It's like, just moms and their kids I think. They sit around and drink coffee and eat and chat. That's what it says. Just a way to meet people. There's milk and juice and cookies for the kids. And toys and games, little cars for them to ride. Anyone can come."

She was rambling and Amethyst didn't look remarkably interested. There again, Amethyst wasn't expecting a second child to complicate her life. Amethyst had even started talking about going back to work someday, her world well-organized, well-planned, while Lydia shrank in fear at the thought of coping with both hands full.

"I promise I won't try to make you religious. Honest."

Amethyst laughed. "You mean like that priest-fellow promised before we got married there?" She explained how she and Steve had to meet with Pastor Bill before the wedding. "Oh, what a name, like *Builder Bob,*" she laughed. "I suppose we should all be glad he's not *Pastor Pasqual.*" After regular meetings, agreeing and signing forms to agree they understood what church was about, and marriage, and blessings and all the other stuff, they'd been allowed to book the building. "It was just the week after yours, Lydia." After the wedding they got letters and postcards and visits from parishioners, gifts of meals and flowers. "Even you came around to see us, just after you moved into your place. Don't you remember?"

"Hey, come on. We visited 'cause we're neighbors, and we'd bought your house."

Amethyst ended her diatribe with a smile. "Sorry. I'm just not churchy. It's just not me."

Lydia smiled agreeably. But please would Amethyst come anyway and meet the other moms and give her moral support.

"Moral? I thought me and Steve living together before we got married proved we weren't that." She smiled, taking the sting out of the words, and agreed to give it a try.

Tuesday afternoon sunshine poured down when Lydia came to Amethyst's door. Alison snoozed in her stroller, so the two mothers walked to church through the brisk fall air instead of using the car. It wasn't far. The movement made Jeremy doze so he'd doubtless be awful tonight, unless he ran off lots of energy.

They hung up coats in the hallway. Walls echoed with loud adult voices and shrieks of children, and Jeremy woke. Lydia set him down on the blue gym mat, but Alison quietly drooled into her coat and didn't blink. "Can't believe she's asleep in this!"

They sat on two fold-out metal chairs, uncomfortable and cold, with the mother of that strange older kid Amelia, too tall for a toddler, too vacant for a child, sitting close by. The mother looked fairly normal, fairly stressed. Her daughter just looked wrong. Moms formed a circle around the tots on the gym mat, castle wall with legs providing safety. Lydia smiled at someone she thought she'd seen in church, didn't know her name. Another stranger pointed to Jeremy and laughed. "Sweet little guy." It wasn't so bad.

Toddler group was one of the few committees Savannah Steepleton didn't attend, which was probably why Lydia hadn't heard of it before. At least she could sit down in peace and didn't have to check for her mother spying on her. One of the committee ladies scurried around the outside of the circle, offering drinks from her tray. A sweet old grandmother mustered older children into a separate room with paints and glue. Lydia waved and smiled while Jeremy, still too young, stayed on the mat. *Mom's friends*, she thought, hoping she wouldn't give them cause to complain.

The door swung open, bringing draughts of cold air and exhaust fumes as another mother entered. Lydia shivered. Then a ball of fluffy white fur slipped between her ankles onto the mat.

"Hey, Garnet."

"Oh heavens. Garnet!" Amethyst jumped to her feet, too late. The cat leapt onto Alison's lap, and startled screams ensued.

"Oh I love cats." An elderly helper swooped down, trailing a scent of soap while she reached to pet Garnet. Excited voices twittered. Alison calmed. Then Savannah Steepleton's nemesis, great leader of the toddler group committee, announced her loud protest.

"No animals in here. Children are playing."

Lydia whispered to Amethyst that she had a thing about cats.

"Well she has a point." Amethyst lifted Alison out of her seat. "Someone might be allergic."

"It's all my sister's fault," Lydia explained. "She makes those pictures with the flying cat and sells them for church funds."

"Those ones in Blake's? They're neat. What's wrong with that?"

"Well, some people are pretty sure guardian angel cats are pagan and they'll corrupt us."

Amethyst frowned, the same expression she wore when Lydia first mentioned church. Perhaps Lydia shouldn't have mentioned Sylvia's cats. Meanwhile Garnet curled into the vacated stroller and closed her eyes.

Other mothers watched and listened with puzzled frowns. "Did you know I call Garnet my *guardian angel*?" Amethyst volunteered, a little too loudly.

"No, how so?" said a sandy-haired Mom, blowing over her coffee.

"I was going out to dinner with my husband once, way back when. It was raining and a cat like Garnet kept me from stepping out in front of a car."

"Cool," said someone, around a mouthful of cookie.

"And Steve was heading for where the bridge was out but a cat made him stop, or a squirrel I suppose."

"Wow. A real guardian angel. I remember reading it."

"Lydia's roommate had one too," said Amethyst, smiling broadly but Lydia demurred, didn't want to spread the tale.

Mothers drank coffee and ate cookies, sharing memories of the day the bridge washed out, moaning about storms they'd known, and watching while their children scrambled and played. Even strange Amelia's mother joined in the conversation—Evie Callaghan, she said her name was—while Amelia herself stared hypnotized at the cat. Garnet had broken the ice, true guardian angel that she was.

Coffees drunk, Lydia and Amethyst turned their attention to the kids and watched the diaper dance. "Lots of spares in the back hallway by the ladies' restroom," a new friend told them. They walked together, carrying kids in companionable silence, till a picture on the wall provoked the conversation they'd both avoided—a red-robed man surrounded by children, green grass and white clouds, with a halo on his head.

"Churches," said Amethyst, turning away from the image scornfully.

"Hey, I thought you were enjoying yourself."

"Yeah, but churches. You know…"

"What about them? It's okay here isn't it?"

Amethyst began to list the many ways churches made her mad. Firstly it annoyed her when the church told people they couldn't be Christians if they used their brains. She slapped a dirty diaper into the bin.

"That's not what it says!"

"Well, not if they use their brains to study science or history, right?"

"It's not…"

"It is!"

She dropped a clean diaper—one provided by the church—under her child, adding how she hated the way church people worried more about guardian angel cats than the homeless.

Lydia knew she shouldn't have mentioned Sylvia's cats. "We serve food in the park every other Saturday."

"Yeah, some of you do. You make them pray for it first though, like making them beg."

"No we don't."

"I'll bet you do." And when the world ended—"which you all think's going to be tomorrow or else the day after, so roll on Armageddon"—then people like that anti-cat woman would probably beg God not to let half their friends into heaven, instead of begging on behalf of their enemies.

"I'm sure she wouldn't," said Lydia, though her lips twisted into a smile imagining the scene. Amethyst had a point. Still, "I'll beg God to let *her* in when He turns her away at the door. And you, as well."

"Gee thanks." Amethyst fastened the final button on Alison's suit.

Toddler group finished at lunchtime. Some parents had kindergarteners and needed to pick them up. Afternoon naps had to be catered for, and shopping. Pastor Bill came in for the last ten minutes, walking around to greet everyone, delighted with every new face, and magically remembering Amethyst's wedding and her husband's occupation. "Is he doing okay? And you?" He congratulated Lydia on her brother's promotion, asked after Troy, and promised to send his van in to be fixed as soon as he could. He reminded Amethyst she was welcome, "any time," in church. "And so's your cat."

Garnet, who'd claimed Alison's stroller as her bed and stayed there ever since, sniffed his fingers in greeting, then patiently allowed him to stroke her head.

Different

Pastor Bill had a kind face and would do anything for anyone. Everyone knew that. Evie Callaghan, though not a church-goer, had come to rely on him. Ever since little Amelia was first diagnosed. Ever since her husband left them on their own.

Amelia began to scream as they packed up the toys from Moms and Toddlers. "Have we taken something of hers?" someone asked, but Evie shook her head, displaying the ubiquitous rabbit and red-dressed doll. She felt that deer-in-the-headlights terror flow over her again—couldn't quite believe Amelia had behaved so well all morning—probably the cat's influence.

"Don't worry," said a helper. "Lots of kids are like that." But lots of kids were *not* like Amelia.

Evie dragged her screaming daughter outside, leaving others to tidy up. She watched mothers with well-behaved toddlers strap them into car seats and strollers. Amelia was too big for a stroller now; Evie didn't want and couldn't afford one of those big *I've-got-a-handicapped-kid* monstrosities. She wanted a life and a future. She wanted things to be all right.

Meanwhile the person who helped with Sunday school was leaving town, taking away another slice of Evie's rare cherished freedom, and the local elementary school had nothing to offer.

Pastor Bill, with his kind face and gentle manner, invited Evie to sit on a stone bench outside church while Amelia calmed down.

"I don't know what I'll do," Evie said, clutching tight to her daughter's hand, a grip well-practiced, firm enough to hold but not quite hard enough to bruise. Her fingers felt like she'd trained them into a vice. "When Amelia goes to Sunday school, it's when I catch up on stuff, you know." She rocked to and fro as Amelia matched the motion. Amelia's fingers pushed up her sleeve and stroked the skin of her elbow, doll and rabbit temporarily discarded. "I know everyone thinks I should be in church and all that…" The pastor shook his head. "It's one of the few times I really know she's looked after, and now there's no one… I don't know."

"Someone else will take care of her, Evie. Don't worry."

"But Amelia won't like it. She won't cope. It won't be the same."

Pastor Bill said he was sure she'd settle down, but what did Pastor Bill know?

"She gets so difficult."

It wouldn't be a problem.

"She'll run off."

The doors would be closed said Pastor Bill, and Amelia hadn't yet learned to lift the bar to the fire escape. Actually, he claimed to be more worried Amelia might be trapped in a fire, said she needed to learn. Pastor Bill had a very kind face and a very nice smile. He just didn't quite understand. "So how was toddler group?" he asked.

"I don't think it helped her socialize. She just stared at the cat."

The pastor smiled. He'd meant how was it for Evie. "Did you make any friends?"

She ignored the question. "Of course, she doesn't want to socialize does she? She just wants to be alone." The cruelest blow—knowing her daughter didn't need her, except to keep her warm and fed, knowing a mother's love was surplus to Amelia's requirements.

Pastor Bill offered comfort, his job of course. He told her you could see it in Amelia's eyes, how she loved her mother. Pastor Bill saw many things; *he probably sees God*. But sometimes, late in an evening, when Amelia sat on the sofa—one thumb in her mouth, the other rubbing softly on Evie's elbow—sometimes Evie almost thought she saw love in her daughter's eyes.

She'd prayed, before her husband left, for their little girl to be healed. Then she stopped praying because nothing happened and the world started falling apart. Now she let Pastor Bill say the words, his warm hand resting on the restless girl's head—she who hated to be touched—and his gentle eyes closed. He prayed for understanding and love, for the feel of God in their lives, for help and support. Then he prayed with thanks for the beautiful child whose perfect features and innocent gaze brought such light into the world. *What light?*

"Will you be back next week?" he asked.

Evie thought of the crowded hall, echoing voices, plastic car-wheels scraping on concrete floors, shrieks and squeals and sing-along music, the clatter of coffee cups, chatter of mothers, and absence of the cat. She couldn't imagine Garnet would come back, and who would calm Amelia without the cat's strange hypnotism? Sounds were an avalanche. Friendly faces made jigsaw puzzles with a few too many pieces. She felt a curious sympathy for the child and shook her head.

"Well, on Sunday then."

"If you're sure."

"Of course I'm sure. Just bring her along as usual. She'll be fine."

Second Child

Turning Point, Nine Months, Get a Life, The Babysitter

Their relationship reached a turning point. She brought Thanksgiving decorations for their little wooden shack, homey touches for a place not meant to be home, as if she thought they might build a driveway someday and a garage for a car. She took the sleeping mat home to wash and brought it back smelling of powder and chemical flowers. She brought teacups in bone-white china and a kettle and picnic stove. He imagined her playing house as a child, stuffing a cushion up her jumper and pretending pregnancy, asking her teddy to baby-sit the dolls.

Peter remembered the woman in the motel with an aching desire. She'd known about undemanding love. Sure, she'd left him but she hadn't tried to glue herself to him. If another woman like her should appear at the garage…

But I'm not my father he told himself. *There's nothing wrong with me*. He didn't need a dozen different lovers to keep him kind and sweet. Just needed the one. Unfortunately, *she* didn't seem to be the one. Just like Mary hadn't been before. With the right woman though, he'd live the right life.

Garage guy, he knew nearly all the local women. They brought him their cars and he flirted politely while counting the wheels and the cash. He couldn't afford any dalliances though—they might hurt his clientele. *Someone without a car perhaps?* He closed the till with a crash, sealing off his thoughts of her.

On the street outside, car horns echoed an angry orchestra. "Hold the fort, Troy." Peter stepped out the door to see if he could help. A bus blocked the light, drivers and pedestrians milling around to complain, stamping their feet and blowing on frozen hands. Peter adjusted his tool belt like a movie hero and stepped into the fray.

"Got a problem here, have you?"

Women whispered, "Hey, it's the garage guy." He preened inside.

"Stalled," said the bus driver, lifting his head from under the steaming hood. "Don't want to start."

"Let me try it. Tell me what you see."

Peter didn't wait for a reply. He climbed on the bus and stared triumphantly at worried passengers. *Women who don't drive cars perhaps?* The mother of that strange kid sat by her vacant-eyed daughter, china doll dripping drool in her lap and clinging to her elbow, rabbit and red-dressed puppet in her other hand. Behind her the nervous woman who lived near Troy and Lydia sat hunched behind a shopping bag. Watery eyes blinked through wire-rimmed glasses and wouldn't hold his gaze. Wispy hair stuck to her face, making her look like a child pretending old age as she chewed her lips. Near the back, that Carla child swayed seductively—young David's girl, posh waitress at Benson's and scurvy check-out clerk at the supermarket—woman for all seasons but she was taken.

The driver, predictably, had left his key. Peter turned it but the engine barely stirred. He climbed down to change places. "You turn her over. Let's see what I can do."

His tool-belt of secrets might touch an engine's heart, but what had Peter to do with knick-knacks in a dolls-house wooden shack? Still, the stirring in his loins as the engine woke made Peter itch and know, he'd have to call her; they'd have to meet; they'd have to share their bodies as they always did. A man, even if he's not his father, has needs. It's not as if Mary would offer to satisfy them.

Turning Point

Mary didn't drive a car these days. Besides, it wasn't too far from her house to Lydia and Troy's. It felt good to walk, kept the circulation going and made her remember feeling young.

Lydia greeted her at the door—"Should have let me pick you up"—and led her into the kitchen. Jeremy sat at the table drawing trains, surrounded by scents of fruit juice and coffee, while Lydia sat down to snatch a cookie from an opened pack.

Mary waved temptation away. "I'm trying not to get old and fat."

"You'll never be fat."

"Look Gramma. Train. I finish," Jeremy announced in ringing tones. His juice tipped dangerously as he climbed from his chair and Mary steadied it. He was growing fast, but Mary struggled to imagine a baby sibling.

"Does Jeremy know yet?" she asked, looking down at Lydia's bump.

Of course he wanted to know right away. "Mommeeee. Tell Jemmeee. Tell meee."

They retired to the living room, where pieces of trains lay scattered over the floor. Lydia wanted Mary to sit on a comfortable chair, but she wasn't so ancient yet. Instead, she maneuvered herself to the stained red rug by the electric fire. One arm cooked, while the other laid pieces of railway in circles and lines. Her hips creaked quietly.

"Points," said Jeremy proudly, holding a y-shaped piece.

"Do you want me to put points in for you?"

Jeremy beamed.

Lydia wouldn't sit, of course. She tidied papers from the sofa and table, always tidying. "You don't need to do that for me," Mary volunteered, "or I can help if you really think it needs doing."

Her daughter-in-law smiled. "You're helping anyway, keeping Jeremy happy. Besides," she sighed "it's not you. It's

Mom. She's coming around later and you know how she is."

"I'm sure Savannah's used to a bit of mess," said Mary comfortably. "She had three of you to look after, you know."

Lydia knew, she said, but Savannah would offer to help, would tidy up for her daughter and make her feel useless. "She always does."

"She doesn't mean it that way. She's just trying to make things easier."

"Yeah, I know."

"She means well."

"I know."

Mary moved awkwardly on the floor, trying to cook different parts of her sleeve and extend the railway track. Lydia turned down the fire. Outside, the autumn winds were cold, still howling, tossing leaves against the window.

"Did you know some scientists say the world's getting warmer?" said Lydia. They laughed at the thought.

Jeremy's railway fanned into sidings and sheds, one track leading to a turntable missing its center. He searched for it while Mary fitted interlocking curves into continuous lines.

"You're so good at that." Lydia sat on the sofa and cuddled her stomach.

Mary laughed, filled with memories of Troy long years ago.

"You're so patient."

"You should ask Troy about that."

"But you brought him up, all on your own."

"My mother helped."

Warm dusty smells of wooden tracks and trains mingled with the haze of cookie crumbs—it was comfortable here, calming, though Jeremy screamed when the train wouldn't go straight. He threw a car with a tantrum across the room and Lydia rescued it.

"I gave my notice," Mary announced quietly.

"What? You quit your job?"

"Getting old. I retired."

Lydia complained Mary couldn't be that old. After all,

Peter wasn't retiring.

But Mary was tired. "That time of life," she said. "It gets to you. It's different for a woman."

"Maybe you'll find something else to fill in the time."

Mary didn't want anything else. "Perhaps I'll babysit for you." She watched Lydia hold the bump as she sat down again. "Do you know if it's a boy or a girl? Would you tell me?"

"Mary! It's secret."

Jeremy pulled the train tracks apart, patterns changing, breaking, and reforming under his hands. Lines led to nowhere and ended at the wall, table, or door. *There's always new routes to be made*, Mary thought, new resting places and turn-arounds, new adventures beyond the corner. She picked the turntable up and rotated the handle in her palm.

Opportunities abounded.

Perhaps she'd help in toddler group at church. They might need another pair of hands, with Jeremy and Alison racing around and the baby coming soon. She could always make coffee. "What do you think Lydia?"

"I think you'd be great."

Nine Months

Nine months felt like forever. It should have been easier, no college, no work, but mothers with children at home have it harder than their husbands. *The wives deserve the fat salaries and bonuses*, Lydia thought.

Nine months ago the sun shone bright, cold air scented with spring and possibilities. Nine months ago little Jeremy was the sweetest child, image of his father, temperament of an angel. Even the brightest day couldn't shine as wide as the smile on his face. Now her gentle first-born stormed through terrible twos and threes, while Lydia crawled through trials of pregnancy. Her back ached endlessly. Her mother determined to organize her life. And her husband, ever-working, ever-helping, created chaos.

One afternoon in the park Lydia tried again to persuade her mother not to join the toddler group committee.

"I'm sure your group could use my help."

"I'm sure they could too, Mom. But don't stretch yourself too thin. You've got to let other people learn to do stuff." *And give me some peace.* She didn't say that.

Conversation meandered with their footsteps, ending at the swings with the question of the soon-to-arrive second grandchild. "Boy or girl?" Savannah asked.

"I don't know."

"I thought everyone knew these days." Savannah paused then announced it was bound to be a boy. The way Lydia carried him, the shape of her bump gave it away. "What will you call him?"

"I don't know."

"Call him Jason, for Daddy and your brother."

Wouldn't Jason Junior want the name for a child of his own some day? "Besides, the baby's a Markham, not a Steepleton, Mom."

"Yes, well. A little Jason would still be nice. And your dear brother shows no signs of getting married." Lydia's brother, not Savannah's son? Things that didn't go her mother's way were always Lydia's fault.

They'd picked Jeremy's name—Jeremy for a boy, Julia for a girl—with all those tables and charts, plusses and minuses and scores. They'd had time to talk uninterrupted then, but things were different now. Lydia struggled with Jeremy all day. Troy spent his time at the garage. How could they plan?

"It's got to have a name," said her mother urgently. But Savannah wasn't carrying the child, wasn't burdened with the need for choice. She didn't chase Jeremy as he hunted ducks either. Luckily Amethyst's white cat distracted him before he fell into the water.

"Jeremy Markham. Stop that!" Yes, Jeremy had a name. So did the cat.

"Garnet." Jeremy chased her back to the path.

Soon the aunts and uncles, and even her dear brother,

pressured Lydia to choose. "Jason Junior Junior?" Jason suggested with a rueful grin. Troy was no help. He just waved his hand and said it wouldn't hurt to give in. The baby might always be a girl, and they could call a boy by his second name.

"Jason Christopher? How's that?" he offered.

"And how d'you think he'll ever spell Christopher in school." Lydia remembered her problems spelling Lydia with a *y*. Still, Christopher sounded nice. Jason Christopher Markham had potential. They could call him JC… which even the slowest child would easily spell.

So JC it was, born with the winter's snow.

The christening took place at the village church, pews crowded with neighbors, family huddled around the font. The heating wasn't on that Sunday afternoon because someone had helpfully shut it down after the service. "I'm sorry. I forgot."

Grandma Savannah Steepleton bent her head over the tiny child. "Coochy coochy coo." Her perfume was sprayed on thick as glue and the smell would surely make him cry. Lydia watched her child draw breath. "Coochy coochy, Jason little boy."

He screamed.

Lydia rescued the baby from the stroller and held him to the sweet scent of her breast—comfort restored. "We're not calling him Jason," she said, her voice tight. The baby couldn't possibly understand but he snuggled close, snuffling to the sound of her voice. Then Lydia's mother declared in ringing tones how she hoped her dear daughter wasn't going to be one of *those* mothers. "Which mothers, Mother?"

"The ones who call their children by their second names."

"No Mother, I'm not. He's called JC."

JC seemed so peaceful, listening to her heartbeat. She felt proud she could soothe his world so easily though she couldn't soothe her mother's.

"Lydia Mary Steepleton! Not JC! For heaven's sake!"

"What?"

Behind Savannah, Grandfather Jason stifled an unexpected laugh and rolled his eyes. Over his shoulder, Grandma Mary stuffed a handkerchief into her mouth, while Grandpa Frank clutched her shoulders and shuddered with mirth. Whispers rustled around the church while Savannah glared.

"Why? What's wrong?" asked Lydia.

Her mother lifted a Bible and pointed angrily. "Lydia, there is no way—NO WAY! You can NOT call your baby, or anyone else, JC"

"Why not?"

"Because. Because…" Savannah waved the Bible angrily as if preparing to throw it at her daughter's head.

Then Troy, father of the newly named son, placed a soothing arm around his wife's trembling shoulders. "It's okay love," he whispered in her ear, stroking the baby's soft head. "It's okay. It's just your mom. You know how she is." He took a prayer book from the back of a pew, having guessed the cause for dismay, then pointed out the initials of their Savior's name.

"He's still JC," Lydia whispered back. "We decided."

"Of course he is. It's not like anyone else is worried—not even your sainted dad."

Grandfather Jason suggested they call the child Jacey, which made everyone feel better. "After all, it almost sounds like it's short for Jason." In time, Savannah would file her grandson's name with guardian angel cats, feeling thankful for small mercies. Her children might not show proper reverence, but at least they still went to church.

Get a Life

Jeannie Collins, Troy and Lydia's car-less semi-invisible neighbor, didn't go to church. She didn't go anywhere if she could help it, just home to work to home to work again, public transportation, private silence all the way. She didn't like the way the bus driver looked at her, still less that haunted gleam in the garage man's eyes—the way his gaze seemed to strip her woolen overcoat and wire-rimmed glasses away, proving her unworthy. *What's his problem? I* am *unworthy.* Jeannie shuffled from bus stop to house, barely venturing a glance to either side so no one would see her…like a child who's forgotten to unclasp his hands after playing peek-a-boo.

Children saw her of course, because children see everything, dark-haired toddler with summer smile and her tiny red-haired boyfriend from down the street. Their parents never noticed her, just another unknown neighbor in the unknown crowd.

Jeannie trembled at the sight of the toddler-girl's cat crossing the road. She imagined, out of all her neighbors the cat might be her friend. But cats can die in the street so Jeannie trembled, pressed herself close to the wall, and tried not to see.

Tires squealed. Brakes shrieked. White cat, another of its nine lives sold, disappeared.

Jeannie's bag weighed heavily. She needed to get home to make dinner. Dinner for one. Just food. The fuel of life. *Move Jeannie,* she told herself, staying instead by the lamp post, stuck. It happened sometimes. Some passing thought would throw her into scenes from memory. Arms and legs would freeze into place and she'd have no choice but to wait.

Remember when you were young she thought, fresh out of college feeling ancient and freaky. There was something inherently wrong about dressing in tight jeans and tee-shirt, bangles dangling on wrists and ankles with a body that couldn't move or respond to the beat. So she began to dress old, stopped styling her hair, wore wire-framed glasses again instead of chasing fashion. She hid herself in the folds of her elderly mother's shapeless coat.

"I'm okay, Mom," Jeannie said on the phone, glad she'd got a job somewhere else and moved away.

"I'm fine," she told colleagues, without giving them her new address.

To neighbors she was just a wandering shadow without a car.

Back when it started, Jeannie felt frustrated and scared. Now she just watched the stories in her mind, time-outs a part of life, until the clock ran forward again.

This memory came from long ago, when her mother brought home a kitten. Jeannie called it Coal. Its black warmth comforted her in bed every night, and it woke her in the mornings. Jeannie remembered paws touching her nose, whiskers tickling, purring rumbling in its throat. She tried to move from her lamp post, but the story wasn't done.

Coal grew fast, his body sleek, his eyes snakelike, hypnotic. She watched him hunt, bringing birds and mice, even a squirrel home to her mother. Mom really didn't appreciate the treats, and Jeannie, ever practical, grew well accustomed to removing bloodstains from carpets and body parts from rugs.

In the present she still couldn't remove herself from the lamp post. Squeal of tires. Shriek of brakes. A thump and her childhood treasure died. Blood and precious body parts in the road. Then Jeannie, ever practical, packed them into a shoe box for burial.

"Coal," she whispered, deep in her well of memory, tears on her cheek. Then a hand landed, so softly, on her arm.

"Here, let me help you."

Suddenly released, Jeannie woke to see the face of an elderly man—long white hair, dark-skinned wrinkles, tidy beard.

"Let me carry your bags."

"No I'm fine," Jeannie muttered, but he didn't seem to hear. He was old. Perhaps he was deaf.

"Name's Frank," the stranger said, his voice gravelly and low. "I've got family on this street. Let me help."

Jeannie recognized him now she was awake enough to see. He often pushed the red-haired boy's little brother in his stroller. She bent to her bags but Frank picked them up and carried them to the door so she had to let him in. Then they drank coffee, Frank asking why a pretty young thing like Jeannie would hide herself away. Then, because he looked old and safe and maybe deaf, but probably not, Jeannie told him her tale.

"I know folks like that." Frank trailed black-nailed fingers through the fringe of his mustache.

"Yeah, and I bet they're not young."

"They're people. They've got lives."

Jeannie smiled, embarrassed, but Frank talked on, unoffended, unconcerned. He asked about her medications—seemed surprisingly familiar with the names, side-effects and dosage. "My wife has it," he explained. "Real bad."

"Your wife? I'm so sorry." Even more embarrassed now.

"No problem."

When Jeannie told him the doctor said she'd just have to live with it, Frank was ready with a perfectly sensible answer. "You get on with your living then, little lady. What do they say, *Get a life,* while you can?"

Jeannie laughed.

"Well, you do it." He thanked her for the coffee and set off for his grandchildren's house. "And you go see our Lydia someday, Young Lady. She'll teach you to make real coffee."

Next day the mailman knocked on Jeannie's door, "Just to say *Hi*."

Soon Frank's gardener was calling around with plants, "In case you can use them."

Frank's friend from the senior center brought her son to visit. "He's new here. I wonder if you'd show him around." Embarrassment again. *I'm new here too.*

Joe and Karen Grainger invited her to bridge but she refused. Amethyst with the eight-lived cat, asked her to baby-sit instead.

"What if I have an episode?"

"Have you had one recently?"

"Not in a while. Not since the doctor changed my meds."

"Well, there you go. We'll not be far away. Just over the road at Joe and Karen's. And at least we'll know what can go wrong instead of having to guess."

Jeannie guessed she'd got a life.

The Baby-Sitter

"Jason, will you sit the kids while we go out to bridge?"

Jason juggled the phone. "Didn't even know you played."

"We don't. Steve and Amethyst do and they invited us." His sister laughed, the sound tinkling on the line. "They got a different sitter 'specially so we can give it a try."

JC was a baby still, no trouble to anyone, though Jeremy was a terror. Jason knew what he was letting himself in for. He arrived early, drank coffee, confirmed where the diapers and pajamas were, then shooed his sister and brother-in-law out the door.

It was summer which meant, "You need to close the curtains really tight or JC will never sleep. He can't stand the light." Lydia offered her confident advice.

"I'll be fine."

"And if Jeremy wants to play out that's okay I guess." She sounded suddenly oddly uncertain. "But you have to bring him in by eight and get him to bed."

"Ah, so late." Jason smiled, half-afraid and half-glad at the unexpected permission to stay outside instead of keeping doors locked.

"Yeah well. He's growing up."

He waved his sister and brother-in-law off as they walked across the street to their neighbor's house. You'd think they'd have given up worrying long since. Jason had babysat plenty of times. But then, maybe parenthood turned every easy-going well-poised little sister into a mobile panic attack. Or maybe she was just scared of playing bridge.

Lydia looked back, frown lines between her eyes, while Jason waved again. "Go, Sis. Go win some bridge."

Then Jeremy, holding Jason's knees, looked up to ask, "Is Mommy building castles and d'awb'idges?"

JC was such a peaceful baby, Jason thought. He lay asleep in the stroller while Jason and Jeremy constructed their own complex bridge—twigs and bits of candy-wrapper balanced across a lake of spilled orange juice. Jason was fairly sure Jeremy spilled the juice on purpose, but he didn't complain. The ants liked it. "Like fish aren't they, little Germ?" The tiny cars were ready to make their first trip when Jeremy suddenly leapt to his feet shouting, "Hey look! There's Alison."

"Come back!" ordered Jason, as Jeremy conquered the garden gate—in a single bound—and set off down the street. "Jeremy, get back here!"

Alison, it turned out, lived just at the end of the cul-de-sac, so Jeremy wasn't going far. Jason had time to kick off the brakes on the stroller before he went to fetch him.

"Hello," said a dark, hunched figure from the neighbor's door, so quietly Jason hardly heard her voice.

"Are you Alison?" he asked.

"No, she is." A trembling hand pointed to the child running after the cat.

When she moved into the light the hunched figure seemed intriguingly beautiful—dark wispy hair, slightly swarthy skin, shy smile. Her name was Jeannie and she was baby-sitting the neighbor's four-year-old, Jeremy's friend Alison.

"I'm Jason. I'm meant to be sitting for this little tyke—his uncle for my sins. He seems to like your Alison."

Jeannie smiled and Jason melted into her gaze. Something stunning glowed behind her eyes, something he'd never seen before, piercing through wire-rimmed glasses. "Shall we join forces? Just till eight?"

Jeannie seemed unsure but her frown slowly faded. "Okay. They can play here."

More orange juice spilled, more bridges were built, then more cars and even some dolls drove merrily across. It should have been chaos, two four-year-olds, one large cat, one sleepy baby, and a couple who'd never met before. But it worked and they planned to do it again, baby-sitting next week perhaps, if Troy and Lydia went to another bridge night. Maybe they'd meet for coffee in town at the weekend "with no kids to look after."

Babies are sweet, Jason thought as he cradled JC in his arms back at Troy and Lydia's house, in the bedroom with the curtains tightly closed as prescribed. And toddlers are terrors. But this was the first time he'd ever tried imagining children of his own.

School Days

Best of Times, Quick Learner, Feeling Blue, Winning Moments

Her perfume called him, every meeting still the best of times. Her china-doll sweetness, delicately breakable, like comfort and proof he'd never end up like his father. Imagine if he held her too tight, how she'd bruise. But Peter would never cause her pain because he knew, he was sure, he was not his father.

Her perfume, even the thought of her perfume, even the memory of her perfume in their ridiculous little shack in the woods by the stream made his body long for her. He looked at the sleeping mat stretched on the floor and imagined her, winsome, naked, lying and waiting for him. Arms wide, pert pointed temptation trembling where he'd press his lips, she'd stretch like a cat, even purr. Her body learned to sing for him.

He imagined extending himself over her, cold but knowing his blue flesh would soon warm. He'd press his lips against her neck, feel her pulse, his own pulse eagerly matching it—a race, he'd win. Then kneeling, poised over her, he'd glide his hands slowly, sensuously, from fingertips to palms to soft-shaved silken underarm. He'd cup her sweet-tipped mountains, trembling. Then down, so smoothly down he'd move his mouth to the hollow of her waist. Lips would slide and glide, down, down and down. He imagined her legs spread wide before him on the mat, kitten-mouth, silk-furred, opening to him, the taste of her.

He imagined—*why was she late?* He nibbled the back of his hand and thought of all the other women strolling out in the woods. None of them could taste quite the same. He never brought them here because, despite the knick-knacks and cleanliness, she really was the one that completed him.

"Dad, where do you go every lunchtime? You take forever to get back."

"None of your beeswax, Kid."

Best of Times

It was the best of times, it was the worst of times. Yes, that probably described it, Lydia thought. Her tiny son, once a baby, then a precious, precocious little boy, had just walked into school, hand in hand with his girlfriend. Lydia was left to cope with his toddler brother. Ah freedom—*is that what it's called?* Life without Jeremy for a whole morning.

"Well, that went okay," said Amethyst, giving a final wave at the school's closing door. "And don't worry. Alison will look after Jeremy. Want to stop for a coffee before we go home?"

Lydia nodded, though the newly opened coffee shop wasn't exactly on the way. JC would have to be bribed with the promise of playtime in the park. Lydia strapped him into his stroller while Amethyst talked with other parents, then they set off together.

"I don't know how you manage," Amethyst declared, looking, rather obviously, at Lydia's early bulge where child number three resided.

"Me neither," Lydia agreed and they laughed.

Other mothers strolled from the school gates now. Some slipped back into low-slung daddy-cars, others into mommy-mobiles. Some, like Lydia and Amethyst, simply set off to walk. "Walking's good for us." By the time they'd reached the coffee shop they were alone.

"I'll go in," said Amethyst. "We all know how much JC likes to wait in line."

Lydia bent to the child. They'd already arranged that, when Amethyst returned to work, Lydia would take over bringing

Alison to and from school. It would be no problem, she said, except suddenly she'd go from chasing two children to three, then four with the baby. Not that the tiny one would need much chasing yet she thought gratefully, imagining a kick inside. *Wonder who you'll be.*

With coffee cups balanced in the holders Troy had rigged on Lydia's stroller, the mothers crossed the street to Paradise Park.

"I said my sister could join us. Hope you don't mind," said Amethyst.

"Your sister?"

"Yes, she's got a little kid here too, Alison's age. I meant to introduce you but, you know, in the rush… He started out at one of the downtown schools but she moved him here instead." They headed for the path. "She's got a little girl as well," Amethyst added. "Same age as your JC."

The stroller bumped on the uneven track as they took the short cut under trees, and JC complained. "Dark, Mommy."

"Be out soon. Don't worry."

Shadows strayed and spooked them till they emerged into cool morning sun. The grass was damp. Bright light reflected from the pond. Ducks splashed and quacked while drifting through the reeds.

"Feed duckies," JC announced.

"We haven't brought any food."

"I want."

"Next time, little one."

There were benches by the pond, in sun and shade, and others near the top of the hill where a fat man sat, king on his throne, eating a sandwich—early lunch perhaps? Amethyst and Lydia settled by the wooden climbing frame. Then JC, released from the straps of his stroller, waterfowl temporarily forgotten, scrambled off while his mother sipped her drink.

"They said they'd take me back at my old job," Amethyst volunteered. She looked worried, as if unsure their previous agreement still stood.

"Good for you."

"And you really don't mind?"

"No trouble. It's fine."

The coffee tasted warm and sweet. The day, insects buzzing, distant ducks, sun beaming, was warm and sweet too. Both mothers leaned back, eyes closed for a moment's relaxation, ears open for the sound of JC's footsteps and sparkling voice.

Car engines thrummed as more visitors parked by the trees. Two women, half familiar to Lydia, sat down nearby. Amethyst introduced the one with the dog as her sister. "Sapphire Greenwood, Nate and Tracey's Mom." The name seemed vaguely familiar.

Sapphire smiled, the dog lay down, and the newly-introduced Tracey ran to the slide behind JC, obviously delighted to be free.

The fourth mother, small and dark, introduced herself shyly as Marcie Kopp, mother to Robert, wife to Darryl. Then Amethyst and Lydia finished off with their names.

In the sudden silence Lydia asked if Sapphire wasn't that journalist she'd read in the local paper. "Yeah that's me," said Sapphire.

"Why didn't you say, Amethyst?"

Sapphire asked Lydia why she looked familiar.

"No idea. I'm nobody special."

"But her mother's Savannah Steepleton," Amethyst volunteered to Lydia's furious gaze.

"Oh wow," gushed Sapphire, smelling news. "So your sister must be the guardian angel cat girl."

"Cat girl?" Marcie asked.

"No, guardian angel cats." Lydia turned back to Sapphire. "And you're the one who writes about them, right?" She found herself describing the story of her old college roommate…

"Where is she now? Did she graduate?"

"No idea."

"And where's your sister?"

"She's off at college."

Amethyst told of her engagement night and dinner, much

delayed, at Benson's in the rain. Garnet featured prominently in both tales.

"Not the same cat surely?" Marcie asked, as if trying to make sense of a nonsense conversation. "And why would anyone see it in the dark?"

"Because it's white," Lydia interjected. "And fat and fluffy. And 'cause Garnet's always wandering in the park."

"Garnet?" asked Marcie still catching up.

JC toddled off toward the trees and Lydia leapt up to chase him.

"So is it true there's some pervert lurking in the woods or is that just a rumor?"

Lydia kept half an ear listening for Sapphire's reply but the conversation veered in other directions.

With JC retrieved and wiggling under her arm, Lydia returned to her seat. Then, as if she'd heard her name mentioned, the great white wanderer Garnet herself appeared. Paws stepping rhythmically, daintily, she strolled along behind an older woman who looked harassed and scared. Sapphire's dog raised a lazy nose and nuzzled down to sleep.

"Have you seen my daughter?" the woman asked. All the mothers looked up. "Amelia—she's about so high," hand held out by her waist. "Pretty smile, kind of stares at you. Carries a doll and a rabbit? She's autistic. Always wandering off."

Lydia had seen the woman around church she thought, not a friend or fellow worshipper so much as someone to be prayed for. She'd never really looked at her though—you don't when something's wrong—wouldn't have recognized her.

Garnet suddenly scurried to the trees with a scrabble of gravel spraying behind her flight. JC wobbled after her. "GaGa. GaGa."

"Come back here."

"Tracey, stay," said Sapphire, as if her child were obedient as her dog.

When Lydia and JC got back, Amelia's mother was explaining her concern in short sharp gasps, watery eyes flickering distractedly, thin hands clutching at each other in lieu of holding onto her daughter. She seemed to be in pain. Lydia tried to imagine how it felt not to know where a child had gone. It was painful enough not knowing exactly what Jeremy was doing at school.

"It's so hard," Evie said and the other mothers nodded sympathetic agreement. They were glad, and couldn't say so, that their own children were normal and safe.

"Do you have to home-school her?" Sapphire asked.

"Sort of. I do what I can. She has therapy in town."

"I could write an article. Get some publicity."

A burst of laughter and splatter of paws distracted them. Sapphire's dog raced toward the trees. Garnet and a squirrel chattered angrily high on a branch. JC and Tracey sang Ring-a-Roses around the tree-trunk. And sweet Amelia, rabbit and rag doll in hand, stared totally absorbed. When the children shouted, "All fall down," Amelia sat primly on a patch of dry grass as if joining in.

"Guardian angel cat," said Lydia, pointing and nodding solemnly, then laughing. "Must be Amelia's guardian angel too." She retrieved JC who was rolling in the undergrowth, swings and slides ignored, and looked down at her watch. "Time to get back. This boy needs to catch *Thomas* on TV or he'll never go to sleep."

The mothers separated and went their various ways, agreeing that maybe they'd meet again, Karen Grainger looked like a great teacher as well as good neighbor and bridge-player, fall would come soon, and it was indeed the best and worst of times, sending your first kid off to school.

No one stopped to ask what Evie thought.

Quick Learner

Sweetheart, darling, baby… *That's what parents call their little children.* Evie tugged Amelia away from the trees and called her by her real name—anything else would be too confusing. "Amelia, come along now. We're going to catch the bus."

Amelia hummed a tune, *The wheels on the bus go 'round.* "Good girl, Amelia!" While those wheels rotated, Evie could lead her child unprotesting to the stop. "Here we are. Let's wait for the bus, Amelia."

Amelia strode ahead and stamped her feet. "Sweetheart." *No, don't say that.* "Amelia. We have to wait."

Humming louder, Amelia pulled from her mother's hands, but the blue cord tied to their wrists wouldn't let her go far. "Come back here. Now, Amelia!" Evie reeled her in slowly so as not to overly dismay, and Amelia busied herself stroking the fabric of her rabbit and doll. Luckily the bus arrived promptly.

"Let's get on the bus, Amelia."

Wheels on the bus went around and around while Amelia hummed her tune, sitting docile and sweet, toys placed with rigid symmetry one on each knee. She let her mother take the seat next to her. Behind sat the lady who kept missing her stop, round glasses and thick winter coat hiding body and face. *We're the oddballs* thought Evie. In front, teens shouted slogans at each other. Amelia ignored them and Evie hoped she wouldn't change her mind.

Would a car be easier? Would a husband and father help? Evie didn't know. Through years with her husband, through years alone, nothing had changed except the child grew larger and more beautiful, her clothes didn't fit—and she didn't like anything *new.* Amelia didn't like differences, or people, or strangers, or scratchy material or buildings with freshly painted walls. But she liked buses.

"Time to get off the bus now, Amelia."

Amelia fought and Evie overpowered her into the aisle. One day she'd be too small and her daughter too big. One day these battles might go the other way.

One day at a time Evie told herself. She'd live one day at a time. And if one day, she woke and her child was normal, she'd wonder had the world turned upside down.

A sign pasted to a lamp post caught Amelia's eye and she read aloud, reciting words, enunciation perfectly learned, punctuation and meaning non-existent: "Grand meeting of the board and all interested members of the public to discuss repairs to Paradise Elementary School and funds for outside activities seven p.m. on Saturday thirteenth don't miss it we'll be in the ground floor library coffee served." As they turned away she summed the words, a small frown creasing her brow, then announced the total, "Forty-five."

Feeling Blue

Children sat on miniature chairs with elbows on child-sized desks, heads bowed over crayons, except for Alison's head which was bowed over Jeremy. *Not fair,* she thought. The cat on Jeremy's page had eyes, nose and mouth, and a jewel in its collar, just like Garnet. Alison's picture seemed more like a furry lump in comparison. *How dare he be better?* He'd only just started school. She scrunched her paper into a ball and drew a house with blue door and bright sky instead. She knew she could draw that.

"Time for math," said Mrs. Grainger in her school teacher voice, so much louder than the one she used when talking about bridge with Mom. Today's helper handed out counting blocks while Mrs. Grainger collected their papers. "Very nice Alison. Jeremy…"

Alison sorted her blocks into piles and Jeremy built a spaceship. "That's not what you do."

"Why not?" But of course, genius Jeremy could count without blocks. He added spaceport buildings, even some blobs that might be people, while Alison stared, entranced. So much more fun than counting sets of ten, but her mother had told her to *look after* Jeremy and he'd have to learn, you don't play in school. She raised her hand for the teacher.

"Really?" said Mrs. Grainger, staring down at Jeremy's scene. "Maybe this is too easy for you, young man. How many children in this class?"

Jeremy counted. "Sixteen."

"And if Alison wasn't here?"

"Fifteen." He paused, then pointed. "Sixteen."

"Say again?"

Alison turned to follow Jeremy's gaze. The classroom door stood open and green eyes watched from a bundle of white.

"Oh heavens!" Mrs. Grainger scooped up the cat. "What's Garnet doing here?"

"Please, Mrs. Grainger, can't she stay?"

"No, Alison. You take her to the office and call your mother."

As Alison left, cat flopping over her arm, Mrs. Grainger bent over Jeremy. Her voice was quieter now, almost purring like the cat's. "You're the Steepleton's grandson all right, young man. Just like your granddaddy. You'll go far."

"But I can't go till Mommy gets me." Jeremy's ringing tones echoed down the corridor.

Alison returned just in time for story time—poor Garnet would have liked that. She made a sad face, wishing the cat could have stayed, but then she saw Jeremy looking lost and led him to the mat, sitting big-sisterly beside him and holding his hand. It made sense. She couldn't look after Garnet and Jeremy both at once.

"Well, children. Who wants to help with my story today?"

Alison tugged Jeremy's hand. "We can help." But he just stared at the floor in front of his feet, didn't even look up when Alison pranced like a pony to the front and begged "Me, me!" *At least I'm better at story time than he is.*

She was better at lunchtime too and knew exactly what to do when Mrs. Grainger lined them up by the door. "Jeremy comes home with me. He's my friend."

"That's nice, Alison. Now let's wait for your mommies."

"D'you think Garnet will be there?"

"Just wait and see."

Jeremy's mother had JC in his stroller with Garnet curled on his lap. Alison's Mom stood beside her. "Look! There they are." Alison ran, begging eagerly, "Mom, can we go in the car?"

"No, dear. We're walking."

"Why?"

"Cheer up. 'Cause it's nice. Blue sky and sunshine. And we can walk together."

Why do parents have such a thing about sunshine? Alison plucked a blue flower from a straggling bush for Jeremy. She gave him her picture too, pointing to the stick figure by the blue door and saying, "That's JC. Can you play at my house?"

"Not today." Jeremy's mother answered for him. She sounded strange, like Alison's Mom when Alison made her sad.

"Why not?"

"First day of school—Jeremy's tired. He needs a break."

"I didn't break anything Mom!" Jeremy stomped his feet.

"That's not what I meant. We just need to go home."

Mom needed. Jeremy didn't.

"There's chocolate chip cookies."

"Can Alison have some?"

"She's going home with her mommy."

Which she did, leaving Jeremy to stomp on every step of the path and twice on some, just to show how he felt. Alison knew exactly why he was angry. Jeremy didn't know she knew, and barely spared her a glance.

The blue door slammed closed behind him, and Jeremy flung his bag to the floor.

"Bring your lunchbox in the kitchen."

"Why?"

"So I can clean it."

"Why?" He thumped it on the counter.

"Here's your drink." Mom sighed. "And your cookies."

Jeremy climbed on his chair, kicking the table with his feet. The kitchen did smell nice though—not dinner nice, but cookie-nice, sugary and chocolatey. He felt a reluctant smile tug his face. The fridge hummed softly. Birds sang outside. Peace and quiet soothed him after the frantic noise of school. He told his mom there were nine steps on their path but one was cracked so it looked like ten.

"Careful." His cup began to tip.

"I am careful."

"Careful," said JC sticking a cookie in his ear.

Mom grabbed the tot and lifted him into his chair. "You two sit here and talk about what you've been doing."

But what could Jeremy say to a pre-school kid? "Work," he answered, his voice suddenly serious and low. "I've been doing work."

"I play." JC sang.

"That's 'cause you're a baby. Babies can't work."

JC thumped the table and screamed. Jeremy cried. His mom gave him a hug. Then Garnet hopped in through the window. Mom snatched the cookies away. "Never mind, Jeremy. JC's just jealous." She patted JC's head. "What sort of work?"

"I did numbers and a picture. And Garnet was there. Then we listened to a story. Alison danced."

"I dance," said JC, climbing down from his chair.

"Not just now." Mom held him back and turned to Jeremy again. "So why the glum face? Why so blue when you've had a good day?" *And why is my voice cracking?* And why was she hugging the cat to her chest and cuddling it so tight?

Jeremy shrugged, tugging the flower and the picture out from his pack. "I'm not a color. This is blue."

"Blue door," said JC.

Lydia sighed. Perhaps it was she, not her son, who really felt blue.

Winning Moments

The sun shone on another bright school day, a special day, Sports Day, highlight of the year, and Jeremy really did feel blue. Not the newest kid in class anymore, Jeremy was the Genius, the Math Prof, or the Germ. He opened his eyes miserably, wishing he could catch some germs. In the bathroom he scrubbed his face extra hard. If his cheeks looked red, Mom might think he had a temperature, but she'd just use the thermometer to measure it. No point pretending.

Jeremy's lunch box stood to attention next to his juice and cereal on the kitchen table. His backpack leaned against his chair at an angle close to thirty degrees. He wished he could relax like the huddled bag, but little boys on Sports Day have to pretend to be lunchbox straight.

"You okay?" asked his mother.

Jeremy allowed himself a moment to imagine she might let him stay home. "Yes Mom. I'm fine."

The doorbell rang, Amethyst bringing Alison around before work. Jeremy glugged his juice.

"Time to go then, kids."

They rode in almost-silence in Lydia's car, Alison and Jeremy sitting in the back to either side of JC. Mondays, Wednesdays and Fridays were Amethyst's work days, though Alison whispered her mother was coming home early to watch the sports. She looked like she expected Jeremy to reply but he said nothing. His mother filled the silence with unimportant questions like, "Have you remembered your notebook?" and "Did you sharpen your pencil last night?"

"Got your PE stuff?" she asked as they arrived.

Jeremy scrambled out. "Yes Mom."

"Both of you?"

Alison waved her PE bag in the air as she ran off.

"See you after lunch then, kids."

Jeremy slumped up the path and into class. He wanted to do some extra math problems with the teaching assistant, but she just talked about how excited he must be. "It's Sports Day, Jeremy! And the sun's shining too," as if he might not have noticed it for himself.

Mrs. Grainger tested their sums. "And anyone who can't answer four questions will have to stay in and work instead of doing sports." Ah, if only Jeremy could get the answers wrong, but his mouth spouted numbers before his brain could stop it. *There's no way out.*

At last they ate lunch. It was meant to be a treat, eating in the same room as the first grade kids instead of going home.

Jeremy tried to finish as fast as he could, thinking he might throw up, but he couldn't even do that right. Soon, far too soon, the children lined up at the classroom door, all dressed in PE shirts and shorts, all full of excitement, except for Jeremy.

They marched down the corridor and out to the field. Robert and Nate started a fight. "I'll send you two in if you don't behave," threatened a teacher. Jeremy wondered if someone might fight with him.

His mother was there of course, standing behind the kindergarten finish line, camera ready, waiting to capture those glorious winning moments for posterity. She smiled for two because Jeremy's face had frozen to a miserable frown. JC waved hands up and down like tiny hammers, face red, as he sat in his stroller. Jeremy wished he could change places. Where were Garnet and Alison's Mom?

"On your marks!" *Lunchbox straight. Shoulders back.*

"Get set!" Jeremy crouched like a backpack on the floor.

"Go!" *Why not just count from one to three?*

Everyone started to shriek. Jeremy screwed his eyes tight shut because he couldn't close his ears. Tripping over his feet, he stood, opened half an eye, and set off wobbling, one foot after the other.

The crowds screamed. They shouted and cheered. Then they grew quiet, murmured and started talking among themselves. They thought he couldn't hear. "It does that Jeremy Markham kid good to be taken down a peg or two. Lets him know how other kids feel, always parading how good he is at math and everything."

But Jeremy wasn't last to finish. Soft footsteps behind were a four-legged cat, even slower than Jeremy on two. Probably Garnet wasn't trying to win, but her presence made Jeremy feel better. They said, "It's not the winning that counts," when he finally crossed the line, so he turned to Garnet, repeating the words generously. Say it often enough and maybe he'd learn to believe.

"Poor kid. Just like his Uncle Jason was."

JC still struggled and screamed when the race was over.

Watching his fists, Jeremy thought how he'd like to flail out at all the mothers who'd laughed at him. If he couldn't run, maybe he'd learn to fight. He'd scream and shout and everyone would wonder what the fuss was about. But Garnet jumped into JC's arms to calm him, and Jeremy walked quietly behind his classmates, back into school to pick up his backpack and lunchbox before going home, just Jeremy the Germ who can't run and jump but does math like a third grader.

Life and Death

Perfume, Rush, Drip, Life Death and a Cat

"**Y**ou're taking your pills aren't you?"

"Of course."

Peter wasn't quite sure why he asked. The way she looked at those kids rushing along with their mother on the path made him nervous though. Her eyes seemed hollow, hungry.

Of course, Peter smiled, his eyes might harbor hunger too—that mom was quite a looker. He turned his head, trying to catch the scent of her perfume, but knew he had to stay in the moment. Talk quickly. *Don't let anyone know we're together.* "You're sure you're taking them?" *Just as long as she doesn't plan on having kids.*

"Of course I'm sure."

Life's too short for more.

They wandered separately into the trees where leaves dropped lazily. Peter pretended to go one way while she took the other. They'd meet at the shack. Meanwhile a cat's green eyes swiveled to see.

Perfume

She smelled of *Sweet Innocence* and roses, with a hint of sophistication way beyond his league. Her scent walked through the trees before her. Her pheromones called to him as he watched in the dark, in that secret wooded place he'd built for them.

"Why don't we meet at your house sometime?" she asked.

"Why? Would you come there?"

"I don't know. Would you let me? Or at your work?"

He laughed, bending to the task of undressing her. Fingers nimble and delicate on each perfect button, he slid her sun-scented garments out the way. Her skin felt soft against his palms. Smooth-soaked flesh poured out of her silky blouse. Then she stepped back, folding her clothes in a pile on top of her shoes to keep them clean.

"Why don't we meet at the art gallery?" she asked, lying down and stretching her arms above her head.

"I'd never fit in." He hovered over the rising mounds of her.

"No, I suppose you wouldn't."

Then he pressed down crushing her body to the ground. "Besides," he added, pushing into her—was she gaining weight?—"keeping me secret's half the fun for you, isn't it?"

She purred, sounding unsure.

Andrea's combs and mirror, make-up and perfume were stored in her purse. Afterward no one would know a thing about where she'd spent her time. She'd make her way back to the sunlit path, walk into town, and return to work, sweet sophisticate, with a secret all her own.

But for now, she pressed her tongue deep into his mouth, accepting the familiar taste of him against her teeth. She ran her fingers down his chest, clutched tighter, squeezed him closer, deeper in.

Then he left her, rushing away, and she walked slowly back to the shop, feeling secrets grow heavy and sticky between her thighs.

Rush

Sylvia ran from the stock room when she heard the tinkling bell of the gallery door—only her boss, back from yet another lunchtime in the park. But On-DRAY-uh-the-perfect looked distracted, even slightly disheveled, the skin around her eyes puffed and red as if she'd been crying.

"Are you okay?"

Andrea rushed past, leaving a whiff of perfume tinged with clay and the scent of leaves.

You shouldn't go down to the woods on your own Sylvia thought but said nothing. You can't babysit your boss. Then Andrea returned from the bathroom, still distracted, carrying her purse.

"Going out to the shops."

"You can't. You've got…"

"You hold the fort."

Some summer job this was turning out to be, but at least Sylvia would be back at college soon.

Drip

Andrea Blake had eaten alone at Benson's last night. Carla remembered watching her pore over the menu. She stirred food on her plate like porridge, scarcely touching a bite, and rushed to the restroom over and again. When the bill came she glared, ignoring Carla's worried "You okay?" And she didn't leave a tip.

Now she rushed along the supermarket aisle, looking lost and afraid, snatching boxes and packets and a stack of metal coat hangers. She stopped by Carla's checkout, staring as if they'd never met before and suddenly demanding, "Is there a bathroom? A bathroom somewhere?"

Carla pointed to the gray-painted door at the end of the checkout stands.

Music played on the radio, interrupted by sound bites of local politics. Something dripped incessantly, or perhaps the clock was ticking or a wire had come loose in the speakers.

"You hear that?" Carla asked the girl on the next check stand.

"Hear what?"

"That ticking, dripping, whatever?"

"Can't say's I do."

A politician said they ought to do something about cleaning up the park. *Is it dirty,* Carla wondered? A mother complained she wouldn't let her child play there alone and Carla thought, *If I had kids—if David was willing to have kids...* Tick tock, a woman's clock.

"D'you need me to bag that?" she asked her customer. "Did you find everything? D'you want help out with those?" Questions dripped like a faucet prone to leaks. She pulled the groceries over the shiny red scanner, one per drip, steady, unthinking, till the first-shift manager marched over with his big bold frown.

"Speed it up a bit."

Carla struggled to go against the flow, hard not to follow that beat that drummed in her head. "I need a bathroom break," she muttered but didn't want another reprimand.

Soda, apples, cookies, cake...

"Oh puh-lease, Carla!" The manager ran over to her. She'd rushed a creamy cake across the light a little too hard. Cream smeared on the chrome checkout where the plastic cracked open. Her boss apologized to the customer and promised a replacement, while Carla reminded herself she was perfectly capable of making her own apologies.

She really needed the bathroom though.

Familiar faces smiled around the store. Carla tried to smile back. Lydia, wife of David's workmate, pushed through the doors. Heavily pregnant, she towed two small boys—was it really so long since her wedding?

Lydia'll need the bathroom, Carla thought, watching jealously. She saw her rush, one child in her arms while the other clutched her skirt—didn't even stop to pick up a cart. Then Lydia waited, doing the bathroom dance outside the gray painted door. Funny, Carla thought. She'd had the ladies' room on her mind all morning and was sure it was free, but must be mistaken.

Lydia tapped on the door and waited some more. She turned around, scanning the store with strained look begging for help. Carla checked another customer through, then waved her hand to the glaring manager. "Ladies' bathroom," she whispered, pointing, then continued passing groceries over the scanner, her metronomic drip falling suddenly silent.

A crowd formed around the bathroom door. The manager pointed to the back office, maybe offering Lydia the private restroom. He knocked, leaned against to the door, and shouted, "Anyone in there?" Through the window Carla watched Joe and Darryl park their police cruiser outside—lunchtime coffee or had the manager called for help? They joined the crowd at the end of the checkouts, Darryl bending low over the lock while Joe pushed people back. Then time froze.

Later Carla couldn't remember how they'd opened the door, didn't know if anyone screamed or if the sound was just in her head. She remembered the scene though, red on the floor, the sudden certain knowledge of which packets Andrea Blake had carried with coat hangers into the stall.

Why would anyone die in a public bathroom? How could anyone sit on a toilet and bleed to death without calling for help?

A bloodied and bent coat hanger dangled from Andrea's hand. An opened pregnancy kit lay in the pool, blue-lined for sure. Carla didn't see the blue, just knew, maybe somebody told her. Two deaths in one.

Home—had she come home early? Had someone driven her home? Carla sat in her chair hearing a faucet drip and hating the sound. She screamed, hands clawing at her hair, then grabbed the phone to call her boyfriend. "Fix the faucet, David.

Just fix it!" So he did. He left the garage right away and Carla sobbed in his arms.

"You couldn't have known," David said, stroking her hair. But she could have found out. She could have taken a bathroom break herself; then they might've opened the door in time.

"You couldn't have helped." *But if they'd found her sooner she might have survived.*

"It wasn't your fault." She'd fumed while a stranger sat dying. It *was* her fault because she should have known.

David helped her undress for bed, gave her cocoa and sat by her side. As soon as Carla closed her eyes, she saw cake sliding across the checkout again. She saw the box crash, splitting open, then blood instead of cream smeared onto chrome.

Life, Death and a Cat

It was Thursday, so Alison's mother had picked her up from school, bringing her home in the mommy-mobile instead of letting her walk with Jeremy. Now Alison sat on her doorstep, cuddling the cat and waiting for her friend. Aunt Jeannie's car pulled up at the curb down the street—maybe she'd know where he was. Glancing back at the kitchen window for permission, Alison ran toward her, cat paws dangling unheeded over her arm.

Jeremy climbed out the car.

"Where you been?"

He ignored Alison's question, announcing proudly to the world, "I saw a dead person!"

"Really dead?"

"Really."

The children ran back to Alison's house while adult voices arranged how long Jeremy could stay. Yes, Lydia was fine, just a little shaken, and JC would be no problem for Jeannie to handle. Would Amethyst please send Jeremy home as soon as she tired of him?

They charged around the back while Jeremy's aunt drove away.

Alison's mother didn't keep their back yard tidy—not like Jeremy's Mom. Grass was knee high, damp with recent rain, and tickled the children's knees. Garnet reached her paws up, clutching Alison's shirt, then climbed on her shoulder.

"Really, really dead?" she asked. "Where? Tell me!"

Jeremy tugged plastic cushions from the patio, laying them out on the overgrown lawn. Alison sat cross-legged with Garnet in her lap, while her friend flopped on his stomach, feet in the air, one ankle held in his hand. His mom had driven to the store after school but she needed the bathroom before they even started shopping. She needed it even more than JC these days. She was getting fat.

"'Cause of the baby in her tummy," Jeremy explained. It was all very strange. "So we stood there at the bathroom door and Mommy couldn't get in."

"Why? Was someone inside?"

"Well, it was locked." They carried on waiting till a man in a uniform came.

"What, like a policeman? Like Mr. Grainger?"

Three men, Jeremy explained—Mr. Grainger and another policeman, and a fat man from the shop. The shop man led Jeremy's mother and JC away while the policemen knocked on the door. But Jeremy stayed. He wasn't the one needing the bathroom anyway and he wanted to see. He peered through everyone's legs, watching a policeman break open the door, then staring at the blood all over the floor.

"And a dead person?"

Jeremy nodded solemnly.

"Really dead?"

"Really, really dead."

Suddenly strangers pulled Jeremy away, eyes staring, white faces asking if he was all right, fingers poking and prodding, strange perfumes and flapping skirts. All Jeremy wanted was a closer look.

The shop man pushed the assistants back while an unknown lady declared they should "Give the boy some air." Then someone picked Jeremy up around his waist, legs dangling helplessly, while his arms flapped like wings. He found himself rushed into a dusty-smelling office and plunked on a chair.

"Did you cry?"

"No. Not really. But it was scary. And he kind of hurt my tummy."

The fat man led Jeremy's mother to sit beside him. She didn't know what the fuss was about, but Jeremy wasn't allowed to tell her. Instead people shushed him and whispered hushed phrases in the doorway, like *terrible* and *sorry*. "Then the policeman came and asked lots and lots of questions."

"Was it Mr. Grainger?"

"No, the other one. Robert's Dad." Jeremy's auntie was called and drove him and his mother home. "So that's why I was in Auntie Jeannie's car, even when she really hates driving, and that's why I was late."

Alison still cuddled the cat, fingers buried deep in thick white fur. Garnet had curled in her lap to listen. When Jeremy stopped talking, she stalked away across the grass, back arched high to keep her fluffy stomach out of the wet. The children crept behind.

Garnet walked toward the wooden fence, stepping neatly over a line of Popsicle sticks that angled from the ground. She began to clean herself. The white cat's penchant for mice and small rodents, and even once a young squirrel, had fed the children's imaginations. Now there were shoe boxes, stuffed with tissue paper and tokens of affection, buried under the sticks in their secret graveyard.

As Garnet licked her paws and wiped her face, Jeremy lay himself down perpendicular to the fence. His feet stretched beyond brown soil onto the grass.

"She'll need a much bigger grave," he said solemnly.

"Silly," said Amethyst. "They don't bury people in back yards."

"That's 'cause they wouldn't fit."

"And they don't use Popsicle sticks."

"That's 'cause they're too small."

Garnet finished her grooming and continued around the house. Jeremy struggled to his feet while Alison chased the cat, scooping her up with dangling legs over her arm. A quick meow and the dangled feline pretended to be a purse. They sat on the step in front of the house, looking out at the road.

"A real dead person," Alison repeated in tones of awe.

"Yeah. And blood too."

When a car engine slowed at the turn-around, they looked up to see two policemen staring back. Joe Grainger stuck his head out the patrol car window.

"You okay, young Jeremy?"

"Yeah."

"Well, ask your mother before you eat these, all right?"

Jeremy and Alison caught the candies Joe tossed aloft. A quick look back at the kitchen window confirmed they were allowed to snack. Then Garnet walked back to the house in disgust, seeking feline treats, or more mice to add to the Popsicle burial ground.

Aftermath

School Visit, Hard Labor, Little Eyes, Growing up

It was hard to believe she'd died. Peter labored over an engine, pretending not to listen, not to care, while Troy and David discussed the news. Killed herself? Pregnant? Just trying to get rid of the baby? Perhaps she was scared of being a single mom or something, couldn't bear to have an infant growing up, school visits and all that. It wouldn't have done. No one could imagine picture-perfect Andrea Blake with a child, or lying dead in a public bathroom.

"Show some respect!" Peter spat.

"Sorry, Dad."

But she'd died. She'd really died. Just like his mom.

I'm not my father, Peter swore to himself, then hoped the sound of machinery drowned his words. Not his father—she did it to herself. Peter hadn't made her, asked her, told her… He hadn't even known and he wasn't his dad. He couldn't have guessed and she'd promised she was taking the pills, so it wasn't his fault.

On the radio, neighbors and townsfolk and commentators, shoppers and clients and friends still whispered her name. They speculated, *Who was the father?* and, *Why didn't she ask for help?* Truth to tell, thought Peter, *it might not even be me.* What if Andrea was like his dad, and Peter was just her little bit on the side? That might be it.

He punched the wall, timing the blow with Troy's hammer, and almost broke through. Chipped paint fell down. But it wasn't so bad. Really. Things could be worse. She was gone from his life and he'd been thinking, hadn't he? Tried to fool himself but he'd known it all along. *She's not right for me.*

Besides there were plenty more in the woods where she'd come from, younger fruit like ripe peaches, ready to be plucked. He wasn't his dad and he'd never hurt anyone, so they were fair game.

Next lunchtime Peter pulled down the shack, didn't want to leave a reminder of her being there. He buried her treasures under the mud of the stream where they'd never be found. Then he hid himself in the dark under trees, where little eyes couldn't see him. Even the cat that warily dogged his steps wouldn't know where to look. He stayed alone where plants and memories waited and he thought of her. He thought of others too.

School Visit

Robert's father was Darryl, Marcie Kopp's husband, renowned for saying children should be seen and not heard. He wasn't the ideal choice of speaker in school, but Karen's husband had insisted. "He's getting bored with the job. It'll be good for him. Get him to interact with the boy as well, know what I mean?" Karen Grainger wasn't sure but wasn't unsure enough to disagree. Besides, what could possibly go wrong? The kids always behaved themselves for Joe's talks. Just as long as she could persuade them not to make jokes about cops called Kopp—poor Robert would never hear the last of it.

Robert, usually third or fourth in line for noisiest child, became still and silent when his father walked into the room. Policeman Darryl marched proudly to the front, eyeing the unusually quiet children, unusually tidily seated, as if he commanded their attention by divine right. Karen felt tiny next to him, almost invisible. She introduced him then stood under the window to watch him speak.

"Policemen keep you safe," Darryl began. Everyone nodded, open-mouthed. He told them policemen protect property. Karen could see some of the children wondering why pencils and erasers would need protecting, but she kept her smile, and her charges, under control.

Darryl told the children policemen look after people who need help.

"You mean like doctors?" asked Jeremy Markham. "My mommy keeps going to the doctor."

"Not exactly like doctors." Darryl tried to explain. He talked about a woman who needed the rest room in a supermarket.

"So you're, like, the supermarket guy?" asked a voice from the back.

"My mommy needed the rest room and it was locked."

Not a suitable story for elementary school—Karen pantomimed a change of subject and Darryl nodded at her. "Policemen catch bad guys," he said.

"What bad guys?" asked Nate Lee. Then Darryl, with predictable lack of tact, began to describe a grisly murder scene. Karen jumped in again to rescue him, but the children were way ahead of her.

"We don't talk about things like that," they said. "Not in school. Not in class." Just to prove the point, one little girl turned green and threw up on her desk.

"E-e-w!" Jeremy Markham tried to wriggle away. Another child accused Darryl, rather loudly, of making his friend sick. Someone else wanted to know if Darryl looked angry and would he arrest them now?

"I want to go to jail. Please, please! Will you 'rest us? Have you got your gun?"

Poor Darryl was totally out of his depth, children definitely heard as well as seen on all sides of him, while laughter echoed around the room.

Poor Darryl? thought Karen. *Poor Joe* when she got hold of him tonight. Next time he suggested someone else should do the police talk for the children, she'd not agree so willingly.

Hard Labor

Markham's Paradise Motors rang to the sounds of spanner, electric winch and air pumping out of machines. David had gone home because Carla still felt shaky, and Troy buried his head in an engine. "We're doing it, Dad. No arguments."

Peter snorted disapprovingly but his son shrugged his shoulders. Lydia had an appointment with the doctor again. Amethyst, Sapphire and Jeannie were all out at work. Grandma Abigail was having some kind of health crisis so Mary had to stay by her side. And there was no way Lydia would ask Savannah, so Troy was next in line. No problem. It was Troy's garage just as much as his dad's. Troy's family too.

The children's faces were smeared with peanut butter when they arrived. They'd had to eat lunch in the car because Lydia was running late, because she felt sick. Troy told her not to keep apologizing. He was just sorry he couldn't go with her and hold her hand, but instead he held the kids. While his father continued to drip disapproval in every shifting glance.

"Are you sure it's okay?" Lydia asked.

"He'll come around," said Troy. "Take care. Drive safely. Good luck."

Conventional words felt too frail to carry all he meant as he waved goodbye. The children held tight to his hugs. The thought occurred to him, not for the first time, *how on earth did we imagine we'd cope with three?* Troy's Dad wouldn't be much help.

Troy had set the old playpen up in the coffee room. It took a contortionist to walk around safely, but he hoped it might keep the toddler out of trouble. JC played there with his toys for all of the first five minutes, so things started well. Then Troy heard him rattling the bars.

"JC wants you, Dad," said Jeremy who was holding a flashlight illuminating dark corners of an engine's innards.

"He'll have to wait a minute."

"Shall I go to him?"

Dark corners became black again, though Troy could see as well with fingers and didn't need the help. He mumbled agreement, then heard, "Daddy," as Jeremy rushed back.

"Yes, son."

"JC de-fin-ite-ly needs you."

Troy smiled at his son's pronounced enunciation. "And what does he definitely need me for, Jeremy."

"He needs a diaper change."

"Oh."

Lifting the smelly child from his pen, Troy made his way out to reception. He gave the receptionist his most hopeful look.

"No way, pal." She shook her head.

"But the guys' bathroom is all smelly."

"Tough luck, Troy. You'll cope."

Into the smelly room Troy marched, a soldier into the fray—walls patched with oil, floor covered with drifting scraps of paper, one wailing child. When he owned the garage, when his father passed it on, Troy would *definitely* upgrade the facilities.

Meanwhile Jeremy climbed into and out of the playpen, boosted himself to the counter, and stole cookies from the cupboard. The receptionist caught him before he fell. She told Troy he was cute. Troy added more garage snacks to his lengthening list of things to buy.

"No climbing, Jeremy. It's not safe." *There again, is anywhere safe for a six-year-old in a building full of cars.*

Troy's father slipped back into the break room later and the children grew suspiciously, pleasingly quiet. Troy moved his head to observe.

Peter leaned against the doorframe, eyes fixed with something close to adoration on two little boys who seemed contentedly busy in their wooden cage. Outside on the floor were the toys Lydia had brought, ones Troy had kept trying to push back in. Inside the playpen the boys were absorbed with a shiny metal bowl, gallon water jug, clean funnels fresh from the packet, and a brand new towel roll. Perhaps Granddad knew a thing or two about children after all.

Did he used to look at me like that? Did he give me things to play with? Did he smile at me? For a moment, Troy remembered being lifted up in confident hands. Was it real or just a dream?

JC began to cry and Jeremy looked up. "Hi, Granddad Peter. JC's done it again."

"Troy! Get in there. You're needed!"

Troy didn't ask what he needed to do—the smell could put you off coffee for a season. But how would he ever cope with three.

Little Eyes

It's time… It's here… It's a boy. *You're a mother of three!* Lydia struggled to open her eyes and gazed at her baby son's face. A lifetime seemed to have passed in a flash, while everyone else assured her the world would go on. *No way. No way.* Warm lips sucked leaking milk and Lydia asked herself, *Do all mothers close their eyes when they feed their babies?* Somehow eyes, hers, the baby's, seemed more important than anything else. The baby's eyes were fastened shut, damp arcs of lashes on his cheeks. She didn't even know what color they were.

Mother of three? No way. She wouldn't think about that.

If anyone asked about Lydia's eye color, she'd refuse to answer. Yucky and mud-colored maybe—not an option on forms—or greenish brownish bluish gray. She could never remember which box she'd checked on driver's license or passport application. One day someone might collect all her data on computer and decide she was fake, because the answers disagreed.

Occupation: mother of three. *Open your eyes. Close them. Feed the child.*

Lydia's oldest son had beautiful blue eyes, like his father's and grandmother's. "They'll change," they told her when he was born, but they didn't. Nearly seven now, blue-eyed, red-haired, narrow-faced Jeremy was the image of his dad, apart from the hair—he even loved the same subjects in school. Daddy's boy, for sure.

Lydia's second had deep gray eyes to draw you in and trap you like bottomless pools. His chin was square not pointed, hair dark brown, wide nose, flat cheeks. "You're not him," she'd say as she changed his diaper, but it wasn't Troy she meant. JC was the image, though nobody noticed, of Lydia's deeply resented grandfather, who passed away before she was pregnant. She didn't dare believe in reincarnation. "You're not him. I know you're not, and I love you, little guy." Then deep gray eyes would gaze up into sky.

This third infant, contentedly sucking her breast, was unique—an accident for a start, not planned like the others. Jeremy just settling into school, JC testing everyone's patience, Lydia wasn't ready to be pregnant again, nor was Troy financially. There again, who is?

Lydia sighed, adjusting the questing mouth. She ached, tired, so much worse this time than before.

Carrying JC, lifting Jeremy, even getting her pregnant body into and out the car had worn her out. Visits to the doctor, constant sickness and weight loss, days when she had to leave the boys with their father at the garage... Great-Grandma Abigail got sick. Grandma Mary spent all her time at Paradise House, and Lydia was banished. Carrying life, she spent her days fearing death. But Abigail pulled through just as the baby came due. Feisty as ever, the old woman lived on, wordless and helpless as a newborn child.

Lydia's water broke early while Troy stayed late at the garage. The ambulance driver wore a black armband because health workers felt underpaid. Nurses at the hospital wore bad moods, all asking where Lydia's husband was and not waiting for her reply. The heart monitor slowed its beep with every contraction. Then Troy arrived. There were forms to sign, and needles and doctors and noises and everyone scared. *Fetal distress?* Why had nobody else noticed the monitor's beep? Why hadn't she said? They called the elevator but someone pressed *hold* so it didn't arrive and the doctor swore.

A voice in Lydia's head began to sing, *Take good care of my baby.* She wondered *can a song be a prayer*?

Lydia's bed crashed wildly through the doors of the operating room. Green blankets like Troy's green overalls. White lights and clockwork men. It would all be all right because Great-Grandma was going to be all right. It would all be all wrong. She fell asleep while the doctor counted down from ten.

When Lydia woke she lay alone, tucked tight into a hard narrow bed. She struggled to sit, a transparent box beside her and inside, the child with little eyes looking out. She worked her feet out from the covers, heard the beginning of a cry and lifted him up.

There are little eyes upon you, Lydia thought, wondering where she'd heard the phrase before. Her baby opened them now and gazed in deep and glorious adoring trust. Brown eyes. Deep beautiful earth-colored eyes. She knew you shouldn't have favorites among your children, but little Joshua suddenly held her in thrall.

Growing up

Jeffrey Irons sat on the hill watching time go by—two toys kept him company on his bench today. Sometimes it was one, sometimes none. Four mothers, two children down by the duck pond changed to three and three as months turned to years. Two mothers sat with one child now. One little boy lay asleep in a stroller with one large dog at his feet. Six ducks swam in one muddy ring, closely observed by one white cat. Jeffrey gazed but couldn't see if the mothers were drinking coffee or feeding the ducks, or if Amelia's mother was nearby. He listened but heard only bird calls, the drone of traffic, an occasional quack or splash. He finished his sandwich, left

Amelia's rabbit and rag doll waiting on the bench, and rolled back to work.

Amethyst and Marcie had both taken jobs, leaving Lydia and Sapphire alone after the morning school run. JC and Tracey were in kindergarten together, Joshua the only child at home.

"I can't believe they've grown so fast," said Lydia.

"Seems impossible," Sapphire agreed, leaning back and stretching her neck against wooden slats while her hand stroked Mason's ruff.

Lydia wondered aloud if three years made a big enough gap between siblings. Jeremy and JC seemed happy enough but would they always be friends? Were Nate and Tracey? "Did you plan the three-year gap?"

"Not really," said Sapphire. "Young Tracey was a bit of a surprise."

"Like this young man." Lydia gestured down at the stroller with her cup, careful not to spill.

"You planning any more?"

"Not likely," Lydia replied, smiling down at her toddler.

"Ah, the littlest. He's special then." Sapphire held a tiny embroidered handkerchief in her hand. Little Tracey had given it her to look after during school, afraid it might get lost. She stroked her fingers against the stitches, like a child finding comfort in the smoothness of satiny thread. "Definitely special."

Lydia bent to stroke her small son's head. He gazed, brown-eyed and beautiful, from his laid-back stroller, shriveled thumb in mouth. She wondered how quickly the future would make him grow.

After school, Jeremy interrupted their slow walk home with a loud announcement. "Robert's Daddy is going to join the army." *Robert? Marcie's child?* Wasn't Marcie's husband a policeman, Joe Grainger's partner? Lydia felt quick sympathy for the younger woman.

"Will my daddy join the army too?"

"I certainly hope not."

"But it's good to join the army isn't it, Mom?"

When Lydia didn't answer, Jeremy assured her, and anyone listening, that fighting is good as long as it's not in school. It's good to kill bad guys and good to be a soldier because God wants us all to be good little warriors in his army. Lydia sighed, too tired to argue the point. *Too many soldiers, too many guns and battles in this world.* Meanwhile JC and Jeremy pretended their fingers were weapons and shot each other.

"Careful, boys."

"It's okay, Mom. It's only pretend."

JC's bombshell came later. He and Jeremy walked either side of Joshua's stroller, holding tight to the bars, and he suddenly stopped.

"I don't want to be JC anymore."

"How d'you mean?"

"I don't want to be JC. Auntie Jeannie says Jay's a good name, so I want to be Jay."

"Okay," said Lydia, weakly, another battle wearing her further down. Aunt Jeannie was an admirably dependable babysitter, so how could she complain. Still, she stuttered through the rest of the day. "JC, stop that."

"I'm not JC anymore."

"JC. Jay, whoever you are…" till she started calling each of the children by strings of unintelligible sounds.

When Troy got home, he understood straight away, making Lydia feel hopelessly inadequate. "Isn't there a girl called Tracey in JC's class?"

"Yeah. So?"

"So, I'm guessing Jacey sounds too much like Tracey to him. Maybe somebody teased him and said he was a girl."

"But I liked JC."

"Never mind. You'll like Jay too. Just give it time."

Time was something Lydia had plenty of, and never enough. She gave it to Jeremy's homework, Jay's reading, Josh's toys. She filled it with cooking and cleaning and shopping and washing. She helped in school, in playgroup, in the library. *I'm turning into my mom.* And sometimes, once in a while, in rare moments of freedom, she dreamed of painting pictures while her children grew.

Part 6

The Crime

Finding Amelia

Whispering Trees, Alone, Secret Child, Amelia Hides

He walked alone under trees, hiding where memories whispered and tears dried to dust. He didn't want to think how she'd died because, after all, he really wasn't his father and wouldn't have hurt her. But her voice buzzed its mosquito-drone on the tight-skinned drum of his life and he couldn't squash it. Instead he watched strangers walk in the park to remind himself there were children and parents and families still alive.

Mothers pushed their babies in strollers, drank coffee, talked to each other and ignored him. Children hopped and skipped and let him pass without a glance. Even the ducks gave their favors to others, his bread not good enough. So he walked off the path because being invisible hurts less when you're alone.

Sometimes he strolled alongside strangers, hiding under branches and undergrowth. Once in a while someone would turn. "Who's out there?" Usually at night, in the dark when he'd never be found. Sometimes people strolled off the path—a child to hide or pick flowers, lovers to kiss, a teenager shedding tears of secret pain. Once he saw a couple undressing each other, felt emptier than ever watching them.

There'd been a girl, a long time ago—tight top with her womanhood just showing, her skirt so short he wondered why her mother let her out like that, such blatant temptation. *Her mother? Yes, he knew her mother, didn't he? Didn't want to be seen but he did feel sorry for the child.* Her backpack weighed like a car from the way she carried it.

She sat alone, eating chocolate sometimes—so bad for her complexion but she was young. When he came close he could see those silver tears on peach-blossom cheeks. He wanted to hold her, make everything all right, but knew she might be afraid.

One day in the pouring rain, she'd seemed so lost he couldn't stay away. He approached her in a clearing with the sun on his back. His shadow stretched ahead and glorious light flowed around and through him, as if he were an angel rescuing her. He clutched her to him, felt her body shake and sob. Then he turned her around and pressed her face to his chest to comfort her. Later she lifted her head to the sky and he kissed her sweet wet lips, saying nothing, but thinking all the while, *It's okay, little girl. It's not so bad. Don't cry.* When she soothed he, perfect gentleman and kind, left her there and walked away.

He saw her waiting again, a few days later and soon after that, as if she really needed the comfort he gave. She didn't cry against his shirt anymore, just rested in his arms, welcoming kisses with smiles and tight little gasps.

He wondered if she knew who he was, but felt that angelic power come over him, an angel of comfort sent to wear his flesh. So he hid his face, lest it distract from grace.

Her breath smelled of chewing gum. When he washed her cheeks with his tongue he tasted soap and salt, sweet scented, tinged with flowers. Inside her mouth the open space welcomed him, soft and warm.

He grew to love finding her there, tried to see her every day. He stayed longer, held her tighter, gave her ever more of his time and love. Running his fingers through silken hair, electric fire in his chest, he tried so hard not to let her know the way his manhood stirred—*do angels love this way?* Her beauty thrilled him, but he might frighten her.

Those buds of breasts, so small with their tiny points, he cupped them through the silken bra, his fingers under her blouse. He touched the smooth pure softness under the bra and it made him hard.

One day he pushed her gently against a tree, steadying her with his weight while hands explored. His fingers slid beneath her pants—that small excited cry. She was warm, damp there where flesh met flesh, so perfectly ready for him—he longed for her. And still she waited, loved him, welcomed him, until he knew it must be okay.

One day he laid her gently on the ground, a cradle of leaves to cushion her soft head. He undid her clothes with nervous, angelic reverence, fingers fumbling, thumbs all clumsily. Slowly, *don't scare her, don't go too fast,* he undid his clothes where his manhood strained for her. He kissed her, leaned over her, pulled down her pants, then folded his aching sword into her sheathe, lost in the moment, no angel holding him back. Then she started to fight.

Small fists punched his ribs and squirmed with bony knuckles, sharp edged nails to cut till he pulled away. It was so hard to leave her now, so hard to fasten his clothes and turn from her. Sweet, soft and vulnerable, she lay on leaves, but he couldn't finish it, could neither fill her nor empty the pain in himself.

He left because he had to go, because he couldn't hurt her. He wasn't his father. He never saw her wander the woods again where whispering trees still tried to comfort him.

Whispering Trees

Do trees whisper or is it the wind, or animals, or dreams? Amelia stretched her arms to feel the touch of air and drifting cobwebs, bark-dust singing, butterfly wings. Red sunshine warmed the lids of her closed eyes as she started to spin. Her feet scuffed earth, where stones or skeletons of leaves slipped into socks and caught between her toes. She moved as fast as thought while the air, pine-scented, grew earthy and cloudy, scratching in her throat till she fell down. Then wrists and ankles drummed the cold dry ground until they hurt, warm like the sun, crusted like earth, fragile as butterflies.

"Amelia," her mother called.

Amelia knew this voice. It belonged to the warm person who filled her with food, didn't hold too tight, and gave her elbow for comfort in the night. She bent her legs and crawled back onto her knees. But sunshine dappled, whispering through the leaves. Amelia stretched her arms to cradle earth and air and sky, embracing life.

"Amelia!"

When the voice gets louder it means you're going to be filled on the outside too. They'll wrap their arms around and hug till you can't touch the breeze. They'll make you sneeze with other people's smells to fill your throat. They'll say your name and too many sounds will flit and refuse to be words, noise crushing you, no space for whispering trees.

Amelia turned to face the voice and walked back through the woods. Heavy footsteps were her mother running, afraid her daughter had wandered off again. Amelia didn't know that. Heavy breathing announced her mother's panic while Amelia knew no fear.

She knew the trees, the animals, the wind, the whispered dreams, and they were good. But now she must leave because she was a *people*, not a tree.

Amelia didn't know she was autistic, fragile as a butterfly, beautiful and frail as the summer sky.

Alone

Alone in the trees, watching, he knew he couldn't wait forever. His body needed the touch of another's flesh. It had been so long. He needed love.

He watched the students walking back to their dorms, envying couples, following those who were alone. *Had he done this before?* He touched the ones who left the path, touched and kissed, and stroked smooth flesh. Usually they ran away. Once in a while someone would stay with him. A bright young thing might let him play, but her hands would steer him the way she chose, this far she'd say and no further, granting no freedom. Once in a while he'd think he'd found true love, then she'd never return, or else there was solace in one who asked payment in cash.

He watched the tight-dressed, summer-dressed, and imagined their forms underneath. He watched the wide-wrapped, winter-dressed and imagined silk and sugar against their skin. He pictured himself peeling off their layers of clothes, imagined how his body would warm to their heat.

And she? He'd watched the bright smart owner of the art gallery, who stumbled from the path in high-heeled shoes and lost her way. When she called for help he was there for her, and her kiss, her promise to return, were ample reward. Willing and warm, his secret high-class girl, she threw herself naked and wild and welcoming. His manhood restored, life was good. He built a home for her.

Then one day, high-class perfect girl smeared make-up with low-class tears on bleary face. She told him she wanted, she needed, she had to… She told him *he* had to, his fault, and his choice. She said she wanted a child with him, and he couldn't be a father again. *I'm not my father* he told himself *and I'll not risk being anyone's father again.*

She told him, ordered him, bossed him around till her flesh became stone in his hands and her lips turned sour. He dried her makeup with a handkerchief, held a mirror while she cleaned and painted herself. He backed away from the coldness of her touch and couldn't stroke her hair. Smelling the earth instead of her perfume, leaves instead of flesh, he didn't notice when she left.

She died, his secret high-class girl, a secret low-class death. She never came back. His ache without her was greater than ever and crueler than lonesome will. The woods were his only safety these long years now, his secret place where he sighed and dreamed and touched and waited for longing to be filled.

Secret Child

"Amelia!" Evie called her daughter's name again, the story of her life. Thirteen years she'd followed her strange child around. At least Amelia knew her at last, and mother knew child, not quite so vacant, not so completely separate as they'd been. In thirteen years they'd never held a conversation, but the snatches grew more—periods of words making sense to both, more than empty phrases now. Then Amelia would wander off in a dream, painting shadows on air, her mouth delighting to sounds or scenes remembered from cartoons. Or else her mother would walk away in despair, jobs to do, salaries to be earned and lives to be ordered and arranged.

The park was Amelia's favorite place. As a small child she'd undress herself under the trees then walk out naked, all unaware as other children stared. Her mother would cover her quickly in spare garments, carried in her bag. Then she'd walk back into bracken and leaves till they found the missing clothes. "It's just a phase," the doctor said.

When other children learned to talk, Amelia only learned to watch TV. She watched cartoons repeatedly, her favorites bought on tape because they alone kept her misery at bay. Her first words were to recite the whole of a scene from a children's show. It didn't make any sense to Evie, but seemed deep and meaningful in the ears of her child. Evie told herself it didn't matter if she didn't understand. They'd work it out.

When other children went to school, Amelia stayed home. Evie home-schooled with the help of therapists, but not much teaching went on. Amelia understood the strangest things. Writing posed no problem—reading neither, but she knew no meanings to words. She matched pictures to letters and sounds, knew all the flags of countries and states, all the birds and foods and monuments, but didn't know a state was where somebody lived. After all, a state's what little girls get into when they roll in leaves. Amelia knew words can't be trusted not to change their meanings.

At first Evie prayed for a miracle. Then her husband left. Prayer groups adopted Amelia, raising money for trips to doctors and healing conferences. But the prayers weren't answered and people grew tired of hoping and made schedules instead—"Whose turn is it to take Amelia out of Sunday school? Who's willing to give Amelia's Mom a break?" Slowly Evie's prayers changed too. Because Amelia was a real person after all, a child in her own right, different, but herself. Soon Evie wasn't sure she even wanted her daughter to change. Amelia without the autism wouldn't be Amelia.

Does that make me a bad mother?

Each night, Evie prayed for her daughter's safety and her own sanity—each night, and mornings too. "Guard her when she wanders off, Lord. Help her grow up enough so she'll cope when I'm gone. Please don't leave her on her own." Each Sunday she left her child in Sunday school and went home to clean. Each week she wondered, *does that make me a bad Christian?*

Sometimes she prayed she might stay healthy forever to care for her child—her special, holy child. And maybe God answered.

Then for peace, refreshment, and sunshine they'd walk together to the park. Amelia would wander off alone, the trees her company. Sometimes she carried her rabbit and rag doll. Sometimes she left them, always on the bench up on the hill— Evie never knew why and was never allowed to move them but that was all right. She could pretend to be a regular mom, sitting at the bottom of the hill by the pond, talking with other mothers, with regular kids. She enjoyed the innocent screams of joy—sounds that terrorized her child. She delighted in hands reaching trustingly for hugs. She reveled in everyday conversations, diapers and milk and which child was learning to share. Park mothers didn't offer to pray. They didn't wear sad faces and serious frowns. She was still *poor old Amelia's Mom,* still interestingly different, but she felt close enough to the same, close enough to be sane.

Sometimes she called for Amelia and pretended she wasn't afraid. She tried to sound like any other parent, just a mother calling her child. She tried not to panic for all was bound to be well. All *was* well, until it ended.

Amelia Hides

Amelia wasn't hiding. She knew where she was. If you know where something is then it's not hidden.

"Amelia," her mother called, believing it a game. When Amelia walked out from the trees, her mother would say, "I've found you," like she always did—the magic words—*game's ended, time to go home.*

But Amelia wasn't playing a game and she wasn't trying to hide.

Dry leaves and twigs rustled under her feet. If she took off her shoes they'd wrinkle between her toes, but Amelia had learned over the years, taking off your shoes without mother's permission is generally thought to be wrong.

Damp leaves brushed her face. They hung by single delicate legs from traceries of branches like lace across the sky. Amelia liked lace. She liked holding pieces of lace over her face and blowing them. She liked to lace her fingers over her eyes letting light shine through. She drew endless patterns of lace in bright colors on rainbow paper. The leaves enthralled her, so she stepped with her feet, still wearing shoes, in a circle on the ground, face lifted to sky.

Warm sunshine makes the light outdoors. *Cold* light bulbs shine inside. Amelia knew this, though even cold light bulbs are hot. They're not as hot as the sun of course. If they were they'd burn everything up. She'd learned that too, and knew not to try holding light bulbs between her hands. But she *could* hold the sky.

Birds sang music, fluting, high. Children's voices danced in the park beyond the trees. Her mother's voice too, but Amelia tuned it out.

"Amelia, isn't it?" said a voice she didn't know. A man she hadn't seen spoke dark and low. Amelia stopped twirling and turned to him. He wasn't someone she'd met before and she wasn't supposed to talk to strangers.

"Amelia." The man walked toward her, outstretched arms holding tight to emptiness. Something wasn't right. "Amelia, child."

Amelia's feet began to tap. Her hands moved up and down and up and down. Her head shook wildly, hair flying over her face. She closed her eyes. The voice in her mind, the one trying to drown the sounds of the world, said *Go away go away,* but the only sound from Amelia's mouth was a gentle, steady wail. "Ay-ay-ay-ay."

The man came close while Amelia's eyes were closed. She felt his palm on her cheek, fingers pressing her mouth, driving her whimper to silence. She felt his hands, too many hands, stroking and pushing and bending and clasping her. She felt the bark of a tree leave its pattern on her back. *Don't touch. Go away.*

And she was lost.

Thick wetness pressed and slid on Amelia's face, covered her nose, pushed tight-closed lips apart and filled her throat. Thick roaming hands and arms and legs and knees pressed her body to earth.

Amelia *was* hiding now, far far inside her head, where sounds and breath can't touch and she'd never return.

"Amelia, where are you? Amelia!"

Losing Amelia

Park Bench, Scent of Blood, The Mother, Choice

Amelia, he watched her. She'd grown from infant clinging to mother's arm, to child in the woods, undressed and dressed, to the promise of womanhood. *Amelia*, her body nearly formed, innocence complete. *Amelia*, who drank the rain, danced with the leaves and took breakfast with the sun.

"Amelia," he sighed, the perfect bride, untouched, untouchable.

He saw her that day and kept far out of her way, because Amelia wasn't right in her mind. He couldn't talk with her, nor touch her budding flesh—forbidden fruit. Still *she* came to him. She came so close he could smell her berried shampoo over the vines, tasting her fragrant soap over dry autumn leaves. So he knew it was ordained after all. Amelia was his angel, sent for him.

"Amelia," he said. She turned that sweet, oh so sweet, innocent face, that sweet sweet smile.

"Amelia, isn't it?" He held her gently, standing so still, she like a butterfly cupped in his life-giving palms. Her wings vibrated.

"Amelia." He laid her down so softly on the ground, watched the flash of her tiny limbs drum the earth with delight. He stroked and gentled her. He kissed and lapped at her delicate throat, at the hollow so sweet and so round.

Warm flesh she had, translucent, soft as silk, thrilling with life. He moved the cruel restraining clothes aside, handled, sucked, and filled, released himself. He covered her mouth as she cried out, held her with his secret silence, pressed her with his bright eternal power. Ethereal limbs pushed back with unnatural strength, but he knew what she wanted, knew she was made for this, he savored ease.

When he pulled back, when he shifted his weight, the butterfly stayed too still. Amelia lay too quiet on the ground. No pulse under her bruising neck, no throbbing heartbeat pumping in her chest. No breath came out, nor questions in her loosely opened mouth. The scent of blood was ash on fallen leaves where her garments lay discarded.

He dressed rapidly then, faster than ever before. He started to stretch the girl's clothes back on her flesh, but the limbs moved all wrong. With his nails, with palms, with fists, he scooped a hole down under the leaves, dug deep in dirt like a dog hiding a bone. Then he buried her, buried her clothes with his dream, and ran away.

No one knew. No one would know. No one would ever know.

And the mother, still calling Amelia's name in the distance, would never see.

Park Bench

Jeffrey sat in his accustomed place on the park bench on the hill. He bent down awkwardly at the waist, loosing Shamrock from the leash. The child's doll and stuffed rabbit shared the wooden slats with him again. He hoped Amelia wouldn't disturb his rest picking them up. Afternoon sun felt soft and warm on his face, red as wine on the backs of his eyes, while Shamrock's padding paws faded to distance on the grass. Sunday afternoon, in the park, in the sun, sleeping off breakfast—what more could an aging executive want?

Ducks cackled on the distant pond, a whir of insect wings, a splash, and children's voices laughed. He could have been a father here, with children playing at his feet. *If I'd stayed. If I'd married Savannah.* He could have guarded toys for an errant daughter, shared a teddy bears' picnic with rabbit and doll. He dreamed it as he'd dreamed it before, and smiled.

In the distance, penetrating dream and muse, Jeffrey heard Shamrock bark. Perhaps the dog was chasing the white fluffy cat. Jeffrey added images to his dream—father, daughter, son, white cat and a dog. But the barking continued. A woman shouted, urgently, "Amelia." Pretty child, often lost, nothing to worry about. Her mother would stop total strangers on the path, asking with serious face if they knew where to find her. Today the search took longer. Less familiar voices caught the refrain, "Amelia, where are you?" Jeffrey stirred.

Shamrock's barking rose to a frantic crescendo, demanding to be heard. *Better see what's going on.* Jeffrey struggled, swaying, to his feet. He leaned for strength against the back of the bench, looking down on the toys. How long had he slept? He turned to the trees.

A crowd had gathered in the playground down the hill. The white cat streaked toward them from the forest, splashes of red on its fur instead of its collar. But perhaps it was leaves. Jeffrey rubbed his eyes, knowing some nightmare alarm had forced its way into daytime's peace.

The sun, once warm, hid behind a cloud. Jeffrey sagged. In his shadow the toys looked lost and forlorn, as if their missing owner would never return. The doll's red dress turned brown in leaden light. She hugged the rabbit tightly as if afraid.

Something was wrong with the sound of Shamrock's barking. Jeffrey walked down the hill, an aging man, overweight, overtired, overburdened, and wearily concerned. Somewhere the child in his memory wondered if the wrongness was all his fault. Had he dreamt it, with the red sun's blood and red on the white cat's fur, had he dreamed a nightmare?

People shouted, pointing, whispering. Jeffrey joined their throng.

"She's in there. Buried they said."

"The dog found her."

"The cat."

"Who would do such a thing?"

Sirens wailed. Brakes screeched. A police car tore to a halt leaving jagged ditches in soft green grass. Flashing lights reflected red and blue on the darkening sky. Young Kopp, or Grainger, came out from the trees holding Shamrock by the collar.

"Is this your dog, sir?" the policeman asked, Shamrock straining to wrap herself around Jeffrey's knees. Jeffrey fastened her back on the bright red leash, tears on his cheeks because she was found and Amelia lost, such a beautiful girl.

The cat—mud, not blood, in its fur—returned and sat silent to watch. Shamrock lay at Jeffrey's feet. The crowds fell quiet while up on the hill, small doll and rabbit waited. In the trees a mother sobbed hysterically while paramedics soothed.

Scent of Blood

The scent of her, the taste of her, sweet breath through parted lips before she died… Her eyes' pale light, the innocence of her gaze, her darting glance… Ethereal skin, translucent, petal-soft…

The only images his memory could conjure now were flat dead eyes and skeletons of leaves to cover them. He breathed her scent on the breeze but tasted blood and saw decay.

They'd find her soon, find him. They'd find him out.

I am my father after all.

The Mother

Peter sat in his living room, pressing the backs of his hands into his eyes to hide his face. He remembered the smell of his father's breath and the ringing sound of his voice. He remembered the sodden thump like wood on wet earth, his mother's whimpering cries like a kitten in distress. He remembered the taste of blood in the air and thrust his thoughts away with straightened arms. This wasn't right. This wasn't him.

"Don't leave." Was someone calling him? His mother? But she wasn't here. His frantic gaze took in windows—*cover them*—door—*make sure it's locked*—table and chairs. Dreams and reality mixed then tumbled like dinner spilled on the floor. Cold air should wake him. *Go out. Go shopping. Put an end to this.*

He tugged the door awkwardly then stopped, trapped somehow in a gap between yesterday and tomorrow, between outside and in, clinging to the post. Warm air wafted behind from the furnace, cooler breezes ahead. He remembered hiding outside in the cold, under the picnic table in unmowed grass. His body had grown almost too tall to fold into the tiny space. A rotten plank, fallen free long ago, lay splintered by his hand. He thudded it on the ground. "Take that. Take that." Couldn't drown the sound. Later his mother let the cat out—*white cat, black cat, cat with a bright red stone like an eye in its collar*? Peter crept through the yellow light spilling from his parents' back door. He hugged his mother's battered knees as he passed, smelling sweat and blood. Then he stepped around the hulking shape of his father before climbing upstairs.

In the morning Dad still lay like a sodden log left high in the flood. Mom rested under the table, hiding as Peter had outside. He thought she was playing.

"Hey Mom." He tried to share the cramped space but Mom wouldn't move, didn't want him anymore.

"Hey Mom." He kicked her angrily, his booted foot knocking her knees aside. She wasn't dressed underneath. There was blood on her thighs, pooling a sticky puddle on the floor.

"Hey Mom." He pulled the hem of her dress and it tore. Tugging again, he looked in her eyes, blank, unmoving, made of clay, then he knew his world had changed forever.

Outside, he wandered down to the park. He sat on the swings while rain washed away tears. Police cars drove past.

They took his dad. His grandparents took him. And Peter had a happy, normal life, sitting and dreaming of sunshine on park benches, ducks in the pond, and children playing in the rain.

He closed the door behind him and went shopping, not so hard. Then he came home to bed.

Choice

Tires squealed. First noise of the morning. It was time. Peter knew more vehicles would come, but this was just the neighbor's son seeing how fast he could go, the morning ritual. Distant sirens wailed in the crisp morning air. They'd come too, with screeching brakes and voices shouting loud. They'd come, *but not yet*. Not until Peter was ready. It was time.

He'd opened the blinds earlier, but closed them now, perhaps to shut out the sirens, silence the alarm. All they shut out was the faint gray light of day, letting shadows bar the room.

The air smelled fresh and cool. It drifted through the window, past the blinds, bringing birdsong with scents of grass seed, roses, and dawn. Fresh air would help. It would show he cared, make it less unpleasant later. It was time.

Peter stepped back from the window and walked to the bed. He bent down carefully to touch the still form nestling in the center of the covers. He'd expected cold hard steel, alien gray and heavy, dull and solid. Instead it felt cool with the morning's gentleness. He ran his fingers over its silky surface, pressed them into softly rounded edges, oiled, almost damp. He smelled coffee. Before he sat on the bed, he picked up the gun, reverently touched its waiting mouth to his lips. The tip of his tongue tasted it, sweet smooth caramel and something else, deep earthen and cool.

He lay back luxuriously then on the bed, feeling the softness of the duvet, the back of his head cradled with love against the lace-covered pillow. His free hands held the gun over his face, turning it slowly around in front of his eyes. His gaze lingered, longed. He'd never really held a gun before, or looked closely at one—well, maybe once in the shop, but that wasn't him, just the image he projected, Peter the garage guy, wanting to buy some protection.

"Can't be too careful these days, Pete. It's a good decision."

"Yeah, I know."

"Things sure have changed around here."

"They sure have."

Then, the metal had been cold and heavy, even rough in his hands. Now, he smoothed his fingers over silken gray, unblemished and pure, desire stretching and tugging his breath, tensing the muscles of memory under his flesh.

Police sirens echoed on the morning breeze. It was time.

He stretched the moment, imagining how it might play out, reading the future like memory. Would they come today, when he didn't turn up for work? Tomorrow maybe, to see if he was ill? Not his son—his son never came without calling. A stranger then? A neighbor? They'd notice he was missing and call the police. Or the police would come anyway, coming soon.

The open window might keep down the smell. But they'd still come.

Peter touched the gun to his lips, caressing it, savoring one last taste. It seemed almost alive, almost loving in his grasp. He wrapped his mouth like a kiss, close around its shape, swallowing, filled, his finger so very light on the trigger. It was time.

Tires squealed and he heard no more.

***

The car jumped the curb, halting sharply, driver and passenger turning startled eyes to each other.

"What was that?"

"I'm not sure."

"I could swear I saw a flash."

"Where?"

"Up there. In that house. The bedroom I guess. I thought I heard a gun."

"No way, Steve; you were driving."

"I could swear." A white cat marched in front of them, red jewel flashing from its collar. "Hey, that's your cat."

"You could swear? You could dream, Jason. Get going. We're late for work and the cat'll be fine. Garnet knows her way home."

"Yeah. Sorry. Let's go."

***

Tires squealed again in the evening, in the dark, in the gathering gloom. Sirens wailed. Emergency lights flashed and reflected from windows, street lit for Christmas in July. Hard voices shouted, questions rang, complaints and worries and orders poured and shattered the night's reverie.

The truth is the dead have no control over the future. Nothing afterward piped the tune Peter had planned.

Part 7

The Punishment

Hours

Bright Lights, Sorry, Leaving, Soldier

The phone rang just as Troy was getting ready to leave the garage. It had rung all day in fact—just one of those days when nothing seemed to go right. The garage was filled with delayed business, cars and vans to fix, tires to rotate. And Troy's father hadn't turned up to work. Troy called Lydia in the morning. "Just pop around, please. Check if my dad's okay." But she said there was nobody home.

"Did you go in?" She didn't have a key. "Sorry, love. Busy day. I'll see you."

The phone kept ringing with customer orders, deals to be made, deliveries and complaints. Troy soldiered on, long after David and the other new mechanics had gone, long and late till darkness fell and street lights blazed outside. Then he switched the buzzing workshop sign to closed, stripped off his green overalls and locked the door.

He had just waved goodbye to David's Carla, newly employed as night manager, when she called, "Sir, Mr. Markham." If she'd been working there longer she'd have known not to bother Troy now, not when the day's done, but she held out the phone. "Sorry, Mr. Markham. It's a Mr. Lee, says he's got to speak to you. He says it's urgent. Please." So Troy took the call.

He wondered at first. *Mr. Lee?* He wasn't a customer, not one of today's customers anyway. Troy didn't think he had any friends called Lee either.

"Troy Markham, right?" said the stranger's voice. Troy agreed, cautiously. "It's Dyson Lee. Your wife knows my wife,

Sapphire Greenwood? She's on the newspaper? Our kids, my Nate and your Jeremy, or Tracey, or, I dunno—they're in the same class, right?"

Then Troy recognized him, or at least he recognized the names of his children.

"Your Lydia's taking the kids to our place," Dyson said, then hurried on, not leaving time for complaint. "I can be with you in five minutes. I'll pick you up."

"What?" Troy asked. "Pick me up why? What's going on?"

The stranger asked if he really hadn't heard—said he hated to be the one to tell him. Dyson Lee, who Troy barely knew, announced Troy's father's suicide.

Troy held the phone away from his face in shock. *No way!*

Words dripped down the line. "Sapphire heard." *What sort of a name is Sapphire?* "Heard through the paper. Got contacts I guess. I really am sorry." *Sorry for what?* The phone fell silent and Troy held onto the receiver like something broken, beyond repair.

Bright Lights

Colored lights splashed and reflected off windows in fairground abandon while emergency vehicles blocked the road. Dyson drove slowly past the junction with Troy, gazing out the window, hunched in the seat beside him. A little further and Dyson pulled the car to a halt under a street light, turning to his passenger.

Troy wasn't even a friend, just an acquaintance, his sister-in-law's neighbor, but his presence dominated the car. His body filled the small front seat, sickening the air with fumes of oil and grease. Troy's hair hung limp over hooded eyes while long-fingered hands clenched on the dash. He made no move, scarcely breathed.

"So what now?" asked Dyson.

"I don't know." Troy's voice spat sparks.

Dyson gazed out the window, unsure what to suggest. "You

should call your wife," he tried eventually, holding out his new cell phone, but Troy shook his head. "Okay well, how 'bout I call Sapphire instead?"

Dyson pulled out the aerial, pressed buttons, listened, and spoke. "Yeah," he agreed. "Invite them to stay over. You can fit them all in can't you?" As he hung up, he faced his reluctant guest. "You're all staying the night. Sapphire says it's best."

Troy didn't reply.

Cars passed in the dark, no one looking, everyone heading someplace else where authorities don't lurk. But Dyson knew someone would notice them soon. He put the car in gear, drove slowly forward, while Troy stayed still. Then he spotted an alleyway and stopped.

"Troy." Dyson tapped the younger man's arm, making him look up through his curtain of hair. Troy's eyes seemed lost. "Listen Troy, I know a back way. D'you have a key?" Troy continued to look blank. "A back door key? To your dad's? Do you have a key?"

Troy shook his head, rubbing thin fists against his eyes.

"Doesn't matter I guess. The police'll let you in. But you can skip the gauntlet of neighbors if you go around the back." Dyson explained the alley connected with one behind Troy's father's house—too much time spent studying real estate with Charlie paying off for once. "Just turn left at the *T*." Troy struggled out the car, his body too long, too stooped for the confined space, and too defeated. Then Dyson offered a flashlight. "You might need this."

He watched through the window as Troy disappeared. Flashes of red and blue still lit up the clouds. Heavy clouds. Heavy fear. Though the young man wasn't a friend, Dyson feared for him.

"Call me," he shouted, flinging open the door and stretching over the car so his voice would carry. "Use your dad's phone. I'll wait for you."

Troy looked back, nodded and straightened, as if a phone call felt solid enough to wake him from his dream.

Dyson sighed. This was a nightmare. He rested his head on

the steering wheel, wishing he could have told Troy the whole story, the one Sapphire poured out when she asked him to help. But Sapphire only called it suspicion. Not the sort of suspicion you raise with a man who's lost his father. Dyson couldn't have said it, still hoped it wasn't true.

So now, all unknowing, Troy entered the nest of vipers. The police wouldn't be as gentle in their telling. Dyson sighed—could have given him a warning, a hint. *How do you hint something like that?*

The leather cover of the steering wheel pressed into his forehead, filled his nose with its scent. Dyson whispered an unaccustomed prayer. Then, though grown men don't cry, though Troy was barely an acquaintance and his father a stranger, and though Dyson hadn't even known the dead girl, he started to sob.

Sorry

Troy stumbled, flashlight in hand, to the back of his father's house. Fresh air woke him, but he'd rather have stayed asleep. *Dad's really gone?* The splash of red and blue over the house looked like a warning, his ending of days.

He reached over the gate for the catch and pushed his way in, walked up the path, lights blazing, house wide awake when it should have been asleep, smelled sweet lavender and cool damp earth.

A policeman opened the door to him. Not someone Troy knew. Not Joe Grainger, bridge-playing neighbor, though Troy thought maybe he could hear his voice somewhere in the house.

"I'm Troy," he introduced himself. "I'm the son."

"We've been looking for you."

"I wasn't hiding."

He found himself escorted through his father's kitchen, offered water. Not coffee. His father hadn't put coffee on even though he had visitors. *That's because he's dead. He'll never put it on.* In the living room they offered Troy his father's chair. Someone else sat in his. Someone he didn't know.

"We'll take you upstairs in a minute, sir." Who would take him? Why?

Troy heard a familiar cough nearby.

"Hi Troy." His neighbor acknowledged him, lifting a reluctant hand. "Sorry about this." Joe said something about identifying the body and they all went into the hall, upstairs, up Troy's father's stairs, not part of the house where Troy was accustomed to tread. In the bedroom, the body had his father's hands and ring—why did he bother to wear it?—blood on the bed-sheets and wall.

Troy gagged. Downstairs again, he had only a stumbling memory of how he'd got there. They talked about evidence, suspicions, *things* they'd found. He didn't listen, didn't care. "Troy, you have to hear this, son. I'm sorry."

Not your son. "Have to hear what?"

The other cop, Darryl, too young, too smooth, too smiling, seemed slickly sure. He sat Troy down and talked about the girl in the park, Paradise Predator changed to Murderer, and witnesses.

"Who? What?"

"Where was your father the afternoon of…?"

How should he know? What witnesses?

They talked about the dead girl's underwear, which made no sense. They'd found her pants in a drawer, lots of pants, lots of girls. *What girls? What did they mean?*

Someone had coffee in a thermos and gave Troy a cup. It tasted plastic. Then Darryl shook his hand and said he was leaving. Troy hadn't strength to check his watch. *Leaving what? Time to go home?*

He stared around the room. His father's cup should be on the table, not those bright reams of paper. His father should be in the kitchen where strangers walked, too busy in too bright lights, all staring at him. He gazed at the blinds—did his father close them, or the police?—at the television's empty face beneath its rabbit-ears, at videos they'd shared. His father should sit on this sofa, not Troy, should be eating takeout and watching the news. But perhaps he *was* the news.

Knowing nothing, less than nothing, Troy wondered if anything he thought he knew was real. But he answered questions, mouth on automatic pilot, brain asleep.

"Good luck," shouted Joe as Darryl left.

I'm the one needing luck.

Then Joe said he'd drive Troy to the station.

Why? "I've got a friend," said Troy, remembering Dyson. "Waiting for me."

"Call him then."

Troy went to his father's phone, on its table under the window, but Joe offered his. "More private," he said, though Troy guessed he just wanted a record of the number. He had to stand in the back yard to find a signal, skulking in shadows next to yellow light still streaming from the door. Then he didn't know Dyson's number, scarcely knew his name, or how to find it.

"Sapphire Greenwood?" he suggested when Joe offered to help. Joe brought the number out scribbled on paper, then stood in the doorway while Troy talked. *Is he listening? He's my neighbor. Doesn't he trust me?*

"We'll go the back way," Joe said afterward. "No need to go through the house." They set off together down more dark alleyways till they got to Joe's car. Troy wasn't even sure which road they were on. More bright lights, streetlamps illuminating truth and interrogating pain. At the station Joe drove to the rear parking lot. He told Troy to sit up straight "like you're meant to be here. Don't let the jackals spot you."

The station itself felt like school. Tiled floors disappeared into shadow. Strip lights shone overhead. Cream-painted classrooms were stacked with tables and chairs, and the smell of disinfectant bled everywhere. Joe showed him the bathroom—"Go clean yourself up"—then led Troy to a table where more plastic coffee and store-bought cookies waited, too sweet, too sticky with vanilla in the air.

More questions, more papers, more signatures. Troy was

cold and tired and lost.

Afterward Joe offered to drive him home though Troy would just as happily have laid his head on the desk. "Not home," he answered sitting halfway up with long hair covering his face. "We're staying with friends," but he couldn't remember the place, had to look it up in the phone book.

"It's good you're not going home," said Joe. "I called Karen. Press camped out on your front yard. Have been for hours." As they left he made Troy hide his face and crouch down in his seat, just in case *they* were looking. "No reason to make it easy for them. No one to follow if they don't see you."

Leaving

The papers were full of stories about the girl. Everyone knew. Television too. *Little girls shouldn't die*, Marcie thought, *and husbands shouldn't go to war,* but perhaps it was heartless and cruel, to think of herself at such a time.

Newspapers quoted Joe and Darryl saying nothing, silent policemen investigating heinous crime. *Policeman Darryl. That's what you are,* Marcie thought, *what you've always been.* But Darryl's only conversation these days centered on packing and planning and going away. He'd leave her tomorrow.

"I got held up," he'd said on the phone. She'd come home early to make a special dinner and he got held up. At least he'd phoned. The TV was scrolling a message of breaking news in the Paradise case but Marcie couldn't be bothered to turn up the sound.

She'd put down the phone and stood by the dining room table, their goodbye dinner going dry in the oven, candles burned to ribbons of wax while wine glasses gathered dust. It looked like dust anyway. She wiped it with a finger, left a smear, wiped the smear with a tissue. Then, because the newspaper was there—she always left it by Darryl's plate; he always wanted to read it—Marcie turned her attention to the front page.

They'd printed a good picture; fat man Jeffrey Irons from the big construction firm in town—she'd seen him around the park sometimes, lumpy blob on the hill on his tiny wooden bench. His dog sat at his feet, the red setter's fur offsetting the owner's incipient baldness. A human interest piece at the side told why he'd named it Shamrock for good luck. *What's luck got to do with it?*

Meanwhile a newsman on TV pointed glaring lights at the front door of a house. *What's he saying?* Marcie crossed the room to hear. "No news yet about the family…" *When did no news become news?* She turned the sound down again.

Evening fell. The dining room's yellow light dripped through the window onto bones of dead grass. She should pull the curtains, or wish for four-leaf clover in the lawn. Luck to keep her husband home. Luck to protect *her* child.

"You'll cope fine without me," Darryl told her over and again.

"How do you know I'll cope?"

"You don't need me. You always say I'm never here."

So why did it hurt so much that he was going?

"I'm serving my country, Marcie. I'm doing good."

Why not do good for your family instead?

Car tires scraped on gravel outside. Car radio music flared and went silent. Darryl was home.

Marcie listened to the key in the lock and leaned over the paper, pretending absorption. It really was a catchy headline she thought. *Death in Paradise.* They must have been thrilled at the excuse to print it.

Darryl threw his coat on the chair before announcing, "Guess what? We caught him."

"Who?" She tried not to look interested.

"The Paradise Murderer. It's Peter Markham. You know, the garage guy."

"No!"

"Oh but it is." Darryl sounded so smug. "We got proof. *And* he killed himself."

Marcie drew back with a gasp, trying to process the words.

Peter Markham was young Jeremy's granddaddy surely, grandfather to their own dear son's best friend. Didn't Lydia's husband work in the garage with him too? Didn't Jeremy and Robert play at the garage sometimes? Bile filled her throat.

"No Darryl, no!" Too many truths, too many ramifications to comprehend. But Darryl sat down at the table with the paper as if he didn't care, just waiting for dinner.

"The candle needs relighting," Marcie said hopefully. Darryl didn't move.

Marcie carried the food from the oven, thick gloves over her hands. She almost forgot to put it down. *Peter Markham, as unlikely a killer as the fat man on the hill.* He played catch with Jeremy and Robert in the park at the last school picnic. He gave Robert a handful of shiny metal washers when Marcie's car broke down. He played ring-a-roses, though not willingly, with Robert at Jeremy's party. He'd stood separate from Jeremy's grandmother, who smiled at another man.

Okay, so they weren't a completely normal family, but they weren't so strange. They weren't killers. *Killers don't have grandsons who play with your son.* She began to hope she'd never see them again.

And that ordinary house on TV where camera crews waited, where no news was news? Was that Lydia's house? *I've been there. I've drunk their coffee.* It couldn't be.

Still Darryl insisted Peter Markham had killed the girl then killed himself.

So now... thought Marcie, the casserole hot and heavy in her hand.

So now... She almost let it drop as she placed it next to the newspaper on the table.

So now... When the safe world around her was falling apart—when a coffee-drinking friend, who shopped at the same stores as her, was married to the son of a murderer—when her own sweet child who hardly knew his dad was best friends with a murderer's grandson—*so now* Darryl was off to fight foreign wars because the travails of home weren't enough for him?

They didn't discuss the murder or the army over dinner, just ate in silence. In bed Marcie held her husband so tight she might break him. Maybe she'd break a nail to remember him by.

Soldier

Darryl slept through the alarm in the morning. His last lie-in. Marcie looked down at his sleeping face, eyes closed, dark lashes in smooth half-moons, hair cropped like Robert's after a hair-cut gone wrong. She couldn't bear to disturb him because once he woke she'd know he was leaving.

Breakfast took place among the detritus of last night's dinner. Marcie kept the radio and TV turned off because she didn't want Robert hearing the news. In the silent room her thoughts switched from murder to war to betrayal to school. Warm scents of last night's steak hovered over the milk. Unwashed pots filled the sink.

"Eat your breakfast, Robert." The boy pushed flakes around their bowl with his spoon while Marcie kept up the pretense of an ordinary day. Transformers on his lunch box posed bright and dangerous, flashing guns with explosions red and black. Their own private war. The clock ticked on.

"Time to go." Marcie handed her son his bright backpack, heavy with books he barely even glanced at when doing his homework. She kissed the top of his head, remarked how he'd grown, and told him to take care.

"Will Dad still be here when I come home?"

"I don't know son. I don't know what time he leaves."

"D'you think he'll say goodbye?"

"He did, last night."

"I was asleep," Robert protested. "Will he say it again?"

Marcie sighed. "I don't know, sweetheart, but you've got to go. You'll miss your bus." She should have woken Darryl up for the boy's sake after all.

He walked the path, head down, shoulders sloping under the weight of his father's betrayal and his pack. Marcie stood in the doorway feeling lost. She could have walked with him just this once. He would have let her join him today, wouldn't have minded her standing with him at the bus stop while he waited. Then she could watch and keep him safe because the world was falling apart, and little girls died.

But Darryl would wake up soon. If she wasn't here he might just leave forever without saying goodbye.

Heavy footsteps on the stairs drew Marcie's gaze from the street. She threw a final wave to her son—he'd almost reached the corner—then turned away. Darryl's hand pressed on her shoulder. His voice boomed past her ear. "'Bye, son. Be good. Take care of your mother while I'm gone."

Robert waved, sorrow and joy warring in his little soldier's face as the bus approached, and Darryl closed the door.

"So Marcie. Aren't you proud of me, Sweet?"

She fell into his arms and cried.

Days

Friends, Chocolate Kisses, Circus, Hiding Place

Dyson, his friend, gives him a beer, cold and fresh, straight from the fridge. Troy drinks it down. Sapphire offers coffee. He drinks that too. Sometimes Sapphire gives him food. Sometimes Lydia tries to give him a kiss.

Sometimes Troy has to move from the sofa. He switches the TV off or goes to sleep. Children cry. Troy hides behind the beer and crazy circus of childhood games. No pattern's left to anything in life, no night or day, no yesterday or tomorrow, only this, and he'll take another beer. "Yes. Thanks." Maybe he hears his father's voice in his head, his father's intonation in the sound of his speech. He doesn't like hearing.

Pop the lid with a smacking sound and lift the can to lips. Drink might drown the memories and carry him away, or bury him.

Remember Dad lifting me high in the sky? He's flung me down.

The dining table has too many plates, too many knives and forks. Nothing makes sense. And a man whose father kills is hardly a man.

Friends

Pattie's husband tossed the newspaper across the table. It landed by her breakfast plate, narrowly missing the cereal bowl. "Wasn't he married to that friend of yours?" Dan asked accusingly.

"Who?" Pattie glanced down. The headline read *Death in Paradise* in large black letters. Underneath was something about a murder suspect committing suicide. Dan really didn't bother with sensational tales, so she turned the paper over in her hands, seeking some innocent side column with mention of someone she knew.

"No, Pattie." Dan pointed to the middle of the page. The spoon Pattie held clattered to the table. "Ring any bells?"

Peter Markham, she read in amazement. *Poor Mary's husband.*

Food turned to dust in Pattie's mouth and she gulped for air. Cereal, forgotten, dissolved into murk in the milk. The scent of coffee grew sulfurous. She let it steam untouched and forced her eyes to read the column, barely remembering the words as each sentence crawled by, then returning to the start.

"Drink your coffee." But the cup shook too much when she touched it.

"I didn't mean to upset you." But he wouldn't understand.

Dan cleared the table noisily around her. She heard the whir of the disposal trashing sodden cornflakes, listened to the sucking sound of the fridge, the perilous thunk of last night's wine-bottle falling over in the door. *Will Dan remember to prop it up again with the milk's half-gallon?* She didn't care to ask.

The dishcloth rustled and squeaked as he wiped the table. Dan *never* wiped the table. Then he tugged the paper from Pattie's hands and pointed to the phone. "Go talk to her."

Pattie wanted to refuse. "She'll not want to talk to me," she muttered, standing lost, halfway between her chair and the wall. When Dan protested that of course she would, Pattie continued lugubriously, "We exchange Christmas cards, Dan. That's all. We used to meet before Dad died but not anymore. Mary quit her job. I didn't need to visit. There just wasn't the occasion." She would have said the same words whether Dan was listening or not, Peter's name in the paper bringing back memories in a way notes on Christmas cards couldn't. Mary wouldn't talk to her *ever* again, or exchange cards.

Pattie remembered Mary's first trip to Paradise. She saw her surprise again at the hopeful name on the sign, the light of possibility dawning in her friend's dear eyes—she could live without her spouse, *but maybe Peter couldn't live without her.* Mary's suspicion of the old folk's home, Mary's nervousness around her dishy neighbor, Mary in love, her supremely confident step when they visited parents together at Paradise House, her loving support when she attended Pattie's father's funeral.

"You'll stay in touch?" They'd hugged tautly, determinedly, making promises only Christmas cards would keep.

"Come visit sometime."

And so these days they exchanged their empty messages seasonally, memories of friendship. Pattie didn't know how to change those memories into fact. *So, your ex-husband's a murderer is he?* How would you even imagine starting such a conversation?

Pattie tossed the paper into the trash and Dan rescued it. He turned it over with barely another glance at the glaring headline. Pages fluttered. His morning dose of puzzles.

"Six letters. Word for a cat?"

"Feline." Pattie answered automatically. Dan wrote it down.

"Red stone."

"Ruby? Garnet?"

"Perfect place."

"Heaven I guess." *Paradise has too many letters,* Pattie thought, *and too many sins.*

Her hand hovered over the phone on the wall, not wanting to call her friend. She wanted her mother, a phone call through time, a message from the dead. If Pattie was a child, perhaps she'd just cry, something precious broken, *Mommy, mend it.* A child wouldn't feel like the snake who'd sent disaster to Paradise. A child wouldn't have betrayed her friend with a kiss and stolen joy. She wanted to cry sodden tears on her mother's ample bosom, be a little girl again. "It's all right," Pattie's mother would say, and Pattie would sob till tears washed her sorrows away. Then friendship would mend and rebuild itself as childhood friendships did.

Dan, who of course would never understand, wrapped his arms gently around his wife. He rested his chin on the tight gray curls of her head. "It's all right, Pattie," he said. "It's not your fault. It's nothing to do with you."

His arms held comfort. His love survived and didn't change. Pattie realized he might understand after all.

"Phone her," said Dan. "She might need a friend. That fellow she goes around with, he might not be who she wants to talk to. You might be just the tonic she needs, our Pattie. Just give her a call."

Her fingers remembered the number, even though her mind had forgotten. Then the phone rang so long Pattie was ready to give up, till the receiver clicked.

"Hi Mary." She almost shouted the words in her hurry to be heard.

"Pattie? Is that you?" Her friend's voice whispered, dull and lost, dispirited. "Good to hear from you." *Not so good.*

Pattie stumbled, wondered what to say. "I just thought…"

"Peter killed someone. I can't hardly believe it."

"Me neither, you poor thing."

"And then he killed himself."

Mary sounded so vacant and far away, it wasn't hard for Pattie to think what to say. "D'you need a place to stay?"

"Oh Pattie. Would you?"

The two friends sobbed down the long trailing lines of the phone as Dan went to the car.

"Mary love, we'll come and get you. Be right there."

Chocolate Kisses

In the school playground, Nate Greenwood announced that Jeremy was now his little brother.

"Not so little," said Jeremy, looking slightly disturbed.

"Why not? I'm older than you."

"Not by much you're not."

Young Robert Kopp stood in a corner of the playground to watch.

Karen Grainger was on playground duty today. She knew Robert's frown. He was mad, justifiably mad. His dad had only just gone off with the army, and now his best friend was hanging around with someone else instead of him. There'd be trouble soon.

Meanwhile Jeremy's little brother Jay struggled to get away from young Tracey Greenwood over by the swings.

"Jacey's my big brother now," Tracey sang merrily, her voice a younger version of her cousin Alison's, her face the same except for coloring and eyes.

"No I'm not." Pugnacious fists grew tight.

"Jacey sleeps at my house."

The smaller boy stiffened as crowds gathered around. "I'm not Jacey. I'm Jay," he complained, but the chants started up as they'd done when Tracey first joined kindergarten.

"Jacey's a gi-irl. Jacey's a gi-irl."

Karen coughed loudly and stared at them, the bow-and-arrow stare of a teacher preparing to let loose, so the children fell silent. Jay and Tracey began to discuss something else, and the others wandered off. *Disaster averted.*

Meanwhile the noise from Jeremy's end of the playground grew louder. Robert had come out from his corner and mouthed something fierce at his friend. Karen struggled to hear.

"…murderer. Your daddy's a murderer."

Not his father—his grandfather, Karen thought. Jeremy didn't react except to retreat to a safe place behind Nate's shoulder.

"Your daddy's a bad, bad man. He's a sicko. He's evil."

Robert circled Nate and Jeremy as he spoke. Others joined the song. Karen sped toward them as shouts began. "Fight. Fight. Fight. Fight."

Suddenly Robert lay on the ground with Jeremy standing over him.

"You going to murder me then?" Robert squealed, losing control of his voice. "You're a murderer too!"

Nate pulled Jeremy back, but he broke free before Karen could take over. Both boys began to punch and brawl and Karen tore them apart, scarcely bigger than they were but with more authority.

"Robert Kopp," she bellowed. "Go stand over there." She pointed toward the older kids' corner of the building. "And Jeremy Markham, that way," pointing to the younger kids' corner this time.

"But I didn't…"

"It was him…"

"He started it."

Karen's breath blew wild and heavy, pumping the sound of authority into her voice. "I don't care who started it," she bellowed, "but I'm telling you it's finished. Now!" The children weren't used to little Mrs. Grainger shouting. They hurried obediently to their spots, stumbling in confusion and dismay.

Karen drew breath—long, slow, deep breaths. She hated pretending to lose her temper with the kids. Poor Jeremy hardly knew what was going on, and couldn't go home because of all the reporters camped in his yard. And Robert? The poor child's world was falling apart—just falling in different directions from his friend's.

Jay stared aghast at his brother's disgrace. The younger boy's lip began to wobble. His little world grew fragile too, with his perfect big brother suddenly in trouble, his beloved father silent with a grief no one should suffer, and his grandfather dead. Karen called him over and reached into the depths of her purse.

"Here Jay." She scribbled a note for his teacher. "I need you to take this to Mrs. Williams please. Can you do that for me?"

Jay nodded solemnly, while Karen finished the words. *Jen. Can you cheer him up? Give him something to do. He's having a tough time.*

She reached two chocolate kisses from the bottom of her bag and tucked them in the note. "Those are for when you get there," she said to the wide-mouthed, wide-eyed boy. "One for you, and one for Mrs. Williams. You got that, Jay?"

Small dark head nodded, hair flopping over his eyes just like his father's, just like his grandfather's. Then Jay skipped off as if life were suddenly lighter. Jay was young enough still, Karen thought, safe enough still for chocolate to heal everything. Jeremy though, scowling red-faced under red hair at his friend—he'd have a harder time.

Circus

Amethyst made sure they walked on the opposite side of the road after school, away from the cameras and media circus laid out on her neighbor's front lawn. *They'll squash Lydia's plants, break her rose bushes*, she thought. It distracted her from other things on her mind.

"But Mom. When's Jeremy coming home?" Alison tugged her arm, pointing, getting noticed by the crowds. Amethyst tried to silence her behind a car. "But Mom."

She crouched to whisper to her daughter, "Later. Don't talk here."

"Why not?"

"Because they're listening."

"Who?"

"The newspaper people. Out there on Jeremy's lawn."

"But Auntie Sapphire's a newspaper people too."

"I know. Please hush."

Someone had seen them. Footsteps crunched as Amethyst rose to her feet. A stranger thrust a microphone toward her face, his voice talking faster than her weary brain could process. Alison had grown way too big to be carried, long and lanky, mop-topped weed with knobby knees, but Amethyst lifted her like a shield and hurried on. "Excuse me. We're going home."

"But… but…" She refused to hear.

In the house, after slamming the door, Amethyst set her daughter on the floor. "Sorry, love," she muttered and leaned with her back to the frame and the wide world outside.

Alison rested hands on hips, asking again, "So, when's he coming home?"

"Kitchen." Amethyst steered her through the doorway, drawing the blinds at the window though it was still day. She poured soda into a glass and placed it on the table in front of her daughter, then set the coffee gurgling. Alison slurped through a bendy straw while Amethyst wrapped her hands around an empty mug and drew breath.

"Jeremy's grandpa did something bad," Amethyst began.

"Yes Mom, I know that."

"So Jeremy's family is hiding."

"Why?"

"Because…"

"They didn't do anything, Mom."

Ah, the innocence of youth. She tried to explain to her daughter, or the coffee maker, or herself, how the media worked. She wasn't sure it really helped to know Sapphire was part of their world, even if her sister was doing her best to help.

Everyone wanted to talk to the family now, Amethyst explained. To Troy and Lydia and Jeremy and Jay and Josh— to Amethyst too, it seemed, and Alison, and anyone else they could find. Everyone wanted to ask how they felt, or tell them how to feel, to wonder if they knew and ask how they thought they couldn't have known. The media wanted someone to blame, and people to turn into victims. They wanted tears and anger and sound-bites and quotes. They wanted pictures.

"We've got pictures Mom. We could give them some and then they'd go away. Then Jeremy'd come home."

"They want pictures of him crying love, not playing in the yard."

"But that's not fair."

"That's why his family's hiding."

Alison slurped to the bottom of her drink and wriggled down from the chair. "But Mom, couldn't they just find them when they go to school instead?"

"Let's hope they don't. Maybe there's a law against it. Maybe they don't know to look for Auntie Sapphire's van."

Alison set off with her backpack upstairs.

"Homework before toys."

"Yes Mom. I know."

Amethyst looked at the phone, a squat green frog on the windowsill. She'd been shopping during her lunch break earlier. Just a quick dash to the supermarket. Poor Savannah Steepleton was there, hiding her face behind that ridiculous scarf, racing down aisles as if she hoped no one would recognize her. Amethyst wanted to ask if she'd heard any news, then realized she'd sound just like a reporter.

"Mrs…"

"Shush." Frozen peas, frozen stare.

"I'm sorry."

"I'm not here." Frozen lips, frozen frown.

"Yes, okay. I see."

"I'm just praying nobody thinks to talk to the children." The older woman danced to unheard music of a funeral dirge.

"How d'you mean?"

"The children in school. The papers are going to get them."

"I hope not."

"You should pray for them too." Her voice cracked earnestly. "They'll be after your little girl. You mark my words."

Maybe Savannah wasn't really so mad. Maybe everyone should hide their faces these days. And maybe Amethyst really should worry about school—especially if even Alison thought it a problem. But she wasn't into prayer. Still, she could check with her sister later, see if she knew why the newspapers hadn't moved to the school gate, see if Lydia wanted clothes picked up for the boys. She didn't know how she'd get into the house if she did. Maybe leap over the garden fence—send Garnet to sneak through a window somewhere. She smiled at the thought, then felt guilty for not feeling bad.

Would Sapphire and Lydia be home from school yet with the children? She picked up the phone.

Hiding Place

A generous offer, impulsively made—Sapphire was constantly amazed at how small her once large house now felt around her, like living back in their old apartment again. She'd just talked with her sister on the phone. Now she tapped out an article on her office computer, trying to meet a deadline. Nate and Tracey ran wild underfoot. Jeremy sulked in a corner. Jay and Joshua chased the dog who staggered, far too old now for such games. Lydia tried so hard to help in the kitchen, but never put anything back in its right place. Meanwhile Dyson and Troy sat watching everlasting television shows.

When the canned reporter's voice fell silent, Sapphire knew the news must be about Troy's Dad again. Dyson always turned down the sound to protect the kids. She strained her ears then went back to typing. The article finished, Sapphire checked, rechecked, then plugged in the phone. *Imagine if you could write to friends as well as employers this way.* Time to get the dinner made.

Their kitchen was Sapphire's pride and joy, newly remodeled just before they bought the house. A brightly-lit room with sunlight streaming through windows during the day, flat lighting at night, it loomed dark and gloomy now—too crowded, too disorganized. The island felt cramped with so many plates, so many mouths to feed. Cupboards opened in all the wrong directions. Drawers were too close to the floor— she'd had to move her knives to the worktop to keep them from Joshua. Now she worried Nate and Jeremy might play with them.

It was a kitchen made for a house, not a hotel, but she'd had to let them stay. Sapphire knew how things worked. But for the friendship of children and parents, she might have camped on their lawn like everyone else, awaiting the perfect picture, the earth-shattering interview. Visiting reporters had come from all over the state—even some nationals. TV crews had staked their space too, but at least they'd moved on, their lights and uber-cameras needed elsewhere. Only reporters remained.

Lydia looked like a puppy whipped once too often whenever she saw the TV or a headline. She couldn't even watch children's programs or read a magazine. So Sapphire welcomed her unwelcome help, wondering if her friend was going to break, or if she'd make it after all.

The TV sound turned up suddenly and they heard Peter Markham's name. Lydia and Sapphire caught each other's eyes. Beneath their hands were plates of chili and rice. Between their eyes was the knowledge, this couldn't go on.

"Switch that thing off!" Sapphire shouted. Dyson leapt to obey while young Jeremy slunk away into a corner.

"Dinner's ready," added Lydia, neither servant nor guest. Then everyone sat, elbow to elbow, around the big dining table.

"Can we go home soon?" asked Jay, eating a mouthful of beans.

"Soon," said Lydia.

Sapphire suddenly guessed a way to make it true. "Can I talk to you? When the kids go off?"

After dinner, they fought the usual evening battle sending children to sleep. The older boys shared Nate's happy room, Nate in bed and Jeremy on cushions on the floor, next to Nate's railway. Jay and Joshua shared the single pink bed, one small head on a pillow at each end, in Tracey's room—*no playing with the dolls*, Tracey commanded—no touching anything. Tracey slept on an inflatable mattress in the walk-in closet. It took forever to settle them all down.

Troy and Lydia sat on the sofa together, hands never

touching, motionless eyes, like Nate's model robots when the batteries ran down.

The muted TV muttered its weary drone while Sapphire and Dyson strolled in from the kitchen after washing up. "We need to talk," Sapphire said again. Dyson faced her, questioning, but Troy lolled listlessly. "If Lydia gives me an interview…" She held out a hand to silence instant objections, making them wait. "I'm saying *if*. But *if* she gives me an interview and *if* they print it, maybe the press will go away. No scoops to wait for anymore."

Lydia stared, blank-eyed, betrayed.

"I'm just saying. Then you could go home."

After talking, they agreed reluctantly it might be a good idea. Troy still said nothing, eyes never leaving the safety of the flickering screen. Troy's hands held the beer can, moved it to his mouth and back, no need to swallow because it was empty. Both Sapphire and Lydia struggled not to cry when they looked at him.

"Need a refill?" Dyson offered and Troy held out a hand, no word of thanks.

"You think we might even get home this weekend?" Lydia asked, eyes gleaming with a first faint glimmering of hope.

Sapphire nodded, and they retired to the computer, planning what to say.

"It'll be good for the kids," said Lydia, rolling her wedding ring nervously around on her finger. "Be good for you too, but you've been marvelous."

A generous offer, impulsively made, Sapphire wasn't trying to get rid of them, but life had to get back to normal or else she'd go mad.

Weeks

Chipped Teacup, Garage Days, Love Promises, Broken Chairs

Troy loved them, but there comes a time when you wonder if love is enough. He saw the hurt in his family's eyes—all his fault. His father's son, he haunted their lives the same way he haunted their home—not *his* home now. Deserving nothing he told himself they'd all be better off if he went away.

Give him the chipped teacup at dinner. Sit him on the broken chair. Send him out to the garage to work and know he'll break every promise love ever made.

Deserving nothing, he dug a hole for memories all turned false. Dad dropped him and he'd never fly again.

Chipped Teacup

Lydia found her husband in the back of the garage, sitting in an old broken chair they'd meant to throw out. He cradled his head in his hands, feet resting against a box on the floor, chipped teacups, cracked plates, the detritus of years. She had no words for him.

Standing by the kitchen door, warm sunlight shining from behind, cold darkness ahead, she peered into the gloom. Now she'd found Troy, crouched in the shadow of the car, she felt like she wanted to keep searching. Not here. Not in the dark. Not in the smells of rubber and oil with cobwebs catching her hair. She didn't know where she wanted to find him, but she knew she needed light to comfort her.

Words of greeting clogged her throat like a dirty dishcloth.

Troy didn't move, didn't even raise his head, though he must have heard her there. Did he wish her someplace else, wish her out of his life? Would he wipe out the whole of their existence together, and was that what his father had done, their oldest son barely older now than Troy when his dad left. Was it over? Was it done?

Lydia saw the paper jammed into the crack between box and wall, almost hidden at Troy's side, another newspaper article pushed away. Something else he didn't want the children to read.

"But they don't read the papers," she'd protested before. "They're too young."

"They'll never get to read it."

"They will when they're older."

"They'll never know."

"But they already know."

Her fluent tongue was dry with dust, so she turned back, coughing, into the kitchen. She stumbled to the sink, turned the faucet with fingers suddenly shaky and weak and cumbersome. Cool water flowed fresh on her hands, on her face, smooth and soft on her tongue. She sipped from cupped palms, chipped cups of living flesh. Her body trembled as she leaned against the cupboard for support, smelled the drain and decay, chlorine's sharp incense washing tears away. She smelled soap and dish detergent, stale coffee, and she gagged.

When Lydia returned to the garage he was gone, leaving the paper, the box of chipped crockery, the chair, the shadows and the cobwebs. And the car.

Garage Days

His father was dead. His mother had fled. His world dissolved into nightmares. Troy phoned Dyson and Sapphire from the garage. Of course they'd lend him their inflatable mattress. Did he want anything else? He took a pillow too.

Snacks from the garage shop, heated in the microwave, money in the till for every meal because he wouldn't cheat, would do no wrong... *I'm not a criminal. I'm not my dad...* Troy even paid for his coffee.

Every night, Troy filled the mattress with his own breath, only right it should hurt. He slept behind the car lift, then squeezed the plastic flat in the mornings before any customers arrived. He stayed out of Carla's way when she took the night shift, didn't want to admit he was there. Blankets made for cars gave him feeble warmth.

Troy kept the bathroom sparkling clean, the garage his inheritance now. But there was no shower so he borrowed Sapphire and Dyson's. They loaned him a towel.

Love Promises

Ironically, it was Frank who sent Troy home—Frank, the married boyfriend of Troy's absent mother—Frank who visited his wife each day then slept with the woman downstairs—Frank, despair of church and town and breaker of all love's promises.

Troy went to visit his grandmother. He'd given up—family, garage, the lot. Time to leave and he didn't care where he went, but he had to say goodbye, to honor tradition. His mother always used to say, "Don't leave till you've said 'Bye to Grandma." Not that she'd spoken to anyone before she left for Pattie's and didn't come home.

Back in the days when life was simple and Troy just a child, Grandma had ears to hear and a voice to reply. Now she lay still, didn't speak and was barely alive. Brown paper cheeks accepted Troy's Judas kiss without complaint and he turned away.

Frank met him in the corridor. "You need to go back to your wife."

"Like you're the one to tell me."

"You need to go back."

Light from the hallway window framed Frank's image, black on white. Troy wanted to punch him but that would just confirm everything and make it worse. So instead Troy stood and trembled and held himself back.

"You have to, son."

"Shut up! I'm not your son." The words burst out as though he'd eaten them and they'd made him sick, bile and anger building in Troy's throat. "Shut up, Frank. What do you know?"

"I know you love her," Frank said in a voice quiet as air. "I was there at the wedding, remember? I know love makes promises, and you meant them."

Windstorms roared in Troy's ears, and the blackness of Frank's image devoured his light. He felt like a shadow in a tunnel, disappearing into fog behind the train. The trembling stopped and his legs grew weak—if he moved he'd fall to the rails and electrocute himself. Frank continued to speak.

"Love promises to try. Love promises to care. Love promises you'll share everything and never run away. Go back to her Troy. Go back to your sons. You know you'll never forgive yourself if you don't."

Troy couldn't move, hypnotized by his mother's live-in boy. "What about Mom?" he asked. "I don't see her coming back. Will she forgive herself?"

"She'll be back," said Frank as calm as the soothing sea.

In the tiny bedroom, its door still open, her frail body prone and still in the white-paned bed, old Abigail listened. White hair fanned on the pillow like silk—combed each morning, washed each night. Her bird-boned wrists lay just within sight on the cover over her chest. Her eyes lifted unblinking to the ceiling where all was quiet. Her mouth didn't quiver or even drool. She heard the gentle water of Frank's words on Troy's thunderstorm. She heard the drum-rolls quiet to distance and light, torrential rain dissolving into trickles and musical streams. Then she knew it was all right.

If Abigail could have smiled, she would. Young Troy might look like his father but he still had his grandmother's eyes. He'd even passed them on to his oldest son. Troy wasn't his father. Troy was okay. And unlike his father, Troy would go home before it was too late. Abigail relaxed. It was good and she wasn't mistaken.

Broken Chair

Lydia stepped down from the kitchen into the garage. Her nose wrinkled at the smells of mechanical parts, the scents of Troy. This was his place. Her eyes peered into dark recesses, shadowed, cobwebbed, forgotten. She stood by the broken chair where Troy sat the last time she saw him. When she leaned down, it rocked against her foot. Perhaps a ghost sat there—she pressed her hand to its seat. Then she sat in Troy's place and opened the battered box of crockery. Days' worth, weeks' worth of papers, hidden away from the children, crammed the corner between crumbling bricks and wet cardboard. Her gaze slid to the headlines despite herself. Meanwhile the children watched TV and she had to be ready to entertain in a minute when the program ended.

Cardboard crumbled in Lydia's fingers as she pried the lid from the box. Smells of wet dog and old compost mingled with sprinklings of earth. She ran her hands over edges of broken china, tugging three cups from the relics, one for each child. Each was chipped in its own unique way, each with its history, each from a different set. Memories of dropped drinks, silly distractions while tidying the table, accidental falls, a married life, was she really sure she dared touch them?

Cramming the cardboard down again, Lydia carried her prizes to the kitchen. She wasn't even sure why, but some part of her brain, lost in the past perhaps, still operated, still planned new occupations for small hands.

"Mommy Mommy Mommy." The children raced to greet her.

"Mommy, where you been?"

"Mommy, where's Daddy? When's Daddy coming home?"

"Mommy, Joshua hit me and it hurt."

She hugged and answered each in turn then sat the kids around the table. "We're going to do a project," she said because she was good at projects and because some part of her seemed to have a plan. Her mind ran on autopilot while her heart stayed weeping in the garage.

"What we gonna do, Mommy?"

"We're going to plant seeds."

"How, Mommy? How?"

She sent Jeremy for papers from the pile by Troy's recliner in the living room. "Won't Daddy want to read them though? Doesn't Daddy like to read papers?"

"Daddy's not reading just now, sweetheart. He doesn't mind if we use them." Lydia's voice sounded surprisingly normal, surprisingly fluent again. *Would Mom be proud? Would Mary? If either of them cared.* She watched herself from the kitchen doorway, watched her arms lift the youngest son onto his chair, watched her hands guide the middle child's fumbling fingers, watched as she spread papers over the table to protect it. She watched herself smile sweetly—*but how could she smile?*—and listened to her gently fluid voice praising the boys.

"What we doing now Mommy?"

"We're going to put some earth into these pots."

"They're teacups not pots."

"They're old teacups. But they'll make good plant-pots too."

A bag of earth leaned against a wall of the garage. Lydia

felt split in two, part of her stepping aside to watch while Lydia-that-walked took the children one by one, past the car, past the spiders, and helped them dip their cups. They carried them back brimming with blackness, sticky and dark. Watching-Lydia was surprised when she saw the seed-packet in her hands. *Where did that come from?*

"Three seeds each," said walking-Lydia. "Tuck them in, like they're in bed." Grubby fingers tucked. "Now we water them just a little drip under the tap." She helped, lifting the littlest one up so he could stand on a stool.

You'll break that chair, Troy's voice said in her head, Troy's voice from the broken garage chair, from memory. She saw him sitting in the dark again and blinked away tears, watching-Lydia and walking-Lydia come together as one. She didn't want to fall apart.

"Now we put them in the sun." Her voice almost choked as she spoke. "Then we can watch them grow."

"What we growing?" asked the littlest one.

Autopilot answered, though walking-and-watching-Lydias had no idea. "Flowers, for Father's Day."

Then a key turned in the door and Troy came home.

Months

Photograph, Don't Move, Reconciliation, Corner Stone

Home. It didn't feel like home, more like a photograph. Or maybe Troy just didn't feel like a person meant to live there. The children were too good for him, Lydia too sweet and kind and forgiving, too eager to reconcile. The rooms were too big till the corner stone slipped and the walls started to bend and close around him, squeezing him out like toothpaste from a tube. He could neither move nor stay in one place.

The car. The garage. The smell of engine oil like blood coating the back of his mouth. Blankets were nests of leaves with a child beneath. Memories were lies. He was home. He just didn't know how long he'd stay.

Photograph

Jeremy looked at the face in the photograph, so like his father's face, so like his own. Bright eyes gazed out from deep dark hollows, watching from the newspaper's columns of words. The narrow chin, slight smile quivering on lightly parted lips, the tousled hair... Jeremy turned his eyes toward his father, watching from the doorway. Dad wasn't smiling. His father's thin-lipped mouth closed tight. Eyes frowned, turning his face into a stranger's though he wore his father's clothes. Jeremy's father wasn't even standing straight but leaned against the door as if scared to come in. He looked like a little brother, caught in some childish plot, like a math question where all the numbers add up to something wrong.

Jeremy's mother sat beside him at the table. "You don't have to read if you don't want to."

"But everyone else has read it," said Jeremy.

"I'm sure they haven't."

"They say they have." Saying they'd read it was more than enough. It was printed in the paper so it must be true, because their parents said so, and their grandparents. But that didn't make it right. "It's about Granddad Peter isn't it?" Jeremy said. "Because he's dead?" Then he read aloud, "Peter Jeremy Markham," and added, "I'm called after him aren't I?"

"Sort of, I guess."

Jeremy was ten, easily old enough to read the paper. His fingers grabbed at words bouncing over the page. Those things they said, they didn't belong with Jeremy's picture of his granddad. The background they painted didn't match his memories.

"Is it true?" Jeremy asked after a while. "Really true? Just like they say?"

"Yes," said his mother but Jeremy ignored her. He stared at his father who said nothing, who wouldn't even lift his hooded eyes to look back at his son.

"So Granddad did something really really bad, just like they say?"

"Yes," said Jeremy's mother again. His father's breath sighed, feet shuffling restlessly as if he might run away again.

"And he killed himself?"

"Yes."

Jeremy paused to process the thought, pondering what to do with it.

"I expect he felt so rotten about what he'd done," he pronounced solemnly, gazing down at the paper on the table, at the photograph. "I expect he felt like nothing could ever make it better and it wouldn't go away." He felt his father's gaze bore into his head and looked up. "I expect Granddad felt like it wasn't really him and he was sorry."

His father groaned and Jeremy saw him grow tense, no longer leaning, ready to run. He knew it was down to him to find the right words and say them *right now* and his tongue began to race.

"It's like you always tell us isn't it, Dad? Like we all do bad stuff, but you still know we're good and you still love us. That's right isn't it? That's what you always say?" He tried to hold his father still by force of will. "That's what I'll tell my friends," Jeremy said. "I'll tell them I know my granddad did something bad, but even if it was really really bad he's still my granddad and I still love him."

Was that all? His father still looked ready to leave. Didn't they say in church there was something else—something you do when somebody's done something wrong—something you have to do? Jeremy tried to work it out. "I *won't* tell them I forgive him." The decision made him feel grown-up and stubborn and proud. "Just that I love him and always will."

His father shuddered and struggled to stay on his feet, trapped in the doorway between dining room and kitchen, broken and lost. Somehow it seemed right for Jeremy to get up and run to him like a tiny child. He didn't think about words or numbers now, or anything else. He clasped his dad around the waist of his jeans, buried his face with his own wet tears in the rough leather scent of his belt. He felt his father's arms circle his head. Water, his father's tears, dripped down his neck. Then Mom completed the circle behind him, the warm dry scent of dinner, the flowery cleanness of her clothes, the smells of home washing over him. They held each other, a circle of love, till Jeremy's little brothers started to shout in the other room.

"I'll go to them," said his mother.

"I'll unpack," his father replied.

"Then phone your mom."

Maybe Jeremy's fractured world would come to the right answer after all.

Don't Move

Marcie woke abruptly from the dream, violent images vivid in her eye. She felt frozen to the bed.

Don't move, Marcie thought. *Don't even blink.* If you do nothing, acknowledge nothing, then nothing will be true. *Don't let it be true.*

It was how she'd responded when Darryl first told her he wanted to join the army. She hadn't even dared say "No," because he'd only defend his own position and prove himself right. *What does the world need armies for anyway?* Marcie had held her hands in front of her face, mouthing silently *stop*. But Darryl hadn't stopped. He'd filed the forms. He'd passed the physical. He'd gone away.

So now she woke still shaking from the dream, holding her hands above her chest, pushing away images of death. Young Robert lay safe in his bed, not in the park. Neither stranger nor erstwhile friend would cause him harm. It was only a dream.

She tossed in a bed grown too large, bedclothes too tangled, the room too empty and silent without Darryl's presence at her side. She wanted him back. She wanted her life back where it had been before. She wanted the house, the street, the subdivision to be safe again. Listening to refrigerator hum in the night, ticking clocks, the clicks and sighs of street and house, she longed for a world where husbands don't go to war, soldiers don't die, and nobody murders little children in the park.

But most of all, climbing out of bed and shivering in her nightdress and slippers, Marcie wanted her son. She crept to his room and watched the rise and fall of his bedcovers, saw lashes curled and dry on his cheeks, no tears tonight, and blew kisses in the stubble of his hair.

Robert stirred, clutching the bedcovers, small fingers brushing his chin and handsome lips bubbling to smile. Marcie backed slowly out the room, returning to her large empty bed with its echoes of fears, back where the dream could be banished for another night.

Darryl was still alive, fighting some foreign war. Little Amelia who lived down the street was still dead. And Robert's friend's grandfather was still a pariah and purveyor of death.

Reconciliation

It was Pastor Bill's idea. Such things usually were. He said they should have an all-church service, invite their neighbors from all the other churches across town. He said they should pray for healing and God would bring their community together. Then Paradise Park might be Paradise again.

"Who will invite Evie?" asked the ever-practical chair of the women's committee.

Their oldest member volunteered but Bill knew she wouldn't be a good choice. He wanted to ask Savannah Steepleton, but she sat lumpen and sad. He wasn't sure how well she'd be received either. "My job," he said because he could do it safely.

"And who invites the Markhams? Have they even been here since…?" Voices trailed helplessly away. Since then, since that incident which cannot be mentioned, since events left Savannah sullen and silent at her end of the table, only half pretending presence at the meeting. Since murder and suicide filled the papers and TV with smut and speculation, cruel truths better left unturned.

"I'll tell them," said Savannah, "but I don't suppose they'll come."

"My job," said Pastor Bill again.

Several of the women were turning Sylvia Steepleton's guardian angel brooches around in their hands, as if they thought they might magically heal the world. The mother of Sylvia's best friend busied herself making coffee and opening packs of cookies, her hands never still, as if their motion spared her the need to think.

"What will we do?" It wasn't clear if they just meant at the service or life in general.

"We'll pray. We'll heal."

Savannah was assigned to ask Sylvia to make posters. "She can paint them and mail them to us." Pastor Bill would make photocopies. Someone else would carry them to shops and galleries and businesses all around town.

No one specified the pictures, just the words: *A call to Paradise—Reclaim our neighborhood—Reclaim our park—Everybody welcome.* Sylvia added cats, several at the top and one guardian angel crouching under the words. A thirteen-branched halo hovered over angel-cat's wings, thirteen circles drawn around *everybody*.

"Why thirteen?" Savannah asked.

"Because it's unlucky and it isn't meant to be about luck," said Sylvia on the phone. It might have made sense to her but it meant nothing to her mother.

The signs appeared all over town as the date approached, but the school principal wouldn't take one. "Some families might be offended," she said.

Pastor Bill didn't mind. "But I hope you'll make it clear," he said, "if anyone asks. Everyone's welcome. It's not an outreach or anything like that, just a chance to bring us all together—get on with caring for the living."

He even visited the leader of the synagogue, and the Muslim imam. They said they'd be there.

The day dawned bright. Sunshine. Clear blue sky. The wide open spaces of Paradise Park were packed. Choirs sang, from every church and denomination and every faith, lifting music to heaven. Prayers were offered in languages old and new and barely known. Speeches were made, about the dangers of the modern world, the need for more lights under the trees, town politics and campaigns and promises. It wasn't outreach, didn't feel like church. Then Evie Callahan and Lydia Markham took the stage together. Evie held the microphone.

"I lost my daughter," Evie said, her voice catching, confidence fading backward into the trees, then reflecting back.

Too much has happened underneath those trees. "I lost my daughter right over there." She pointed. "And a dog found her and dug her up. She was buried like a bone. So then we put her in a coffin. Were you there? Did you see? She was so beautiful."

Evie's hand almost dropped the microphone and she began to cry. Lydia held her till she was ready to continue. "You know what I prayed sometimes?" Evie paused after the question, eyes wide open, questing over the crowd. "For my Amelia? You know what I prayed? You know what she was like." She challenged them to remember the real Amelia, autism and all. "I prayed God would protect my little girl because I wouldn't always be there for her, because a mother's meant to die before her children isn't she? I never expected I'd have to bury her."

Evie sobbed again. "I thought, you know, the same things you all thought—about how she'd never cope on her own. How she'd never... And I asked God to help. So I guess God must've decided she wouldn't have to cope. I guess God took her away. I don't like how it happened. I'm sure she didn't like it. But God took her away and now my Amelia's okay. Now she's never going to suffer anymore and I don't need to be scared for her." Evie's voice faded as she wrung her hands and held the microphone too low. Lydia helped her raise it up.

"I guess it's me who has to cope on my own now," said Evie, "not Amelia. And I just want to ask you all to help, 'cause it's so very, very hard."

When her voice fell silent, Pastor Bill hugged her, pulling her gently to the back of the stage while he pushed Lydia forward. "You go now."

"I don't know what I lost," said Lydia, facing the crowds uncertainly. She held the microphone up with one hand and clutched at her stomach with the other. "I lost my father-in-law I suppose. And then it was like he'd never really been there for me to lose, like I'd never really known him. I feel like everything's sliding away, like everything's an illusion. Nothing's certain anymore."

She looked around the crowd, so many faces, and confronted their knowledge of him—their mistake too. "Did you take your cars to him? Some of you did, I know. If you talked to him in the garage, if you met him on the street, aren't you wondering the same things I am? How could we not have known?"

How could they indeed?

"I lost my memories of my children's grandfather, and my husband's father. That's what I've lost. All the things I thought he was, things he could have been, things he should have been. And then my little boy comes up to me and says, 'I still love him.' So what am I meant to make of that?"

She saw people turning to face each other, anger perhaps on their faces, disgust or something else. "He still loves him," she announced firmly, with Jeremy's face in her mind for confidence. "His memories, my son's memories, he's still holding onto them. They *were* real, those things he remembers; they're part of him. And I'm thinking maybe that's all right because I'm not sure how to say it's all wrong."

She paused again. They were looking at her, puzzling, forgiving her maybe, but she still had to finish. "Everything that's happened, all these awful things, they don't change the past. The only thing changing is the future. Jeremy loves the granddad he remembers. He treasures the memories they made together. So maybe I can still love him too, love the man I thought I knew. I'm just not sure if that's the person we buried."

"I wonder," she asked, "can someone be two people at once? And then I wonder, in the end, what do we ever really know about anyone? My son doesn't forgive him. I don't think anyone can ask for that. But he still loves him."

Pastor Bill led closing prayers. He prayed that God, who knows everyone fully and completely, would sort out all the stuff none of his children can comprehend. He prayed that people who think they know it all would realize they don't and be kind. Then he prayed that if God could make Evie and Lydia stand together in this place after all that had happened, perhaps the rest of the community of Paradise could stand together too.

The service didn't mend anything but it was a memory the community could use as a corner stone while they set out to build the future.

Corner Stone

They put a new bench in the playground by the park with Amelia's name on it. They strung new lights along the path and labeled it the *Amelia Callahan Memorial Walk*. Troy Markham took his father's name off the sign at the garage and made it his own. And Peter's gravestone read: "Beloved father, grandfather and sinner."

"There again, aren't we all," said Pastor Bill.

Years

Intrigue, Rainbow, Edited Memories, Funerals

"Keep the children in," said Troy. Today was to be a special day, and luckily the sun was still shining.

"Don't worry, Love. Jeremy'll keep them in order. He won't let Joshua see."

Troy carried heavy machinery around the side of the house and into the yard. He set it up on a flat space cleared of leaves, pulled the cord, and got the motor running.

When his dad was ten, Troy's grandfather killed his grandmother. When Troy was ten, his father walked out. When Jeremy was ten, the world was almost ready to fall apart again. And now… And now…

Troy watched the flaccid plastic taking shape, a mound of nothing with gasses blown in, building itself into mystery and intrigue, a castle made of air. He thought of children jumping high, sky and ground turned all around, and found himself suddenly, quietly remembering. For a moment he felt his father's presence, strong hands lifting him around the waist, up up into the sky, up where the ceiling was painted blue with the world laid out below, and he wanted to cry.

"Are you up there, Dad? Is there forgiveness and heaven even for you?" He hoped there might be because time had proved Jeremy right despite his doubts. It took Troy longer to work it out, but he really did still love his father, for who he'd been once, for who he might have been, for who he remembered.

And maybe in heaven there are memories built like rainbows, forgiveness threaded with beads made from the tears of funerals. The castle grew and Troy drew breath into himself and smiled and knew. He wasn't his father or his grandfather. He was dad to three sons, he was Lydia's spouse, and he was Troy.

And he was building a house in the back yard for his youngest son's party.

Intrigue

"What's that smell?" called Joshua, rushing downstairs from his bedroom. The living room was dark, curtains hiding the window.

Josh's brother Jeremy blocked his path and bent to ruffle his hair. "Grass clippings, little brother."

"Engine oil," said Jay, blocking his way.

Josh pushed past toward the kitchen. "Mom, what's that smell?" But the door was closed and he knew better than to open it. Whatever his mother was making, she obviously didn't want any help. In particular she probably didn't want help from Alison's large white cat that sat by the door frame, purring contentedly.

"Garnet, d'you smell it?" asked Joshua, burying his nose in the cat's furry ruff. He got no answer. "Hey guys!"

Joshua's brothers ran upstairs laughing. Their bedroom door banged shut. "Hey guys!" Josh chased after them but they wouldn't let him in. Rustles and laughter escaped with sounds of sticky tape torn from its roll. He ran downstairs again. "Mom." No answer. "Dad." Perhaps his dad had gone out somewhere. "Hey, what you guys doing?"

He should have smelled cake. There should have been fanciful cards and presents waiting by his plate at breakfast. It should have been Josh's birthday, but everyone seemed to have forgotten it. So he sat in a lump on the floor and hugged Alison's cat. "You haven't forgotten me have you?" he said. Then the cat walked away.

Joshua's mother cracked the kitchen door open and smiled at him. "Sweetheart, there's someone coming up the walk," she said.

"So what?"

"So will you answer the door? I've got floury hands."

Joshua walked reluctantly to the front door, pulling it open before the bell could ring. There were his school friends, boys and girls from his class, even Jay and Jeremy's teenaged friends Robert and Nate. They stood with gifts, bright-wrapped, all with smiles, all with cheers. "Happy birthday, Josh!"

Jeremy and Jay ran downstairs with gifts in their arms, fresh-wrapped as well. Then Joshua's father came in from outside to usher everyone through, through the tidy living room, through the wide patio doors, flinging open the curtains as they passed. Outside there were tables and chairs and decorations and even a bouncy castle—*How had Dad done that?*—all set up on the grass.

"So, ten-year-old. Double figures," said Joshua's Mom.

One of the girls grabbed his hand and counted ten fingers for ten years. "So, ten-year-old. Happy birthday, Joshua!"

All Joshua's favorite foods came out on plates piled gloriously high. All his favorite music played on the CD player. All his favorite smells scented the lunchtime air outdoors. Grass-clippings from the fresh-mown lawn clung to their legs as they danced. Engine oil was the scent of the motor powering the bouncy castle. And the party was the *bestest gift* that Joshua could ever have imagined.

His new girlfriend was the *bestest girl* in all the world too, just for today. So Josh took off his shoes for the castle and let her add up his toes.

"Our little boy's growing up."

Rainbow

It rained the day of the Senior Prom. It rained all day, drumming on roofs, splattering from wheels of cars, crushing flowers, dripping wet and weary, everlasting rain.

Jeremy drove the two doors from his house to Alison's and raced up the path. He held his hand over his head to keep the water from his eyes. Then Alison's mother reached out through the open door with an umbrella.

"Thanks Mrs. Walker."

"You're welcome." She slid back inside.

Alison was a vision in pale blue lace, perfectly matching the corsage Jeremy brought. "It's beautiful," she said. Her mother watched Jeremy struggle to pin it on. They exchanged final vows and promises to take care, drive safely, and of course, have fun.

Jeremy held the car door for his date. He'd never done that before. He tried to hold the umbrella too, but over her head, not his. His hair dripped hopelessly by the time he got into the car, spilling over his eyes.

"Should've brought a towel," Alison laughed.

Jeremy laughed too, though he knew his voice sounded strained. "Are we really doing this?" he asked.

Alison touched his hand with hers and said yes. They were really about to graduate high school. They were really going to dance at their Senior Prom.

At the end of the street they turned right and Alison asked why. "I thought you'd go through town."

"Nah," said Jeremy. "The forest road's faster."

"Yeah but…"

"It'll be fine."

The forest road skirted the park, running through trees in a place all the locals still avoided, not for the bridge over the stream that used to get swept away, but for memories of a crime they preferred to forget. Jeremy, of all people, should have known, but he seemed unconcerned. He drove steadily, turned at the light, and headed for the hill.

Windshield wipers blurred the view, back and forth, swishing back and forth. Trees loomed darkly, wet road gleaming black like an evil snake, and distance obscured. The road flattened out where the stream was high, too close to the surface of the bridge, running wild. They heard rushing water even over the whooshing sound of their tires while Jeremy drove on.

Alison grabbed the handle of the door as Jeremy steered around the corner, relaxed and calmly in control. At last, they crested the hill into gray mists of clouds. Jeremy pulled the car to the side and stopped. Alison asked why.

"You'll see. Just wait."

As the window misted, Jeremy pulled a tissue from his pocket to wipe it clear.

Suddenly, the sun came out. Bright light poured from leaden clouds, flowing down to settle over streets and streams, trickling with rain from branches waving on trees. A rainbow spanned the valley from town to sky.

"See that?" said Jeremy.

Alison clutched pale hands to her mouth and sighed. "It's beautiful."

"So are you." Jeremy kissed her lightly, politely, on the cheek. He turned away quickly and started the engine again. "My Granddad Peter used to bring me up here. The rain always clears and there's always a rainbow; nowhere else you can get the view quite like this. And everyone avoids it."

"Sad," said Alison, though her voice was quiet and puzzled as her look. Jeremy's grandfather was the reason people avoided the forest road. "Everyone but the tourists," she said softly.

"Everyone but the tourists and the free. I want *you* to be free."

They drove down past the fields and farms that thronged the side of town, then back toward the school and hall and dance. No pot of gold waited at the end of their rainbow, but a golden nugget settled in Alison's heart, planted by Jeremy. *Forgive and live.*

Edited Memories

"Tell me about your childhood," the psychologist said. She sat on the official side of the desk, exotically dressed in sparkling sari, red dot glowing on her forehead. A pen balanced between her exquisitely painted fingers, hovering over plain lined paper lying yellowly, miserably out of place among decorative paperweights and neatly stacked files. Her name, Doctor Mary Phillips, PhD., stared out from the nameplate facing Sylvia.

"What d'you want to know?" Sylvia stared back.

"Anything. Just start at the beginning."

Sylvia took sparse breaths and looked down at her hands, fingers twisting in her lap. "I dunno," she said slowly. "I've got one brother, one sister—Mom and Dad—grew up in the subdivision, Paradise Mansions; we moved there when I was small—went to school. What d'you want me to say?"

"Were you happy?"

"Yes, I guess."

"Always?"

"I guess." Sylvia tried to keep her gaze unfixed. She glanced at the wall, the desk, the pen, the doctor's twining fingers but never her face. She heard the quiet Indian voice start to speak and interrupted quickly. "We used to fight sometimes. Me and my brother and sister. But not a lot. We were always good friends in the end. We looked after each other."

"How about at school? Were you happy there?"

"Yes. Mostly. I had some friends."

"Good friends?"

"Just friends." She thought of ones who moved away, others who teased her, team captains who never really cared for her, Sharon with the hunky big brother. She smiled in memory.

"Would you say you were a bit of a loner perhaps?"

"Maybe," Sylvia agreed. "But I was okay."

The conversation stalled again while Sylvia thought how pointless it all seemed. Everyone always asks the same questions and the answers are always the same. *There's nothing wrong with me*, she thought. Nothing wrong except I can't cope and I keep crying, but that's just life. *So why am I here?*

"Secondary school?" Dr. Phillips asked in her soft, slightly foreign voice. "Were you happy in your time at secondary school?"

"Yes mostly, I guess."

"Junior High? Senior High? And at university?" Sylvia nodded. Her head was getting used to this. "You met your husband there?" She nodded again. "And when did you marry?"

Sylvia told her it was right after they graduated, ten years ago.

"And you have how many children now?"

"Three."

"How old?"

"Four and two and the baby."

The questions carried on the same, still leading nowhere, inexorably. Sylvia squirmed in her seat, moved her sleeve unobtrusively with her wrist so she could see her watch—ten minutes to go. She hoped Dr. Phillips hadn't seen what she was doing and kept her gaze fixed down.

"So, did anything happen to you, Sylvia? When you were young. Say ten or eleven, twelve maybe? Something you don't like to talk about?"

Sylvia didn't answer.

"When you were thirteen?"

Time froze. The watch, the wrist, the arm, all suddenly belonged to somebody else. Looking around, there were splashes of color, all unformed, the world unmade. Sylvia's heart beat louder than her breath, and a scent of something sour lurked behind the warmth of furniture polish. She started to cry.

This was the question, so specific, so simple, that no one had asked before. It tore through her edited memories and opened the dam.

Dr. Phillips pushed a box of tissues toward her, decorated with pink-flowered fabric, and said nothing at all.

Funerals

Funerals, funerals and more funerals. Eventually they all ran into one, the dead all gathered together by the altar and the living waiting to join them, just a part of growing old. Pattie's father, Mary's mother, and Peter—*no*, Mary wouldn't think about Peter today.

Troy looked distinguished, standing firmly at his mother's side, arm linked with hers while Frank, bent with age, held her other hand. Lydia and the children weren't there, but then, who was Grandpa Frank's lost wife to them? She'd been dying for years and was finally gone, gliding with the angels while Frank's younger lover felt age begin buckling her knees.

It's a bit like swimming, Mary thought. You kick your legs to stay afloat while the dead slide gently at rest. Then the pastor speaks a blessing over the waters. *Dangerous waters,* with Peter's ghost circling like a shark, teeth snapping, waiting to bite even after the years.

Mary had read about sharks. If you look them in the eye, they think you're a predator and run away. Swim away. Whatever. She didn't know if it worked with fish, but it seemed to work with Peter's memory now. She looked in his eye, determinedly, watched him drop his gaze, then saw him fade as the church full of mourners shaded back into focus. Words and prayers were formless as if spoken underwater, Mary trapped between drowning and fighting marauding memories.

Frank's thin fingers tensed on hers. Was he needing or giving comfort? She turned to smile, heard the susurration of whispers water the walls, strangers talking about Frank, or about her. Frank was a good man, a good husband. He'd always loved his wife. *But what am I?*

Lots of people didn't talk to Mary these days, and the silence hurt, stinging even as years went by. "Don't be silly," Pattie would tell her in their weekly phone call. "If everyone talked to you, Mary, you'd complain you weren't getting any rest."

"Oh that's easy for you to say."

"It's no easier for me than for you. Just say it."

"If everyone talked to me…" And they laughed.

She'd stayed with Pattie when Peter died, time out of time—not friendship quite, nor even companionship. Pattie's house offered a place where Mary could pretend to be invisible. Pattie and Dan had left her undisturbed. Afterward they'd promised to stay in touch, and done nothing about it, as if embarrassed to remember the last time they met.

Mary's mother's funeral brought them together again. Freed suddenly by different memories, they talked as if there'd been no yesterdays, Peter's name scarcely mentioned. Just neighbors and friends and children and retirement concerns. Since then, they'd taken turns to phone each other every week.

"Your Frank's a good man."

Yes, Mary knew. But Peter's shark bared its teeth in a grin, approaching her again. Peter had once been a good man too, a fine father and lover. She looked in his eyes—sweet lonely predatory eyes while the teeth snapped on her hand. Troy hugged her tight.

They rode in cars to the crematorium, Troy and Mary and Frank in the second one, driving just behind the coffin. She imagined Jeremy beside them, though he wasn't really there, smart in his first real suit as he'd sat at his great-grandma's funeral. She saw Troy alone, holding her hand, as they drove to bury Peter. No cremation for him. No pomp. No ceremony. Just a stone declaring him a sinner in the graveyard plot he'd bought for them both. She would never lie there.

When the procession turned into the wide curving drive, Mary looked to the copse where she knew a pale mauve rose bloomed for her mother. *Ashes to roses.* It seemed appropriate.

The day dripped, cool and gray, with rain adding water to tears. But the scent in Mary's nose carried ashes of memory, dirt left behind by hope and Peter's betrayal. The grass, fresh-cut, lay in globs of sticky green. *Dirt sticks to you.* Mary wondered again what people said behind her back.

Somehow she got through the ceremony without drowning. She gazed her shark in the eyes as it circled. She drove it away and away and away again. Eventually she found herself outside, alone under trees, watching black-suited strangers shaking hands with the man she loved, while her only son had vanished.

A hand touched her arm. Not Troy. It was Pastor Bill.

"Frank's a good man," said the pastor and Mary agreed. Then he continued. "Must have been a blessed release for her at the end." *For Frank's wife* she guessed. "So long in dying. Ours not to reason why…" He repeated that Frank was really a very good man.

"I know what you're thinking," said Mary, sharply, not willing to be deceived.

"Really?"

"You're wondering… But I won't. I won't marry him."

"I know you won't."

"How d'you know?"

"Frank told me. He's a very good man."

Mary sighed. "That's the point isn't it?" The pastor's presence made a cone of silence where she could speak her mind. "He's a very good man, is Frank. I know. And I couldn't ever risk me changing him. I'd not be good for him."

"You do know what happened with Peter was never your fault."

Mary touched her head with a dripping hand in damp agreement. "Yes I know. Up here in my brain. But you can't help wondering can you? If I'd been a better wife… If I'd stayed with him… If I'd never moved to Paradise, maybe kept my mom at home…"

"If Troy had never gone to look for him?"

"Oh no; it's not Troy's fault." *It could never be that.* "But maybe if I'd been a better mother, Troy wouldn't have needed to look."

"It really wasn't your fault."

Mary touched her head again, almost like a salute to the shadow of truth. "Yes Pastor. I know. But I wonder sometimes if I changed him. I've got to wonder. His father was no angel, I know, but he didn't have to be like him. And he wasn't. Not before. Not even when he was away from us, not so's anyone's said. So why did he change?" She placed her hand unsteadily over her heart then looked up through tears. "Knowing in my head's not the same as in my heart."

The shark circled again, but Mary kept her eyes on Pastor Bill. His open line to God might keep the predator out of reach.

"It would make him happy if you would," Bob said. "I promised I'd tell you."

"Frank you mean?"

"Yes, if you'd marry him."

Mary twisted the garnet ring—her *promise ring* Frank called it when he gave it to her, because his wife still lived and they couldn't be married. "You think I'm wrong?"

"I'm not saying that."

"It's just…" She struggled to find the words. "It's just, as long as I don't change anything, I won't feel like I'm to blame for anything changing. It's just…"

"But things have changed."

"Not because of me." Mary settled her shoulders squarely casting away doubt. "I'm sorry, Pastor. I am sorry but I just can't do it."

The hand-shakers had moved away. Troy, back from wherever he'd been, stood together with Frank and looked across at her. Mary's two strong men—Pastor Bill gave her a smile and a gentle push toward them. "Don't worry Mary," he said from behind in a low voice just for her. "Frank's a very good man, and he'll love you just the same with or without a marriage license."

"Me downstairs. Him up?" Mary turned to answer briefly.

"Same as always. Nothing has to change."

"And God doesn't mind?"

"The law was made for man Mary, not man for the law. I'm sure God doesn't mind."

Epilogue

The Son

Jeremy

Visitor, Return, Rebirth, Reconciliation

Things hadn't turned out how his family might have expected, his teachers either, but that was okay. Brilliant mathematical Jeremy, he felt comfortable now in his life as if reborn. He belonged at last, no longer just a visitor walking in his shoes. He'd even returned to live in Paradise. *I'm not my father, nor my grandfather* he thought, *not my great-grandfather either. I'm me, born to be me,* reconciled to his past. He would hurt no one and leave no one and his mission was to heal. Meanwhile a whole subdivision of people depended on him for care, his congregation instead of family. The high-ups had wondered if people would accept him here as a pastor, given what happened, but Jeremy never doubted. He set his feet on the path of Pastor Bill.

Visitor

The visitor sat near the middle of church. Not at the back—he'd be in the way there if anyone came late. They'd have to decide if they wanted to sit next to him, and it was embarrassing watching the thoughts in their eyes. He didn't sit near the front either, because the weight of all those gazes on the back of his neck might make him perspire. But here, in the middle, near the end of a row—this was good. It was good enough anyway. Jeremy would see him.

Behind him, an old fat man spilled over the edge of a pew,

making the wood creak. His coat trailed the floor, shabby and loose as if he'd lost weight. He coughed repeatedly, but didn't sound infectious. Maybe the dog hairs on his collar irritated his throat.

In front, a group of elderly ladies whispered secrets, plucking juicy bits of gossip from the air. Teenagers sat by the altar, bright-colored shirts like an offering to their god, though tradition might claim holey jeans lacked respect. The youngest children pranced in their Sunday best, frilly dresses, white shirts and bowties, bouncing happily and chattily in the aisles before service began.

The professor had been in many churches like this. He'd seen those looks on people's faces as they saw his pale linen trousers, long silken jacket with embroidery around the neck, the red jewel in his collar. His hair stood out, he knew, like a halo around his head—Einstein decorated with a ponytail. His dark skin, cool and exotic, set off the outfit, dark wrinkles a fitting backdrop to the smoothness of linen and silk.

He didn't belong here so he sat all alone, watching others watching him. He hadn't come for comfort, rather to offer comfort to his student, his young friend, math dropout, Jeremy. He would listen with more respect than the children and the gossips, he'd stand and sit with more ease than the fat man at his back, and he'd read the holy book with sincere reverence. He'd listen to music and imagine eternity's choirs.

Conversation stilled, Jeremy, still recognizable beneath his sacred robes, processed up the aisle to the front and the service began.

Return

Dr. Jeremy Markham, it said on the church bulletin in his hands. Jeremy wasn't sure he'd ever get used to it. Teenagers called him *Pastor Germ* and the older ladies still referred to him as *Lydia Steepleton's boy.*

He saw his old professor sitting near the aisle in the middle of church, pure and white in a sea of bright colors. His head bent down over his bulletin, as if afraid his gaze might distract his former student. Jeremy wondered what he made of his favorite dropout being a *Doctor*.

The service was planned with care, each tone and prayer and supplication. A teen in scrappy red sweater with holes in the sleeves read the passage from the Bible. Old ladies in blue jeans served communion. Jeremy preached his sermon to the whole congregation, but found his eyes seeking his professor's approval and his mind losing track. Eventually he determined to speak to the walls and keep his face to the door.

Still, "Nice sermon, Pastor," said his old neighbor Mrs. Grainger, when it was over. She shook his hand with her bird-like grip and bobbed her head like a beak. Jeremy thanked her, gently encouraging her to move on before she trapped him in too long a conversation.

"Pastor." One of Grandma Savannah's friends nodded, still going strong, the palm of her hand pushing the small of another lady's back. It wouldn't do for crowds to get too thick around the church door. Another woman gave Jeremy a smile of acknowledgement as she slipped out the side to supervise coffee.

Evie Callahan—everyone still called her *poor Amelia's mother*—walked in at the same time. Jeremy smiled. She didn't come to *church,* Evie always said, she came to help, and Jeremy was one of the few people who would still talk about Amelia.

Today she had Carla and David's little twins, late-born surprises, tugging her skirt as she scanned the room. "Try the meeting room," Jeremy mouthed over the crowds, then shook another hand.

"Nice job, Jeremy," said his old friend Nate, arm twining luxuriously around his latest girlfriend's waist.

"Good to see you," said Nate's mother Sapphire, just visiting again—she'd been *just visiting* Paradise church for the last six months so perhaps she'd stay.

Jeremy's heart beat faster as his own long-awaited visitor approached. He hugged the white-haired professor in the cramped doorway, embarrassed but overflowing with enthusiasm, warmed by his presence.

"Good talk," said the older man, "but I can't help thinking you're wasting yourself."

"Not at all," said Jeremy. "This is where I was always meant to be."

"A local church? A congregation of what, two hundred people, going nowhere?"

"Two hundred eighty-five."

"You could have had my job, boy."

Jeremy smiled. "But I wouldn't want it."

The rest of the congregation, those who hadn't escaped earlier, crowded restlessly behind. Jeremy asked someone to walk his friend to the meeting room. "See you there soon." Then he smiled politely, accepted further thanks for his half-forgotten sermon, expounded on the reading as briefly as he could, and saw the rest of his flock walk out into the sun.

"It's a lovely day, Pastor Jeremy," said a quiet, sad woman, Robert Kopp's widowed mother, Marcie.

"It is that." Any other Sunday he'd have walked the grounds with her, talked of Robert and Alison and school, and Darryl's sacrifice. Instead he turned away, too busy today, heading along the path.

"You're not really going to stay inside in this weather?" "Drink coffee in this weather?" "Work on a Sunday?" But Jeremy said he had a special visitor waiting in the hall.

"Who would that be?" Marcie asked sharply.

"My old math professor. You saw him in church."

"One of those atheist university types then, is he?" One of Grandma Savannah's old friends overheard and stopped to complain on her way to the store room for more cups.

"Not at all," said Jeremy. "He's one of those Muslim university types if you must. We have a lot to catch up on."

In these days of war and terrorist attacks, Jeremy had wondered how his professor's faith might be construed by the congregation. In truth, he didn't care. *Might as well wonder how his grandfather's crime was construed. Life isn't fair.*

Soon he escaped and hurried to the manse. He changed his clothes and tugged out the satchel of notes to show his professor. In the church hall, they sat together drinking coffee, ate cookies and spread Jeremy's papers over the table. It was his book, the one he'd dreamed of writing all the way back in college, the one that tried to explain how a son doesn't have to become his father, how love and forgiveness don't always hold hands, and how the infinite possibilities of disaster can resolve into a future. He'd never have finished writing it if he hadn't settled down into a nice quiet life in a quiet village church.

"Still pushing the Christian point of view," said his professor pointedly as he turned a page.

"Still wanting to argue it?" Jeremy asked with a smile. They agreed to differ, as they'd agreed before, in the days when Jeremy first left his professor's math class for Bible College. They agreed the book might have something good to say, and Jeremy's life was good, and God is good.

Rebirth

"Glad to see you didn't entirely give up on math." The professor laid a page covered with diagrams onto the table. Dusty light reflected from the jewel on his collar as he frowned at sharp-drawn labels and lines through rising steam from his coffee.

"Do you think it's too much?" asked Jeremy, smiling apologetically. "The graphs? Will readers understand?"

"You could try *moment of decision* instead of *singularity.*"

"Except that's kind of the point." Jeremy shook his head. "I didn't want to call it a decision because we imagine it's all beyond our control."

"*Decisive point? Point of change?*"

The jewel winked red through a gray steam of coffee. Jeremy waved his hand, working out his reply. "A point where the world falls apart, that's what I meant. Infinite possibilities. Somehow we forget it's still up to us to decide which way to go afterward. Blame genetics. Blame fate. Say God's betrayed us when we're really betraying ourselves. When we should be fixing it."

"You're sure it's not too personal?" Jeweled fingers reached for the pages again while piercing eyes looked up.

"That's why I asked you to look at it, sir," said Jeremy. "I know I've got something personal to say, but I want to make sure it reads right for other people."

The professor nodded slowly. "Didn't you tell me your mother quoted you in some sort of service back then?"

"Yeah. But would *you* quote me, sir? If the book ever gets published? If you knew someone…?"

"You're the one who lived through it."

"Death of a subdivision." Jeremy smiled.

"And rebirth. That's what *you* taught *me,* noble student, there's always rebirth."

"And God of course."

"Of course. And there's only one God." The professor sighed, slipping the manuscript pages from table to bag. "I'll read it through, Jeremy, when I get home. I'll let you know, but I'm sure it will be good. Let's shake on it."

They reached across the plastic-covered table, leaning over coffee cups and crumbs. Pastor and professor braided their fingers together in solemn vow, promising hope and a future for a broken world.

Reconciliation

Back in the sunshine, standing on grass near the church, Jeremy and the professor watched parishioners walk to their cars. Parents picked up children, youngsters waited for parents, Sunday lunchtime rituals continued.

Alison Kopp arrived to take her son and daughter home. Jeremy wondered if he'd ever get used to her surname, now she'd married Robert. "We still on for lunch, Jeremy?" she asked through the window of the car.

"Be there soon." Jeremy turned to the professor, who nodded agreement.

"It'll be good to catch up on Alison again," said the old man as she left. Then he added, "You know, I always thought you two…"

"No, we were just friends. More like siblings really." Jeremy called after the disappearing car, "Hey, Alison! Don't forget to save some milk for Garnet."

"Garnet?" The professor fingered the jewel in his collar.

"Well, Garnet the fourth I guess. She's a bit of a mascot around this place."

Marcie Kopp heard the remark and made a tutting sound. *Where had she come from again?* But she wandered back into the hall to clean up after coffee, carrying condemnation under her arm.

Jeremy's Aunt Sylvia ushered his youngest cousin down the steps from the youth room. The ten-year-old held a large white cat in his arms and called loudly, "Pastor Uncle Germ! Can't I kidnap Garnet? Please?" Jeremy laughed as the fur ball struggled free. The professor stepped back.

"It's all right. She's friendly."

"That's what I was afraid of."

"So?" Jeremy asked when the cat had climbed his legs and settled like a blanket over his shoulder. "Shall we walk or drive to Alison's?" He offered the professor his arm and Garnet jumped down, trotting serenely ahead, sure of her way and her place.

"Let's walk."

The Paradise they walked through hadn't altered much over the years. Subdivisions ran together and split apart, new houses and old, new roads, new traffic lights. The church had built a big new hall. But it was still the same old place, the town where Jeremy and his brothers and friends grew up, where Amelia died—one precious thread tied off in the tapestry of life.

Jeremy had left and changed and then come back, but part of him was still the little boy whose grandfather killed the girl. No one hated him for it now. No one forgot, but no one blamed. The people remained, young and old, good and bad, all making their own decisions, all mixed together, served warm or cold, with a dash of human kindness holding the promise of mercy and hope.

And a boy doesn't have to grow up to be his father, after all.

I hope you've enjoyed your visit to Paradise.
If you want to learn more…

read Sylvia's side of the story in ***Infinite Sum***
and meet Amelia's absent dad in ***Subtraction***.

If you want to help the author, please recommend this novel to your
friends and leave a book review.

And thank you for reading ***Divide by Zero***

www.ingramcontent.com/pod-product-compliance
Lightning Source LLC
Chambersburg PA
CBHW030532190726
48283CB00006B/1886